The Dragon's Prison

The Dragon's Prison

Marshall Pickens

Corvid Publishing

This is a work of fiction. All characters, organizations, and events portrayed in this novel are either products of the author's imagination or are used fictitiously.

The Dragon's Prison

Copyright 2022 by Marshall Pickens

Again and again to Stacy
for helping with editing
and catching all the missing and
misplaced punctuation.

Chapter One

It was late, and only one small table lamp had been turned on, illuminating the corner of a massive mahogany desk. The diminutive light couldn't hide the opulence of the room, and Amr was surprised they'd even let his cousin and himself in. Deep burgundy carpet cradled his feet like a newborn babe while heavy wooden bookshelves lined the walls. The books, he'd noticed when walking in, were all arranged by color and size, making it look very impressive, but also giving the distinct feeling they'd never been used.

Compared to the room, Amr was dirty. No, not dirty. That word carried with it the idea of poverty and need. He was dusty. They had been out scouting the site and hadn't had a chance to clean before coming here. There had been only one man waiting for them when they'd been ushered in. Amr was sure he'd been told the man's name when they'd met but he hadn't found it important enough to remember and so just referred to him by his most notable feature. Even now, at some time around two in the morning, he stood there in a perfectly tailored three piece pinstripe suit. What stood out to Amr wasn't the suit itself, Amr's people were fastidious as well when it came to meeting guests, but that they, he and his cousin who was second in command, hadn't called ahead to plan this meeting. They had just shown up. Did this man sleep in a suit?

The man in the suit stood behind the desk, using it to keep Amr and his cousin at a distance and said, "What do you mean you won't do it? Aren't we paying you enough?"

Glancing over at Miro, his cousin, for moral support Amr adjusted his wire frame glasses and said, "It is not the money."

"That's nonsense," the suit said, "it's always the money."

"We would be too exposed," Amr said. "We looked at the site today. Well," he shrugged, "we looked at it from far away with large binoculars, and there is no way to get into where you want us to get into without being seen."

"The understanding was that it would be dangerous." The suit's voice was calm, "That's why we're paying you so much."

Amr ignored him and pressed on, "Also, we couldn't find a second way out. If we go in we're trapped. It's not dangerous, it's suicide."

"And what about you Miro. Do you agree with your cousin?"

Miro shifted on his feet and crushed his felt hat in his hands. He didn't like the idea that this man knew his name. He hadn't told the suit his name, and as far as he knew, they'd never told him they were cousins. Not wanting to contradict Amr, and get a beating later if he did, he just shrugged and said, "Amr is in charge."

The suit sighed and turned his back on them. Walking toward one of the book cases he said, "I thought you would be willing to do this for the money. I know your plans require large sums."

Amr straightened up, "What do you know of our plans?"

Shaking his head the suit replied, "Your plans are no mystery Amr. Anyone watching a news channel could figure out your plans. As I was saying," he pulled open a false section of the bookshelf revealing a small safe, "I was hoping the money would be enough, but I do also know you have a bit of the mystical in your religious upbringing, so maybe that will convince you."

Opening the safe he extracted something then turned to them. What he placed on the table was a box about the size of a deck of playing cards. "Go ahead," he gestured at it and stepped back to allow room, "open it."

Amr looked to his cousin then back at the box. He expected a trap or trick of some kind, but the suit needed them and was trying to convince them to help. Why do something to hurt that possible relationship? However, he couldn't imagine anything that might be in the box able to convince him to head into that cave. The money was good. No, the money was amazing. The suit was right about that. What he planned couldn't be done for cheap, and there had been no way to get the necessary funds. What the suit was going to give them would cover it all and more, but there was no way to spend money when you were dead. He knew for a fact the Americans kept a satellite pointed to this very part of the world looking for people like him and his cousin. They could go at night, but recent events had proven the cover of darkness to be no help against the all seeing eye of an American satellite. In the end he would turn down this job and find another way to get the money, but there was no harm in seeing what was in the box.

Reaching out he picked it up. It was light. Something like a stone rattled inside. The box was of a simple wooden design and the lid slid open easily. As it opened, light peaked out as if a firefly were trapped inside. It flickered between shades of red and pure white, making the shadows dance around the book lined room and reflected from the lenses of his glasses. Amr found himself looking down at a jagged sliver of crystal. Looking up at the suit he said, "What is this?"

"That is the piece they kept. It took us years and millions of dollars to track down the truth of that little shard."

"But what is it?" Amr's gaze was pulled back to the flickering heart of the stone.

"It's a leftover piece and a warning light of a sort. As long as the light shone, they knew the prison still held."

Miro shuffled forward and looked over his cousin's shoulder, "Held what?"

The suit stepped forward, reached down into the box, and picked up the stone. "If you won't do it just for the money, will you do it for this?"

Amr looked up at him, "You expect this," he waved his hand at the glowing piece of crystal, "this unknown sparkly rock to convince me to place all our lives in danger? At least tell us what it is."

The suit sighed, "It might be easier to show you." With a quick step and a fencer's lunge the suit rammed the tip of the crystal into Amr's belly. Twisting it he spoke three words, each word sending a crack through the room. Twisting it again, the light flared creating a circle around Amr. Miro could see through the circle of light and what he saw rooted his feet to the lush carpet. A sand dune spread out under a clear blue sky. The light of it illuminated the room they were in causing Amr's shadow to cover the suit leaving him undefined, his face hidden. The suit pulled the crystalline shard back, then with his free hand he reached forward and pushed. Amr tumbled through the glowing circle landing on the sand and sliding down the steep incline.

Miro blinked and the circle was gone. Only a glowing after image remained burned onto the back of his eyes. The small flickering of the stone lit the suit's hands and the underside of his face, leaving him as a ghostly figure in the room. "Well, Miro. It seems you are in charge now. I will gladly up the amount we are willing to pay you…"

"Will you tell me what it is?" Miro knew he should be outraged at what just happened to his cousin. Culture and upbringing screamed at him to take revenge for the killing of Amr, but the dancing light, curiosity, and desire overwhelmed him.

Chapter Two

"Lieutenant Bishop?"

Bishop turned away from the view out the open door of the Blackhawk. The waves of the south eastern Mediterranean were turning from an inky black to a dark turquoise as the sun rose on the port side of the helicopter. He was glad for the distraction, the view had been a bit too hypnotizing, and after being hastily pulled from a deep sleep he was already fighting to keep his eyes open. Dragging them away from the water he looked at the pilot, "Chief?"

The voice crackled over the helicopter's headset, "Coming up on the border of Libya. About twenty minutes till the LZ."

"Roger that Chief." Glancing around the interior of the Blackhawk he took in the ten other members of today's little excursion. They sat or stood, rocking with the familiar motion of the helicopter. Seal teams like this one had become almost mythical in the consciousness of the United States. A small band of highly trained soldiers silently taking care of problems around the world. Today was no different for them. For him, however, this was not a normal day, but normal or not he had a job to do.

"Gentlemen, quick review." He felt ridiculous going over information they already knew, but SOP was what it was, and you didn't get promoted by ignoring it. They all dutifully looked his way while behind him, out the open door of the blackhawk, the desert of eastern Libya rolled by. "At approximately oh-seven-hundred an unknown number of confirmed terrorists were spotted entering a cave system on the border of Egypt and Libya. Satellite coverage is spotty, and by the time a drone could reach the area they'd already entered the caves. We know it's at least ten but likely more. A cave is an easily entrenched position so plan for hard fighting. It's at this point," he briefly made eye contact with each of them, "that I'm supposed to tell you what your job is. I feel that would be insulting to professionals such as yourself."

"Except Jacobs." A voice from the left made Bishop turn his head.

"True," another chimed in, "he has no idea what's going on."

"Poor new kid, gonna die on his first mission."

"LZ in one minute." Bishop was glad for the pilot's interruption.

"All right, you know your business. Even Jacobs." Bishop turned and faced out the door of the blackhawk and watched the ground rise up to meet them.

There's a cliche out there which says practice makes perfect. In the military he'd learned that really wasn't true. You could practice and practice and still get something wrong. There was more to it than practice. You had to have at least a touch of natural aptitude for whatever it was you were doing. Also, you needed to bring a certain amount of sober austerity to the practice. If you weren't serious about it, nothing would be gained by the practice. Finally, and maybe most importantly, you had to practice doing it correctly. If you practiced doing something wrong then, yes, that practice would make it perfect, perfectly wrong.

The men around him dismounted the blackhawk and set about their business with perfectly practiced ease. They had been through this exact scenario dozens, and in some of their cases, hundreds of times. What made them experts, however, wasn't how many times before they'd done it, it was how many times they'd done it perfectly. Jacobs was the newest member of the team. This was only his third mission with the group. Which meant they all tended to keep an eye on him, because, as he'd stated earlier, there was a chance he'd practiced something wrong and they would need to correct for that, or they could all die.

Silently they set out toward the mouth of the cave in a V formation with Bishop at the rear. In other situations time would have been taken to send up a portable drone, but since they would be entering a cave he didn't think it would be a good use of their time. The previous flyby of a UAV had shown no defensive measures set up outside the cave, and a quick sweep of the area from a high point by the LZ had confirmed it.

Air whistled through Bishop's gritted teeth as he scanned the rock strewn desert around them. A mottled brown lizard poked its head out from behind a leafless sun scorched bush proving there truly was no place to hide. As they approached the cave entrance he thought about giving orders, but decided to leave specifics to the Senior Chief. Bishop wasn't about to pretend he was the one in charge, and as Senior gave clipped directions he realized no one else was pretending he was in charge either. He might be the Lieutenant, and technically the officer in charge, but also, and not so technically, he wasn't even supposed to be here.

The O3 who was supposed to be in charge was currently in the med bay with various nasty fluids coming out both ends. Bishop had told his friend not to eat the street food when they were on R and R in Alexandria. Walking into the cave backward, he checked their six o'clock making sure no one was going to box them in. Glancing to his right he watched Rodriguez set up behind a pile of rocks with a good field of view through the entrance. Gotta keep your exits secure.

Turning, he looked down a natural hallway made from a rock fissure. About twenty feet farther it took a hard bend to the left, and Bishop couldn't see around the corner. Four men were lined up on the right wall and four on the left. One was kneeling and watching back toward Rodriguez and Bishop while the final one was poking a bendable snake camera around the corner. With a silent wave of his hand the camera operator sent the team on into the waiting darkness.

Bishop's earpiece crackled at him, "Lt, come have a look at this."

Moving forward in the darkness of the cave, his vest light fell on the back wall and the problem the Senior Chief wanted him to have a look at. Bishop sighed and said, "This must be the reason for all the recent activity." A crack slightly shorter than himself and only just wide enough to squeeze through sideways grinned at him with stone teeth. "It must have opened up because of that little earthquake they had recently."

"That's all well and good sir, but how do we proceed?"

Bishop looked at the crack and knew this was technically his decision to make, but he didn't like it. Only one man could squeeze through at a time, and while he was moving through he definitely couldn't have any weapons out and ready. The only good news is this seemed to be the only way in or out so there wasn't much chance of the bad guys collapsing it with explosives. "Did you try to get a look through?" Bishop indicated the soldier with the snake camera.

"It's too deep. Camera doesn't go that far."

Well, thought Bishop, lets hope no one's secretly claustrophobic. Pushing yourself through that crack while hoping no one starts shooting at you could give the best soldier problems. His options were limited. If they threw a light through to see if anyone was waiting it would just announce their presence and tell people to start shooting. Separately, it was truly dark on the other side of that crack. Standing here there was still a little bit of filtered light coming in through the cave entrance behind them, but through there...

The Senior Chief nodded toward the crack, "They'll have posted a guard."

Bishop nodded. Of course there would be a guard. You would have to be an idiot not to post a guard. That didn't mean they got to just pack it up and head back to the blackhawk and call it a day. He really wasn't supposed to be here. It wasn't that he was scared. Sure he was scared, you would have to be mentally damaged to not be scared in this situation. It was the weight of the decision, and the whole team knowing he wasn't the man who should be making these decisions. He wasn't even the second choice. Lieutenant Chavez was the backup for missions like this, but no, he had to fly out yesterday because his wife was having a baby. Which meant here he was. The third string quarterback. Except in this case he was sending someone to his probable death through a crack in a cave wall.

He looked back to the Senior Chief, "Two options, and please correct me if I'm missing something Senior. We either send someone through, or we all go home."

The Senior Chief simply nodded.

"All right. I'm not as familiar with your men so who's the pick to go first?"

The Senior Chief walked the line of soldiers, stopped and tapped one on the shoulder. The man moved to the front of the line. Bishop thought for a moment then waved the rest of them up, "Here's what we're going to do. Figure out a way to block as much light from the entrance as possible and," he turned to the soldier who would be first through, "you have a balaclava?" The soldier nodded, pulled one from a pouch and put it on. Bishop glanced at his uniform to see if he could read the soldier's name, but it was too dark and he couldn't make it out. "Also, who has the highest powered flashlight?"

They all looked at each other and shrugged. "You're telling me," Bishop looked them over, "that none of you bring your own super over powered flashlight?" A sigh came from the Senior Chief and he handed over his personal flashlight. It was black, of course it was, thought Bishop, and was about as big as two fingers put together.

The Senior Chief nodded toward it, "Lt's right. The crack's too tight to carry a gun in your hand, but you can hold that. Flick it on and it'll blind anyone sitting in the dark on the other side."

Bishop nodded his thanks, "Whoever's sitting over there most likely knows we're here by now, and hopefully he's going to wait till you're exiting the crack before taking a shot at you so be ready with the light." He momentarily thought about sending two through, one right after the other, but if something went wrong he only wanted to lose one guy not two.

Four soldiers lined up across the cave tunnel to block out more light and give the darkly camouflaged figure a better chance, while the rest lined up silently next to the crack. Bishop watched as he slid his way in and was consumed by the cave mouth and swallowed by the darkness. They could hear the scrape of his uniform and Bishop realized he was holding his breath, mentally trying to hold back any extra noise that might give their sacrificial lamb away.

The scraping sound of uniform on stone stopped. A silent ten seconds ticked down in Bishop's head followed by a flash of light. A gunshot rattled his already frayed nerves and was quickly followed by two more. Next to him the Senior Chief grabbed the nearest soldier, "Squeeze through and back him up."

Bishop looked at the huddled mass of soldiers, "Medic."

A soldier stepped up to him in the darkness, "Sir?"

Before giving orders Bishop glanced at the Senior Chief who nodded back at him, sensing his question. "You go through next. There's a good chance..." He trailed off not feeling like he really needed to explain that at least one Seal was shot and waiting for help on the other side.

With a nod the medic began the uncomfortable and what Bishop assumed was a terrifying trip through the crack in the cave wall. He knew this was their job, but he was still amazed every time one of these men walked into mortal danger without so much as a blink. If someone asked him to be the first through that crack, or even the second, he would have at least needed a moment to pull himself together. He would have needed a few, or maybe a dozen or more, deep breaths, and a prayer so the good Lord knew he was imminently expected. For these men it was more than a state of mind, it was constant practice. Again, practice didn't make perfect, but it did make permanent. Once this facing death on a daily basis mindset was permanent, how did you go back to any kind of normal, quiet, family life?

The radio in his ear quietly told him it was safe for the rest to come through, and after the Senior Chief stationed another soldier to cover their exit from what he was now thinking of as The Crack, they proceeded to squeeze through. On the other side the warm glow of red flashlight filters flickered along the walls like ancient torches. Bishop squeezed out and into an open space about nine feet wide with the ceiling roughly ten feet up. Two things immediately struck him. First, the medic was tending to a bullet wound on the seal who'd gone through first, while everyone stepped quietly around the body of the terrorist with a knife sticking from the side of his head. Second, the reason they were ignoring the guy with a knife for a hat was the space they'd stepped into.

Normally the team would be decked out in night vision goggles and everything would have a haunted green glow. This time, however, was different for a very scientific reason. They didn't want to get blinded by the same method the first seal through the crack had used on the enemy. A couple of them would flip down their goggles and check around them every once in a while to see if they'd missed something, but for now they were going with the red flashlights. Scientifically speaking red was good because it didn't damage your night vision, but on the other hand blue light didn't travel as far and wasn't as easily visible to someone wearing night vision. It was a trade off depending on what the mission parameters were. Being in a cave with absolutely no sunlight filtering in meant they would have to figure out the lighting question as they went, and since the Senior Chief had a lifetime more experience, Bishop was glad to leave those decisions to him.

The spot they'd squeezed out of was obviously a crack in a surprisingly man made wall. The recent earthquake in the region must have opened up this new way in. The walls were made of cleanly cut stones that reminded him of Myan pyramids he'd seen when they'd been in port on the Yucatan Peninsula of Mexico. The stones were of all different sizes but had been fit together perfectly. The floor was similarly paved, though covered with dirt, and looking up he saw most of the ceiling was covered with cut stone blocks as well. Some had been damaged and fallen, leaving gaps, most likely at the same time as the crack had opened in the wall they'd entered through. To his right, what he was thinking of now as a hallway, had collapsed entirely, and to his left it curved so he couldn't see more than thirty feet.

"Boston," the Senior Chief whispered, "you take point. Lieutenant cover the rear."

Technically the Senior Chief, though years ahead of Bishop in experience, was below him in rank and shouldn't be giving him orders as if he was just another one of the guys. In this case, however, Bishop was willing to let it slide. He couldn't, however, stop himself from doing his job. "Medic," he knelt down and said in a low voice, "how's he doing?"

"It went through, and I've got the bleeding stopped. He should be fine to head back through the crack in a few minutes. I'll have him send Rodriguez up here and he'll take his place as the rear guard." He paused for a beat, then, "If that's alright with you, sir."

"Perfectly fine." He glanced over at the injured Seal, "Very well done in a crazy situation."

The soldier nodded, "Just doing my job sir."

Bishop stood back up and nodded at the Senior Chief, who'd taken this slight delay as all part of the plan. The Senior Chief turned and motioned to who Bishop assumed must be Boston. He didn't know if that was really the Seal's name or if it was some kind of moniker based on past events or his hometown. For all Bishop knew, there could have been a Seal team barbeque where this poor soldier hadn't done well with the baked beans and the problem had become a nickname. Either way, Boston led the way to the left and down the hallway. As the team spread out, Bishop watched them disappear around the bend until there were only a few left in sight.

Most of the soldiers in the lead had opted to flip down their night vision. The tunnel was small enough that the projected infrared would cover most of the visible hallway, lighting it up a horror movie green. Bishop decided to stick with his red lensed flashlight attached to his tactical vest. It wasn't necessarily better, he just figured someone should be different in case something happened. If the bad guys had flares set up, or any kind of bright light, and you were wearing those goggles, you'd be blind for a good while. Then, the one guy with the red flashlight could step up and save the day, or at least shoot a few bad guys, hopefully.

Once he'd gotten around the bend in the hallway, Bishop noted a change in the stone walls. He allowed himself to become distracted because, let's face it, he thought to himself, I'm the rear guard and no one is behind us, and I'm very definitely the third wheel on this date. There had been an obvious line in the wall where the normal stone had given way to larger flat areas that he could see, on closer inspection, had carvings on it. Bishop remembered from his ancient civ class in college, and from the tour he'd taken in Mexico, that the Maya had a type of pictographic language. Because of the type of stone used on the walls, he'd begun thinking of this place as Myan, but he now realized that was ridiculous. They were in northern Africa, and while the original Europeans who'd discovered the Mayan ruins in the jungles of central America had believed the Maya had come either from Egypt or were survivors of the sinking Atlantis, they all knew now it was its own separate and unique society. What he was seeing here was unknown to him, which wasn't saying much. His one ancient civ class hadn't prepared him to figure out languages carved into a hallway in northern Africa. It didn't look phonetic, like sounds you put together to make words. So, that just left pictographic like the Chinese or ancient Egyptians. Egyptian was much more obviously pictographic, since they really did look like pictures. Whereas Chinese just looked like a bunch of lines. What he was looking at here was some kind of cross between the two. There were pictures, but they were connected with different markings.

After a few wall panels covered in the unknown writing there was one with faded pictures. The red of his flashlight, while great for not interfering with the IR goggles, wasn't so great for showing the finer details of faded ancient wall paintings. What he could make out was ancient mythological looking. There was something big with wings. At first he thought it might be a dragon but it was standing on two legs and looked like it had arms. It was surrounded by smaller people, or he assumed they were people since they were mainly just dark lines with little lines that were probably arms and legs. In the next picture the big not a dragon thing looked like it was being tied down by the stick figures, but he couldn't really tell with the lack of good lighting and the centuries of being buried underground.

"Contact." The softly spoken word broke Bishop from his distracting studies of the wall. He immediately crouched down and checked their exit for any problems.

"Rodriguez?" The Senior Chief's voice carried an entire conversation of expectations in that one word.

"All clear here." Came the reply. It's meaning was layered and Bishop parsed through it as quickly as the human brain could. It meant there was nothing blocking their exit if things should go badly and they needed a quick way out. It meant the injured soldier was out of the way and taken care of, so they wouldn't need to worry about that as they were pulling out. It meant the medic was ready and standing by for whatever happened. So much meaning in just three words, and what was more amazing to him was how quickly all that meaning was absorbed and understood by everyone on the team.

"Lieutenant, you need to come see this." The Senior Chief's statement again carried more than just the words. If the rookie, third string, lieutenant needed to come up and see what was going on then things had just gotten either really dangerous or really weird. Also, it meant he needed to switch over from his flashlight to his goggles so he didn't give their presence away. Chief seemed to read his mind, "You won't need your goggles."

He switched off his light anyway and counted to ten to give his eyes time to adjust. Hints of light from around the next curve started giving an outline to the walls and soldiers around him. The bad guys up ahead must have something going on and weren't worried about being seen. Squatting down, Bishop shuffled his way to the front, tapping the shoulder of each soldier on his way by to let them know he was there, and to let the last guy in line know it was now his job to watch their backs. As he moved forward the light intensified and the hallway opened up onto a large room.

Senior Chief and who Bishop still assumed was Boston were crouched behind a collapsed portion of wall just off to the left of where the hallway opened up. Bishop wanted to stop and stare, but training, and his desire not to give them away and get them all killed overruled the feeling and he continued on till he was covered by the debris. Once safely behind the broken pieces of wall he took the time to really take in what the Senior Chief had called him forward to see.

The chamber the hallway ended in was roughly natural with a few parts obviously carved out to form more of a circle than the original cave must have been, but cave it was. There were stalactites and stalagmites, he never could remember the difference, but there were both so it didn't matter that much. The space was a bit more than one hundred feet across both ways and could easily have fit a college basketball court in it. Parts of the wall glistened with moisture and moss had obviously been growing for quite some time. The air, now that he was paying attention to his surroundings more, was humid and heavy with the smell of a closed in, derelict pool. Light played off the moisture on the walls giving it all the illusion of movement.

It was the light that really caught his attention, and the people forming a circle dressed in robes. First, before dealing with the people, his mind needed to come to grips with the source of the light in the cave. He'd assumed the terrorists had set up camp in here with battery powered flood lights of some kind and were using the area to build a type of dirty bomb. What he was not expecting was a glowing crystal about the size of a good floor lamp. The thing was almost six feet tall and maybe two feet in diameter, but those were just numbers, and Bishop wasn't sure if numbers really mattered right now. What mattered was the flickering white and pink light coming from it like some college kids' lava lamp left on for too long.

A shout snapped his attention from the pulsing shard of crystal, and a rifle report clarified his attention. Looking to his right he saw his squad flowing through the door and taking positions behind broken blocks which must have originally been finished man made parts of the walls and ceiling. Gun fire flickered from the shadows at the back of the cave followed by deadly response from his own men. It took him a moment to really see past the light cast by the standing stone and into the shadows, but eventually he saw the tell tale shapes of crouching figures with rifles tucked to their shoulders. He'd assumed the robed figures circling the light show were the terrorists the Pentagon had identified going into the cave. That assumption was wrong.

The glowing weirdness going on in the cave needed to be ignored for the moment, Bishop thought to himself. Their job was to deal with the known terrorists. Kill or capture was the order. This should be easy, he thought to himself. They were trapped in a dead end cave with the only exit he could see being held by his men. Then an RPG flashed through the cave leaving a glowing orange line across his vision. The thump of it hitting a wall behind the right hand section of the squad matched his heart rate as he looked and tried to count if any men had been injured. He started to move to get a closer look when the Senior Chief grabbed his arm and pulled him back down. "There's nothing you can do over there. Cover us while we swing over to that pile of rock." He indicated a mass of broken rock forming a perfect hunting blind. If the Senior Chief and a few others could make it they could set up good intersecting lines of fire with his soldiers on the opposite side.

Bishop raised his MK16 and opened fire. The flickering light and multiple shadows of the cave caused him to doubt what he was aiming at, but at this point it didn't matter. What mattered was putting rounds down range. He wished for a moment for a grenade launcher attachment, but then wondered about the wisdom of possibly bringing the roof down on them. After squeezing off round thirty, which he was mostly sure hit someone on the other side, he popped out the magazine, rammed home a full one, and flipped the switch to load the first round. Scanning to his left he saw the Senior Chief and two others ensconced in their own little castle and laying down a hail of bullets.

With that taken care of, Bishop reverted back to lieutenant mode. Scan the field of battle, assess everything going on, and try to coordinate it all for the best possible outcome. He knew he had fire from his left being laid down by the Chief and his buddies. Slightly to his right he could see some of the longer range MK16's poking out from around the edge of the doorway taking calculated shots across the open space to the targets on the other side. Farther to his right, and spread out behind individual chunks of debris, were the rest of the squad. Now, with time to really focus, he could see a few of them laid out behind the rocks being worked on by other members. He assumed, or more rightly hoped, one was the medic who'd moved forward after dealing with the knife fight back at their entrance point. So far only one RPG had been fired off. He could almost hear the conversation on the other end after it had exploded against the back wall. Someone must have yelled a lot. Bishop wasn't sure what language they would be yelling over there, but he was almost certain some swear words would have been flying at the guy who decided to try and bring the cave down on them.

The main issue he was running into was their ability to continue to move through the cave and eventually kill or capture all of the targets. They were devilishly hard to see from this side and since the only cover was along the walls they were also hard to get to. He considered rushing through the open area in the middle. It would be quicker and have a good chance of success, but they would absolutely take casualties, and that wasn't acceptable. In the end, slow and steady around the edges would win the day, but did they have time to be slow and steady. This group was holed up here for some reason that had yet to become obvious. Was that reason almost done? Did it have something to do with the crazy glow rock in the middle of the room? That, lieutenant obvious, had to be true, he thought to himself. Why else would they be here if not for whatever that thing was.

In fact, he took another good look around, the guys with the robes were still doing the circle shuffle in the middle of the cavern. No one was shooting at them. Well, no one was intentionally shooting at them. They hadn't pulled out any weapons. They hadn't done anything threatening, and as such his team had seen no reason to take the focus away from the actual bad guys shooting at them. Bullets flew past the men in the center, and he was fairly certain one had been hit, but only accidentally because he'd moved into the line of fire. That was his own fault.

So, Bishop ticked points off on his gloved right hand, we have heavily armed terrorists firing from the far side of the cavern. They're dug in behind chunks of rock and stalactites and will be hard to extricate without the use of more force. Maybe some smaller hand grenades will be in order eventually. Next, we have random people who are obviously working with the terrorists to accomplish some unknown goal revolving around a glowing crystalline rock in the middle of the room. Adding to that thought, he raised finger number three, we came down a very old, perhaps ancient, man-made hallway leading to this very specific spot. It told him this thing might be valuable, but if it was then why not just grab it and get out? Sell it for millions and fund your insane jihad for a few years.

A flash of light followed by a concussion brought him back to the moment. One of his men on the right had decided the grenade idea was a good one. Glancing to his left he saw the Senior Chief and his group take advantage of the momentary confusion and rush the terrorists positions. A few gunshots latter the Senior Chief's voice came through his headset, "Position neutralized. Also, whoever threw the grenade is going to get a talking to for not communicating his intentions to the rest of the squad."

"Yes, Senior Chief. Sorry, Senior Chief."

Bishop let the hangdog tone linger for a moment more before saying, "We need to round up the non-combatants in the middle and figure out what their intentions are. Who's still standing and close enough to get that done?" Bishop could just make out the shadowy shapes of the Senior Chief and a few men on the far side of the room.

"We got you Lt." Bishop glanced to his right to see three men slip out from behind the rubble directly to the right of the entryway.

They formed a perfect V as they headed toward the closest of the robed men. For the first time Bishop counted eight robed figures. As long as they weren't armed it shouldn't be a problem to round them up and get them back to the LZ. Standing and moving around the rocks he'd been crouching behind he scanned the unidentified men as his own soldiers approached slowly, one saying in a clear voice, "Place your hands on your head and get on your knees." When there was no response the three soldiers stopped and the leader said, "We will shoot you. Place your hands on your head and drop to your knees."

Bishop didn't know why, maybe it was his training actually doing it's job, but he didn't watch the unfolding drama in the middle of the room. Looking around the open area in the center of the cavern he noticed an odd rock out of place. It quickly changed from a subconscious rock to a consciously focused rock then onto a very focused claymore mine. He could see the shadows cast by its little stick legs shoved into the ground, and could imagine the raised letters spelling out "this side toward enemy" on the curved green surface.

Turning and running toward the three soldiers he heard himself yell, "Claymore…"

While at the same time another voice bounced around the cavern, "You will not have it!"

Bishop knew he should get behind something because terrorists don't yell crazy threats like that unless they're ready to blow something up. Normally it's themselves and whoever's around them, and with this being a claymore situation it was going to be a good chunk of the room that was hit. His brain quickly assessed the potential damage and noted the Senior Chief and his group would be out of the line of fire, and the other soldiers were still crouched behind the debris and safe. That left him, the three seals in the open, and all the robed guys.

He couldn't see it but he knew someone in this cave was holding a trigger for the claymore and was at that moment closing the lever that would send the signal to the C4 causing fire and concussion and seven hundred little metal balls to go flying and bouncing, turning this into a very messy kill zone.

Bishop collided with the front most seal intending to knock them both to the ground where, hopefully, they would sustain less life threatening injuries than if they were still standing in the full blast. Unfortunately, he couldn't outrun the concussive force of one and a half pounds of C4, and simultaneously something punched then stabbed him in the back.

Chapter Three

It was hot. Seriously, uncomfortably, hot. Bishop tried to shift and kick the blankets off, but something was wrong with the mattress. He was laying on his side with his hands curled up under his face. Slowly he flexed the fingers of his right hand and stopped when the world wasn't right, when sand shifted between his fingers and ground against his cheek. His eyes flew open with such speed that his eyelashes created tiny sand tornados spinning out their two second little lives in front of his disoriented gaze. Struggling to get his hands and feet under him in the shifting sand Bishop worked himself onto his knees and looked around.

The sun was up and melting its way through an empty blue sky intersecting a broken horizon. The sand he'd been laying on was the top of a short dune. More dunes of varying height extended off to his right and left while in front and behind him they flattened out onto a plain of cracked and curled up dirt. The dried out earth created geometric shapes extending out into a wavering heat haze.

Expletives learned over years in the military flew from his mouth, and if the age-old adage had been true the air would have turned a deep shade of blue around him. Maybe it would have been thick enough to create some shade from the sun now threatening to bake him into a very overcooked Thanksgiving turkey. Unfortunately the sun continued to beat down, and as he ran out of verbal abuse for the world around him, he decided to take stock and try to realign his present world with reality.

"Okay, okay..." He looked down at himself kneeling on the sand and shifted to a sitting position with his legs stretched out in front of himself. "First aid check. I'm responding and awake, I think. Maybe I'm not." He looked around. "Maybe I'm actually asleep and this is all some crazy dream, but..." Trailing off he scooped up some sand and let it stream through his fingers. "I can't operate on the premise that it's all a dream because... well just because of reasons, lots of reasons. So, bleeding..." Looking down at himself he started patting anything he could to see if there was any blood or anything crusted that might be dried blood. He remembered something hitting him in the back and tried his best to feel around from his shoulder blades down to his tailbone. Not finding anything, and getting sweatier and more sunbaked by the moment he moved on to head injuries or broken bones. Finding nothing there, he flexed all his muscles one at a time to make sure everything was working as well as possible.

"Nothing's wrong." Staring at his hands he shook his head. "Nothing's wrong, and that's wrong." He looked out over the dune and watched the sparse breeze pick up a few grains of sand and carry them down toward the cracked pancake expanse of plane in front of him. In a hundred years this might move the entire dune two or three feet forward. It was like a dirty, hot, glacier.

"Everything's wrong." The self check had been a temporary band aid over the actual injury. He wasn't supposed to be here. To the best of his knowledge there were no holes in his memory. Nothing was fuzzy or distorted. He absolutely remembered the action in the cave, the rush toward his seal team, and the claymore going off. The pain of the explosion hitting him full in the back was camera flash bright in his mind.

Nodding, he said to the sand and the sun, "Maybe I'm dead. The claymore killed me. That has to be it. It shredded me like extra swiss cheese and here I am in the worst afterlife imaginable."

Laying down flat on his back the sand shifted and formed to his body like the worst version of a memory foam mattress. He stared up at the sun and wondered why it was so hot and uncomfortable if he was dead. Sighing, he closed his eyes, and pain exploded across his back. Frantically he gasped, his eyes popped open, and he tried to sit up. Hands held him down and voices yelled over the thump of helicopter rotors, "We got you LT. Don't try to move." The inside of the copter was filled with camouflage and faces. A plastic mask pressed into the skin around his mouth and nose and the cold bitter taste of oxygen flooded in. "We need to sedate him. Hand me that needle." He briefly saw the Senior Chief's worried face as he passed a hypodermic needle to the medic. A prick in his arm was followed by ripples of cold spreading, and spreading...

It was hot, again. Raising his arm from the sand he shaded his eyes before opening them. "Seriously..." He was pushing himself up to a sitting position when a bird landed next to him. It was black and sleek like a businessman getting out of his BMW in downtown New York. It was too big for him to classify as a crow so, even though he'd never seen one in his life, he was going to say it was a raven. "Well, Mr. Raven, it seems this is all some mental delusion brought on by my injuries."

"That sounds convenient."

Bishop stared at the Raven. The Raven stared back. "Did you just..."

"What?"

"That."

The Raven looked around and seeing only sand said, "I'm worried about your state of mind."

"You're worried about my state of mind? I'm worried about my state of mind." Part of his worry was the absolute normality of the Raven's voice. "I'm sitting here getting sunburnt and talking to a raven."

"Well, you started the conversation."

"That's true." Bishop nodded, and not quite knowing where to go with the conversation reverted back to his original thought. "So, I was hurt pretty badly by a claymore explosion, and…"

"What's a claymore?" He hopped a bit, and his voice changed tone.

"Well, it's a…" Bishop started to make a shape in the air then said, "Why don't you sound like a raven?"

"What? You mean all croaky and squawky?"

"Yeah…"

"Can we talk about my lack of proper raven grammar while we find a way to get out of the heat? I mean it's all very interesting but I'm wearing all black and dying out here."

"Uhhh, well, sure, but I have no idea where I am or where to go. The last time I looked around there wasn't even a tree to head toward."

The Raven bobbed its head and hopped a few feet toward the edge of the dune, "When I was flying over here with plans to eat you…"

"You were going to eat me?"

"Look," the Raven turned one eye toward him, "no offense, but normally people that end up out here are dead and rotting. Like that guy." He bobbed his head toward the base of the dune and Bishop could just make out the wink of sunlight on glass. "He showed up screaming his head off and tumbled on down. I had to wait a bit for him to stop squirming, and the glasses were a bit annoying, but once I moved them his eyeballs were nice and warm. Just how I like em. Now if you're done interrupting," the Raven paused and waited for a beat, "I was going to say I'd seen an oasis that way." He twitched his glossy black beak toward the desert flats.

Bishop stared at him and wondered what part of his psyche had come up with all this. His practical sense took over and spoke before he could mentally wander too far away, "How far?"

The Raven turned back and looked at him, "Seriously? I don't know. I flapped a few times. I drifted on a good heat updraft for a while. My sharp amazing eyes spotted a possible dead guy on top of a dune. What do you want me to say?"

Bishop thought about it. A raven wouldn't be wearing a watch to know how many minutes or hours away it was, and he definitely wouldn't know how many miles it was because when would a raven ever learn the concept of miles. "That's a reasonable point."

"Thank you."

"So in your estimation," he wiped his sleeve across his forehead to stop more sweat from burning a path through his eyes, "do you think we could walk there and actually make it before I die from heat stroke?"

"Honestly? My experience with people walking has a lot to do with them stumbling around and never going in a straight line. They fall down and crawl for a while, and I wait to peck out their eyes."

"So is that a yes or a no on getting there before I die?"

"No way to know unless you try, and either way it's a win for me. You make it there and it's a free ride for me back to water. You don't make it and I get to eat your eyeballs."

"Why the eyeballs?"

"Lots of water in those suckers."

"Well," Bishop stood up, "my hallucinations are logical at least."

The Raven hopped and fluttered his wings enough to get direction then landed on Bishop's shoulder. "Ugh, it's a good thing I'm used to carrying packs cuz you are not light."

"Kinda the point." The Raven leaned over and poked Bishop in the side of the head with his beak. "Since I'm not a hallucination."

"Ouch." He rubbed his head and looked at his fingers to see if he was bleeding. "Well, since I know for a fact I'm being transported back to the ship with claymore shrapnel embedded in my back and an oxygen mask strapped to my face I'm going to disagree with you."

"Then why are you walking to find some shade and water?"

"Cuz you're right, and there's no good reason to sit here and sweat when I could be sitting and not sweating, even if it is all in my head."

"Ahhh, is that why you didn't freak out at the talking bird? Most people seriously freak out at a talking bird."

"Yep, that's why."

Bishop turned sideways and half slid half sidestepped down the hundred feet of shifting sand. Every once in a while the Raven would flap and move on his shoulder to keep its balance, but during the descent he stayed silent. He made a mental note of the spot where he'd seen sunlight glittering off a pair of glasses in the sand and avoided it. Using the total silence of the desert Bishop tried to organize his thoughts. For one thing this was the most realistic dream he could remember, other than the talking raven. That didn't mean much though because every dream felt absolutely real while you were in it. It wasn't until you woke up that all the little idiosyncrasies really popped up. So, what he was going with, at the moment, was this was a hallucination brought on by his injury and medical attention. Sure, he thought, he'd never had any kinds of dreams before when going through medical procedures. In all those cases, however, he'd had anesthetic. On the other hand they had stabbed him with something that felt very anesthetic like right there at the end of his helicopter memory. He shook his head trying to clear it. Every thought was shifting and sliding through his brain like the sand under his feet. They were all important, and they all made sense, but he couldn't keep a hold of them long enough for any one of them to really be a permanent solution to what was going on. This all felt too real. The weight of the Raven on his shoulder. The pain in the side of his head where he'd been pecked. The overwhelming heat of the sun beating down on him.

It reminded him of the training center at Fort Irwin. Little towns built to simulate terrorist interactions, but actually filled with the hatred and anger of the sun trying to kill every soldier quicker and more painfully than any ISIS bullet ever could. When he finally stepped from the sand onto the hard packed drought curled ground he was no closer to having his current situation figured out than when he'd taken his first sliding steps at the top. Looking back he was sure he should be able to turn the whole thing into a great metaphor about something happening in his life, but his brain was just too hot to even try.

"So," the Raven's voice was abrupt and startling after the silence of the descent, "now that you're not concentrating so hard on not slipping, falling, and dying buried in the dune, you can tell me what a claymore is and why you think this lovely place isn't real."

Normally, he was trained to keep information about missions and the actions of the various seal teams on his ship to himself for obvious reasons, but here and now he was fairly sure a talking raven in his dream or hallucination wouldn't divulge military secrets to the enemy. So, shrugging, he began the story of a third string lieutenant, a glowing rock, and the explosion that brought the two together.

Chapter Four

An involuntary groan escaped his lips and Bishop tried to look around. His last memory was finally finding a trickle of water seeping up between the broken pieces of a shattered stone, getting a drink and falling asleep under the only bush tall enough to provide some shade. It wasn't the oasis the Raven had promised but it had water and less murdery sunshine, so he'd collapsed and shut his eyes.

His current effort to look around was stymied by gunk cementing his eyes shut. He tried to raise his hands to wipe it away and felt a tug on the back of his right hand as if he was connected to something. Prying his eyes open with a force of will, the liberal use of his left hand, and aided by the corrosive effect of military vocabulary, he was finally able to see where he was.

White plastic walls held together with vertical metal strips reflected back the light of the halogen fixtures behind their frosted plastic panes. Crisp white sheets covered him and an IV sprouted from the back of his right hand. The door swung open and he turned his head to see the white shirt of the ship's doctor come into the room.

"What's…"

The doctor held up his hand, "Hang on Lieutenant Bishop. Let me check some things first then I can answer any questions you have." Leaning over Bishop he pulled out a small pen light and pointed it into his eyes.

The light, Bishop thought, the sunshine, the heat. Was it all just a fever dream?

"Your pupils seem to be back to acting properly. For a while there they were just tiny little pinpoints. Couldn't figure it out. The medic assumed you had a concussion along with everything else, and I can't blame him. The problem is, a concussion makes your pupils larger, or they just don't match with each other. Yours were like you were looking into the sun." The doctor lifted Bishop's arm, pressed his fingers against the inside of his wrist, and looked at his watch to count the beats.

Looking into the sun? It certainly had felt like it. The desert had been so real, but now, like every dream, the cracks in that reality started to show up. A talking raven, a desert that wasn't there before, none of it added up to reality.

"Your heart rate's right on the mark." The doctor walked over to the desk sitting in the corner of the room. It was cramped. The bed Bishop was lying on and the desk were just about the only things that could fit. The rest of the room was taken up with medical equipment that had hoses snaking from them, or lights dangling over his head. A door on the opposite side of the room, Bishop knew, led to the other section of the infirmary with simple beds for the sailors who had more normal maladies. A broken arm because you weren't paying attention and fell down the stairs, puking because you ate the street food the commander had told you not to eat, or even a broken nose from the fight when you lost at poker, would all end you up in that section of the infirmary. This room was reserved for real medical issues. Like getting blown up by a claymore in a cave in northern Africa.

Bishop looked back over at the doctor sitting at the desk writing notes. "How's the rest of the squad I was with?"

"Well, let's see." The doctor reached over and grabbed a manila folder and flipped it open. "We have a few gunshot injuries that are healing up nicely. One injury from a rocket propelled grenade exploding close to him. He's going to have some hearing loss as his main problem. Then there's you and a few others that were caught in the main explosion. From what I understand there was a large rock structure in the middle of the room that took the brunt of the explosion. You shielded a soldier with your body, very noble of you, and he didn't suffer any injuries. The two on either side of you took some rock shrapnel and sustained injuries comiserit with that. Nothing serious, they're already out on their own recognizance."

"And…"

"And what about you?" The doctor rolled his chair over to the side of Bishop's bed. "Your main injuries came from flying shards of what I thought were glass, but the medic from the Seal team told me were chunks of some type of quartz crystal. I'm not a geologist so I'll believe him on that. They removed the larger chunks and stopped the bleeding on site before transporting you, but I had a serious time getting all the little broken pieces out of your back. You've got a few stitches back there and a few dozen band aids."

"So, nobody died?"

"No, although I would say if you hadn't put yourself between the blast and that soldier he might not have had such a good time of it. A face full of glass shards isn't something I want to try and fix, nor is it something anyone wants to try and survive."

"Well…" Bishop let out a breath and tried to force the tension out of his muscles. The conversation about the mission helped to finally sweep away the dreamlike trance he'd felt. The desert, the Raven, it was all still fresh in his mind, not fading like so many other dreams. He could still feel the oppressive weight of heat along with the annoying weight of the Raven sitting on his shoulder. Again he pulled in a deep breath and let it slide slowly out his nose.

"All in all," the doctor rolled his chair back to his desk and stood up, "I think you've come out of this fairly well. I'll go let the Captain know you've woken up. He said he wants to talk with you."

The conversation with the Captain was predictable. The military was predictable. It was one thing most people who joined, and decided to make it a career, liked about the military. The whole thing was one big if-then statement. If you did this in your job then this would happen. People quit the military because at some fundamental level that statement hadn't worked out for them. They had done all the correct if things but the then thing had never shown up. The promotion hadn't come after years of good service, or maybe they hadn't been able to do the if part and knew the then part would never happen. The point was, his Captain had been happy with his service in a bad situation and would be putting him in for some commendations. A purple heart for sure, but also a bronze or even a silver star. That would be nice. The purple heart was something in and of itself but a silver star would be a real career mover.

After his standard chat with the Captain, Bishop tried to let himself drift off again. He figured he deserved some rest after getting blown up. Unfortunately every time he tried he couldn't shake the feeling of something reaching for him and just as he was about to drift off it would touch him and he would twitch so hard he almost fell out of bed.

A few hours and multiple failed attempts at sleep later the doctor came by and checked him over again. He said Bishop was fit to head back to his bunk. Bishop knew this was only partly true. He was fit enough to head back to his own bunk, but just barely. The doctor was ever so politely kicking him out. There was only one bed in this serious section of the med bay, and he was no longer considered serious enough to inhabit it. So, he unplugged himself from the IV, slowly dressed himself in a pair of sweats they'd collected from his locker, and hobbled back down the gray metal halls to his quarters.

Calling them his quarters was a stretch. He slept there and kept his clothes there, but so did three others. Most of the time they weren't all there together, but since he was told by the doc to take two days of recuperation he would be seeing a lot more of them. Normally it was two on two off and he would only be sleeping in the same room with one other officer since the other two had opposite duties. Bleakly he thought about the only one of them who snored, so far he'd been lucky enough to have the opposite shift, but now... He shrugged and hoped that was the worst of his recuperation.

Settling into his bunk took some time. A navy bunk was never going to be accused of being overly comfortable, and in his present situation with stitches and gauze pads tapped on he was finding it difficult to settle in. Every twist made something tug or pull and worried him that he would wake up in a pool of his own blood from multiple popped sutures. Not to mention it just plain hurt. It's strangely hard to fall asleep when it feels like something is stabbing you in the back.

For what seemed like the twentieth time a sharp jab just below his shoulder blade jerked him awake. Worried about things coming loose he reached back to check and leveraged a stick away that had been digging through his shirt into his skin. His mind froze. A mental break caused parts of his waking mind to argue with each other. While he was aware and amazed at how quickly the human mind can work through a problem he was also aware there was a problem. There shouldn't be a stick in his bunk, and while it would be possible his cabin mates had played some kind of a trick it wouldn't explain the dirt also pressed against his face and the smell of sage coming from the bushes around him. Which also led to the question of where the bushes around him came from. Confusion swarmed his brain like tiny ants crawling in mass through his head.

Starting to turn, a voice over his shoulder whispered, "Shhh, don't move. He's coming."

Trying to look without moving he said, "What? Who..."

"Shhh, seriously, if he finds us we're dead. Not just as good as dead, but actual dead."

The outline of a bird against faint starlight brought back memories of a desert and a raven riding on his shoulder. This place. But it had just been a fever dream while he was being transported. The words came out before he could consciously process them, "Who's coming?"

"Shhh, I'll tell you later."

Shifting just enough to see out through the branches of the sage brush he'd crawled under to get out of the sun he tried to look for anyone approaching. Apparently this nebulous person must be someone big, so he shouldn't be too hard to spot. Nothing was on the horizon coming toward them. Bishop had learned in some past training not to look directly at something in the dark. Your night vision was best on the edges so he scanned the horizon looking for something blocking out the star light. With no city lights to wash them out the stars were a powerful force in the night sky here in the desert.

It would have been easier, he thought, if the clouds hadn't blocked out the moonlight. Glancing up he realized it wasn't a cloud. Something was moving in the sky, something big. Looking at it, a thrum, like the plucking of a bass guitar string, started in his head. It turned, and the feeling pushed, a deep vibrating, from the base of his skull up and out. The skin on his scalp tightened and behind his eyes fingers of pain tried pressing out and up through his forehead. Burying the heels of his hands over his eyes he pressed trying to block out the pain.

"Crap, Crap, Crap," the Raven hopped toward him, "he's getting closer. Did you do something? Did he see you?"

Bishop gritting his teeth, feeling them grind against each other. His breath puffed out in tiny quick gasps as the pressure in his head spiked causing him to twitch.

"What is wrong with you?"

A scream ripped through him. Hands grabbed him and pushed him down, holding him flat. The thing, he thought. The thing in the sky. It's got me. He thrashed and fought against the hands. His head still pulsed and pounded, but his training, and what was left of his rational mind told him he needed to see. He needed to know what he was fighting against.

The room around him was at once his bunk onboard and the sagebrush. There were men in uniform trying to hold him down while a great shadow blocked out the moon and stars.

A voice, "Lieutenant? Can you hear me? Lieutenant Bishop?"

The raven, "Well, bloody eyeballs, he's headed this way. Sorry man, but I'm gonna hide over there. If there's anything left of you when he's done, I promise to be polite when I eat your carcass."

Another voice, "Doc, he's gone into some kind of… What is that? Are those horns on his head? Careful he kicked a hole in the bulkhead…"

The darkness settled, blocking out his quarters, and silencing the voices. Then it spoke, "Who are you?" It was as if cold had a voice, as if the deep night of uninhabited mountain sides could speak. "I can feel you. Are you a way out?"

Bishop couldn't speak, couldn't think of what to say even if he did feel up to uttering a retort to the madness. Lashing out he tried to push it away but a hand caught his wrist.

Again the deep thrum vibrated through his head and the thing said, "I need to know."

A sharp pain in his shoulder caused cold to flood through him. The smell of the sage brush slowly dimmed. The darkness retreated. His quarters became fuzzy around him. Finally, it all went away.

Chapter Five

Peter Bishop woke up strapped to a table. It took him a good while to realize this, and the realization came not from feeling the straps but from not being able to roll onto his side. The world was foggy and all he wanted to do was roll over and curl up because laying flat on his back for too long had left an ache in the small of his back. If he could just curl his knees up it would stretch out and he could get another hour of sleep, but it wasn't working.

Squirming in bed, his body tried to figure out the problem while his brain was still searching in the haze for the on switch. Nothing seemed to make sense. There were loose ends in his memory, but that didn't matter. Only the now mattered, and in the now he couldn't roll over. His heart started racing and he could feel panic rising like bile in the back of his throat.

"Bishop?" A hand was on his arm, pressing down, telling him to be still, but how could he when he was trapped and he didn't know why. "Peter, you need to be still." He paused at that. He didn't hear his first name much anymore. For years now he'd been Bishop or Lieutenant, not Peter.

His eyes tried to focus. The light was dim in the small room, and after a moment he recognized the medical bay on his ship. He was on his ship. He was in the medical bay. He remembered being injured in the cave when the terrorists had set off the explosion. Was he here because of that? There had also been a large black bird talking to him, and he was irritated at it because… Because why? And hadn't he made it back to his bunk? Why was he back here? Finally, his eyes came to rest on the other person in the room. "Captain?" His voice was a rough whisper, but in the silence of that small room it carried.

"Nice to see you back, Lieutenant."

Bishop licked his lips and tried to swallow. His mouth was so dry. "What happened sir? Why am I…" He tried to look down at himself but couldn't sit up enough to see much. The thick cloth of the straps pressed into his bare arms and across his chest with others across his belly, thighs, and shins.

"Well," the Captain hesitated, looking up at the ceiling, "there was an incident."

Bishop knew it must have been bad. The Captain of the ship didn't just sit in your hospital room waiting for you to wake up because he missed you. It's not that he wasn't a caring man, he was, at least as much as the commander of a naval ship could be, it was that he was also a very busy man. If a sailor had been seriously injured the Captain would definitely find a moment to poke his head in and check on the poor soul. That's what made him a good Captain. He cared about his men. However, it was a big ship, with lots of sailors. "Why are you here sir?"

The Captain looked around the dimly lit room devoid of any other person, most notably devoid of a doctor. He nodded and understood Bishop's implied meaning. It wasn't, why are you personally here, but more along the lines of why is the Captain of the ship sitting here watching over me while I'm strapped to a bed. "This incident..." The Captain hesitated then started again, "There were some unusual..." Again he paused.

Bishop chuckled as much as he could, "Sir, I'm strapped to a bed and don't really remember why. If you could just get to the point. Am I in trouble? Did I do something?"

"Yes?" The question inflection at the end of that single word told Bishop a lot, but at the same time wasn't helpful. It meant the Captain was here because he needed to know something. He was hunting for information. Rolling his chair closer to Bishop's head the Captain leaned toward him, "Do you remember what happened in your bunk?"

Yep, Bishop thought, the Captain's fishing for information. "Well..." Bishop tried running through things as chronologically as he could but his memories were still foggy. "Was I drugged, sir?"

"Right," the Captain stood up and moved out of sight above Bishop's head, "the doc said you might need this to get you going again." Bishop tilted his head up as far as the restraints would let him and could just make out the Captain adjusting something on an IV line he hadn't even realized was leading to his arm. Priorities, he thought. I was so focused on being tied down, I didn't even realize there was a tube sticking out of my arm. "There," the Captain sat back down, "Doc said that shouldn't take too long to kick in. He said if I needed to ask you anything I should use that."

A memory of getting home from basic training sprung to mind. It was a vivid memory because traumatic events, like basic training, tend to stick. He'd been home for a few days and decided to call a girl he knew and see if she would go out to dinner with him. Being back from basic was a great excuse to ask anybody to do anything because he'd just gone through something and they wanted to know about it. Why not put it to good use and see if she liked him. The dinner was nothing special, and their conversation and interaction had faded to almost nothing in his mind, but what he did remember was the soda. For months on end at basic then again at advanced training he'd been drinking only what was deemed healthy. Milk, water, and such things were the only things on order. Every once in a while they were able to get something like orange juice and that was amazing. Then he'd gone on this date and decided to celebrate by getting a highly caffeinated beverage. Turns out, if you haven't had caffeine in a while and then you do, it really has an effect on you. He remembered not being able to stop tapping his fingers on the restaurant table, but he couldn't remember anything they'd talked about.

Whatever chemical the Captain had released into his bloodstream did its work. Everything around him seemed to have edges sharp enough to cut a steak. The cloth of the straps tingled against his skin making him want to itch. The desk lamp on the doc's table buzzed then hummed then buzzed again.

The Captain checked his watch, "According to our good medical professional you should be all hopped up by now. How do you feel?"

"Uhm…" Bishop licked his lips, "I, uhm…" his mouth was so dry, "Is there…" he looked around for anything to drink.

"Oh, right. He said you would have a wicked case of cotton mouth after everything." The Captain leaned over and grabbed a water bottle with a straw sticking out.

Drinking from it brought home to Bishop the insanity of the situation. He was strapped to a table on his own naval ship with his own Captain leaning over him. What exactly had happened? He wanted to know. Swallowing, he tried to start at the beginning, "I remember being blown up down in the cave." The Captain nodded at him. "I woke up here with the doc and a bunch of stitches in my back." That was clear to him. The conversation, being released to head back to his bunk and get some rest, wondering if he'd be able to because some of his bunk mates snored. "I got back to my bunk and had a hard time falling asleep because the stitches kept pulling and I was worried about them. Then…" There was a raven, but he didn't want to say that out loud. That was crazy. But, there had been a desert and a raven. He'd walked through the heat and finally found a place to sleep under sagebrush. The smell of it mingled with the wet earth around a puddle of water he'd drunk out of before collapsing into fitful sleep on the ground. There had been something there. Something blocking out the stars. The Raven had left him, which was why he was annoyed, but that was all he could remember.

"Something wrong Bishop?"

"It's just," he wiggled to get a little more comfortable under the straps, "are these really necessary sir?"

"You kicked a hole in the metal bulkhead by your bunk so I'm going to leave them for now."

"I'm sorry, I did what?"

Taking a deep breath the Captain leaned back in the wheeled office chair, "Sometime around oh three hundred there was a report of a fight in your room so some guys were sent down to investigate. When they popped your door open they found... well..."

"Sir," Bishop tried to keep his voice as calm as possible, "I'm strapped to a bed and don't know why. Just tell me."

"Strange things happen on this job if you're here for long enough."

"Straps, sir."

"According to the eye witness reports you were thrashing as if something was trying to attack you. They called for the doctor thinking something had gone wrong with your meds or you had been infected with something from the explosion in the cave."

"Right, but..." Bishop rolled his head to say get on with it. Obviously he wouldn't be strapped to a bed in the infirmary if this was all just him fighting off a fever because of some cave slime.

"The side of your bed is connected to the bulkhead running down the length of the hallway." The captain paused again, as if this statement about the position of his bunk would answer all the questions swirling through Bishop's head. Rather than state the obvious yet again about the conversation Bishop decided to stare at the captain in the hope this would somehow move things along better than his previous remarks. Looking up at the ceiling the captain finally continued, "They were a bit worried about you injuring yourself by kicking the metal bulkhead. At least they were until you kicked a hole in it. One sailor standing at the door to move lookers along said he saw your foot come through the other side."

The statement about his foot seemed to be the pebble holding up the dam because when he'd finally gotten it out everything else flooded behind it. "One report says you grew horns for a few minutes. Another claims you were speaking in a language none of them recognized. When the doc got there he claimed to hear multiple voices, and that you levitated off the bed for a moment. Technically he refused to say that in any official capacity, but he was unofficially freaking out."

Taking a deep breath the captain broke eye contact with the ceiling panel directly above him and looked at Bishop. "Honestly, I didn't know what to do. By the time I got there the doc had administered some kind of sedative and was in the process of strapping you down." He looked around the room as if there would be an answer stenciled on the walls. "I've seen men do crazy things over the years, and I've had reports dropped on my desk of everything from UFO sightings to unexplained underwater lights so I know there's crazy out there."

"So, wait," Bishop stared at the captain hoping somehow he could get reality back on track, "you're going to just believe that I, what, that I grew horns? That I, somehow, kicked a hole in a slab of steel?"

"Well," the captain leaned forward, putting his hands on his knees, "I have a few options. One, I can believe them one hundred percent. Which to me, and by the look on your face, to you as well, would be a trip to crazy town. The real problem with option one is what to do about it. The doc doesn't have medical experience dealing with," he raised a hand from his knee and waved it at Bishop, "all of whatever that is, and it's not like I can honestly write a report up about it. Option two, I can say it was all some crazy kind of epileptic seizure brought on by your encounter with the terrorist cell down in that cave. However, there are problems with that option as well. The main problem being the hole in the bulkhead by your bed. I don't care what kind of allergic reaction you're having, no one can kick a hole in that wall, and yet..." He shrugged expansively.

Something shifted on the bed accompanied by a rustling like feathers. "So you believe them?" Bishop couldn't wrap his mind around the conversation they were having.

Next to his ear Bishop heard, "Why wouldn't he?"

Bishop twiched. That voice. He whispered, "You left me."

"Well yeah." The feathers rustled again and the weight on the bed shifted slightly closer to his ear. "You did see how big he was, right?"

"Lieutenant?"

Bishop stopped. He stopped breathing. He stopped struggling to turn his head and look at the stupid Raven who'd left him to deal with that monster alone. The moment froze. He was strapped to a bed in the infirmary on his ship. He was a lieutenant in the United States Navy. He'd been injured on a mission to deal with a known terrorist cell. He was hearing a raven talk to him. A raven that should only exist in a dream he'd had about a desert. Turning his head he looked at the captain. "Sir. Something's wrong sir."

The captain gave him a short nod. "That brings me to option three. You see, lieutenant, as I said before, if you're in this line of work for long enough you see some strange things. Things that aren't always easy to talk about or explain. I know you don't want things to be strange, but sometimes you don't get a choice. I'm not sure I believe the horns part, but I have to believe the kicking a hole in the bulkhead part, which tells me something's wrong. Now you start talking to things that aren't there, and you want to tell me something is wrong. That's two wrongs in a very short amount of time. So, let's take the easy way and you tell me what you think is going on."

He felt the Raven hop once next to his head, "Yeah. Tell him all about it. I'd kinda like to know why I'm sitting here and not back in my nice eyeball eating world."

Bishop breathed in and smelled the feathers. For the next ten minutes he tried to explain what was happening, but the problem he kept running into was that he had no idea what was happening.

"Wait, wait," the Raven pulled at his hair, "you were in a hallway with what markings again?"

The captain was leaning back in the office chair and obviously didn't hear anything the Raven had said, "I don't remember seeing anything in the official report about markings on the walls in the caves."

"Honestly sir, I was just getting in their way. You and I both know I was only there as a placeholder. The mission legally needed an officer present and I was the only one available at the time." The captain nodded. "I didn't want to mess things up by pretending I was actually commanding the mission, since I wasn't, so I admit I spent a little bit of time examining the area while they did what they do." When the captain didn't argue with this position Bishop continued, "The tunnel we were in was obviously man made and old. It wasn't carved, or at least if it was then the carved parts were covered up by cut stone. In some areas the stones were larger and covered with pictures."

The Raven bounced on the bed next to him, "What kind of pictures?"

"Well, there was writing that I obviously can't read."

"Right, right." He could feel the Raven hop next to his head.

"Then there were pictures of a big thing with wings being pulled down by little people with ropes."

"Oh, oh, like the thing…"

The movement of the covers created a picture in Bishop's head of the Raven hopping from foot to foot, "The thing?" A giant black shape cut a hole in his memory. Wings blotting out the sparkle of the stars as it dropped lower.

The captain's voice cut through his thoughts like a bad brain freeze, "The thing? Lieutenant, you are making less and less sense as this conversation goes on, and are you really talking to someone I can't see?"

"Sir, I," Bishop hesitated. His ability to complete any sentence that would help this situation make sense had abandoned him, melting away like snow thrown into a furnace. "I've got nothing sir. This is all wrong. I've never had an issue in my life like this. Just look at my file, sir. This isn't me."

"True," the Raven's breath tickled his neck, "you are stunningly boring. Well, except for that moment when it came down and didn't eat you. That was exciting."

"Bishop," the captain sighed and rubbed his jawline with his right hand, "I believe you, and I've looked at your file. I've even taken the time to talk with your shipmates. You were on the fast track for a promotion, now..." He stood up, walked over to the door, opened it and leaned out. Bishop could hear him talking with someone, but couldn't make out the words. Anxiety flooded through him, riding on a cold wave of adrenaline. Who else knew he was strapped down in here? Was some rumor spreading through the ship about him having hysterical fits? Something like this could ruin his career. It would follow him as a joke wherever he was assigned. The captain closed the door behind him and sat back down.

"Sir?"

Raising his hand the captain cut him off. A moment later a knock sounded on the door. Standing back up the captain let in a single sailor. Bishop amended that thought to a marine. He didn't personally know the marine currently closing the door behind him, but knowing he was a marine was as easy as checking the time on your watch. The uniform, especially the hat tucked into his right pocket, would have given it away, but even when not in uniform just the way he stood would have said marine. It would have shouted Marine except this particular one looked like he didn't need to shout. He was maybe six feet tall, putting him a few inches shorter than Bishop, but probably outweighed him by a good fifty pounds. Where Bishop was tall and thin like a track star, this guy was a brick wall built by a very experienced mason.

"Corporal Sidney, take a seat." The captain glanced between Bishop and the new soldier, "The corporal is on loan to us from the department of defense. He finished his other duties and is now free to help me out with this little fiasco."

The corporal pulled up a folding chair and Bishop listened to it creak as he lowered himself into it.

The Raven whispered next to his ear, "Now that's a guy. I mean I know he's a guy, and you probably know he's a guy, but I mean he's really a lot of guy. Can he hear me? Cuz, I mean, I can't really fly away in this place, and if he gets upset at stuff... Actually, I'm still a little fuzzy on what's going on with me right now."

Bishop totally agreed with that sentiment. He was listening to an invisible raven who, he was pretty sure, had only existed in his dreams until an hour ago. It was quickly coming to the point where he would have to make a decision about his sanity. At this moment the easiest decision, being strapped to a bed and all, was to do nothing.

Freaking out about hearing voices would only make things worse. So he laid there, strapped down, agreeing with the invisible raven on his bed as the marine corporal took a seat.

The captain started pacing across the room, "Here's the deal." He went out of Bishop's line of sight then a moment later walked back into it. "This situation is all kinds of messed up. Sometimes as a commander you need to be able to admit when you don't have all the answers. At those moments you learn to delegate to the best people you know. Lieutenant, you and Corporal Sidney here are going on a mission. The official record will show that you were injured beyond the capacity of this ship to handle. Sometimes the best stretch of the truth is the one that's closest to the actual truth. We will be dropping you off at a hospital in Rome to seek specialized medical care and relaxation. The paperwork will be heavily redacted, officially because of the assignment you were on when you were injured. There will be no original in existence. Corporal, unofficially you are to act as the lieutenant's bodyguard. Officially you are simply escorting him to the hospital then taking some well earned R and R in Italy before heading onto your next assignment. Finally, and let me make this clear to the both of you, if Lieutenant Bishop gets out of hand in any way that you, corporal, deem over the line and dangerous to our national interests, you have my permission to shoot him."

The captain stopped pacing and made eye contact with them both.

"Sir?" The corporal leaned forward in his seat.

"Yes, corporal."

"I'm going to need a little bit of a briefing on," he waved a hand at Bishop.

Bishop sighed and dropped his head back onto his pillow. He would love it if everything could be resolved with a simple briefing. Open the right paperwork, maybe some nicely colored maps, some charts or graphs, color coded would be best, and explain exactly what was going on with him. Staring at the pockmarked white dropdown ceiling Bishop thought he'd been handling all of this remarkably well. All things considered, and there really were a lot of things to consider, he thought he'd kept himself from absolutely losing his mind. According to the captain, and maybe he was right about this, he had lost his mind, but Bishop didn't feel like that was true. What did it feel like to lose your mind? Did it feel like an invisible raven making a dent in the bed next to your left ear? Did it feel like, or rather smell like, sage brush and mud when he knew for a fact he was on a naval ship in the middle of the Med?

If he was going crazy what should he do about it? Fight it? Pretend the voices weren't there? Try to go about his life like everything was good to go? Or, should he roll with it?

Bishop listened to the captain try to explain to Corporal Sidney what exactly was going on, and he was impressed with the poker face the corporal held. What would he do if the captain was calmly telling him that one of the junior officers was showing signs of, what, possession? That's what it sounded like the captain was implying. Horns popping out, strange languages coming out of his mouth, strength enough to kick a hole in metal.

"So," the corporal used the word to fill the air for a moment after the captain finished. It hovered there like the blade of a guillotine waiting to execute Bishop's fate. "What exactly are we supposed to do?"

"Exactly," the captain had sat down to explain the issue to the corporal and now stood back up waving his hands in the air like that would help move the problem of his possessed lieutenant away from him faster, "I contacted a friend of mine at the Vatican."

"As in, The Vatican." Corporal Sidney emphasized the words so you could hear the capital T and V.

"Yes, corporal, the head of the Catholic church Vatican. The only people I know with two thousand years of experience dealing with this kind of stuff, Vatican."

"Sir," the corporal hesitated as if he really wanted to ask the question but wasn't sure if it was appropriate. Eventually, Bishop could see the decision come across his face that given the case at hand any question might be appropriate. "Have you dealt with this kind of thing before?"

The captain stopped pacing and looked up and the ceiling, "There was an incident in the first Persian Gulf war. Someone found something out in the desert on the way to Bagdad." He dropped his gaze and held eye contact with Bishop. "Let's just say this time has gone a lot better than that one."

"How's that sir?"

"For starters, no one's died yet, and I'd like to keep it that way."

Bishop tried to decide what to do with his face as the captain's eyes and statement drilled into his head like a good old 1920's lobotomy. Should he smile to show the captain that everything was just fine? Nope, he tossed that idea aside for its sheer creepiness. Should he try to present an air of steely resolve, like they were all in this together and he'd be certain to fight his way through it? He settled on that idea, but by the time he mentally made it there all he was able to do was try to minimize the look of sheer terror and overwhelming

38

confusion. Normally, as an officer, he was great at hiding his true feelings. It was a normal skill when you're sometimes surrounded by young, inexperienced, idiots with access to guns. This time, however, things were different.

"Hey," the Raven whispered in his ear, "I think I've done a pretty good job of not butting into what are obviously some heavy issues, but I think I need to tell you something."

Bishop stopped himself from answering on the grounds that he didn't want to look even crazier to the corporal. But he did nod in a way he hoped would come across to the invisible raven who might actually just be a projection of his broken psyche. He didn't feel like he needed to answer, for the before mentioned reason, but even if it was all in his head, there was no reason to be rude to his own demented illusions. After all, if he could dream this all up then who knows what might happen if he pissed things off.

"I'll take that as you wanting to hear what I've got to say, but first," Bishop felt a short bounce of weight next to him then distinctly felt two bird feet land on his chest. "Hey!" Bishop twitched as the Raven's voice echoed off the walls of the small infirmary room. "Fat captain, and stupid faced guy! If you can hear me do something!"

Neither of the two twitched. They continued with their conversation, laying out the details of transportation to the military airport closest to Rome. "Well then," the Raven hopped a few times on Bishop's chest, "this is awkward. I can see everything. I can move around. You can see me, right?" Bishop lightly shook his head. "What? You can't see me? This whole thing's getting more and more bonkers by the second."

Bishop wanted to reach up, grab the bird, and shake him while yelling something like, really? Really? You think this is bonkers? I'm strapped to a bed and my CO is talking about me being possessed.

"By that twitch in your face I'm assuming you agree with me. However, before we get into a conversation about the existence of multiple planes of reality and me seeming to be stuck between them, I think I need to warn you about something."

Bird feet hopped on his chest. Back and forth. One foot to another. "Something else is here, with me. I mean, with us."

"Lieutenant," Bishop had been staring at the blank space on his sternum where he could absolutely not see the Raven he felt there, and the captain's appearance next to his bed made him twitch.

"Sir." His arm started to move involuntarily to salute. At some point in a soldier's career certain things moved from conscious thought to pure muscle memory. Other things, however, were older, deeper in the psyche, burned into his personality from a young age, and unfortunately, sarcasm was one of those. "Are you two finally done discussing how you're going to shoot me? Because I'd love to get off this bed. These straps are really starting to itch."

The captain stared down at him, and for a moment Bishop worried he'd gone a step too far, but the corporal with his sidearm drawn told him that, no, he really hadn't. If things were going to spiral out of control then he was going to say something about it.

Shaking his head the captain started undoing the straps. "At least I know your personality hasn't changed, lieutenant. Hopefully that means," the last strap came off and Bishop sat up, "everything will be fine and all of this will just be a strange memo in your file."

Rubbing his arms, Bishop swung his legs over the edge of the bed. The corporal started to raise his weapon and the captain waved him back irritably. Bishop cocked his head and met the corporal's eyes, "Sidney, actually I'm just going to call you Sid, if you keep thinking about shooting me every time I sit up, this relationship is going to be a difficult one." Standing up Bishop stretched and touched the ceiling panels. It wasn't an amazing feat. Naval ships, any ship actually, just had low ceilings. Space was at a premium, and unless you were on some super yacht, you weren't going to get nine foot, or even eight foot, ceilings.

Bishop stood at just over six feet tall with short cut brown hair. Standing there in his PT uniform shorts and t-shirt you could tell he had military amounts of muscle, but he wasn't going to be mistaken for a bodybuilder. He was a bit on the extra fuzzy side with enough arm and leg hair that it would actually sun bleach if he was on deck for too many rotations. Corporal Sidney, on the other hand could pass for a bodybuilder. It wasn't that he was short, but his mass made his height seem irrelevant.

"All right boys," the captain stepped into Bishop's line of sight, "you don't need to stare each other down. Hopefully nothing will come of all this." Turning to look over his shoulder, "The lieutenant's right corporal, if you twitch your trigger finger everytime he moves this will turn into a fiasco. Give him the benefit of the doubt. If something crazy happens, you'll know it."

Sid nodded and holstered his weapon, "Well, if it's alright with you sir," the captain nodded at him, "I say, the sooner we get going, the sooner this is over with."

Chapter Six

The sun filtered through the sagebrush and left artistically dappled shadows dancing across Bishop's face. Sand dug into his cheek, and he rolled over to brush it off. Realization hit him like, well, like a bag of sand. "Son of a…"

"Yay!" The Raven hopped into view. "I'm real again!" One final hop landed him on Bishop's outstretched leg. "You have no idea how weird it was to be someplace I'd never seen before, and on top of that I was invisible. Right? I was invisible, right? And, no one could hear me. Well, except for you, and you really couldn't say much because whoever that other guy was, he was super sure you were bonkers crazy, and a smart raven like myself knows you don't want people to think you're any crazier than you need to have them think you are…" he trailed off as his sentence started to wrap itself back around like a climbing vine.

Clenching his teeth just served to make his jaw hurt, so taking a few deep breaths, Bishop rolled onto his knees, not caring if the Raven was disturbed, and crawled out from under the mass of sage he'd slept under. Did he sleep under it? Had he actually slept? Maybe he was sleeping right now. The last thing he remembered was strapping into the helicopter for their ride to Italy. It had been decided that landing at a military airbase would take too long and involve too many interactions with people who didn't need to know what was going on. They would have to catch a train and make multiple stops on their way to Rome, or they could just land at the airport in Rome and call it good.

Getting out from the sagebrush patch only achieved scratches and more irritation. Standing and shielding his eyes against the rising sun he swore. Normally he didn't. It's not that it was totally a choice, some of it was, but it was mainly just a lack of habit. However, there were times and scenarios he reserved for swearing. This was one of them. He was good at swearing. Partly this was due to his overexposure to the words and usages of them in his chosen workplace, and also it was due to his lack of normally swearing. Sometime in the past he'd made the subconscious decision that if he wasn't going to swear normally, when those few times came around for it then he might as well do it in style. So he swore, and he swore again but this time longer. He called the expansive desert in front of him names that should only apply to demons who've come to eat your children.

"Wow." The Raven landed on his shoulder. "Just wow. I mean, I eat dead things on the regular and am known around the world as something of a bad omen, but that right there…" He pecked him on the ear.

"Hey," Bishop twitched sideways, "what was that for?"

"Someone has to do something about that potty mouth of yours."

"Seriously?" Bishop waved his hands at the world in front of him. "This is the wrong world."

"Well, I think…"

"I don't care what you think," he waved his arms hard enough for the Raven to flap irritably off in front of him and land on a broken off piece of sagebrush. "I am being accused by my commanding officer of being possessed by a demon. I am somehow having a recurring dream of being in the worst place possible. And the only person I have to talk to about it is you, and you don't seem to have any answers to what is happening to me."

"I might."

Bishop stared at the black feathered harbinger of doom and wondered if it would help to throw something at him. Was it even a him? It might make him feel better, but he also wouldn't have anyone to talk to at that point, and that wasn't helpful. "What do you mean, you might?"

"Have you ever asked?"

"Why would I ask? You don't know me. You seemed just as confused as I was when we were back in the infirmary."

"True, true, but I might, and since you never actually asked, how would you know?"

"Well?" Bishop was fairly sure this was proving to be an actual descent into madness, and he wouldn't blame Super Soldier Sid for shooting him at some point. Then he mentally congratulated himself for the good use of alliteration in his nickname of the corporal.

"Well what?"

"Are you kidding me?"

"Maybe a little, but still it would be nice to hear you actually ask."

"So you're saying you don't want to find out why you were invisible in a different plane of reality?"

"Oh, now you're turning it back around on me are you?"

"Fine." He still wasn't sure if any of this place was real, or all in his head, but what was the harm in asking. "Do you know anything about what's going on around here? Specifically with me, and why I keep being here, and not where I'm supposed to be."

The Raven puffed himself up, "I know this is going to be a terrible thing to say, but…"

"Let me guess," Bishop threw his hands in the air, "after all that, you don't actually know anything."

"That is not what I was going to say. What I was going to say is, we should walk and talk because I really don't want to be stuck out here in the sun all day. Again."

"That..." he felt his jaw clinch again.

"That what? That's a great idea? I'll assume that's what you were going to say. Anyway," the Raven fluttered up and landed back on his shoulder, "I know the oasis is a bit of a walk in that direction." He pointed forward and slightly to the right with his beak. "It's what we were heading for yesterday but we ran out of time. Well, you ran out of time. I could have kept going."

"Great." Bishop started walking. "I might as well have fun getting imaginary sun stroke while I talk to a raven who might just be a figment of my imagination."

"Could a figment of your imagination do this." Grabbing his hair with his beak he pulled.

"Ow! You son of a magpie..." Bishop swatted at him.

"Woah, hold on there," the Raven caught a draft and hovered a few feet over Bishop's head. "Now you're just getting mean."

"Am I?" Continuing to walk, Bishop unbuttoned his over shirt and pulled it off, "You haven't answered any questions. All you do is talk and poke." He draped his shirt over his head then wrapped the sleeves around and tied them at the base of his neck, making a giant bandana. "I carried you from the dune, and the one time I needed help you hopped off to safety and left me at the mercy of whatever that was."

"First of all," the Raven tacked back and forth in the air, attempting to keep pace with Bishop, "it's almost impossible to stay with you if I'm flying, and I was worried about you dropping dead on me. Well, worried isn't really the right term. I wouldn't have minded too much if you died, cuz, you know, eyeballs are tasty. Second," he squawked to keep Bishop from interrupting, "this is where we get to what I know, but I need to land. Because talking to you while trying to keep you in range of talking to you, while concentrating on the updrafts caused by the heat given off by the sand, is going to drive me insane."

"Oh, you mean like how I feel popping back and forth while having some overeager hallucination take over my brain?"

"I'm telling you, it's not a hallucination. I know you don't believe me," he landed on Bishop's shoulder, "but this is real."

"It can't be real."

"Why not?"

"Well," Bishop stopped walking, "it just…" He waved his non bird carrying arm at the desolate landscape. With the sun coming up in full force he could see there was more to the desert than just sand and rock. Scrub brush and grasses popped up. Most of them dry and wilting, but some showing a colorful resilience, holding out hope there would be something other than a hot dry death. He started walking again. Heading toward what looked to be something in the distance.

"I assume," the Raven inched closer to Bishop's ear to center his weight, "you're trying to express the idea that simply because you've never encountered something before means it can't exist."

"Well," Bishop's mind filled with examples of things he hadn't encountered but he knew were real. Whales, penguins, and cuttlefish were the first things to pop into his head. "The difference is that while I might not have personally encountered things, other people have. We've documented the natural world. We know what's out there."

"And just for one moment let's pretend someone did get here. Let's pretend they then tried to tell people about it, to document it, as you say. What," the Raven hopped, "would your people say about all this?"

"The exact same thing I'm saying."

"Head a little more to that way." The Raven nudged him to the left, "There's some closer water there."

For a while they walked in silence. Bishop ran back over everything from the last few days. The only other person he'd seen while in this place had been the dead body back at the giant sand dune. He had no answers. There were two obvious choices. First, he was dreaming, or hallucinating, or something like that. With the injury he'd sustained on the mission it could be the case. Second, this was all real. Another world existed. It was a sucky desert world, but another world altogether. Somehow, he traveled back and forth between them whenever he fell asleep. That all sounded like the worst storyline to a budget movie.

"You said you had answers."

The Raven bobbed his head, "I figured I'd let you be in your own head for a while. All this stuff must be hard. I know it was pretty crazy for me when I was in that little room and no one else could see me. I'm still not quite sure how that happened. I feel like I should know. Like, it's right there and if I just wait long enough the answer will just show up. I feel like it's something I forgot."

"Well?"

"Well what?"

"Answers."

"Oh, sure, sure." Hopping into the air the Raven extended his wings and glided over Bishop's head to land on the other shoulder.

"Here goes. That thing from the other night. You know the one. It's the only other thing that's happened so far."

"Right," Bishop nodded, "the big black thing that I thought was going to eat me, but decided to talk to me for some reason."

"Yeah, that thing."

"Well?" Bishop was starting to make a decision. It was slowly bubbling up in the back of his mind, influenced by years of movies and TV shows. He'd been sliding down a hill of silent desperation ever since he'd woken up in the sand, and he was almost to the bottom. His conscious mind was scanning the rocks and scrub brush around him, the distant shadows of unknown trees or hills, and even the sky for any threats. His subconscious mind, however, was still freaking out. Lists were being made and discarded with talking ravens, and massive shadows blotting out the moon and stars at the top of that list.

"It's a dragon."

Yup, his subconscious said, and his conscious mind replied with a situation report of the skies being all clear. That does it, Bishop thought as his subconscious and conscious minds finally came together and agreed on the situation. I'm hiking through an imaginary wasteland talking to a raven about a dragon.

"What?"

Bishop realized he'd been mumbling to himself. "A dragon. A talking bird."

"Raven, thank you very much."

"Sure, sure." He turned and started walking in the opposite direction. "I agree with the captain that something strange did actually happen. I wasn't awake for it so I do have to take his word for it, but there's no reason for him to lie. To the best of my knowledge he's never even pulled a prank on anyone, so I can't chalk it up to that."

"Why are we going this way?"

"There was absolutely, positively, a big glowing crystal rock thing in that cave."

"A what?"

"Caves are known to have strange things growing in them. I mean, we all know there are kinds of mushrooms that can make you see and do things, just straight up hallucinogens."

"Seriously." The Raven hopped on his shoulder. "The water is the other way."

"And mushrooms grow in caves. That's a well known fact. I'm not saying it was a giant mushroom. That would be crazy. Ha," he picked up the pace to what his drill sergeant back in the day called a range walk, "crazy. This whole thing is crazy, and I think that's what tipped me off."

The Raven leaned over and tried to get eye to eye with Bishop, "Have you lost your mind? I'm trying to tell you something important about a really big dragon, and the really important not dying water, and you're going the wrong way."

"But that's just it, isn't it? Everything always feels real when you're in it. Even if one wall of your old high school classroom is missing and all the chairs have been replaced with tree stumps. You always think it's real right up until you wake up and realize it was seriously kooky dooks. Your house wasn't actually your house, and you know what gives it all away?"

The silence dragged on for a good count of ten until finally, "Fine," the Raven fluffed his feathers out, "if it gets you back on track I'll answer your crazy question. What gives it all away?"

"The fact," Bishop's voice grew louder with every word, "that nothing makes sense."

"Great. Now can we get turned around and headed toward the water? I like water."

"No. I don't think you're real. I think this is all some messed up hallucination caused by some weird fungus that got jammed into my bloodstream when that claymore went off in the cave. I also think I've put up with about enough of this. I'm not going to die if I walk the wrong way in a made up desert, and I'm not listening to the ravings of a hallucinatory talking bird."

"I'm a raven." Pushing off Bishop's shoulder he leaped into the air, and flapping his wings to gain stability, he said, "We are the most majestic of birds, and I don't need to help you. If you want to die off by yourself then fine. I had a feeling like I almost remembered..." a twist of hot air caught him and sent him up.

"Good riddance." Bishop watched him drift farther and farther up, turning to head back the way they'd been walking. "And," he cupped his hands around his mouth to make a megaphone, "everyone knows the most majestic bird is an eagle."

*   *   *

Bishop's headset had slid forward and was partially covering his eyes. The thrum of the helicopter blades seemed distant through the covering of the earpads. In the past he'd always found it easy to fall asleep on a helicopter trip, especially one that took a few hours. The rhythmic thump of the blades created a vibration through the seat that he'd always likened to the purr of a cat. He'd never said it outloud because he knew the term was cliche, but he still held onto it because he missed his cat from home. Misty had been a tuxedo cat, or at least that's how he thought of her. Black with a white neck and chest, she'd loved to snuggle. Her purr would rumble against his legs as he fell asleep all through his high school years.

It was a happy memory to wake up to, at least for the few moments it took for his mind to race back over his final collapse face down in the desert sand. The first hour without the Raven had been good. Not blissful, but good. He'd felt like he'd taken control of his own destiny. Like he'd finally started to crawl back up that hill of sanity. Hope had been high. After all, once you recognize the problem, or in his case recognize that it's a dream, you should have some control over it. Unfortunately, by the time he'd made it to the second hour the sun had really come up. His watch, which was on time with the local sunrise somehow, told him it was only ten in the morning. The meaning of that was clear to him. First it meant his watch was somehow part of the dream, which made sense, and second, it meant it was only going to get hotter.

By the fourth hour, with the sun directly overhead, he'd started regretting his decision. After all, even if this was a dream, water would still be good. Hallucinatory water, or dream water, would still feel as good as real water. Maybe, he thought, if he turned back now he could still find the oasis the Raven had been talking about. Unfortunately, when he turned around he realized there was a problem with that plan. Everything behind him looked the same, and he really hadn't been concentrating on walking in a straight line, meaning there was no way to know which way was actually the way back. On top of that, he really didn't want to admit he'd possibly been wrong and the Raven had been right.

This brought him full circle, and reinforced his drive to keep walking. A talking raven wasn't real. Dragons weren't real. None of this was real. It was, however, really hot, and he was really thirsty.

Sitting, strapped into the seat of the blackhawk transporting them to the airport outside of Rome. He knew he wasn't actually thirsty, but he couldn't shake the feeling left lingering from those perceived hours under the blistering sun. He unscrewed the lid from the gray Hidroflask they always kept stashed between the seats and took three gulps.

"We've still got a way to go."

Sidney, strapped into the next seat, looked over at him. Bishop glared back. Sid's statement wasn't unusual. When you're in a long distance flight on a blackhawk there was no bathroom, and drinking too much could cause problems. Needing to pee wasn't the problem, and Sid making the statement wasn't the problem either. The problem was the very existence of Sidney. He didn't know this soldier. He wasn't even from his ship, and he definitely didn't know what Bishop had just been through. He wanted to question him, wanted to yell that after falling into dirt and rocks multiple times over the last few hours he would drink whatever he wanted to, but all he said was, "I'll be fine. How much longer have we got?"

"Close to two more hours."

"Right." Bishop leaned back and started to close his eyes. It was his default setting in this situation. It was his habit. Then the memory of the desert reasserted itself. He thought about talking with Sid, sitting right next to him, but he really didn't want to. He felt like the soldier had been added just to be his babysitter, and a deadly one at that. The idea of having a gun, even metaphorically, constantly pressed to his head wasn't one he was going to get over anytime soon. What made it worse was how little he knew about Sid.

He knew the big soldier had been assigned to the ship a few months earlier but had no idea why. He wasn't even sure he was an actual marine. What he also knew was that monkeys liked bananas, and sometimes rode around on unicycles. The unicycles definitely were purple, just like the colors sliding past the darkness of his eyelids.

*   *   *

When Bishop twitched his hand clinched. The fact it was under his face and scratching him fed the already overstimulated part of his animal instincts. Rolling, he lashed out. Pain flared through the back of his hand and up his arm and at the same time his eyes snapped open. A solid wooden pole about five inches in diameter stood between the back of his hand and the totally empty air around him.

Pulling his hand back and tucking it into his armpit he gritted his teeth against the throbbing pain. Looking around his surroundings, he wasn't surprised to find himself not on a blackhawk helicopter but instead somewhere that made even less sense than the desert. He was on a bed, but after glancing down at it he decided it was more like a camp cot than a bed. It was more comfortable than any military cot he'd slept on, that was for sure. What looked like handmade blankets covered his lower half or were now strewn onto the floor after his violent attack on what he now recognized as a tent pole. The pole was one of four, holding up the middle living section of what looked like a brown canvas tent. Smaller ones were angled out around the edges where he could also see stakes pinning the edge to the ground all the way around except for one section. Light filtered through flaps, which were tied shut at the moment. The floor of the tent was covered with a multitude of rugs. They varied in color and design from bright red with gold geometric patterns stitched on them to bright blue covered in some kind of hunting scene. Around the edges of the tent he saw one more bed, thankfully with no one in it, a metal stove with the pipe exiting through a hole in the tent roof, and a small table with three chairs.

Throwing off the remainder of the blankets he shifted and dropped his legs over the edge. Not knowing what to expect he was happy to see all his clothes, minus shoes and socks, in the right place. When he glanced down his boots, thankfully with his socks tucked into them, were sticking out from under the cot. This was all great news, especially the fact that he wasn't in the middle of a desert. Maybe this was just your normal, run of the mill, dream. It was obvious he'd fallen asleep now that he could think back. His thoughts had really gotten twisty there for a moment on the blackhawk. He was fairly sure there'd been something about Sid being a monkey.

Pulling his socks out of his boots he busied himself with getting his feet squared away. Once everything was laced up and his leather personnel carriers were ready to go he walked over and found, to his relief a stoneware pitcher of water on the table. His lips felt cracked and his thirst was almost overwhelming. A wooden cup sat next to it and he filled it and drained it two times before heading to the tied together flap he assumed was the door. It really wasn't much of an assumption. It was a canvas tent with only one obvious opening. Assuming the door was the door might not fall under the actual category of assumption.

After untying the door he stepped out into daylight. There was partial shade provided by a built in overhang above the tent door, but he still needed to squint against the sunlight. The door to his tent faced toward a small lake surrounded by palm trees and flowering bushes. Emerald green grass covered most of the ground, but was flattened in obvious patterns where people had been walking. Tents of differing bright colors covered this side of the lake except for one sliver where pack animals were coming down to the lake to drink.

People were everywhere. Adults were carrying pitchers of water from the lake, children were playing the same game any child who finds a long enough stick would play. The thrum of voices washed over him with the staccato tapping of pretend sword sticks puncturing it from time to time.

Smoke and the smell of cooking meat drifted from his right and he turned to see a man walking toward him. A white turban crowned his head with the end of it curling around his neck, and a smile was breaking through a beard that was once dark brown but the gray in it was winning a slow war and turning him from a young man to an elder.

"Good morning," the stranger stretched his arms out and Bishop worried he was going to try and hug him. He stopped a few paces away and bowed low enough that his fingertips brushed the ground. Straightening up, smile still fixed in place, he said, "I am so relieved to see you up and about."

"Thank you," the words and the return bow, though not as low, were an automatic response drilled into Bishop through years of cultural context. He wasn't, however, really sure what he was thanking this man for. This dream, he was still fairly sure it was just that, was very realistic and he had definitely stepped into the middle of a story. What the story was, though, he wasn't sure. "Could you, perhaps, tell me where I am, and what happened?"

"Ah, of course. Come," the man turned and motioned for Bishop to follow him. Leaving the shade of the tent doorway he found himself wishing for his hat. Automatically he reached down to the side pocket on the thigh of his NWU's and pulled his hat out. Putting it on he realized his clothes were extremely out of place. Everyone in the camp was wearing flowing robes of varying shades of white or brown, and here he was with his camouflage Navy workers uniform. He'd always found the uniform to be comfortable and extremely useful. Growing up, the idea of wearing a uniform every day had been the bane of every kid's existence. Being told what to wear, like a high school uniform, was the worst thing most teenagers could imagine. It would destroy your individuality. The uniform would steal your very soul, sucking away your creativity until you were all shades of gray. Looking back on it, he knew those ideas were a slight hormonal over reaction. These days, he found it nice, comfortable even, to know what you were going to wear every day. He never had to worry about his clothing choices, and if he wanted to stand out from everyone else then he needed to do a better job than everyone else.

Here and now, however, the term anachronistic came to mind. The first time he'd heard it was when some of his work buddies dragged him to a ren-faire. People were dressed up as knights and kings and jesters while he was wearing his street clothes, jeans and a t-shirt. He hadn't felt out of place there. The crazy people around him, pretending to be from the middle ages, were the ones out of place. Here, however, he was sure he was the one out of place. They weren't pretending, or dressed up. This was life. The detail of this dream was amazing, and so far nothing had been openly crazy. No talking ravens. No dragons dropping down from the sky.

After some twists and turns, the man led him to a tent whose walls had been rolled up to create a shaded sitting area. There were rugs and pillows covering the ground with a few solid wooden chairs made more comfortable by the presence of a cushion here and there. The chairs were taken by the very elderly, and Bishop understood that. Getting down onto the ground and getting back up were activities for young knees and backs, not for those whose beards or hair had turned all to gray.

"Here, sit," his guide gestured to a section of carpet at the edge of the shaded area. As they settled in, leaning back against overstuffed pillows covered in soft red cloth, stitched over with gold flowing designs, his guide smiled at him again, "I apologize for not answering your questions sooner, but my children are the ones responsible for the meals today and I am overly interested in how they do." His glance drew Bishop's gaze off to the left where tables surrounded cook fires. The smoke drifting toward them carried the smell he'd encountered earlier, and it made his mouth water. The air was so full of the smell of cooked meat and spices that he was starting to believe this might not be a dream, but that was the point of a dream, wasn't it. You didn't realize until you were awake.

"So, to your question. This," his host pointed to the small crescent shaped lake next to which all the tents were stationed, "is Yueyaquan. Once, long ago, there was a temple built here. At least that is what is told. It might also have been a memorial, of sorts, to some long forgotten battle or event. You can find the ruins back from the edge of the lake where the water used to be. Most of it is covered in sand now. As children we loved to climb over its broken walls and search for hidden treasure."

"Did you ever find any?" The words were out of Bishop's mouth before he could even think them. His momentary willingness to sit and listen to the warm tones of his host's voice telling him about something that might never matter to him was the product of his internal military compass. Being in the military meant he was always on duty, except for very brief moments. You had to have a built in sensor, or compass, as he called it, to be able to decide when you could actually relax. This was one of those times.

"Oh, we found some broken pieces of pottery, and a rusty piece of metal from time to time, but nothing that would make our fortune if we traded it in Dunhuang. It had been picked over by so many generations of children before I was even a sparkle in my mother's eye. The only way we would find something is if we dug, and dug deep at that. Fortune to a child is interesting, but not if you have to work too hard for it." Chuckling, he sat up a little straighter and tilted his head, trying to see his children cooking, beyond an elderly woman moving slowly toward an open chair.

"And how did I end up in bed in whoever's tent that was, which, by the way, I would like to thank them for the use of it." Bishop didn't really care how he'd come to be in this dream, but the words, like lines in a play, seemed to be the right thing to say.

"That's simple enough," turning back to Bishop now that he was satisfied with his children's cooking process. "We found you collapsed in the desert about a day's walk from here. We, and by we I mean some of our young men who specialize in tracking the antelope we sometimes hunt in this region, traced your journey. If you had only turned around and walked the other direction from where you'd started, you would have been sitting here at the edge of the lake before noon time."

Bishop stared at him. The words hitting him in the head like a well aimed shovel. Walking in the wrong direction. The sun baking down on him. That stupid Raven telling him to walk the other way. "You're kidding me."

"No. If you had only turned around you might have even seen the reflection of the sun on the water at the horizon."

"I…" His brain trailed off as his thoughts shattered like a rock thrown through a stained glass window. He watched as they spun and spiraled into darkness. This was a dream. He grabbed onto that broken piece and held it tight. It had to be a dream.

"You don't need to worry. That look on your face should be wiped away, and now that your questions are all answered, at least the easy ones, I feel introductions are in order. I am Babar Al Basiq." He paused waiting.

Bishop stared at him for a moment before realizing, "I'm," he hesitated, trying to decide how to introduce himself, and decided on informality, "Peter Bishop."

"Well, Peter, it is good to formally meet you."

"Yes, thank you. You as well. Do you mind if I take a walk around? I just need to figure out what to do."

"Of course." Babar smiled at him and nodded, "They will ring a bell when the meal is ready. Just come and find me when the time comes."

"Again, thank you so much for your hospitality."

He couldn't help but be polite. He was still partially convinced it was all a dream. At least mostly convinced it was. If he was really being honest with his subconscious he was starting to get a little worried about how well he was using the word convinced. The point he was making to himself, as he stood and walked away from his host, was that he had a hard time being impolite. Even in video games he always chose the good path. If this really was a dream he could absolutely be a jerk and it wouldn't matter, but it would matter to him.

Looking around he tried to distract himself with the sights and sounds of such an unusual place. Not that there was anything completely strange about it, but it was out of his realm of experience. He knew places like this existed in the real world. Just the fact he had to differentiate between whatever this was and the real world was a bit startling. Focusing on the surroundings he let his feet take him toward the water. The tents were pops of color against very stark backgrounds. The blue of the sky was total, no clouds broke the immensity of it. The desert beyond the oasis was just as harsh and one dimensional as that brittle sky. He knew from personal experience there was more to the desert than just brown sand, but when so much is just sand it's hard to overlook it. After face planting in it a few times he was sure he never wanted to be up close with the desert floor again.

Had that really happened? He knelt and trailed his fingers through the water of the oasis. It was hard to put it all in context, like trying to pull together the broken pieces of a dropped mirror. He could see himself in all of them, but the perspective was all wrong. He distinctly remembered his argument, one sided though it was, with the Raven, then walking away. He remembered all the moments of heat and thirst, but then there was the helicopter. How could there be both a desert and a helicopter? Not just that, how could the same desert keep coming back? He'd had recurring dreams before, but they were just the same thing on repeat, or the same thing slightly changed. Usually they were stress dreams brought on by anything from a messed up date night to an assignment in school he hadn't finished yet. The worst had been when he'd been preparing to go in front of the promotion board.

Noises brought his gaze up from the shallow muddy bottom of the oasis he'd been staring at. On the other side of the lake a palm tree had, at some time in the past, fallen and was hanging over the water. Kids were climbing out onto it and jumping in. That moment of rippling water casting a bent reflection of the world back at him seemed to encompass everything he was struggling with.

Taking a deep breath he stood and wiped the water from his hands onto his pants. Staring into the distance and trying to come to grips with an existential crisis was all well and good, but how did that help him in the here and now. He turned left and started walking along the shore. "What should I do now?"

No one answered. "Sure," he wound his way around a tight group of palm trees, "when I actually need someone to talk it out with..." he trailed off before he could admit he missed having the Raven around to talk with. Come to think of it he'd never asked him his name, and why should he. It was just a dream, right. "Right?" He asked the sky.

"All right," he stopped and looked around, "let's categorize what we know and if there's anything to be done about it." He'd gone beyond the main grouping of tents. Farther around the lake was another group with cook smoke rising from it, and off to his left away from the water were some very square looking stones. Staring at them he started walking closer and realized this must be the site of the building Babar had been talking about. Maybe a temple, maybe a monument.

He needed to put everything in perspective, to categorize things like a good leader should. "But first," he walked up and touched a stone, "let's distract ourself by looking at cool rocks." Bishop knew he was avoiding the topic and also knew he didn't really care that much. Control of the situation didn't seem to be something he was going to grasp by making a list. This building, however, was at least something interesting. He'd always liked ancient history. The times they'd put into port in an area with some kind of ancient monument, he'd always found time to go and look. He'd seen Mayan pyramids, Greek and Roman ruins. The ruins of Babylon had been high on his list to see, but it just hadn't happened yet. Mainly because it was nowhere near a port.

In front of him, stone blocks piled around each other in various heaps. He could tell some were originally a wall, and in places where the wind blew and swirled against the blocks, paving stones had been exposed. Using the small amount of instinct he had for these kinds of things he figured where the main pathway would have been and followed as best he could. Eventually he came to what he initially thought was part of the hillside, but turned out to be a collapsed wall. Years of local children trying to find a way in had left obvious marks and trails for him to follow, and with a few turns around fallen blocks the size of a Subaru he found a crack just big enough to squeeze through.

A room opened up around him that once had been square, but with the passage of time and the collapse of parts of the ceiling or caving in of walls the shape was now only a memory. He'd worried about it being too dark, but the multiple cracks let in enough light to see most things. However, some corners remained firmly in the grip of subterranean darkness. The video gamer in his brain told him to expect giant spiders to jump from those dark corners. Then if he just pressed the X button over and over as fast as he could it would be kicked off and the fight would begin. There would be dodges and parries with counter strikes to colored areas for extra damage. Bishop chuckled to himself. There hadn't been too much time lately to play games. On board the ship there was an area with a TV and it had a Playstation hooked up to it, and during their limited downtime the guys would do competitions with different games. The favorite was, of course, the NFL. You would think they would be all about first person shooters, but when you live that every day it's really not that interesting. However, pretending to take your favorite team to the superbowl, or destroying someone else in a single game with a score of sixty five to twelve, was very satisfying.

He could tell the main entrance had been off to his left, and walking over to where a giant set of double doors had once been he wondered what had happened here. Time and sun could only do so much damage. The tombs and pyramids of Egypt had been very well preserved over five thousand years of time. Even in conditions that were terrible for preservation, like the jungles of central America, the Mayan ruins were still standing. This looked like it was taken down either on purpose or as a result of something. The lack of scorch marks told him no one had set a fire, plus the damage was structural not cosmetic. It looked like someone had pulled down the sides of the doorway after having removed the doors, then filled it in with sand and rubble. Only through the overeager activities of generations of curious children was there even a way in.

On the fallen pillars of the doorway were carved intricate geometric designs. Interlinked they crawled their way upward to what would have been, literally, a crowning image, but it had been destroyed when the lentil had broken. To the sides of the door and extending around the room were carvings. The closest he could get to recognizing them was to think of them like either Egyptian or Myan hieroglyphs. They were pictures linked together with differing shapes and angles of lines. He assumed, walking closer to the wall, the pictures formed words or phrases and the lines were connectors of some kind. Maybe they represented ideas that couldn't be expressed in pictographic form. Like time or even just simple things like the conjunctions and or but.

Bishop stopped himself. Were they conjunctions? Was that even the right word? It really had been a while since he'd taken any kind of English class. Either way, he knew what he was thinking about even if he wasn't thinking about it in a way someone else would recognize. Because right now, they didn't matter. As long as he understood himself it was all good, but did he understand himself? Something was bumping at the back of his mind. There was some reason, he felt, that he should recognize, or maybe remember this. He'd never been here. He was sure of that. Even in other versions of this crazy dream world he'd been visiting, he'd never been here, so why should he feel like this. Like it was all some kind of delayed deja vu.

He wondered if he could make any sense of the writing, then quickly decided he couldn't. Some things were wrapped in circles, which he assumed meant they were either important or they were someone's name. Other times giant sections were blocked off with fancy borders of crawling vines or flowers. Eventually, on the wall opposite where the main entrance had been he came to another collapsed doorway, but this time little hands had dug away the sand and chunks of rock originally blocking it. Bishop wasn't certain he could fit through the child sized holes, but he decided it might be worth it to stick his head through. Maybe he would see something enlightening, and hopefully there wasn't some kind of desert predator who had decided to make its home on the other side.

Squeezing through as much as he could Bishop paused and looked around. One arm and part of his shoulders were through along with his head, but he wasn't willing to try and pull his other arm through. Getting stuck here with no one to pull him out was not something he wanted to think about. Twisting and looking at the wall next to him led him to realize he needed to wait a moment for his eyes to adjust. There was light, just not as much as in the entryway hall. Closing his eyes he counted backward from twenty. Reaching zero he opened them and looked again.

There it was.

Black human figures painted in bold dark strokes surrounded a monstrous being standing on two legs with wings unfurled from its back. The length of the wall, at least what he could see of it, was covered in pictures representing this thing. He remembered it explicitly. The tunnel leading to the terrorist base. The rough hewn walls of the tunnel giving way to carved blocks. Worn pictures of people interacting with this thing. All of it surrounded by, and the deja vu moment finally came into focus, writing made of pictures connected by lines.

From the figure's wings fell streaks and a village below was broken. In the darkness he couldn't tell, but it looked like red mixed in with the black lines, marking the streaks as burning. Beyond, another picture showed a city with a river running through it. Again, the stark, bold, black lines of the river and the village were broken. The dark figure hovering over the city, this time, seemed to be drawing something to him rather than raining destruction down.

In the tunnel, the picture he remembered, the thing, the dragon for lack of a better term, was being tied down. Craning his head and twisting as much as possible he looked down the length of the hallway. About fifty yards farther on he could tell the hallway opened up into another large room, but without light and the ability to move closer he couldn't tell what it was even supposed to be.

The wall opposite was covered in writing, or what he assumed was writing. Designs of nature and geometry surrounded the words and it stood in stark contrast to the almost paleolithic pictures of the other wall. Most likely, he thought, the writing narrated the actions from the pictures. If what Babar had told him had any truth to it, and he didn't really have any reason to doubt, this place was some type of memorial to an event. That event must have had something to do with humanity's reaction to whatever that thing was.

56

Pulling himself back out of the hole in the wall his mind was reeling, "It's all a dream." His voice bounced off the stone walls and echoed back, mocking him.

Looking around at the brown stone covered in carved flowers and creeping vines he noticed gaps showing where once there had been precious stones inlaid to bring color to the decoration. "A dream. Just a dream that seems to be stuck on repeat. With lots of detail."

Shaking his head he pushed back out through the crack in the wall. The sunlight washed the world white until his eyes could adjust. "What do I do?" Placing his hand on the carven stone of the wall, he hoped the rough tactile feeling would somehow ground him in a kind of reality. As if feeling something solid would bring everything back into perspective. "Do I live it as if it's a dream and nothing I do here really matters?"

That, in his recent estimation, didn't seem to be the best idea. He'd walked away from the Raven. He made a decision based on the dream state. Saying to himself, none of it mattered. Turns out it had mattered. The thirst and the heat had mattered. Now here he was as a direct consequence of that action. How could a dream continue like this? How could a dream bleed over into real life?

"I heard the Raven in the infirmary." He stated it as a witness on the stand. It was a fact being tossed out to the jury of his mind.

"The captain said I kicked a hole in the bulkhead." He shook his head at that. "I'm not sure about that one." Having not seen it, he just had to take the Captain's word for it. He wasn't normally one for ignoring a direct statement from his commanding officer.

"So, what's that leave?"

Looking out over the oasis, he found himself on the opposite bank from his host. He could either walk back the way he'd come, or he could continue on around the other side of the lake. Opting for a different view he started around the side he hadn't seen yet. Not that he was actually paying attention to his surroundings.

"What it leaves," he said to the palm trees, "is life."

And what, he thought to himself as he picked his way around the bank of the oasis, do I mean by that?

"What I mean is, I don't know what's going to happen next. I don't even seem to know what's happening now." He paused then added, "Which is why I'm talking to myself. So, all I can do is deal with each moment as it comes. I guess I should assume this world, this dream, this whatever, has some kind of permanence, even if it's just in my head."

Just do your job. That had been the motto of his crew for a while. Problems had popped up among some of the junior officers because some believed they could do the other's job better and were complaining about it. They'd lost focus on what they were supposed to be doing, causing failures across the ship. So the focus had changed. Don't look at the big picture. Look at your job. Do that amazingly well. Sometimes you just had to admit certain things were out of your control.

A lot was out of his control.

"So here's the new question. What isn't out of my control?" Scrambling over rocks he dropped a few feet down and stood in the shade of some palm trees.

"How I treat people is in my control. Does the raven count as a person?" He wasn't sure if he was joking about that or serious. "Fine, I'll say yes. For now. But, that's not the big issue. The big issue, Lieutenant Bishop, is figuring out what's actually going on."

Leaning against a palm tree he looked out over a scene from a movie. The sunlight had thrown handfuls of diamonds across the surface of the water, as palm trees stood like pillars holding up the immensity of the blue sky. The tents across the lake were a riot of green, yellow, red, blue, and orange. Fading and blending through every shade you could imagine.

"I know what to do in," he hesitated, the words sticking in his throat, "in the real world. We land and head off to talk with whatever expert the captain is sending us to. Hopefully he has some answers, but what about here. What do I do here?"

He didn't mind the idea of simply hanging out in the shade of one of those tents, eating whatever it was that smelled so good, and talking away the day with interesting people. That future, however, left out a big issue.

As he exited the small grove of palms his thought process was interrupted by a single tent pitched in the only flat spot on this side of the lake. There were only so many reasons a tent would be set this far apart. Well, he thought, far was a relative term. It wasn't exactly Alcatraz over here, but there had to be a reason for this one tent being set apart.

If it was religious his host might have mentioned it, and it should have some kind of marker or fancy things showing off the spiritual nature of the area. Some kind of, you are standing on holy ground so take off your shoes, sign.

Another choice was a prison. On first glance, a tent didn't really make much of a prison, but who knows. Maybe they had pillars and chains and stuff inside. What exactly would the stuff be? Mentally he gave himself a weird look. Chains and stuff? Well, he thought about it for a moment, there could be stocks. Sure, like the things back in medieval times where they stuck their head and arms through. The only problem was those were supposed to be a public thing, so if those did exist they should be in the middle of all the tents over there. He saw in his mind people walking by throwing fruit at the poor souls locked up.

"So, you're an idiot. We can agree on that."

Bishop twitched, hands grabbing empty air where his sidearm should have been.

"You know how I came to that conclusion?"

Spinning Bishop searched for the voice.

"It was easy. You, not listening to my brilliant advice, walked the wrong direction."

The Raven stood on a coconut, gripping it by the husk.

"I bet that was fun for you, wasn't it." The Raven tilted his head and looked at Bishop sideways. "All that heat."

Bishop really couldn't believe what he was seeing. Not that he was surprised anymore by talking ravens, but just that the Raven had even found him at all.

"Tell me," the Raven ruffled his feathers, "did they find you before or after you passed out?"

Taking a deep breath Bishop realized there always comes a time when your theoretical thoughts have to become practical reality. It seemed a bit too coincidental that his personal reflections from only moments ago would come face to face with reality this quickly, but it was what it was. Maybe here, in this whatever of a place, coincidence happened more often than not.

Thoughts blitzed his mind. Each statement wishing to be used. Sarcasm was first, of course, followed by playing it cool. Tied were obvious facts and outright lies. What he came to eventually was, "I'm sorry."

Silence. Not real silence. The sound of water from the lake, and the rustle of leaves didn't seem to break the silence as much as point out the actual silence. "I," the Raven looked up at the leaves over his head, then to the side at the lonely tent, "I might have underestimated how strange this whole thing is for you."

Their eyes met and a nod served as the secret signal. Things were what they were. What had been said was done with. "So," the Raven glided down and landed on a rock in the shade, "should I start listing out all the ways ravens are better than those unfaithful, unintelligent, trash scavengers called eagles?"

A laugh momentarily cracked the anxiety coated center of Bishop's mind.

"Whoa there buddy." A black wing flapped like a squadmate reminding him to keep it down while on guard duty. "We need to keep it down a little here or everythings going to go nutso real quick."

"Uh…" Bishop's mind locked up under the pressure of numerous statements regarding the nutso state of his life right now.

"Yeah, yeah," the Raven looked around, "insert sarcastic or cynical statement here. I get it. This may come as a shock to you, but I didn't come here for you. I mean, it's nice to see you alive and all that, and thanks for the apology, but that tent is why I'm here."

Bishop looked back over at the tent and took a moment to do as much of a strategic breakdown as possible. It looked to be a bit smaller than your average Starbucks, with the main issue being the lack of people standing anywhere around it. The entrance must have been on the side opposite the lake because he couldn't see it from where he stood. Maybe there were guards at the entrance. He realized he'd switched to thinking of them as guards rather than just people, because why else would the Raven want him to keep it down, and why else would he be here trying to break into something, except if it was the kind of place to need guards.

"Okay," Bishop said, "then why are you here?"

"I'm going to keep it short for now, because time is a thing. Things started going crazy here a few days ago," he paused as Bishop gave him a look. "More crazy than just you, okay. Not everything revolves around you. It was probably just a coincidence you showed up at the same time, and then the big thing came looking for you specifically, and…" the Raven stared at him. "You know what? We're going to circle back around to that piece of carrion later because…"

"Because," raising both hands and shrugging Bishop said, "I'm jumping back and forth between two worlds and sometimes dragging you with me, and that might be," he flattened one hand out and wiggled it back and forth, "just a little bit important to all of this."

The Raven's black beak bobbed in a quick nod, "Maybe a little. Point being…" He hopped and started to extend his wings, "Could you bend down?"

Bishop walked closer and knelt. The Raven hopped onto his shoulder and turned to face the same way as him. "That's better," the Raven whispered. "So, this particular group of colorful nomads make a good living hunting for particular creatures in the desert and selling them for their parts. Idiots in town believe ground up bits and pieces of certain critters can help them with whatever ails them."

Bishop had first hand knowledge of this from back in, for lack of a better term, his world. His naval group had been tasked, a few years back, with stopping endangered animal smuggling coming out of south east Asia. The biggest one was traffic in Pangolins. They were the definition of odd, and yet surprisingly cute. If there was ever going to be an animal he assumed came from another world and had mystical powers, it would be a Pangolin.

60

"So," the Raven's breath smelled of rot mixed with some kind of nut, "the word is they grabbed something, and it might be important."

"Okay." Bishop nodded, "but why you?"

His feathers ruffled, he hopped, "It's complicated."

"Seriously?" Bishop was getting tired of not knowing what was going on.

"Look, time's a thing right now, so can we come back to this when we aren't in the middle of something else?"

"So, what, you just want me to trust you?"

"I think I might have earned a little bit of that when you decided to try and die in the desert yesterday."

Bishop looked directly into the shining black depths of the Raven's eye, and had to decide between arguing and, for the moment, trusting. Yes, everything was crazy. So much so that the crazy had folded itself like an origami swan back around to some version of normal. The Raven had given him good advice and walked him out of the desert, and for what? He hadn't actually asked for anything, until now. It wasn't like they were robbing a bank. They were saving a poor endangered animal.

"Okay," Bishop looked away and back at the tent, "but they saved me. What am I going to do about that? What is your get away strategy?"

"Well, I was planning to fly."

"Of course you were."

They circled through the palm trees till they could see the entrance. Two men stood on either side of the flap that served as a door.

"Okay," the Raven's feet flexed on Bishop's shoulder, "you do your thing and get the goons out of the way."

Turning his head slightly so he could keep the guards in his peripheral while also being able to glare at the Raven, "That's your plan? If I wasn't here how were you going to get inside?"

"I'm little. Well," he puffed his feathers out and stood on one foot for a moment, "little compared to big bumbling humans. Compared to other corvids or even most other birds, I'm quite large. There're some really ugly headed birds that…"

Reaching up, Bishop tapped the Raven on the head, "Stop."

"Hey," the Raven's head twitched back, "I was just… right. To the point, I was going to duck under the back flap of the tent, let the poor bugger out, then we would make a run for it."

Bishop slowly reversed his course and slipped back around to the side of the tent facing the lake and the thick stand of palm trees.

"Okay, for the most part, that's a fine plan. Do you know if this poor unknown thing can outrun the guards?"

"No idea."

"Right. Do you know if it's injured?"

"Nope."

"What kind of animal is it?"

"Does that matter?"

"Where did you get your intelligence from?"

"Same place everyone else does. A mix of their parents and what God gave them."

"No," Bishop looked up at the sky, and took a deep breath. Who knew talking to a raven would feel the same as a teenage new recruit fresh out of basic training. "Where did you get your information about the animal trapped inside? From other ravens?"

"What? No. Those dummies can't even talk. How would they tell me anything? I'm not a reader of peabrains."

"They can't…" And now, Bishop thought, the weird talking bird is giving me a hard time for assuming birds can talk, "You know what? Let's put that on the list of things we really need to come back around to and talk about later."

"Sure, but why? I mean even you know birds can't talk, right? Or do they all talk in your world?"

"Do they? You know what? Let's just get back on topic. Where did you get your information?"

"People. They tend to talk a lot, and they really don't care what they say around birds, cuz, you know," the Raven looked him in the eye for a long second, "birds can't talk."

"And, here you are, proving them right by not making any sense."

"Oh, snarky. Look, I could've happily pecked your tasty eyes out in the desert, but no, I saved you."

Bishop gave his best poker face, "Are we done? I thought you said time was important."

"I'm not the one making the snarky comments."

"Good use of the word snarky, by the way." A little flattery, Bishop had noted long ago, could go a long way to moving conversations along. "For someone who spends most of their time looking for dead things to eat you've got a good vocabulary."

"Well, thank you. I try my best."

"So," Bishop moved closer to the back of the tent, "the animal inside could be big or little."

"True."

"Might be able to fly, or could be hurt to the point where it can't even walk on its own."

"Also true."

"And your original plan was to have it outrun the guards."

"Yes, but to my defence, I hadn't thought it through very well."

Planning was Bishop's job, and it felt right to be doing something he was actually good at. As a junior officer he was given the overall mission plan by his boss, and from there he had to figure out the details. He didn't want to think of the raven as his boss, but the same principle applied. He had an overall plan from an annoying guy in a dark suit and he had to fix it so things actually worked.

"First," Bishop had learned early in his career to toss a little praise to the higher ups before changing their plan, "your initial idea of sneaking in through the back was genius."

"Granted."

"Now, what needs to follow it up is a little better detail."

"Which is why I brought you along."

"You found me here on accident."

"Maybe, or maybe I planned it this way."

Bishop took a deep breath to keep his next words inside his head. More arguing wouldn't help anything at this point. "You sneak in the back and see what's up with the poor bugger inside. If they can fly then great, just let them out and off you go. I'll distract the guards for a bit and you've made your escape. If they can't fly or they look injured then you'll need to make some noise and get the guards to look your way. Once that happens I'll jump them from behind and, as you said, take care of them."

"I don't know," the Raven looked from the tent to Bishop, "they looked awfully big. I bet they've been fighting off little guys like you since they were out of short robes."

"True." What was also true was how little hand to hand training an officer in the navy received. No one expected a lieutenant on a ship to be kung fu fighting some bad guy. That only happened in the movies. In real life, if the bad guys got onto the ship you used guns, or the Marines took care of it. They were seriously trained in punching people. "But, I'll have the element of surprise, and that counts for a lot. Also, you can seriously mess with them. Do they know you can talk?"

"These chumps? I normally avoid these guys. They hunt special animals, and you can't get more special than me."

"Right," special isn't the way Bishop would have phrased it, "so if you say something, they'll go looking for the person who said it. Then you can fly to another spot and say something, and they'll believe multiple people have snuck in."

"Which gives you a chance to bonk them without getting beat up by guys twice your size."

"Wasn't your earlier plan to just have me deal with them? Since when did you decide I couldn't handle myself?"

"Since I remembered you walked away from water and safety and almost died in the desert."

"That has no bearing on whether I can take these guys."

The Raven hopped and looked at him, "To me, it does."

"Anyway," Bishop pointed to a loose spot at the back of the tent, "that time you said was so important, is wasting. Get in there, and I'll head around the front."

With a slight push the Raven launched himself and glided to the edge of the tent. Bishop assumed it would take him a moment to wiggle under the flap and find whatever was inside. Moving as quietly as he could Bishop looped back around to where he could see the two guards at the front. They weren't as big as the raven was making them out to be, but knowing the lifestyle of bedouins he didn't doubt they could easily beat him to death if it came to hand to hand fighting. Then he noticed the sword hanging at the hip of each man, and revised the earlier thought. There would be no hand to hand fighting. They would just stab him. His knowledge of how to fight someone with a sword was, don't. Get a safe distance away and shoot them. Unfortunately, that wasn't an option here.

Chapter Seven

It had taken patience. As the man wearing the perfectly tailored pinstripe suit squeezed through the narrow opening, ignoring any damage to the double breasted jacket, he projected the image of someone who was willing to be patient. Even as he scraped from the crack into the dimly lit tunnel, he tried his best to act as though this was all just part of a grander plan.

"Sir," a flashlight bobbed drawing his attention, "you'll want to see the tunnel's walls before we head into the main chamber."

Twisting the top of his pen sized maglight, The Suit took a moment to look around and brush some of the more egregious amounts of dirt from his eponymous suit. He knew it was how many of those working for him thought of, and even referred, to him. It didn't bother him. In fact, once he found out about it, he tried to cultivate it. It gave off a kind of Men in Black aura. It said he was always in control, always ready. It had become his uniform, his armor, to don each morning as he prepared to go into battle.

The natural cave, through which they had entered, turned into a man made tunnel. Having been through the Myan and Welsh sites personally he recognized the stone work. Not that it was terribly different from any other ancient site, there was, however, a certain size and cut the workers of the gathered nations had preferred. Apparently when you get more than one culture together they have to come to some kind of engineering agreement.

It was amazing what humanity would argue over when given the chance. Modern churches split because of the color of new carpet in their sanctuary or the difference between sitting in a long pew or a chair. He could almost hear those ancient masons arguing over the right size to carve a stone for best use in a tunnel wall. A little foreshadowing of the United Nations of today.

Sweeping his small light over the wall one last time, he turned and nodded to his guide. A short distance ahead they rounded a curve in the hall and he saw three men diligently snapping digital pictures of a section of the wall. The sound of their footfalls caused one to turn. The Suit nodded at the wall, "What have you got?"

"It's basically the same as at the other sights sir." The man was dressed in black military fatigues.

After the US had attacked his primary crew here, it hadn't taken too long for them to clear out and start looking elsewhere. He'd had to be patient, but it wasn't for too long. Once the CIA had removed any technology from the site they'd seemed content to move on. They believed they could get some intelligence from the laptops or thumb drives they'd found. Unfortunately for them, this had nothing to do with terrorism.

Looking over the pictures on the wall he nodded in agreement. "It might even be the same crew as the one in Wales."

"Yes sir," he pointed at the large figure in the middle. "The overall depiction, and even the type of brush strokes do seem to be overly similar."

"For ex-military, Sergeant Ryan, you do seem to have a knack for archeology."

The ex sergeant smiled, "You hear an egghead talk about the same thing enough times and even us grunts pick a few things up."

The Suit shook his head, "Oh no sergeant, you can't fool me, you are smarter than you let on. Finish cataloging this then join us in the main chamber."

The sergeant nodded and turned back to taking pictures.

Heading down the ancient hallway, The Suit eventually came to the large cavern around which this entire complex had originally been built. While the stones and the pictures on the wall had been similar to other sites he'd come across, the layout of the structure was somewhat different. In the Mayan heartlands it was a pyramid and in the Welsh forests it looked more like a temple, but in both places the general layout was the same. There would be a large entry room with the story written on the walls. That would then lead to a long hallway, or in the case of the Mayan pyramid a stairway, with stories carved on both walls. At the end there would be a grand circular room, almost like the center of a temple. In both cases the building was just that, a building. This one, however, differed in the most important way possible. It was hidden. They'd taken the time to dig and chisel their way under the desert floor. Granted, at the time they'd done it this may have been a savanna. There were other differences as well. There was only one picture on the wall of the hallway, and the chamber at the end wasn't built to be round. His research, and years of digging, led him to believe this was the primary site. All the others had been based on this. The long hallways had originally been the tunnel, and the circular chambers were a copy of this natural cave.

"Patrick," the man waving and coming toward him tripped over the long untied laces of his black combat boots and only just caught himself on a stalagmite before bashing his face into it. He was literally the only person in this room that the Suit would allow to use his first name.

"Mason," Patrick slid his hands over his own suit, feeling the need to straighten it just by virtue of being near the rumpled scientist, "you know you didn't need to wear the fatigues."

"I know, I know," Mason brushed dust from his knees, "but this was important and I didn't want to be the one to blow things because I stood out."

"Well, I appreciate the effort." Here, now, he could stop being The Suit, but only for this moment, and only for this man. There were times he was worried he would forget how to be anything other than the self assured, arrogant, head of this shadowy organization. It was part of the reason he put on the suit. It helped him mentally delineate between who he was and who he had to be. If anyone else had tripped on their own shoelaces in front of him he would've had them fired for idiotic incompatence. If they knew too much about his plans then other options would've needed to be considered. More serious options.

Not Mason, however.

Before any of this. Mason had been the first person he'd asked to be the godfather of his daughter, but now wasn't the time to think about those times. He had things to do.

"So," Mason stopped next to him, turned and waved expansively at the cavern.

"Yes?"

"It took years to find this place. What do you think?"

"I'm not really in the mood for introspection right now, Mason, and the CIA could come back at any time."

"Right, yes. Straight to the heart of the matter. The crystal was here." He started forward and gestured for Patrick to follow. "It was where we expected it to be, and it seems our employees had been trying to set up for the removal ritual when they were interrupted."

"More freelance contractors than employees. I don't really agree with their means, or methods, or motives."

"Then why…"

"I also didn't mind if they were shot."

"So a tool you didn't care about if it got broken."

"Yes," Patrick looked around the central point of the cavern, "I assume the crystal was here."

"Yes," Mason nodded, "was, being the primary word."

"I got that from the message. I also assume the US didn't remove it or it would have been in the after action report."

"I'll get to the point," Mason walked over and patted a cracked and scorched stalagmite. "It was blown up."

Patrick nodded, "The report we intercepted said the terrorists launched an RPG but it was a Claymore that actually caused the central damage."

"That would explain…" Mason pointed at the cavern floor.

Up until that moment Patrick had assumed the gravel on the floor was just what you got in a place like this. Kneeling, he knew these pants would be ruined, but it was to be expected in a moment like this. He peered at the broken chunks of crystal scattered around the central area of the cavern. Reaching out he picked one of the larger chunks up. "Mason, do you have a..."

Mason handed him a magnifying glass.

The color and structure of the crystal matched well enough with the others he'd found over the years that he was fairly sure it was of the same ilk. He wouldn't have a definitive answer until it was put under an electron microscope, but for the moment he would go with his assumption. "So..."

"So, here's a preliminary theory. I want to make it clear I'm just putting things together in my mind right now and some parts of this could end up being wrong."

"Fine, duly noted." Patrick walked over and held the crystal up to one of the lights they'd placed around the cavern.

"Everything we've discovered so far leads me, leads us," Mason emphasized the us, "to believe that this is the originating location. Also, the overall structure, as well as the report from the military we intercepted, leads me to believe the crystal here was the prime crystal."

"I read the report," Patrick remembered the action laid out in black and white. The overall structure of the cavern was only mentioned when it was necessary to place the enemy relative to the friendly forces. The only mention of the crystal would lead someone to believe it was a naturally occuring feature, and it was most likely glowing because of underground phosphorescence of some kind. Like certain types of algae or cave worms.

"Right," Mason reached down and picked up another broken piece of the crystal. "The claymore explosion struck the crystal, shattering it into the millions of pieces you see all around you. I highly doubt they were aiming for it, but those things are area of effect explosions."

"Even so," Patrick turned the crystal in front of the flood light causing refracted patterns to bounce off the walls of the cavern, "we have found pieces of the crystal before, and they were not like this."

"Dead you mean?" Mason nodded. "This is where we get into speculative territory. The explosion directed the shards of broken crystal toward the US soldiers. According to the report, the officer on hand threw himself between the explosion and an exposed soldier."

Patrick remembered the section of the report explaining the lieutenant's injuries, and how the Captain of the ship was recommending him for a purple heart. "So?"

"So," Mason continued, "if we put together the details of the report with the physical evidence..." He moved and stood facing

68

where the crystal would have been, "The good lieutenant would have been here," he turned so his back was toward the imaginary explosion, "and his back would have been hit, not with an explosion, but…"

"With thousands of flying shards of the crystal."

"Correct." Mason held up the broken piece, "And we already know what happens to people stabbed by living pieces of it."

Patrick frowned at this. They did know. The small working pieces they'd found had been tested in many ways. One of those by stabbing it into a person. Most recently the former leader of this, now destroyed, terrorist organization. "But that's not what happened."

"And that's where we run into some problems." Mason nodded and tried, unsuccessfully, to sit on a stalactite. "A portal should have opened and sucked him through it, but unless the Navy is seriously covering things up, that didn't happen. He was injured. Shards of crystal were pulled out of his back. They dosed him with multi-spectrum antibiotics just in case some crazy cave bug got into his system, and that was it."

"Something should have happened." Patrick tossed the shard and caught it. "Something did happen. The power left the crystal and went where?"

Mason shrugged, "Into the lieutenant?"

"That's never happened before."

"Nothing we had was ever even close to the size of this."

"Well," Patrick dropped the crystal, "one thing is sure. We need to talk to this lieutenant."

Chapter Eight

The guard on the left of the tent entrance turned and cocked his head, listening to something. Bishop, from his position in the bushes, could hear the guard say something, but couldn't make out what it was. The other guard shrugged and must have responded but with his back turned Bishop couldn't really tell.

A moment later they both twitched and reached for their swords. The one on the left, holding his sword confidently in his right hand, pulled the tent flap back with his left allowing the other guard to enter.

That was his signal, unfortunately. He still hadn't come up with some amazing way of dealing with two guys with swords. Going back and forth between a good sized rock and a solid tree branch, Bishop had settled on the tree branch. It had a good feel to it and could give him some reach. Stepping out from the bushes he paused and picked up the rock too. You never could have too many options.

The fact they were going through with this told him something important. Whatever was in there couldn't get away on its own. He assumed the Raven could figure out how to open a cage, but if the creature couldn't move under its own power then it wouldn't matter.

Pressing his ear to the slight opening left when the guards had dropped the tent flap, Bishop could hear one guard farther away asking if the other saw anything. The second voice made him twitch when it answered from approximately six inches away.

Bishop's mind raced, going through possibility after possibility. Plans coming together and being discarded as too dangerous or just ridiculous. He had to do something, so he settled on the one with the best chance of not failing.

Kneeling down he lifted the bottom edge of the entrance flap. The guards feet were inches away. Setting down his stick but keeping the rock firmly gripped in his left hand he wrapped his arms as quickly as he could around the guards feet and yanked.

After a satisfying thud the guards feet stuck out from under the tent flap. Bishop flipped the edge of the flap back, crawled up the guards back, trying to use his almost two hundred pounds to keep him down, and swung his rock at the back of the guards head. His forehead bounced off the hard packed earth and his straining muscles relaxed.

A tingle ran up his back, part fear, part adrenaline, part battle rage. Bishop wondered if he'd accidentally killed the man, and a rough voice in a corner of his mind asked if he really cared. His life was spiraling out of control anyway. Pretending calm, he could feel a touch of rage building.

"Hey!" The raven's voice cracked the silence. Bishop looked up to see the remaining guard stop moving toward him and glance toward the sound of the voice in the darkness of the far side of the tent. "Your mother's a cow! A big fat hairy cow!"

Bishop slid off the comatose guard, growled under his breath, and rose to a crouch. His movement caught the guards attention, who turned toward him and raised his sword. The space between them was empty and the body of the first guard laying on the floor seemed designed to convince the still standing one that Bishop really needed stabbing.

The guard advanced toward him sliding his feet across the ground. Bishop could feel his heart thundering as his mind spun through nonsensical ideas. Finally it settled on one. Gritting his teeth against the anger telling him to rush forward blindly he waited for two more steps. As the second step slid across the ground Bishop's right hand twitched and the rock spun toward the guard.

Not waiting for the hoped reaction Bishop launched himself across the remaining distance. Sweeping across his body with his left arm he felt the impact in his forearm as he connected with the guard's sword arm, followed immediately with the solid thud of his shoulder making full contact with the guards midsection.

The guards body flew across the tent as if pulled by ropes tied around his midsection. With a thud he slammed into a cage on the far side of the tent and came to a sudden stop, his head wiping backward and coming to rest at an odd angle. Raising his fists Bishop started advancing toward the still form of the guard.

"Is he dead?"

Bishop flinched to the left and started to swing with his right fist.

"Hey! Hey!" The Raven hopped back a few feet.

They stared at each other and Bishop could hear his breath pushing in and out in the silence of the tent.

"If I'd known you could just toss this guy around like a, like a…" the Raven tilted his head and looked up at the roof of the tent, "I don't know, like a limp dead thing. I wouldn't have taken so much time trying to come up with a fool proof plan."

"I didn't…" a cold flood ran through Bishop's body. His knees felt unhinged. He didn't want to fall, especially in front of the Raven. "I was just angry, and…" he paused. Why had he been angry?

"Hey, I'm not complaining. I just wish you'd told me. I figured you were just a fairly useless sack of human." The Raven flapped his wings and hopped to the top of a cage to the left of where the former guard lay sprawled. "Granted, I think all humans are fairly useless."

Bishop looked back at the guard face down on the ground, then over to the one laying on the cage. He'd expected the second one to flinch when he threw the rock and that was supposed to give him a chance to get in close and tackle him. Bishop figured an upclose wrestling match gave him a better chance of not being stabbed. What he hadn't expected was for the man to go flying fifteen feet through the air. He knew he was in good shape, you had to be with constant PT tests to pass, but not terminator kind of good shape.

"Hey, quit thinking about your belly button and come help me."

Bishop relaxed his still partially raised fists, and shook out his arms. The Raven was standing on an iron cage that had a wooden floor. The bars crisscrossed forming empty squares about the size of his closed fist. The cage itself was big enough to hold a medium sized dog and currently held something that could be considered medium sized dog adjacent.

Whatever it was, it layed curled up on the bottom of the cage. It was black, or maybe in the dark of the cage everything looked black, and seemed to have four legs. Its head was broad and vaguely reminded Bishop of a badger. The legs, although mostly curled up under itself, seemed short and he couldn't see if there were any claws or if they were just paws of some kind. The tail was also tucked and while Bishop could tell there was one, he couldn't tell if it was long or as stubby as it looked now.

"So," the Raven hopped over a few rungs on the cage and tapped his beak on the door, "it's locked. I, if I wanted to, could have figured out how to pick the lock and freed the poor soul, but I thought you would want to feel included so I left it for you to do."

"Right." Bishop glanced back over at the most likely dead guard laying next to them.

"Ignore him." The Raven taped on the bars of the cage making them ring. "If none of this is real he doesn't matter. If it is real then he deserved it for what they had planned for our prisoner here."

Sometimes, Bishop thought, you couldn't worry about whether things were all in your head. The raven was right about that. He'd spent too much time and mental energy already thinking about what was happening. Right now he needed to be a bit more practical.

Bending over the very dead guard he untied the belt wrapped around him. Connected to it was a water bottle, or water skin, he corrected himself, and the scabbard for the sword which was lying on the ground next to him. Both things might come in handy. While it was terrible, and he was actually sorry for their deaths, what was done was done, and he was going to need water and something better to defend himself with. He wrapped the belt around himself and tied it in place. The scabbard hanging on his left and the water skin on his right.

Bishop turned back to the cage. The lock on the cage door was a solid, if ancient looking, metal padlock. Something he felt should only exist on doors from medieval Europe. Wrapping his hand around it he could feel the weight of the metal as the lock filled his hand. It was somewhere close to the size of a softball, but with the heft of an exercise weight.

His hope was one of the guards would have a key on them. He didn't relish the idea of searching their pockets, but when you're an officer in the military sometimes you just did your job and didn't think about it too much. Tightening his grip on the lock he tugged at it. A crack like thick ice breaking was followed by shards of metal falling through his fingers. In the palm of his hand the lock laid there, sad and broken. The latch on it had shattered where it connected to the cage door.

"Well," the Raven hopped to the edge of the cage and looked down into his hand, "that was a terrible lock." He looked up at Bishop, "They really had no pride in their workmanship, or," he danced from leg to leg on the black metal bar of the cage, "some merchant out there is selling junk to poor unsuspecting souls."

Bishop set the lock down on the hard packed dirt floor, reached out, and unlatched the cage door. Most of the front of the cage swung away with the door being large enough to fit an animal in without problem. Reaching in he slid his hands under the creature and lifted it out. He could feel it breathing, and against his arm the thump of a heart beat told him the thing was definitely alive. The fur was consistent with a long haired cat and it wasn't too heavy to carry for a while.

It was too bad he didn't have his rucksack, he thought, he could just put it in there and carry it forever. "All right," he turned and headed to the door, "you go out first and tell me if anyone is out there."

"Right. Scouting." With a jump the Raven unfurled his wings and drifted to the tent flap. Using his beak to push it aside he disappeared into the daylight.

A minute passed, then two. Bishop considered setting the creature down just in case he needed to use his hands. If someone wandered into the tent looking for the two guards he didn't want to have his hands full of unknown animal.

"Hey!" Twitching, Bishop's eyes darted around the enclosure, looking for a place to hide. "It's all clear!" The deep breath he'd been holding whistled out between his clenched teeth.

Using his back to push open the tent flap Bishop exited the tent into brilliant sunlight. Blinking away the temporary blindness he finally found the shape of the black raven standing on a tree branch a few feet away from the path. "You could have come back into the tent and told me quietly."

"Sure I could, but where's the fun in that?" Drifting from the branch he landed on Bishop's shoulder. "Did you flinch? I bet I made you flinch, didn't I? Ravens are naturally hilarious."

"Oh, yes, hilarious. That's exactly what I thought when it happened."

"Ravens are also masters of sarcasm."

"Oh really?" He started walking down the path until it turned back toward the main part of the camp. He'd probably missed dinner. His stomach rumbled at the memory of the smells drifting from the cooking fires.

"We shouldn't hang around here. They'll be pretty mad we stole their thing."

"Not to mention killed two of their people."

"Right, that too."

Bishop glanced over at the Raven. Normally eye contact would help you understand the person you were talking to, but the Raven's eyes were just black pools reflecting the world around him. A conversation about empathy, and caring about the deaths of others with a raven, who happily ate the dead others, would have to wait for another time.

"So," Bishop glanced toward the sun to check how high above the horizon it was, "what now?"

"Well," the Raven fluffed his feathers then settled back down, "I wasn't exactly... uhm, the thing is..."

"You didn't plan this far ahead did you?"

"Of course I did. I just didn't plan on you being here. So, things have to change with the plans I had."

"Is there a spot around here we can hide until the sun goes down? Eventually someone will come around with dinner for these guys and notice things have gone wrong, and with me being the only stranger in the place it won't be hard to figure out who it was."

"There's some old ruins back over there."

"Yeah I already looked around over there, and while it might work it's also a place where kids come and play."

"There's a creek that runs out of the lake and makes a cave..."

"That would be the first place they'd look."

"You're not being very helpful."

"I'm not?" Bishop sucked in a deep breath and started walking. He wasn't sure where. He just wanted to get some distance between himself and the people who were going to be very angry with him.

"Where are we going?"

Bishop pointed with his chin, "That way."

"That's the desert."

"Yup, and any help would be appreciated."

The raven's clawed toes dug into his shoulder before he launched himself into the air. "I'll do the scout thing again."

It was in moments like these that Bishop would normally dive into his own mind to pass the time. He'd found himself in many situations where all he could do was wait. Hurry up and wait. That was the modern military's theme. His mind would wander all over the place. Where would he like to go? What would he do if he won the lottery? In this moment however…

The desert stretched away in front of his feet. Golden brown and sizzling like someone was trying to fry brown sugar. His arms ached from carrying the unconscious animal. At first he hadn't thought anything of it, but after long enough even holding a ballpoint pen becomes a chore. He again tried to run through the events leading up to this situation and find some kind of cause for this effect, but with the heat of the sun beating down on him and the glare rippling up from the desert floor all his thoughts just became another fly buzzing at his ear.

Eventually after he'd left any semblance of a pathway behind over an hour ago, he started making his way around a hill. It would be quicker to just climb over it, but he would have been too easily spotted from miles around as he reached the top, and the point of this was to not be found.

"So," the familiar weight settled onto his shoulder, "why did you help me?"

He hadn't seen the Raven coming. He'd been struggling to not trip over the rocks littering this little valley floor.

"I was thinking about it as I was scouting." The little valley split and he could either continue on to the left and go around the hill or break off to the right where it opened up and flattened out. "Head to the right. There's a good hiding spot with some water."

"It was the right thing to do, I guess."

"You guess?"

Bishop shrugged, "Also, I have been accused of acting without thinking." A memory of being yelled at in Alexandrea after running across a street under fire made him smile.

"That would make more sense. Cuz the idea of it being the right thing…" The Raven fluffed out his feathers.

"Do you have a name?"

"Raven."

"Right, but do you have a name?"

"A raven is better in every way than anything else you could come across. Why would I need to be called anything else but Raven."

Shifting his burden and rolling his neck Bishop trudged on toward, what he hoped was water and some shade.

"See that pointy rock sticking up?"

Bishop nodded.

"Behind and to the left of that there's a crack that leads down to where a spring pops out of the ground. I'll meet you there."

"Where are you going?"

"I wanna see if they've noticed yet."

The walk wasn't much farther, and the brush was easy to avoid. Once he found the spot, unfortunately, the easy part ended. Sand had trickled down the slope making each step treacherous, and the farther he descended the steeper it became. The last few feet essentially turned into a slide. The sides of the crack he found himself in were an arms length on either side, and the blue sky was only a scratch in the air above him. Thankfully, the shade produced by being thirty feet below the normal level of the ground had immediately dropped the temperature.

Ahead of him the walls of the cut turned from sandy and rough to polished hues of red and orange. This did make him worry. He remembered going through some national parks as a kid and learning about how these kinds of spots looked so polished because of flash floods. Tons of water would come crashing through, carrying boulders and trees, and destroying anything in its way. This was the wrong place to be in that situation, but he didn't really have an option.

The water was obvious. He could feel the moisture on his skin. Thankfully, he didn't need to be an expert tracker to find it. In a confined space, like he was in, there were only so many places a puddle of water could be, and around a slight bend he saw a small pool bubbling up from the ground.

Using his foot he cleared away the stones and branches, creating a smooth area to lay his charge down on. Once his arms were free he took a moment to try and figure out if the water was clean or not, then decided it didn't really matter. Leaning over he sucked the water up.

A snuffling noise drew his attention to the animal he'd carried from the camp. It had stood and was leaning over the water. It extended one paw and tested the water, then leaning forward began lapping it up like a cat.

"Good to see you're alive." Bishop's voice echoed down the walls of the little canyon.

The animal sat back and shook the water off it's paw, "Yeah, thanks for that."

They locked eyes. Bishop's blue looking into the brown eyes of the creature. "Really?"

"Yes," the creature's triangular head bobbed, "I couldn't think of a way out on my own."

"No, not that… well, sure, I'm glad I could help, but what I meant was…" he paused and looked around the canyon, "Can all animals talk here?"

"What?" the creature put his paw back into the water then used it to rub his face.

"Because there's this raven…" Glancing around, Bishop half expected the Raven to show up right then.

The creature finished washing its face, "Look, we seem to have gotten off on the wrong assumptions here. Why did you save me? Are you just planning on selling me to the highest bidder or what?"

"Highest bidder?" Bishop took a deep breath. Nothing had been easy lately. "I have a friend. He's a talking raven."

"I'm sorry. A what?"

"A talking raven, and… wait, that's what bothers you right now? You're a talking something, whatever you are."

"Well yeah, but there's a reason for that."

"A reason?"

They looked at each other. Bishop felt they were talking in circles. They seemed to be having two different discussions at the same time. "I saved you because he asked me too. He said they were going to do something terrible and sell you for parts. I didn't like that idea, and I owed him, so I helped."

"Well, he wasn't wrong." The creature leaned back against the wall of the canyon. "Those guys send out hunting parties looking for interesting animals to sell or mix into elixirs to help with back aches or infertility."

Bishop was at a loss for words. Again, he found himself in a situation and was having a hard time explaining how he'd gotten here. Each individual step along the way had seemed reasonable, but looking back, the trail was a mess. He'd rushed into trouble before, and he assumed it was a good thing, but all of those times he'd had a team to back him up.

This situation was all twisted up. He didn't know why he was doing things anymore. He didn't have a direction. Talking animals. Worlds that weren't his.

"Can I have the scale?"

Bishop realized he'd been staring at a spot on the canyon wall for a while. "What scale?"

The creature leaned forward, "Black, about the size of my paw." Holding up one paw he spread it out. "It might have been on a piece of leather?"

Shaking his head Bishop said, "Nope."

"Nope I can't have it or nope you don't have it?"

"Nope, I don't have it. Look," Bishop was starting to get a little annoyed at the situation, "I'm not really sure what's going on here, but in the middle of fighting off guards and trying to carry you away without getting caught I have to admit I didn't look around for any kind of jewelry."

The shaggy head nodded, "That's reasonable." Rolling forward onto his stomach the creature stretched out and put his paw back into the water. "How far are we from the camp?"

"You're not thinking of going back are you?"

"I'll need to rest here for a while, but yeah."

"For this scale?"

The creature nodded.

Bishop stood up and walked away a few steps. Turning he looked down at the badger sized creature. "I don't know what's going on and it's getting more and more frustrating."

"And you need answers." It was a statement, not a question. "How about this, you help me and I'll help you."

"You don't care what I'm talking about?"

"Look," the creature lifted his paw from the water and licked at it, "things need to get done so we do them. It doesn't always matter why. I need my scale and you need answers, yes?"

"Yes?" Bishop still wasn't sure what the scale was.

"What kind of answers you need will depend on where we go after this, but at this moment it doesn't matter because I really need that scale."

"And sometimes," Bishop remembered his drill sergeant looking down at them as they sat on the grass, "you just do the job in front of you enough times that you end up where you need to be."

Looking up at the sliver of sky he took a deep breath and held it for a moment. A mission. He could do a mission. He was trained for that. Why was he here? That's not your problem, soldier. Was this world some figment of his injured brain? That's above your paygrade so just keep your head down and do your job.

"Okay, let's do it."

"Do what?" A flutter of black signaled the return of the Raven.

"We're going back."

"I'm sorry we're what?" He landed next to the creature, dipped his beak in the water and drank.

"Something of mine was left behind." The creature said.

Water sprayed from the Raven's beak and he jumped sideways, "What in the name of Odin's other eye?"

"What?" Bishop looked from the Raven with water dripping down his feathers to the creature.

"What do you mean, what!" The Raven hopped away from the creature, "He can talk?"

"Yes?" Bishop looked back to the creature who was staring into the water of the spring. "Is that a problem? I thought all the animals here could talk."

"I already told you they couldn't." The Raven craned his neck to look up at Bishop, then jumped sideways and whipped his head back around to keep an eye on the creature. "I'm special. I can talk... for reasons." He scooted over till he was touching Bishop's leg. "Animals don't talk. It's weird. He's weird."

Bishop looked down at the Raven and made a decision. Squatting down as far as he could he patted his shoulder. The Raven glanced over, not wanting to take his gaze from the unknown talking creature, then hopped onto Bishop's shoulder. Standing back up Bishop said, "It was your idea to save him, so why the big freak out now?"

"I hear stuff, right? People talk a lot and when you're just a handsome black bird hanging around they don't think anything of it. The talk was..." He looked at the creature. "You know what? Never mind. Let him tell you. I wanna hear his story."

The creature finally looked up from the water and made eye contact with Bishop, "Are you going to help me or not?"

"Help him with what?" The Raven tried to look over at Bishop but the angle made it difficult for eye contact.

"Something important to him was left behind in that tent. At least I assume it was in the same tent we found him in."

"And you don't know what it is, or why he wants it? He's a talking animal." The Raven's nails bit into Bishop's shoulder, "Talking animals are weird, and suspicious."

"Really?" Bishop caught himself sighing and tried to stop, "You just scouted their camp right?"

"I did, after I stopped for a bite to eat."

"Were they coming for us?"

"Most definitely."

"Were you going to tell us that?"

"Oh, they weren't headed in our direction. I picked a perfect hideout."

"So," Bishop looked back at the creature, "while they're headed in the wrong direction would be a perfect time to slip in and find that thing of yours." He wasn't sure why he didn't want to tell the Raven about the scale. He didn't even know what the scale was, or why it was so important, but he'd made a deal with this creature. Help him get his stuff and he would take him to someone who could, hopefully, answer some questions.

"You're just going to ignore me?" The Raven squeezed his shoulder.

"No, but he said he could help me out."

"I'm helping you out."

"So you know where I can go to get answers about why things are happening to me?"

"Maybe."

"Well, two maybe's are better than one." Bishop caught himself sighing again. He didn't remember doing this before. He'd been in charge of idiots in the military and he hadn't turned into an exasperated version of his mother. It was the lack of control, he thought. When he'd been dealing with things before, there had been an obvious chain of command, and plans, and people to help with the logistics of those plans. Here, it was just him, and a whole bucket of crazy.

"I don't like you." The Raven said to the creature.

Make that two buckets of crazy. "I'm going to need you to scout the camp," Bishop said.

"And what if I don't want to help you and this crazy talking thing." The Raven drifted off his shoulder and landed on a stick poking up from the mud on the other side of the spring. "What are you anyway? And do you even have a name?"

The creature stood up, stretched, and looked from Bishop to the Raven. "You can call me Sid, and as for what I am, I'm me. Now, they aren't going to be out looking for us for too much longer. Are we doing this or not?"

"Yes."

"No." The Raven glared at Bishop and ruffled his feathers, "Maybe. Okay, fine, but you already owe us for breaking you out of that place. Now you owe us double, and your helping information had better be really good."

Bishop nodded partly to acknowledge the Raven's acquiescence and partly because he just agreed that the creature, Sid, did indeed owe them. "So, Raven, you'll have the most important job."

"Of course I will."

"Myself and Sid will head back to the tent where he was kept and look for his stuff."

Sid shook himself, "I doubt they kept it with all the cages. They would've wanted to study it and that means keeping it somewhere else."

"Well that's just great because," the Raven flipped its wings up and waved them, "the last time I checked they didn't exactly label all their tents with what was in them."

Bishop put a hand up to forestall the argument, "They aren't going to guard most tents, so we can eliminate those and just focus on ones with guards. Hopefully our master scout can tell us which ones look more promising than others, and also, hopefully, there should only be a couple of them."

The walk back to the oasis was easier because he wasn't carrying something, but also slower because they had to constantly check for potential problems. The Raven would circle out a way then come back and point the safest way. By the time they made it back to camp, night had well and truly fallen. Bishop wasn't sure if the days were the same length here, but it felt like that last one had been longer than the standard twenty four hours.

They approached the camp from the direction of the broken temple Bishop had explored earlier. The broken walls and encroaching dunes gave them more cover, and the edge butted up against the first tents of the main camp.

The Raven landed on a broken low stone wall next to where Bishop crouched with Sid. "Huh, I thought this place was bigger. And there was a dome over there painted white. You could see it for miles."

Bishop looked at him, confused, "Are you talking about this place?"

The Raven shrugged with his wings, "Obviously not. I must have been thinking of something else. I travel a lot, you know."

It wasn't something Bishop wanted to get into right now. As with so many other conversations it needed to be saved for later. "What did you see?"

"Your guess was right. There's two tents with guards. One has torches in front and a lot of fancy stuff hanging around, so I'm guessing it's not that one. The other one smells off, and when I think something smells off then…" his feathers rippled under the moonlight. "If what he said is true about them wanting to look his stuff over, then it's probably in that tent."

"Right." Bishop peeked over the top of the stone wall, "Let me guess, it's in the middle of all the other tents and not conveniently located at the edge of the camp."

"Actually," the Raven bobbed his head, "it's against the edge of the lake, but yes, other than that, it's pretty well in the middle of the camp."

Bishop nodded at the information, "Okay, along the edge of the lake it is. That should provide us with some cover, hopefully."

One man wearing camouflage, a raven flying overhead, and a creature the size of a large badger covered in dark fur, don't stick out much in the dark. This dark, especially, was helpful because it was the dark of the world before civilization tried to permanently light up the night. There were a few points of firelight flickering around the camp, and other than that, it was starlight accompanied by a quarter moon hanging like a clipped fingernail in the night sky.

The raven was a silent shadow blocking off chips of starlight as the others moved along the water's edge. The tent they were looking for was obvious even in the darkness. It was one of the few with torchlight, and the three guards standing at the entry were a solid giveaway. The opening was toward the camp and the back hung over a small rocky cliff of about ten feet which dropped directly into the water of the lake.

It's silhouette was unique with a metal chimney poking through the fabric. Smoke curled from the chimney top telling Bishop someone was probably home. Crouching behind a bush about six feet to the side of the tent Bishop tried to run through his options. A frontal assault would be ridiculous. Again, he thought to himself, I am not prepared for hand to hand combat. He'd come out on top the last time because of luck and surprise. This time there was one more guard to deal with, at least that he could see, and any noise would alert the whole camp.

That thought brought a realization. He hadn't thought of an exit strategy. He wanted to smack himself in the head, but didn't want any sudden movements to alert the guards. This was the benefit and the problem of working in an organization like the U.S. Navy. It was someone else's job to think of these kinds of things. By the time the job reached him the officers above him had collectively run through all these issues and formulated a battle plan with multiple possibilities and contingencies. This time he was just running in blind with a snarky raven as a scout.

On the plus side, the camp did seem mostly deserted. Hopefully they were all out looking for him and even if he did make noise the only people around would be the elderly and moms with newborn babies they couldn't leave.

The generic plan was to grab this scale and hustle back to the hiding spot and hope no one followed. So, again, how to get into the tent and grab the scale. According to Sid the scale was small enough to fit in his hand, so carrying it shouldn't be a problem. Hopefully, finding it wouldn't be a problem either.

The tent was staked down, and Bishop considered cutting through a cord holding one of the stakes. That would loosen up a section enough for him to slide under. He tossed out that idea when he looked at the sword he'd acquired and compared it to the cord holding the stakes in place. It would take him hours to cut through it, and, as the guards checked the sides of the tent every few minutes, that idea was a non-starter.

The back of the tent was unreachable, so that just left a frontal assault. Which he really didn't want to do, but with two talking animals in his squad, he should be able to replicate the previous encounter to give him some kind of an advantage.

Backing away from the tent to a better line of shrubs, Bishop signaled for the Raven. A moment later he landed silently enough to be one of the darker shadows cast by the slim moonlight. "You remember what we did the last time?"

The Raven hopped from one foot to the other, "You mean when I made the humans look ridiculous, like they always do?"

"Sure." Bishop turned to Sid, "You say other animals can't talk, right?"

Sid nodded.

"So you and the Raven here are going to distract the guards. Try to lead them away. The best would be if you could get all three of them to move away from the door long enough for me to get in. What I expect is for at least one of them to stay behind, and I'll deal with him. Once I'm inside, what exactly am I looking for?"

Sid nodded his head and looked toward the tent, "I'll meet you inside."

Bishop looked at him for a solid five count before Sid finally looked over and met his eyes. "I get the feeling you don't want anyone to know exactly what this thing is."

Sid rolled his shoulders and Bishop took it for a noncommittal shrug.

"If I don't know what it looks like then there's no reason for me to even go in there, so..." he paused for a moment hoping the creature would fill in some information.

When nothing happened the Raven let out a little croak, "Well, if we're not going to do this, I'm going to head back to the other side of the lake. I saw some good dead fish over there."

Bishop hoped the Raven was bluffing to help him persuade the little creature to give up some information, but he wasn't sure.

"Fine." Sid continued to stare at the tent. "It's a black scale about the size of a playing card."

"A scale?" The Raven hopped toward Sid. "A scale like something off of..."

"A lizard." Sid finished.

"Right." The Raven looked up as if he expected to see something.

Bishop was reminded of his encounter with the thing from the other night. His mind flickered back to images of something blocking out the stars one at a time until the entire sky was black. Shaking himself to kick the memories he said, "So, it's just black."

The Raven croaked, "If it is what I think it is, no, it's not just black."

Sid glared at the Raven, "In the light it will change color, but mostly, yes, it's just black."

Bishop looked back and forth between the two talking animals, and wondered, not for the first time and definitely not for the last time, how he'd ended up here at a desert oasis trying to steal a lizard scale with these two. "So the plan remains the same."

The two animals looked at each other and seemed to come to some kind of agreement. Bishop knew questions would need to be answered once they were out of here, but at this moment the mission needed to be done. Answers could come later.

Moving back up to the brush closest to the tent he waited for the two animals to make their way to the front. A moment later he heard the Raven say something inappropriate about the guard's mother. Then Sid could be heard from the same direction agreeing with the Raven. The two guards on the far side of the tent turned toward the noise and started a quiet discussion.

They seemed to come to a decision and one of them moved off into the dark of the camp leaving two behind. Bishop took a deep breath. He might be able to hand one, but he didn't think he could handle two of them. The element of surprise didn't work with two to one odds.

A crash brought his thought process back into sharp focus. A yell from the guard who'd followed the talking animals into camp brought a quick response from one more of the three. Looking over his shoulder one guard got a signal from the other to go and at a run he set off into the dark.

Bishop pictured Sid tripping the poor guy as the raven swooped down at his face. Not wanting to waste this chance as the remaining guard was looking off toward the noise, Bishop slipped out from behind the brush and ran at the remaining guard.

The guard glanced over his shoulder a moment before Bishop tackled him. His shoulder drove the guard facedown into the ground. His high school football coach would have been proud of his form. He heard the air rush from the guard as they slammed into the hard packed earth in front of the tent. Sitting up he raised a fist then hesitated as the guard didn't move.

Rolling off the unconscious guard Bishop opened the flap leading into the tent. He assumed someone would be inside, but he hoped it would just be the normal occupant of the tent. Someone whose job was to research the strange animals they found in the desert. Basically, he was hoping for some kind of weak Bedouin veterinarian.

As the tent flap swung back a sword glinted in the torchlight coming for his neck. Dropping to one knee Bishop felt the air move above him as the sword continued its path. Swinging out hard with his right arm he connected with the knee of his attacker and heard a crunch followed by a yell. He had a moment to take in the tent's interior before three more armed Bedouins came at him. It was a smaller space than the one he'd found Sid in. Unfortunately it wasn't small enough to stop all three from swinging at him simultaneously.

Diving forward he split the two on the right and their swords bit into the tent material. Unceremoniously rolling on the dirt of the floor Bishop reached out and grabbed the leg of a table tucked against the wall of the tent. Pulling with his left hand he snapped the leg off. The leg spun from his hand as he pivoted and the broken end slammed into the soft spot under the jaw of the middle attacker.

The sword arm of the one to his left dropped and his eyes widened at the sight of blood coming from someone he'd most likely grown up with. Bishop swept the sword out of any kind of attack position and threw an uppercut to the bottom of the attacker's jaw. His head snapped back, and his feet left the floor. Lunging forward he grabbed the now limp guard by the front of his robe. Pulling him one handed toward him he spun to face his final assailant holding the last one as a shield.

Grabbing his human shield with two hands Bishop heaved the limp figure, causing the final standing one to dodge to Bishop's right. Taking a step with his left foot Bishop pivoted on it and threw his hips into the turn like every coach growing up had drilled into him. Whipping out his right foot, it connected with the guard's knee cracking it and causing him to collapse.

Jumping back out of sword range Bishop looked over the small space. Two bedouins lay gripping broken knees and swearing at him, but alive, while two others were absolutely dead.

"How did I..." Bishop's whisper was cut short as his mind finally caught up with the rest of him and pointed out other important things around him. Smoke had started filling the room as flickering firelight and heat radiated from behind him.

Turning he saw the table he'd broken the leg from leaning against a pot bellied iron fireplace, pressing it into the tent material, which was now joyfully ablaze. Glancing around and seeing nothing useful to douse the flames, his eyes started frantically searching the small space for anything that matched Sid's description of the scale they'd come for.

The broken table had spilled its contents partially onto the ground with others leaning on the glowing fireplace. Doing his best to look over those first before they were consumed by the fire, he was mostly sure the scale wasn't among them. A moment of panic washed through him as he realized he'd forgotten about the two still conscious guards behind him.

Spinning around he saw the one by the door was gone and the other was crawling and had made it halfway out the door. Bishop realized he only had a few moments between the burning tent and the guards about the yell for any help they could get.

Turning back toward the table's spilled contents he dropped onto his knees to rummage through the dropped things. The heat of the fire on his head and shoulders was a good reminder of his need to hurry. In the dust of the floor something glinted, reflecting the light of the fire. His eyes followed the flash and saw a spot of light swirling like an oil slick in a parking lot.

Reaching out his fingers wrapped around it. The muscles in his arm cramped first followed by a wave of nausea. Rolling onto the ground Bishop felt the muscles in his hand clamp down hard enough on the black scale that it cut into his fingers.

Escape!

The thought was a tsunami hammering into his mind on a wave of rage.

You are my door!

A blackness settled over his eyes and blotted out the dancing light of the burning tent.

Chapter Nine

The sound and the feeling happened simultaneously, but were disconnected. The crack registered in Bishop's memory as a gun shot but the thump that vibrated through him wasn't.

"Bishop!"

His eyes snapped open to a world colored in shades of gray.

Kill them!

His fist snapped out and the door to the helicopter buckled, flying outward to hang from one hinge.

"Bishop, what the…" More gunshots snapped around him.

Through the door of the helicopter Bishop could see a black and white world filled with pain. Behind a black van parked across the tarmac, multiple people in tactical military gear had opened fire on the spinning down helicopter. To the left behind a separate, but identical, van, more guns sprouted, promising more pain.

Yes…

Stepping out of the helicopter and moving around the bullets Bishop closed the distance to the first van and brushed it aside with the back of his hand. Reaching down he peeled up a section of concrete and swung it through the remaining assailants who were frantically trying to fall back to the safety of the other van.

Taps on his left shoulder and side shifted his focus to the next van. Four black clad soldiers knelt with rifles spouting flickers of light as the rest piled into the open back of the vehicle. Reaching up, Bishop brushed the bullets to the side, and in one step was among the four kneeling men.

A sweep of his right arm cleared them.

More…

Bishop's right arm hung in the air as the van accelerated away.

Follow them. Kill them all!

Something was wrong with his arm. Patches of skin now shimmed oil slick black, bringing back a memory of a burning tent. Shaking his head, he curled his hand toward him. The tips of his fingers were too sharp.

Why are you stopping?

The voice made him twitch. Closing his right hand he squeezed his eyes shut.

A weight landed on his left shoulder. "Hey!" The Raven's voice was followed by a sharp poke on the side of his head. "Hey! What in the greatest definition of the word "what" is happening?!"

Bishop sucked in a deep breath between his clenched teeth.

"I mean, seriously. One minute I'm watching Sid run into a burning tent and the next I'm here watching you toss guys around like…" The Raven's voice trailed off. "Speaking of guys. The angry looking big guy from before is coming this way?"

Opening his eyes Bishop looked around. Off to his right a black van was crumpled against a hanger wall with a kitchen table sized chunk of concrete leaning against it. What looked to be legs were sticking out from underneath like a terrible version of the wicked witch.

"Lieutenant Bishop, get on your knees and put your hands behind your head."

Kill him. He's unimportant.

"Who said…?" The weight on Bishop's shoulder left and was followed by raven claws digging into his scalp.

Bishop dropped to his knees and watched the Corporal swing around into his field of vision. The bright red of the letter C on the corporal's Chicago Cubs t-shirt stood in stark contrast to the gray tones of the rest of the world. The corporal's sidearm was solidly pointing at Bishop's head. "What just happened?"

The Raven squeezed his scalp and also said, "What is happening?"

You can't hold me in.

"And who is that?" The Raven asked as he hopped to Bishop's right shoulder.

"Lieutenant?" The corporal advanced a step.

Bishop breathed in through his nose and out through his mouth three times. "Corporal, why did we come to Rome?"

The corporal raised his hand gun until it pointed at the sky then nodded. "Right. We better be moving."

Bishop stood and looked around again. "You're not going to ask about…" he waved a hand at the crushed van.

The corporal shrugged, "In my line of work, you just do the job in front of you."

"In your line of work?" Bishop looked the corporal over again as he holstered his weapon.

"It doesn't matter." The corporal said and moved off.

Bishop caught up with him. "We just left multiple unknown attackers dead, a navy helicopter damaged, and, and…" He didn't really want to say the rest.

"And things got strange." The corporal nodded and looked over at him as they wound their way around the main body of the airport. "When your captain signed me on for this, the explanation was that something strange was happening with you and that was why we were coming here. Why should I be surprised when something strange happens?"

"Because I…" he looked down at his right hand then back up again. The color had slowly seeped back into the world around him as they'd walked. His hand had betrayed him. There were times he'd slept on his hand and woken up with no control over what it was doing. It felt like it wasn't his hand. This was like that.

"Because," the voice of the Raven made him jump, "I still don't know what's going on. Why am I here? Why can't I see myself? Do I have a body? Did I leave it back in that tent with Sid and only my mind traveled to this horrible place?"

Bishop's body guard had stopped to look over a map posted on a kiosk next to a main entry door to the airport. Ignoring the Raven, mainly because he didn't want to seem even more unstable by talking to something no one else could see, he tried to remember the corporal's name. Rank was fine for certain situations, but with what had just happened…. He'd heard the captain say the corporal's name back in sick bay, but he'd been a little distracted then too.

A squeeze on his shoulder was followed with, "Are you even listening to me?" A squawk in his ear caused him to twitch his head to the side. "I'm pretty sure you can hear me. I saw you rip up the ground and hit people with it. Then there was this big scary evil presence." The raven dropped his voice to a whisper, "I think it's gone but since I couldn't see it in the first place I can't be sure."

Bishop had to get to the bottom of all this before he went insane. He just had to think of it as a series of steps leading him to talk with this contact at The Vatican. First, get the corporal's name. Bishop wracked his brain but couldn't remember what had been said. He thought about looking at the corporal's name plate on his uniform, then remembered they were in civies. Finally, as the corporal decided on a point on the map, "Corporal, I can't keep calling you corporal. Remind me what your name is."

The corporal stopped and looked at some signs written in both Italian and English, "Ryan."

Bishop hadn't been one hundred percent sure but, "That's not what I remember…"

"Ryan's my first name." He made a decision, headed across lanes of traffic dropping off travelers, and headed toward the parking garage.

"Peter, Peter Bishop."

"Peter and Ryan," the Raven said, "that's nice. Isn't that nice? Yep, it's nice. Now that introductions are over can you please tell me what's going on before I start pecking a hole in the side of your head."

Ryan nodded and checked signs posted on the pillars holding the next level of parking above them. Bishop finally looked over at them. The one they were standing by was bright blue with a big red letter M and the word metro written in white below it. "Been around Rome before?"

"Yep." Ryan settled himself on the single bench next to the concrete pillar.

"I think you're intentionally ignoring me." The raven said. "Actually I think..." The pause was followed by a sound of feathers rustling. "Actually, again, I think you are intentionally ignoring me because no one can see me and things would look even weirder if you started talking to your shoulder."

"Right." Bishop nodded.

They waited in silence for the bus to arrive. The ride into the heart of Rome was just over an hour and in any other situation Bishop would have been ecstatic. He'd never been to Rome. It was the heart of all sorts of things he wanted to see. So many interesting stories wound their way through the eternal city.

At one point he could see the Colosseum, and at another he was sure he saw the pillars of the Forum where Julius Caesar himself had been assassinated. Cleopatra had walked these streets, but so had Mussolini when he'd given birth to the first Fascist political party.

On the other hand... He looked down at his right hand and flexed his fingers. Had it really changed back at the helicopter or was that just his mind interpreting things? Looking over at the Marine who'd been given permission to shoot him if he felt it was necessary, "One thing stuck with me."

"Really?" Ryan looked up from his phone.

"I get it," Bishop saw a Google map displayed on Ryan's phone, "what you said about not being surprised when you've been told things are going to be strange. What I don't get is why you said, in your line of work. Aren't you in my line of work?"

"I am in the military, yes." He tapped some buttons on his phone and pulled up a picture of an older white man dressed in a black robe with the distinctive white collar of a catholic priest. Red stitching outlined the black robe and he wore a belt of bright red with a matching red skull cap.

"He's being dodgy." The Raven said. "Also, since no one can see me, and apparently only you can hear me, I thought about it and have given myself permission to comment on anything and everything. Like how this bus ride is boring, and how do I know what a bus is? I mean, if I've lived my whole life flying over that desert looking for tasty dead things then why do I know what a bus is?"

Bishop wasn't sure how to take Ryan's comment, or the Raven's comments, and didn't feel like pressing the issue at the moment. "Is that who we're going to meet?" It felt strange not knowing all the information. Being a lieutenant he was normally the one with the documents and files, but the captain had decided, in this situation, that Bishop not be given the information. It bothered him. He'd worked hard to be trusted and do his job well. All his reviews were positive. Even the comments from those under his command had been positive. However, he had just punched an entire van out of the way like it was paper mache, so a little leeway needed to be given to the situation.

Ryan nodded, "Cardinal Antonius Sodano. He should be in the governmental offices behind Saint Peters."

The Raven flapped a wing across Bishop's face as he interrupted, "You don't find it strange?" His sharp nails dug into Bishop's shoulder, "I find it strange. I also just realized that I can speak your language. Not that I hadn't realized it before, but now I realize it's strange. Why would I know your language?"

"So," Bishop raised one hand, and the world broke. Out the window of the bus streaks of fire fell from the sky like burning hailstones. Cars crumpled and windows shattered under the fiery onslaught. People caught fire and screamed as he pressed his hands to the window.

I tore it apart. It is mine to do again.

"He's back!" The Raven dug his claws into Bishop's shoulder.

A building collapsed, covering an entire side street with rubble. Bishop looked to Corporal Ryan, "What are…"

Ryan stopped reading a document on his phone and looked up, "It sounds like this cardinal oversees the research wing of the church."

"Don't you…" Bishop waved at the window and they both looked out. A taxi driver stepped out of his cab to yell at a young man on a moped. The blue Italian sky sparkled overhead as Roman citizens went about their daily business.

"And he's gone." The Raven tapped the side of Bishop's head. "Where'd he go? I can see you, and I could feel him like some lurking creepy thing from the great beyond, but now, nothing."

"What?" Ryan looked out the window at the normal Italian day.

Bishop felt the skin on his scalp tighten. He looked back out the window and whispered, "Did you see it?"

"Well," the Raven said, "since you're whispering and being all sneaky, I'm gonna assume you're talking to me. Yes," he whispered back, "if you mean the fire and the smashing and the people screaming, then yes, I saw it. Also, why am I whispering? Also," he let out a caw, "why is your world so crazy? I miss the simplicity of the desert where all you do is wait for something to die. Something always dies in the desert. Then you eat it. Simple."

Bishop half listened to the Raven ramble on about the best aspects of desert life for a carrion eating bird, while watching Rome slide by. He'd seen it. He knew something had happened. Again, he was at a loss about what it was and how it impacted him. It obviously was about him, or connected with him, because no one else was experiencing these things. He felt a compulsion to catalogue all the crazy that had happened to him over the last single day of his life. Had it really been only one day since waking up in the infirmary and being told to head to his bunk?

Chapter Ten

"Sir?"

Patrick looked up from the book he'd been reading. He knew he was supposed to be keeping track of the current mission, but he had people for that, and they were good at their job. Why hire people who are competent at their job then look over their shoulder like you didn't trust them to do that job. Instead, he was reading a biography of Ghengis Khan. Very interesting man. Lots of death and destruction, but it had a purpose. He'd been trying to create a better world. Ghengis Khan's main problem had been his lack of knowledge. He didn't know enough about the world outside his own yurt to actually build a better world, and even with the lack of proper knowledge he did a remarkably good job at the attempt.

Patrick closed the book and looked up at the black uniformed mercenary, "Yes?"

"It was a total failure."

Patrick raised an eyebrow, "I thought we sent more than enough people for a simple grab and go."

"Absolutely sir. To be honest, the amount of men we sent was probably overkill."

"And yet?"

"You need to see the video. It's hard to explain without sounding…" the mercenary waved his hands in the air vaguely.

Patrick sighed and stood up. If you were going to hire good help, then you needed to trust their opinion on the job at hand. Walking the short distance from his stateroom to the operations center gave him a wonderful view of the Tyrrhenian Sea and beyond that the Italian coastline. The ship bobbed slightly as he walked, but the sea was mostly still today.

In the op center he waved for one of the men to vacate their chair so he could get a good look at the monitor. The video feed was marked in the top right corner as being pulled from airport security cameras. He didn't ask how they got it. Again, if you hire people to do a job then just let them do it.

Nodding at the tech seated next to him, the video started. He watched as the helicopter landed and then stared open mouthed as the lieutenant tore up the tarmac and destroyed two whole squads of highly competent mercenaries.

"Well…" he leaned back in the chair. "That was unexpected." Looking over his shoulder at the officer in charge, "Do you know where they went to after that?"

"Yes sir," the officer pulled up a map on a handheld tablet. "We tracked their movements using the airport cameras until they got onto a bus. The line they got onto could take them to multiple locations, so we are currently trying to verify which stop they were headed to or if they changed lines at some point."

Patrick nodded, "Let me know when you've got their location." Standing, he paused for a moment. He needed to project a certain amount of calm and knowledge to those around him, especially with this turn of events. If it started looking like he wasn't expecting this situation then he would lose a bit of the presence he'd been building, and some unusual commands he might have to give would be ignored or not done to the best of their ability.

"We knew this was coming," he said to no one in particular, "it seems we need to move some planning up a bit." He knew the statement was a bit melodramatic, but sometimes things work because those around you expect them to.

As he walked out of the op center he noted some nodding of heads and a general lifting of the unease he'd sensed. They would think it was all under control, and that was all they needed to think.

Taking the first door to the left, Patrick descended the stairs to a separate living quarter section of the ship. He, of course, had the grand room with a balcony up on the main deck. Others were down here, including Mason. Stopping he knocked on the fake wood paneled door and waited.

"Yes?"

"It's me Mason. Can I come in?"

A moment later the door swung inward, "Of course you can come in. I told you knocking was unnecessary."

Mason stood in a rumpled pair of cargo pants with zip off legs and a gray tee shirt with Lake Tahoe stenciled in gold lettering. The room was barely larger than the bed that occupied it, but it did have the luxury of its own bathroom. A clear space on the bed was surrounded by laptops and scattered papers.

"Any new leads?" Patrick asked as Mason made way for him to step into the room. Shifting one pile of paperwork he sat down on the corner of the bed.

"Actually yes," Mason replied as he closed the door. "There's a very promising lead from some new translations at El Mirador in Guatemala."

Patrick nodded, "The Maya always seemed a likely civilization to have the right connections."

Mason climbed over a laptop and settled himself into his clear zone at the head of the bed, "I would have put it at a certainty, but their language is so difficult."

"And we both know the difficulty of assuming something's there and diving into a rainforest to find it before we have all the facts."

Mason chuckled, "I still think there was something hiding along the Congo river."

"I agree with you, and I'm fairly sure the oil exploration teams know exactly where it is."

"I agree," Mason nodded emphatically. "They were clearly not telling us something, but I couldn't tell if it was about oil deposits or some lost temple."

"Most likely the former with a little bit of the latter sprinkled in."

"And with the amount of money the oil companies have to toss around..." Mason shrugged to finish the thought.

Patrick understood. They had very deep pockets for this current endeavor, but not as deep as a massive international oil company. "Changing the subject..."

Mason nodded at him to continue.

"Would the physical interaction of the main crystal with our lieutenant cause him to have..." he paused not knowing how to continue.

"Something happened, didn't it?"

Patrick let out a sigh, "That's an understatement. We caught CCTV of the crew trying and failing to grab him off the tarmac."

"I assume he didn't get away because he's an amazing tactician," Mason said.

"No." Patrick briefly described the scene at the airport, trying his best not to sound crazy, or like he was describing a summer blockbuster.

Mason shrugged, "What did you expect? The main goal of this was originally to decide if the myths of these various places were connected, and once we found the connecting piece..."

"I know, and I know I've talked about it like it was real and certain, but it's hard to wrap your mind around something when it's just a concept. Today I saw the reality."

"You've seen pieces of the stone before, and you've even seen what they can do."

Patrick realized how hard it would be to explain to Mason what was going through his head right then. To Mason it was all facts and numbers. This whole venture had been one long math puzzle for him. If there was a multinational connection between various ancient sites, then there might be some kernel of truth to those sites. If that kernel of truth could be found then it could be accessed. What they had just witnessed was simply proof that it could be accessed.

The fact it was real should have been a relief. It meant all his planning, and all the recruiting, would pay off. So much had been done in the name of the ends justifying the means, and now the proof he was right was staring him in the face.

"I mean," Mason vaguely waved his hands in the air, "the fact that one power set exists doesn't necessarily lead to other power sets existing, but it does lend credence to the idea that the specific one we're looking for could exist."

And that, thought Patrick, was the whole point. The hope that this could be used appropriately. Hope. After years of research and trekking through jungles, deserts, and mountains to look at dimly scrawled cave paintings, he was this much closer to achieving that hope. "You're right." Standing up he straightened his suit. "Now I just have to figure out how to surprise, capture, and hold someone that can throw cars around."

Mason nodded and rested his chin in his hand, "I used to love reading serious fantasy novels. The kind that have nine hundred words and build magnificently complicated worlds. The one thing I kept coming around to was how defenseless an actual wizard was. You get a high powered rifle from a long enough distance and that wizard would be dead before he heard the gunshot."

"I don't want to kill the man. At least not yet. We don't understand his connection to the crystal yet."

"True."

"However…" Patrick trailed off and stared out the small window in Mason's room.

"Yes?"

"Do you know what a feint is?"

Chapter Eleven

The bus pulled to a stop and Ryan gestured for them to get off. From the bus stop they walked down the street until it opened up in front of a huge plaza, mostly circled by a double row of columns. Statues that Bishop could only guess were saints of some kind or another, topped the columns and topped the front of the massive church at the end of the plaza.

"One of them must be Saint Peter?" Bishop vaguely directed the question at Ryan.

"Oddly," Ryan paused and looked through the center of the plaza toward the church that dominated the other end, "even though it's named that, I'm fairly sure none of them are actually Peter."

The center of the plaza, now to their right as they walked by, was dominated by an obelisk. From the base of it, supported by lions, to the tip of a shining bronze cross it had to be at least one hundred feet high. Bishop had seen pictures of the entry to Saint Peter's Basilica, but had never visited. It was definitely a bucket list item for him, and minus every event from the last twenty four hours it was an amazing site. The rows of columns stretched out like arms from the great church of St. Peters, trying to gather in the faithful of the world.

Staying to the left they circled the outside of the columned plaza and stopped at a guarded gate leading further into what Bishop knew was Vatican City. "Whoa," the Raven sounded off with something that was best described as, "Rawk... Do you see those guys?"

Bishop looked around for danger until he realized the Raven was laughing, and the only guys around he might be laughing at, were the traditional Swiss guards at the Vatican gate. They stood stiffly at attention, amazingly clothed in what looked like red and yellow striped pajamas.

"That's going to make my eyes water," the raven let out another rawk, "and I eat dead things."

The guards stopped them and asked for their reasons to want entry and for their passports. Ryan showed them their military ID's and let them know they had a meeting with a cardinal in the Palace of the Governors.

"Are you expected," the guard on the left asked while the guard on the right scanned the bar code on the back of their ID's.

Ryand nodded, "His captain was supposed to call ahead and let the Cardinal know we're coming."

Again, thought Bishop. Earlier it was we're both in the military, or in my line of work, and now it's not our captain, but my captain. Yes, the voice in his head answered back, things are crazy right now but that might be a good reason to ignore simple problems like this. However, the fact that things are crazy could be an even better reason to keep everything squared away. You don't want to be blind sided by something when you're dealing with this level of madness.

"Hey," the Raven whispered in his ear, "I'm starting to get a weird vibe from this guy. So," Bishop could hear him scratch his feathers, "here's the plan. When we get out of sight of the color brigade in pajamas here, you hold him down and I'll peck at his eyes until he tells us what's actually up."

"Hang on." Bishop said while trying to catch up with the corporal's retreating back.

Ryan looked back at him and Bishop stepped over to the right of the paved trail they were following. A waist high fence stretching six feet gave a vague attempt at keeping them from leaning on the giant columns surrounding St Peter's square. Bishop stepped into the shadow of one and waited for Ryan.

"Okay?" Ryan stopped in front of him with his arms crossed.

"Who are you? Who do you work for? And why should I trust you?" Bishop didn't feel the need to play nice with someone who was obviously military. Also, their situation currently didn't lend itself to taking extra time.

"He's not going to answer a straight question." The Raven said. "When he tries to avoid it, knock him down, and I'll start pecking at his eyes."

Ryan nodded, "My name is Ryan Phillip Sidney. I am a corporal in the military. Just not the same military as you, and no I can't tell you which one. It tends to change depending on the mission. Why should you trust me? Because your captain assigned me to this, and I do my job, just like you."

"He's just going to answer?" The Raven's voice was annoyed. "No argument? You can't trust a guy who just answers your questions like that. I should peck out his eyes."

"So," Bishop took another good look at his personal bodyguard, or jailer, "are you special forces or a mercenary?"

"Yes." Ryan looked over his shoulder as two people walked past.

"At least tell me you were a marine at some point."

Ryan nodded again, "Started out in the corps."

"And then?" Bishop asked.

"And then it's none of your business," Ryan shrugged. "We good? Cuz we've got a meeting to sort out whatever's going on with you."

It was Bishop's turn to nod, "Sure, for now. I just punched a van out of the way and I'm still not sure who those guys were and why they were trying to shoot us, so we may not continue to be good, but for now..." he returned Ryan's shrug.

They stepped back out onto the paved pathway and followed the left outline of the massive bulk of St. Peter's church. Eventually making their way to the back of the church they came to an open area with manicured lawns and well groomed trees. The emerald of the leaves and grass was a shock to the eyes after the cobblestone and concrete of the Roman streets. Bishop slowed and let his eyes wander for a moment. To the left a chapel stood at an odd angle, disconnected from anything, while to the right just peeking out from behind some trees was a fountain.

Trying to make out what statue stood at the center of the fountain, Bishop wished the slightly graying trees would move. Then like a painting being washed clean he stared as the color drained from the world. A pinprick of pain started in the top right of his head and spread, throbbing, through his brain.

The cobblestones of the pathway shattered as his knees hit them and the voice cracked his skull.

I will...

A deep rasping croak from the Raven matched the cracking of the columns of St. Peter's behind him.

Break it. Free me and we can break it all. It can only be made new if...

The trees burst into flame causing the grass to curl up and wither. Bishop's fingers contorted, blackening, and digging into the cobbles of the pathway. Pain flared in a stripe across his shoulder blades.

Someone was yelling at him, but the crackling of the flames covered the words.

Eight separate nails dug into his right shoulder and the Raven's beak touched his ear, "Hey," there was a pause then calmly the Raven said, "Peter Bishop." A deep rolling rawk snapped Bishop's attention away from the destruction and pain around him. "This is nothing. Close your eyes. Think on what is true."

You. Of them all, you will not take...

"Don't listen to grumpy." The Raven's head rested against Bishop's temple, his feathers scratching against the skin. "You've got this. Breathe."

Bishop closed his eyes, blocking out the flames, and took a deep breath. Holding it, he mentally pictured all the pain stabbing through him and gathered it all up in his chest. Breathing out he pushed the knotted ball of pain out with his breath.

"See," the Raven croaked, "that wasn't so bad."

Bishop sucked in another breath through his nose and slowly let it out through his lips. Shaking his head, he opened his eyes. The green was muted, as if someone had dusted it all in ash, but the fire was gone. The raven was wrong. That really had been bad. Whatever it had been.

"Lieutenant?" Bishop looked up to see Ryan standing a few paces away with his sidearm pointed solidly at a spot about halfway between them. "Are you..." he trailed off and waved his gun in a small circle.

Taking another deep breath Bishop pushed himself up from the broken cobbles. Looking from them to the world around him, he was pleased to see a few cobbles were the only damage that seemed to be real. "Did you see any of that?"

"Well," Ryan holstered his weapon, "I..." He looked around, "What did you see?"

Bishop considered not telling him, but if Ryan was going to be any kind of help in this situation he needed to know what was going on. "The trees were burning," he looked over his shoulder at the bulk of St. Peter's basilica, "the building was breaking."

Ryan nodded, "I didn't see any of that, but you..." He trailed off.

"I..." Bishop looked down at the broken path beneath his feet and remembered black hooked claws at the end of his painfully twisted fingers.

"Yeah," Ryan's head bobbed over and over, "your fingers were all black and," he raised one hand and twitched his fingers at Bishop, "there was something poking out of your head."

Bishop reached up and ran his fingers through his hair. He didn't feel anything.

"Believe him," Raven said. "Things, like maybe horns or antlers. What's the difference between those anyway. I mean does it make a difference if you start growing one or the other? I think one falls off and the other doesn't. So, it would be better if you grew one and not the other, cuz one would fall off every once in a while and you could pretend to be normal. The other would be permanent, and that would look weird," the Raven sounded a bit nervous as he babbled.

Lowering his hand from his head Bishop looked at his normal fingers. "I need to know what's happening." Looking up at Ryan he held eye contact for slightly longer than necessary to get his point across. "I don't know what your exact mission is, but I need someone to have my back when..." he vaguely waved at everything around him.

Ryan gave one nod, "Well, if you're feeling up to it, let's get on with the only lead we have."

Bishop nodded back.

They turned down a wide pathway marked with cobblestones in the shape of white diamonds, and they were confronted with a four story building that looked as if the engineers for the palace of Versailles had been hired for the design. It was obvious it was a more modern building designed to fit with the rest of the Vatican.

Bishop assumed that over the centuries they'd realized the need to consolidate certain governmental functions. Having to wander all over the eclectic campus, that was Vatican City, looking for one cardinal or the other must have become frustrating.

There was another of the yellow and red striped guards at the door and Bishop sighed as the Raven giggled about soldiers in pajamas. They were directed to the second floor of the building and down the hallway to the left. Eventually, Ryan stopped at a door marked with the appropriate name plate and knocked.

Muffled by the wood of the door they could just make out a voice, "Come in."

Ryan opened the door and led the way into the office. The room was small, less than ten feet by ten feet, and was dominated by three features, a desk, crowded bookshelves, and one large window letting the golden Italian sunlight play across the polished surfaces of the former two. The large wooden desk occupied the majority of the floor space, and was currently occupied by a black clad priest with a simple white collar.

He looked to be in his fifties with deep lines running through dark black skin at the corner of his eyes, and gray attempting to dominate his short cropped dark hair.

"He's not the guy." The Raven whispered in his ear. "He's not even the same color as the guy. This guy's all black, and the other guy had red on his outfit." The Raven chuckled to himself, "I bet you thought I was talking about his skin color didn't you? Well I wasn't. That's why it's funny."

"How can I help you two?" The priest's British accent was a momentary shock, but it reminded Bishop that priests came from all over the world.

Not quite knowing what to say, Bishop was happy to let Ryan take the lead here, "We were hoping to see the Cardinal."

"I'm sorry." He smiled in a patient way that Bishop assumed was a practiced look for a priest. "He's not in today."

"We were told by the guards at the door that he was here," Ryan said.

"Yes, well," the priest looked up at the ceiling, "his absence isn't a scheduled one." Looking back to the two of them he asked, "I am his," he paused to think of an appropriate term, "colleague. Is there something I can help you with."

Ryan hesitated and Bishop was worried he would choose to walk away since their point of contact wasn't here. He knew this was all supposed to be done under the table since the captain, and most likely the entire navy, didn't want people to know about what was happening, but he wanted answers. "We were told the cardinal could help us answer some very delicate questions," Bishop said.

The priest nodded, "On what topic?"

The Raven bopped the side of Bishop's head, "There's not really any way to ask about crazy demon possession without actually asking about crazy demon possession."

Bishop stepped toward the desk, realizing the Raven was right. He wasn't sure how to ask so he just went for it, "Possession."

The priest nodded as if this was the response he'd been expecting, "Of course. Has the person you're asking about gone through the testing process?"

Bishop shrugged, "There's a testing process?"

The priest leaned back and started ticking points off on his fingers, "There are medical tests, psychological and psychiatric tests..."

Ryan stepped up, "We were referred by a good friend of the cardinal's so we would be able to get his expert advice without having to go through all those steps."

The priest sighed and bobbed his head, "Of course. He might be back by this evening, or it might be tomorrow. If you would like to wait for him I would suggest spending some time in the library. You might be able to get some preliminary questions answered before talking with the cardinal."

"So you don't..." Bishop raised his shoulders and the palms of his hands.

"I'm afraid my position doesn't allow me to skip past certain parts of the process. A cardinal can do that." He smiled as kindly at them as he could muster, "I'm just a priest learning to swim through the murky political waters of Vatican City."

Ryan and Bishop nodded at the same time, and Ryan asked, "Which way to the library, and could you let the cardinal know we're down there as soon as he gets back?"

"Of course. Once you leave this building look for a path directly to the left. Follow that behind the basilica till it ends at the back of the Sistine Chapel. Head to the left beyond the chapel and take the first door inside. That will let you into a long gallery. Go all the way down until a large section splits off to the right. That right turn will lead you to the library. The curator will ask to see the pass you were given when you first checked in with the gate guards, and will issue you with a temporary library card. When the cardinal gets back who should I say is waiting for him?"

Bishop had been nodding along with the priest's directions and was momentarily caught off guard by the question. Ryan spoke up, "There's an aircraft carrier captain who said the cardinal owed him a favor. Just tell him we're that favor."

Bishop liked the vagueness of Ryan's statement, but couldn't help but feel like it really would be more helpful if they just left their names.

Exiting the building and following the priests directions they made their way along a tree lined pathway and around the back of the main mass of the basilica. Coming to the door they let themselves in and were faced with the most amazing single hallway Bishop had ever seen.

Stretching what looked to him to be the length of two American football fields, and possibly half the length of the deck of his aircraft carrier, there was almost too much to take in as his brain struggled to parse all the details.

The floor was white marble with gray tiles making geometric patterns, and that was the simplest part. The walls were covered with giant pieces of artwork all of some type of geographic in design. Maps of different parts of the world, which ranged from whole continents to detailed paintings of one bend in a river. Each painting was framed in gold and stood at least ten feet high by teen feet wide. Standing on each side of every painting was a carved bust of some artist or explorer. Stretching the length of each side of the hallway was a single velvet rope placed approximately one foot from the wall, apparently to encourage the multitude of tourists to not touch the priceless works of art. Finally, Bishop's eyes reached the ceiling. It glowed like a perfect sunrise from the luminescence of recessed lights striking the overwhelming amount of gold paint. Every inch if the ceiling was either painted as a gold leaf frame or was a painting done mainly in gold. Standing at one end and looking down the length of that amazing ceiling was a perfect example of the artistic principle of a vanishing point.

Little raven claws tightened on his right shoulder, "So much shiny." The Raven started hopping quickly from one foot to the other, "I, I want to... there's just... I don't know where to look. Do you think they would notice if I just kinda peeled a little gold trim off? I mean, look at this place, it's not like they don't have extra."

It was magnificent, and because they were in no hurry, Bishop smiled at the Raven's dilemma and decided to take his time and look over the artwork as they went along. After a few stops Ryan stepped through the crowd of tourists and said quietly into his ear, "I was just wondering about these episodes of yours..."

He left the statement hanging and Bishop had a mental picture of tourists being thrown through the open windows which were scattered along the hallway as he smashed artwork that was hundreds of years old. An involuntary shiver ran up his spine and the Raven on his shoulder said, "I still don't trust him much, but the guys got a solid point. If old dark and creepy tries to push his way through right now all these wonderful shiny things might get damaged by someone other than me, and that would be tragic."

Reaching the end of the ornate hallway, they made a turn to the right down a shorter connecting hallway. Passing an exterior doorway that looked to head out onto a parking lot they came to a door marked as the admissions office of the Vatican library. They were greeted in Italian accented English by the director of admissions and told that a call had been made about giving them access to the library for the day.

After going through a veritable maze of directions on how the library worked and printing them two library cards, Ryan and Bishop were escorted through the doors, up a flight of stairs, and into the most amazing single room Bishop had ever seen.

He and Ryan stood, overwhelmed by where they found themselves. The first thing to hit him was the smell. Bishop loved the smell of an old book. When he had the chance, which hadn't been much recently, he loved to wander through used book stores. Flipping through the pages would release the most distinctive scent. There was no perfect way to describe it, because it didn't smell like anything other than what it was, and here that aroma of history imbued with age and knowledge was everywhere. It made him happy.

Like the hallway of maps they'd come through, the ceiling was overly ornate. The theme again was too much gold, but this time Bishop really didn't care about the designs on the ceiling. The room itself was the prize. Solid dark wood tables stretched the length of the roughly fifty yard long room with hard wooden stools at each table. He assumed the stools were used to conserve space since they could be pushed all the way under the tables, but they also looked like possible uncomfortable penance after a trip to confession.

Lining the right hand wall were two stories of book shelves. On the main floor, at intervals in the shelving, hallways of more bookshelves led back into the building where Bishop assumed there were even more bookshelves. The second floor was open to the central room with a balcony running along it, and from what he could see was exactly like the first floor. The left hand wall was more of the same except with only one level and the hallways had been replaced with large arched windows letting in the sunshine.

Ryan looked around then to Bishop, "What are we even supposed to do?"

"I've never seen such a useless room," The Raven said. "There's nothing shiny except the ceiling, and that's pointless. Seriously, doing that is ridiculous and just showing off. What do they expect? People are supposed to lay on the tables and stare up? Also," Bishop felt a wing brush his cheek, "there's nothing to eat and nothing interesting and nothing to eat. Yes, I did say that twice, because it's important."

Peter shrugged, "I tried to keep up with the directions she gave us about ordering manuscripts to be brought to the reading room, but..." he raised his hands in defeat. "We don't know what to ask for even if we remembered all the directions."

Ryan slid out a stool and sat down, "It would be nice if they had a computer search system like any library in any small town in America."

Bishop chuckled. He was possibly possessed by something that might have escaped from either an alternate dimension or a giant crystal or both. It was actively trying to escape and destroy things for unknown reasons, and their main problem right now was how to find a book in a library. It was funny, in an absurd kind of way. "What are we supposed to look up? How to not be possessed?"

Together they sat, wrapped in the native silence of what seemed like an empty library. Bishop noticed, a few tables down, a pile of papers held down by a large manuscript bound in bright blue. Some of the things about this place fit exactly with his preconceived expectations, like the gilded ceilings and the dark wood tables. Others seemed slightly off, and that bright blue manuscript was one of them. He'd expected all the books here to be leather bound and slightly covered in dust. He'd also expected brown robed monks to be silently wandering the shelves for no apparent reason. They should also have their robe tied shut with a length of rope.

A predator's eyes were finely tuned to catch movement, and the human is the apex predator. However it didn't take anything special for both Bishop and Ryan to notice the only other person in this section of the library exit one of the connecting hallways carrying two similarly blue bound manuscripts. He paused, nodded at them in the common American tradition of males greeting other males who don't know each other, and set his books down. Placing his hands on his lower back he leaned back trying to stretch out some ache most likely caused by bending over too much.

Having nothing better to do at the moment, and at a loss as to what to do next other than wait, Bishop looked the new stranger over. According to American television stereotypes, military officers like Bishop were supposed to fall into two categories. Either they were bumbling idiots who got their platoons into terrible situations or they were somehow trained to do amazing things. Bishop, however, was neither. The main training he had as a junior officer was in how to do amazing amounts of paperwork, and he prided himself on being detail oriented enough to never get his soldiers into terrible situations.

All of that personal introspection led to him realizing what he wasn't trained to do, estimate the exact height of people. The newcomer was somewhat shorter than he was, but didn't seem to be ridiculously short. That would put him somewhere between five foot five and five foot eleven. Anything below that and it was obvious you were short. Above that and Bishop would say they were the same height.

I'm really putting too much thought into this, Bishop thought. I almost miss talking things out with the Raven.

The stranger was dressed to visit the Vatican library in a khaki pair of dress pants and a button up short sleeve light blue shirt. He had short cut light brown hair and was definitely softer around the middle than most of the people Bishop was used to working with, but being in shape went with the Navy job. Also, he was putting his hands in his pockets and walking toward them.

"Hey," the new guy said, with a smile that shown out like a personal lighthouse, "couldn't help but notice you didn't have anything."

"Have anything?" Ryan replied.

"Yeah," the radiant smile stayed in place and Bishop was starting to think it might be real, "books, request paperwork, stuff."

"Well, we're just…" Ryan was obviously struggling with what to say.

Bishop knew he was more invested in this situation than Ryan was, and the split second decision to ask help from a stranger wasn't one he normally would have made, but as they say in the navy, any port in a storm. "We really weren't sure where to start, and the introduction lecture we got was a bit much to take in."

"Ahhh," he nodded knowingly, then extended his hand to Bishop, "name's Larry."

Bishop, who'd been leaning on the table behind him, straightened up and shook the offered hand. "Peter." He'd had an overwhelming urge to use his last name. The military life had unintentionally drilled into him the use of only his surname. Here, however, he was trying to just be a normal guy. A normal guy standing in the Vatican library trying to look up information on how to not be possessed anymore. Right.

Peter pointed a thumb over his shoulder, "This is Ryan."

"Well," Larry took his hand back and waved at his stack of paperwork and books, "I'm working on my masters thesis and it's not going well, so I could use a little break. Tell you what, over the last few days I've managed to learn my way around this massive place, I'll be your guide. Just tell me what you're looking for."

Peter looked over and made eye contact with Ryan. His shrug gave Peter the nonverbal consent to do a little bit, but don't push it too far. Nodding back Peter turned back to Larry and said, "We were looking into a very specific supernatural case."

"So possession?" Larry's eyes lit up.

"Kind of tangential to possession," Peter said. "We need to figure out what the thing is first and maybe learn some history about it before we can make any assumptions about possession."

"Supernatural historical research. Yes!" Larry pumped his fist in the air as his words echoed around the otherwise empty library. "Well," he turned back toward his own pile of work, and started wringing his hands together like a Disney villain, "first, we are totally in the wrong part of the library for that."

He scooped up his paperwork, placed the books he'd grabbed in a wooden bin attached to the table, and started walking toward the door they'd entered from. "I need to put my papers back in my locker. I'll be right back to lead you on the research adventure of your life."

After he exited Peter turned to Ryan, "Look, my world is falling apart right now, and if I can find some information, any information, I'll feel better."

Ryan nodded, "I've got no problem with doing a little research. We could be waiting for hours until that cardinal gets back and can meet with us. No reason to waste the time. Let's just make sure we keep Larry out of the loop on other matters."

By that he took Ryan to mean they shouldn't talk about their jobs, or at least about Bishop's job. The captain had made it clear he didn't want any of this to come back onto the Navy.

While they waited for Larry, Bishop tried to think of what to search for. He wasn't lying when he said they needed to learn what the thing was before trying to figure out what to do about it. In a way, it was like medicine. You didn't randomly start giving people any medicine you could grab. You had to figure out the disease first.

He wandered over to the book shelves to gain some room from Ryan, "So," he spoke quietly so it would just look like he was thinking out loud, "what do you think of Larry?" There was no answer from the

Raven, and he realized the constant pressure on his right shoulder from the large bird was missing.

For a moment he felt his heart rate go up, and panic started to set in. The Raven was the only one who knew what he'd been through. He'd been with him from the beginning. Bishop took some deep breaths to calm himself down and tried to think about it more rationally. The bird most likely was trying to figure this situation out for himself just as much as Bishop was. He'd probably flown off somewhere, and would be back. Maybe he'd gotten hungry. Bishop had no idea if invisible multidimensional ravens got hungry, and if they did, could he even interact with anything over here?

Shaking himself to release some of the anxiety he tried to focus back on the original problem. How to find information about his specific problem in a giant religious library. He couldn't use anything from the other side. There wasn't much to use from over there anyway. A desert, an oasis, a group of Bedouin's that would be looking to chop his head off, and a large monster he still hadn't gotten a good look at.

He needed to start at the source. This all started in the cave where the explosion happened, but he needed to be a bit more specific than just a cave. What about all of that would act as a kind of historical landmark? The crystal itself was interesting and might show up, so he filed that mental image away for later use. In the hallway leading up to the main cavern, there had been a mural. Now that he thought about it, in a bit more calm and rational way, he remembered the old broken down temple next to the oasis. The mural in there had somewhat matched the one in the cave. That was important, or at least he hoped it was.

"All right, new friends," Peter looked over to see Larry coming through the doors, "what is it we're looking for?"

"Okay," Peter walked over and met him at the table Ryan was still sitting at, "there are two main pieces of evidence we have."

"Right, right," Larry's constant smile was slightly infectious, and Peter felt himself catching a little bit of the enthusiasm, "let's hear it."

Glancing over at Ryan all he got was a slightly raised eyebrow so Peter dove in, "First, there are multiple sights with the same hand drawn mural." He felt that adding the fact of multiple sights would make it seem more reliable and academic, but he wasn't about to say the second site was located in a world that might only be in his head. "Second, the main feature of these sites," he assumed the one by the oasis had a giant crystal, "is a central chamber housing a giant glowing crystal."

"By giant..." Larry motioned with his hands to gauge the size.

Peter put his hand at about the height of his hairline, "It's somewhere around six feet tall and," making a circle with his arms that he hoped was about the right diameter, "about this big around. It was white with shades of red or pink mixed in and would glow."

"Well that's seriously more interesting than what I was doing research on." Larry shook his head and looked around, "I started out looking into Pope Urban the Second's involvement in the start of the first Crusade in ten ninety five, but changed because way too many people have done that. So then I decided to switch to one of the times where there were multiple popes elected at the same time, but again that ground had been a bit too well trodden, if you know what I mean."

Peter did not know what he meant and looked over at Ryan who just shrugged in response.

"One of those stories led me to some information about the Mongol invasion of Europe and the diplomat the Catholic Church sent to try and negotiate with the Kahn in Karakoram, and that was starting to get interesting. Then you two show up with glowing giant crystals and mysterious murals. This is the best."

Larry was still grinning as he led them off, first down one hallway lined with books then through a door and up a flight of spiral metal stairs. "It seems to me that the first thing, the easiest thing, would be to see if the church has records of that particular iconography you're talking about."

At the top of the stairs was another long hallway, and through some windows Peter could see the parking lot they'd seen earlier out the windows of the map hallway.

"Sorry," Larry said, leading them through another door, "this place is a maze."

The room they'd entered was, in a way, more plain and austere than the original library room they'd been in. This one was still full of solid, dark wood tables, and tile mosaics on the floor, but there was only a white ceiling, and the paintings on the walls were in normal frames and simply hung. There were three levels to this room and they'd entered on the second floor. The bookshelves here were lined entirely with manuscripts bound in an off-white leather.

"The research problem you have is the intersection of two popular topics," Larry said as he scanned the backs of the books. "First is the topic of iconography, and there are tons of books written on that. It's not as exciting as those Da Vinci code books make it out to be, but because there's so much meaning the artists put into those pictures people have devoted entire lifetimes to studying them."

He pulled two manuscripts off the shelf and handed them back to Ryan. "The second," Larry strode down the narrow aisle with the shelves on one side and a metal handrail on the other, overlooking the main reading section of the room below them, "is the topic of the supernatural."

Turning down the next connecting book lined hallway they came to an area with books bound in tan covers. "Now the supernatural," he leaned over and squinted at the tiny print on the back of the first book, "is a wide ranging subject. The Vatican gets people in here ranging from ghost hunting cable TV shows, to doctorate degree seekers trying to figure out if ghosts are just demons, or if demons are actually real."

Pulling two more books out he handed them back to Peter. "This should get us started." He led them back out to where the shelves overlooked the reading room, then down a metal spiral staircase, and over to a table with the same uncomfortable looking wooden stools.

"So," Peter looked at the books he'd just set on the table top, "these are in English, right?"

Larry smiled, "Yes, these are in English. What you're looking for," he slid one of the books over in front of himself, "is anything that might remotely sound like your mural. I didn't think there would be any record of a giant glowing crystal so I started with the mural first."

Peter nodded, opened the book, and looked for a table of contents. Time slipped by as he followed leads. There were sketches of different temple sites with scholars trying to figure out what they meant. None even remotely matched what he'd seen. Eventually he closed his book and looked over. Ryan was slowly turning pages and Larry had set aside one book with torn pieces of paper sticking up as book marks, and was almost done with the second.

Nothing crazy had happened while they sat there, including hearing from his missing raven. Peter really hoped the feathery guy wasn't gone for good. The Raven was his only link between the two worlds. It was because of the Raven's presence here, in his world, that he even believed the other realm was real.

Finally Larry closed the book and looked over at him, "Well, I've marked anything that might be what you were talking about, so take a look."

The first two bookmarks were nothing special. They were hand drawn pictures of Hindu deities of different kinds. He was fairly sure he recognized Kali from a previous world history lecture. The third picture looked like a rubbing. It was rough and hard to determine because the picture itself was the negative space left blank as the chalk rubbing was done. Leaning back Peter tried letting his eyes take in the whole picture rather than search for small details.

He saw it. It was more detailed than the one in the cave entrance, but there it was. A large humanoid with wings surrounded by smaller people. It looked like they were...

Tied me! Bound me!

"Stink!" The Raven's voice followed directly on top of the dark words dropping like bombs in his head. "I thought I could..."

I will not...

Peter clutched his head as the color drained from the library. The windows cracked and books began to spontaneously combust.

Squeezing his eyes closed he clenched his jaw.

You will let me...

"Fight it man," the Raven's weight settled onto his shoulder.

Peter's stomach clinched, sending him sliding off the stool. He felt his head hit the table on the way down.

Chapter Twelve

"I don't know how it works." Bishop could hear the Raven talking but it was dark and even though his eyes were open he couldn't see anything.

"So," it was Ryan who was answering, "you're telling me, you two end up in a different world?"

"Yes." The Raven's voice came from off to the right somewhere.

"And, on top of that," Ryan's words came out slowly, "you think the dragon is after him for some reason?"

"Why am I repeating myself?" Now Bishop could hear the Raven's feet scratching on the rocky ground he seemed to be laying on.

That little detail suddenly occupied his whole mind. Why was he laying on the ground, in the dark? On top of that, how was the Raven talking to Ryan? Why weren't they in the library anymore? The library. The picture in Larry's manuscript hadn't been exactly the same as what he'd seen on the wall headed toward the cave, but it had been close enough for the monster in his head to freak out.

Bishop lay there in the cold blanket of darkness, on a hard mattress of stone, and decided that whatever was trying to break his world must be the same as the being in the mural, and was also the same as the gigantic shadow that had zeroed in on him that night under the sage brush. "The crazy just keeps piling up." He muttered to himself.

"Yay," the Raven hopped onto his stomach, "you're awake. Now I don't have to keep repeating myself to this guy."

Reaching through the darkness, Bishop touched the Raven. His feathers were like layered silk cut to a ragged edge. It wasn't soft, by any definition, but neither was it unpleasant. "Where are we?"

"Well," the Raven paused and nudged his head under Bishop's fingers so he obligingly rubbed it, "after you set fire to the tent you were standing in and somehow knocked yourself unconscious, we carried you to this cave to hide out."

"We?" Ryan's deeper voice bounced around in the cave.

"Right," the Raven hopped out from under Bishop's hand, "apparently when you slip off to that other world I go with you, so Sid here had to carry you the whole way."

Bishop's confusion overwhelmed him for a moment. He'd started getting used to the moments of transition from one world to another. In fact, the transition itself was seamless. He never felt anything. It was why, even now to a smaller extent, he'd thought this was all just in his head. The confusion didn't come from that. It was dark, but at least there was a good reason for that. They were in a cave. He remembered the tent getting set on fire, and finding something that might have been the scale Sid had been looking for. There it was, he thought as he sat up. How did Sid, something closer to a badger than not, carry him all the way to a cave, and, "Why does he sound just like Ryan?"

"Hey, Sid," the Raven said, "could you check to see if we're clear to get out of this place?"

"Sure," Bishop could hear someone moving in the darkness of the cave then a grinding of stone on stone followed by daylight curved in the shape of a rock's edge.

Bishop covered his eyes against the sudden brightness as the Raven shuffled close to his ear, "So, there's a conversation that needs to happen, and I want to start with I told you so, and you should always listen to me when it comes to other people."

There was a man pushing aside a thin slice of rock, and as the light intensified to fill the small cavern, Bishop looked around and didn't see Sid at all. "What?"

The man at the entrance to the cave poked his head out into the sunlight, "I don't see anybody, but without someone to fly over the area I can't say if we're clear or not."

"That's..." Bishop pointed to the mystery man and looked over at the Raven.

Bobbing his head the Raven whispered, "That's Sid."

Looking back at the entrance Bishop saw the man, now partially identified as Sid, looking at him. He was crouched in a small space left by the removal of the rocks. "Look," he said to Bishop, "I didn't want to tell you because I was worried you might not stick to your word and give me the scale when you found it."

With the sunlight coming from behind him into the cave, Bishop could only see him as a dark outline against the sharp white of the light. "So, you..." he waved a hand at Sid in a general way.

"Yes, I change shape." Sid turned, and exited the cave.

"And that," the raven started hoping toward the exit, "was all I could get out of him too."

It was a beautiful evening, or at least Bishop assumed it was evening. He had no real sense of direction after being snatched away from his own plane of existence and dropped into a dark cave. For all he knew the sun rose in the west and went down in the east. The sun was lower on the horizon, but without a bit of time to see what happened, he wasn't even sure if it was rising or falling. However, aside from the insanity of the entire situation, it was a beautiful evening. A few high wisps of pure white clouds contrasted with the soft blue of the sky. He could just make out dots of moving shapes high in the sky, and assumed they were birds of some kind looking to eat his eyeballs once he dropped dead in the desert.

The failing sunlight turned waist high bushes into miles long shadows and exposed the rippling nature of the desert floor. The ridges of exposed rock around him had turned from their daytime tan to a myriad of reds and oranges only visible as the low angle of the sunlight exposed differences in the strata.

Drifting on the tiny breeze, Bishop caught a memory and closed his eyes. The brief hint of sage mixed with dust brought back memories of turning a crank to raise the top of his family pop up camper. Setting a fire in a metal ring laid out by the campsite and preparing to roast marshmallows. I may have gone insane, he thought to himself, but I still remember, and it was beautiful.

Letting out a breath he opened his eyes. The Raven was circling overhead, supposedly searching for people who would be trying to find them. He assumed they would be trying to find them after he stole something from them twice and burned down a tent. If the fire had spread it might have been a few tents. Also, he might have killed a few people. All of that after they'd saved him from a horrible roasting death out on the sand.

Turning to look for Sid he froze. Standing a little way off to his left was Ryan. His clothes were different than they'd been in the library, which was nice for him because Bishop just got to keep whatever he happened to be wearing at the moment, but it was still him. "This is great."

Ryan turned to look at him as his words broke the silence, "What? And keep it down."

"What do you mean, what?" Bishop lowered his voice to a whisper and walked over to Ryan. "You're here. This," he waved at the desert around him, "might not..." He trailed off as he thought about the situation. Ryan might just be a part of his mental hallucination, or this was all real and Ryan somehow had ended up here too. "You seem so calm."

"Well, it's not every day I get chased by Bedouins, but it is a surprisingly regular thing when you can do what I do. They seem to think they can replicate my shape shifting if they chop out random parts of me and turn them into a drink."

The Raven landed heavily on his shoulder, "Didn't see any..." A loud rawk was accompanied by his feet gripping Bishop's shoulder tight enough to break the skin. "What the?! How is he here?" He tapped Bishop's head with the side of his own and whispered, "Hey, how'd that guy get here? Did you know he was going to be here? I thought it was just you and my invisible self that did the whole world hopping thing."

"Uhm," Ryan looked them over, "have you two lost your minds?"

"Rawk, what do you mean?" The Raven's voice was a touch louder than necessary, "It's great to see you, guy who's name I don't remember because I never needed to talk to you."

"Look, it's funny I'm sure," Ryan gave them the look that said what you're doing isn't actually funny, "but we need to head out before the sun gets too low or we won't be able to see our direction to town. I've been through here a few times before, but I haven't really needed to sneak my way out in the dark."

"You've been through here before?" Bishop asked.

"Well, yeah." Ryan turned and started walking toward a lower spot between the exposed rock formations around them. "I'm not always a medium sized fuzzy animal. Sometimes I just need to get from one place to another and get my job done."

"Get your job…" Bishop, who had been following, stopped.

"Hey," the Raven was terrible at whispering and his voice bounced off the closest rock walls, "your friend's nuts. Where's Sid? He looked big. We can have him knock this guy out…"

"Wait," Bishop and the Raven both looked up at Ryan, "what do you mean where's Sid? I'm Sid. I mean, I know it was dark in that cave and you were unconscious for some of it, but seriously, how many other shape shifting guys are you working with out here?"

"You're Sid?" The Raven's voice and Bishop's blended into a perfect harmony of disbelief.

"You know what?" Sid, or Ryan, turned and started walking. "I'm headed to town. Thanks for saving me." He waved over his shoulder as he stepped around chair sized chunks of rock.

"Hang on," Bishop called out and started walking to catch up.

"Any idea what's going on?" The Raven was looking around at the scenery.

"Crazy," Bishop said back, "crazy is what's been going on for a while now."

The Raven's feathers ruffled and he let out a low croak, "You ain't kidding. My invisible self was just in some library in a world I keep thinking I recognize and I was fighting off a big black idea of a monster. Why? Why would I do that for some desert snack I don't even know, and why did I decide to stick out my beak and organize a perfect plan to save this ungrateful Ryan, Sid, shapeshifting guy?"

"See," Bishop nodded, "now you know how my crazy has felt for a while now."

Once they were free of the boulders and the majority of the jutting rock escarpments, Bishop started jogging to catch up and the Raven launched himself into the air. Slowing to a walk next to the man who looked like Ryan he said, "So, town's this way."

The sun was setting off to their right. "It's a few degrees off from the setting sun from here. The problem becomes keeping your heading once it sets. You can't just pick a star and walk toward it because they move throughout the night."

Bishop nodded. He knew all that. Finding your way was standard training when you were an officer. The most basic of a Lieutenant's jobs was using a map. Being on an aircraft carrier, or a destroyer, didn't change the fact that you might end up somewhere, on some mission, where you needed to use old fashioned methods to get yourself and your soldiers to the right location.

Granted, he didn't have a compass and a map right now. He wasn't sure they made maps of hallucinatory locations that only existed in your head, but it seemed he didn't need one if he had a guide. His guide was correct that you couldn't just pick a conveniently bright star and walk toward it. The planet rotated on its axis and caused the stars to move. The only real problem being, he wasn't sure if he was on a planet. He assumed the rules held true here because the sun was setting and Ryan/Sid had mentioned the stars moving.

"What I learned to do," Bishop said, "is to pick a landmark you can see off in the distance and walk toward that. Once you get there, pick another one in the right direction and continue that process until you get to where you're trying to go."

They both looked into the distance, searching the horizon for a good point of reference. Bishop noticed a few taller bushes and a single lonely tree here and there, but nothing you would be able to see once the sun went down. Ryan/Sid pointed to a spot where a rising chunk of rock was exposed, blocking out a solid rectangle of sky. "If we keep to the left most edge of that we should be fine."

Landing on his left shoulder the Raven settled in and said, "So, you look just like this other guy we know, and we were a bit surprised because it's dark in that cave and we couldn't see that you looked like this other guy until we were out in the light. Then we were all surprised because you look just like this other guy." Leaning slightly toward Bishop's ear he tried to whisper again, "Did that make sense?"

Bishop nodded, "The Raven's right. We weren't trying to be rude or weird. It was just disorienting to wake up and see someone I recognized. His name's Ryan."

Sid looked over at him, "Well," the sun finally finished it's path and dipped under the edge of the horizon, "I guess with

116

everything happening to me lately that's not the weirdest, but my name is Ryan." The look on Bishop's face was easy to make out, even in the growing gloom. "But," he held out his hands to forestall any crazy theories, "I have never met you before in my life."

The Raven leaned forward, "You said your name was Sid."

"It is, or at least that's what people call me. My full name is Ryan Phillip Sidney."

Bishop thought about it. Then he stopped thinking about it. He needed to focus. Why was this entire situation happening to him? How did he get out of it and back to his normal life? Those were the important details. A guy who looked just like Ryan, could shape change into a smallish furry animal, and actually had the same name, wasn't individually important. It was just part of the larger question of why, and how did he get out of it.

There was, however, one small detail Bishop wanted answered. "If you could shape change into this, then why did I have to carry your fuzzy butt the entire way?"

"And why didn't you just change into a guy and break out of that cage?" The Raven asked.

Sid turned slightly, and in the dying light of post sunset held out the black scale. There was a leather strip tied around it. The rough edges of the scale worked to keep it snug and stopped it from slipping. That strip was connected to a chain dangling around Sid's neck.

Looking at it, Bishop remembered the oil slick rainbow reflection of the firelight in the burning tent flickering across its surface, the rough feel of it under his fingers, and the presence hammering into his mind when he touched it. "Put it away."

Sid shrugged and tucked it back into his shirt. "I couldn't change because I didn't have this."

The Raven had leaned forward to get a better look, "So that's a piece of him?"

Sid nodded and kept walking.

"Him who?" Bishop looked from the Raven on his left shoulder to Sid walking to his right.

Bishop could feel the Raven's feathers fluff out and touch his ear, "You've got a piece of him, so you tell him." This time the Raven whispered perfectly.

Sid's shoulders rose and fell in the darkness, "How do you not know about him? I thought everyone around here would know."

Bishop sighed, "Let's just say I'm not from around here."

"But," Sid looked over at him, "how's that even possible? Wait," Sid glanced at the Raven, "does this have to do with what you were telling me in the cave about other worlds?"

"Look, we'll get into where I'm from later. It gets complicated." Bishop said.

The Raven let out a bark of laughter, "Complicated is too simple of a word for that."

"Anyway," Bishop shrugged one shoulder to get the Raven to move into a more comfortable position, "could you just please just tell me what's going on?"

Sid's head bobbed in the dark and Bishop assumed he was nodding, "He is the dragon. This scale is from him. We don't know if he molts like some kind of reptile or if they just get scratched off from time to time. I found it and now I can do what I do."

"There's a dragon?"

The Raven bobbed on his shoulder, "It's a recent development."

Bishop rolled his shoulder again, "If you're going to ride the whole way, could you switch sides every once in a while? I'm getting a cramp in my neck."

Hopping off, the Raven gave a few flaps to gain some altitude and drifted along, but kept pace with the occasional beat of a wing.

"So a dragon is a recent development?" Bishop asked.

Sid's voice was quiet and drifted through the darkness, "My mom always told me stories about the dragon, but they were old stories. They always started with things like, at the beginning of time, or, when the islands were just formed. Kids would dress up as the dragon for school plays, or painters would use it as a symbol of different ideas or emotions."

The raven's disembodied voice came from the star speckled darkness above him as his black feathers blended in with the night sky, "And then..."

"And then," Sid continued, "a bit ago, everything changed. There was an earthquake. We think that's what started it all, or at least the people in the city think so. I'm not sure which order it went in. Did the earthquake cause it or did he cause the earthquake? There were so many bar room debates at the beginning, but eventually people realized the order of events didn't really change the immediate reality of the situation."

They walked in silence for a few moments before Sid continued, "At first people just saw him flying, and usually it was really high up. Some people assumed it would just stay that way. After all, none of the stories talked about him coming down and eating people, but then he started landing and..." Sid hesitated and Bishop could see him raise his hands as if grasping for the right word. "It was like he was looking for something."

"And that's when you found the scale?" Bishop asked.

"I'd always been, how should I put it, flexible in difficult situations. People hired me to deal with different things. This," he tapped the scale under his shirt, "just opened up more ways of completing my jobs."

The Raven drifted down and landed on Bishop's right shoulder, "I'd seen the big guy a few times, way up, but never really thought anything about it. Then you showed up and he came crashing down on us like a mountain made out of midnight."

"That was him? The other night? When we were sleeping under the sage brush?"

"Yeah. Unless there's another giant black dragon swooping around out there."

"And what about the voice…"

"Yep," the Raven squeezed his shoulder, "he's a talking dragon."

"He talks?" Sid was just a dark contour against the backdrop of the desert sky. "And what do you mean he dropped down on you?"

Bishop caught the hint from the overly tight grip of the Raven, and while he still wasn't entirely sure about the internal motivations of his corvid friend, it seemed to line up with his for the moment. Sid, however, was still a relative unknown. He looked just like Ryan, had the same name as Ryan, and turned out to be something of a mercenary like Ryan. That didn't account for much since Bishop didn't know any of the internal motivation for Ryan either. It seemed he was taking the tack of, I'm just doing my job, but that only gets you so far, even in the military.

Bishop decided he agreed with the Raven, but something would need to be shared with his new comrad. He was in a strange situation, traveling through an unknown world, and he needed help. "We were sleeping outside because I'd made some questionable direction choices. A large shape blocked out the stars then came in for a landing close to us. We overheard him talking to himself, or at least I think it was to himself since nothing else was out there. He was talking about finding it and getting free. We didn't exactly step out to ask him to clarify."

They walked on in silence. Bishop wished he could have a private conversation with the Raven. He may not entirely trust him, but he was the only true confidant he had in all of this. They were connected somehow. They always ended up together, and that was one of the only reasons Bishop had decided he might not be entirely insane.

Instead he turned on his inner dialogue. Back in his first year of college he'd been required to take an introduction to philosophy class. It was one of those things colleges and universities do to try and remind all the new incoming students they should be nice to each other. It makes the world run better, and gives them a better experience at the school. This was his first encounter with some of the works of Plato, and what stuck with him wasn't any of the philosophical ideas so much as Plato's style of trying to figure out the world. Plato would invent another person, or sometimes use the personality of someone he already knew, and pretend to have a conversation with them. This way he was free to try and see both sides of an argument, and to try and solve it. Sometimes this worked and sometimes he just used to it make himself sound brilliant and everyone else sound stupid.

'So', Bishop said to himself in the quiet of his own mind, 'there's a dragon'.

'Yes. Where are you going with this?'

'Well, why is this dragon bothering me? That's where I'm going with this.'

'And,' said his other internal voice, 'is the dragon, who is flying around in this world, the same as the thing that keeps messing with us in the real world.'

'I'm fairly sure it is, since none of that stuff started until after I ran into him out under the sage brush.'

'Okay, so most likely they are one and the same.'

'Right. That's not really helpful in our current situation.'

'We agree.'

'Wait, what do you mean we? Are there more of you in there?'

'Well...'

'That's slightly disturbing, but not relevant right now.'

'We agree. Again.'

'Ugh.' Bishop's internal dialoging self rolled his eyes at his other internal selves. 'So what does he want with me?'

'Well, that's easy isn't it.'

'No, it's not. And how come part of my own mind knows the answer but the rest of me has to ask for it.'

'It's complicated.'

'Everything is lately.'

'Tell me about it.'

'Anyway, what's this easy answer you were talking about?'

'Talking? Thinking? Thinking about talking about?'

'Don't start. Just tell me.'

'Right. Sorry. It just has to do with the order of events. I think, and if you remember with me, it has to do with the explosion that blew up that giant weird crystal back in the terrorist cave.'

'If I remember with you. What kind of statement is that in this situation?'

120

'It's… Look, we're just trying to make this work, okay?'

'Sure, sure. So, Sid was saying there was an earthquake then the dragon showed up.'

'Right, and what if that earthquake was the crystal getting kaboomed.'

'Then somehow I end up being able to pop back and forth between here and the real world.'

'Thus…'

'Mr. Big Scary Dragon thinks I can get him back to the real world.'

'Ta da!'

Bishop shoved the other voices in his head back into the other rooms and grottos of his subconscious before they could start arguing about spelling and grammar.

Basically what he'd come to was the dragon believed he was the key to getting out of this place. What that meant or what that looked like he didn't know, but it explained some of the things the dragon had been saying recently.

Looking out over the desert landscape at night, Bishop let his rambling and cluttered thoughts go. No clouds drifted across the sky to interrupt the brilliance of pure starlight. There were very few times a human, in the real world at least, was able to get an uninterrupted view of the stars. Usually it was light pollution causing the problem, but it could also be smog or a high rise building. Here, it was just pure, unfiltered, starlight.

The dark outline of rock outcroppings, or the twisted frame of a desert tree trying to hold onto life, occasionally blocked the horizon. As the moon rose and his eyes adjusted the landscape became silvered. It was as if the light were reflecting off pools of water scattered throughout the desert. The beauty and the stillness of it helped him to simply walk. With a clear mind, he took in the scenery passing by him, feeling the weight of the Raven bouncing on his shoulder.

They passed their first marker and Sid silently paused to search out another. After passing that one, Bishop realized he wasn't feeling tired. His mind knew it was past the middle of the night, and they had been walking over rough terrain for hours without stopping, but he was fine. He knew some of it was just the physical training required to maintain his position in the navy, but he also knew some of it wasn't normal. It wasn't the lack of physical aches and pains, though that was some of it. It was the lack of droopy eyes, the absolute clarity of mind, and even, yes, how good his feet felt. Something here, something about this place, and now about himself, wasn't natural. He knew it was a stupid, captain obvious thing to think, but there it was.

"There'll be a river you can see from the top of the next rise." Sid's voice was shocking after the hours of silence. "The town will be between that and the edge of the forest."

The Raven, who had been kind enough to switch shoulders periodically during the long night's walk, hopped off and flapped to gain altitude. Bishop watched him go and wondered again what his deal was. The Raven had insisted he was the only talking animal, making him unique even in this unnatural world. He claimed he didn't know anything about the dragon, and yet...

Bishop let it go. He had very few allies in this situation, and he didn't need to be overthinking things. At least not yet.

Once they made it to the top of the next rise the edge of the sun had just poked above the desert landscape and was now reflecting like tossed diamonds from the river winding its way in the small valley below them. As Sid had said, tucked into a bend in the river was a village. On one edge huge wheels were tucked into the rushing water powering what Bishop assumed were lumber or flour mills. On the other edge the village met the fringes of a forest, and even at this early hour he could hear the echoing thunk of axes, somewhere in the distance, hitting wood. Between the two extremes of desert and forest clung a village of dirt streets spreading out in angles and curves with no plan or reason he could discern.

The buildings were of varying designs. Some were made of stone whose color made it obvious it was cut from the desert, while others were log built. The homes on the edge of town were roofed with bundles of long grass, bound together and dried. Toward the center of town, the stone homes were topped with an assortment of things. Some had tile, others had sod, while a few had planks of wood overlapping. All the homes had a chimney puffing out morning smoke as someone inside warmed things up and started breakfast.

One bridge spanned the sparkling expanse of river, and Bishop wasn't surprised to see a shack on the desert side with a board looking guard sitting outside it.

Standing up from a wooden chair that had most likely seen the backside of generations of board guards, he ambled his way to the center of the bridge. "Morning, and where are you all from?"

Bishop had no idea what to say. He'd been told the name of the oasis they'd been at, but had forgotten it in all the excitement, so he stood there quietly and left the interaction to Sid.

"We needed to have some conversations with the Bedouins," Sid said.

A shrug and nod from the guard was followed by, "Toll." He held out his hand.

Sid reached under the edge of his shirt, rummaged in what Bishop assumed was some kind of bag tied to his waist, and produced a copper colored coin. Dropping it into the guards hand he gave the standard head nod, common to most areas of the world, and the guard returned to his ancestral chair.

Reaching the other side of the bridge Bishop heard a faint scream. Looking around he didn't see anything, and decided it must be from farther in town, and hoped nobody was being hurt. He had joined the military to help people, and it didn't sit right with him to do nothing when people were being hurt.

The scream grew in intensity and, pausing on the roadway, he looked around. Sid nudged him and pointed up. Shading his eyes against the rising sun he could just make out a black dot growing in size at the same rate as the scream was growing in volume.

The raven, wings tucked tight to his side, dropped from the sky like a discolored lightning bolt. His scream was one long letter A, and it didn't stop until his wings unfurled and he back beat the air, slowing himself enough to not commit suicide on Bishop's head. "He's coming, he's coming, he's coming…"

"Who's coming?"

A bone shaking roar caused Bishop and Sid to step back. Looking back into the sky Bishop saw it growing over the wooded horizon on the other side of the village. Screams sounded off around the village like fire alarms in a burning building as he watched the dark shape grow.

It's wingspan was easily sixty feet across, and Bishop couldn't understand how, even with wings that big, it could support a body that was, to his untrained eye, the same size as a humpback whale. It's black scales reflected a disturbing oily rainbow of colors back at the rising sun, and as it closed in on the edge of the village he could just make out its eyes looking right at him.

Bishop knew the literally monstrous thing was coming for him. Part of him wanted to run, but that only lasted for a brief moment of pure adrenaline filled panic. The rest of his brain was in agreement, running would accomplish nothing. Where would he run to? If he ran away, it would be back into the desert, and there were no hiding spots there. If he ran toward the village to hide it would see him and where he was going because it would be running toward the dragon.

So he stood. He didn't stand his ground, preparing for battle against a worthy opponent. No, he stood resigned to a fate he couldn't understand. What would it do? Eat him? Suck his soul out through his chest? It's hard to plan for a reasonable eventuality when reality is being unreasonable.

It landed on a nearby single story log home. Thankfully, Bishop saw the family had abandoned the home a minute or so before. The logs of the home were sturdy, but the grass roof was not. The beast had four legs, each of them as big around as a good sized tree, and after putting one foot through the roof it settled its other three on the log structure and, flexing toes tipped with claws as long as his arm, tore two of the walls down.

Standing on four legs its neck stretched up above the second story of some surrounding homes. Its wings tucked in against its body, and a tail at least another twenty feet long drug through the wreckage of a family's life, pulling a bed and some chairs through the destroyed front wall as it moved. It's head was massive and Bishop understood how early civilizations could believe in dragons when they found the bones of a Tyrannosaurus Rex. It wasn't quite the same. The dragon's snout was thinner and longer, with larger eyebrow ridges. Its eyes were easily its most dominant feature, at least this close up. When a dragon is dropping down onto your unprotected village, you don't tend to focus on its eyes. The massive claws and home crushing legs were a bit more preoccupying than the large round and slightly luminous cat pupiled eyes. However, when you're being faced with one as it slowly walks toward you, those eyes were hypnotic.

Carts were stepped on, intentionally it seemed to Bishop, while its tail whipped around and caved in the walls of nearby structures. It lowered its head to something closer to Bishop's own height, so now it was only ten to twelve feet high. Stopping a good twenty feet away Bishop could see the delicate intricacies of individual eyebrows and silvered whiskers around its nose and mouth. Twin black horns rose from its temples and curved in a simple three foot long wave over its head. It was beautiful and terrible.

He could tell when its eyes moved from his to looking at his left shoulder where the Raven dug his nails in, holding on, literally, for dear life.

"Hello, little brother." The dragon's voice was a deep bass that vibrated Bishop's insides, like standing too close to his ship's propellor engines.

Bishop felt the Raven twitch and dig in harder. He was surprised it hadn't flown away yet. Bishop knew if he had wings he wouldn't still be here.

"So it was you." The dragon nodded ever so slightly. "Interesting, and yet it makes sense."

The smooth roll of the dragon's voice was the same as what Bishop had been hearing in the other world, except here it wasn't yelling.

The Raven launched himself with a quick, "I'm out."

A rumble came from the dragon, "Not surprising." Turning his eyes back to Bishop, "You are an oddity, but important to me."

He couldn't win this, Bishop thought to himself. There was no way he could fight this thing. There was no magic sword, no squad backing him up with an AT4. What he wouldn't give to call in a strike from a couple of A10's. Those suckers and their gatling guns would chew this guy up. None of that existed. He was standing in the middle of a dirt road, in a world he didn't understand, facing off with a real, gigantic, dragon, and there was nothing he could do.

The dragon shifted, raised one of its front feet, and extended a claw. Bishop's insides twisted up and everything in him screamed to do something, anything. Run, fight, yell, do something, but the very movement of the dragon seemed to lock him in place. He watched as the claw extended slowly. It wasn't a swipe intended to cut him in half, or the crushing drop of a foot the size of a patio table. It reached out tentatively, as if damage was the last thing it wanted, and for that brief moment Bishop thought he understood. If he really was a key of some kind, then damaging him would be a very bad thing.

One iron black claw tapped him on the chest, and he fell. His arms windmilled as the ground disappeared beneath his feet. Around him dozens of people dressed in dirty gray robes raised their hands and sang. A chunk of stone next to him suddenly flickered to life and began to glow with a warm pulsing light. Screaming, he felt himself pulled toward it. Before he could touch it someone yelled in his ear and a sharp burning sensation shot through his nose and directly to his brain.

Chapter Thirteen

The table snapped cleanly in half. Books flew into the air as Bishop flipped onto his side and swept an arm in front of himself clearing a path. A grunt matched the sight of Ryan hitting one of the library's shelves.

Existence around him was painted in muted blacks, whites, and shades of gray. Rolling onto his hands and knees he saw the tiles crack and buckle under his open palms. Anger rolled up from his gut, clogging in his throat and sticking there, holding back the scream he knew would shatter the world.

His head thundered and sent electric bolts of pain down his spine. A spot on his chest ached as if hit by a hammer. Squeezing his right hand into a fist he slammed it down, turning the tiles to dust and sending ripples like disturbed water through the floor around him.

To his right a scream drew his eyes.

Larry was picking himself up off the floor next to a crack big enough to put both hands in. "What is happening!" Bishop's eyes tracked him as Larry pressed himself against the wall next to a small marble topped table. "Are those horns?"

"Bishop!" Ryan's voice cut through the thundering of his heartbeat. "Lieutenant, you need to stand down."

Bishop swiveled his head and saw Ryan pulling a gun from the small of his back. A small part of his mind wondered how he'd snuck a gun into the Vatican. It was drowned out by the deep bass of anger thrumming in his bones.

Pushing himself to his feet, Bishop stretched. Joints popped and a chair next to him broke into pieces. Turning to face Ryan he could hear Larry behind him, "What? Are you going to shoot him?"

"Lieutenant," Ryan raised his weapon, pointing it at Bishop, "stop. Think. Where are you? What is your name?"

Names didn't matter. This place didn't matter. Escape mattered. Revenge mattered.

"Son," the voice came from his right. It was new. Turning, Bishop found the source. The priest from the office stood in the doorway with his hands raised. "I know you're in there." His black skin contrasted sharply with the white marble of the floor tiles and gilt edged walls. "Your colleague is correct. Remember who you are. Remember who loves you."

Who loves you baby. Who loves you. A woman's voice drifted up from the back of his mind. It pushed its way through the pulsing and hammering of his anger like a rose bud through choking weeds. He could see her face. She was sitting at the dinner table. He'd just come up from the basement to show her the drawing he'd done. She'd hugged him and said, 'Who loves you baby?' She wouldn't let him leave until he answered. You do Mom.

Bishop's knee hit the floor, crushing more tiles, and sending another shock wave through the room. Squeezing his eyes shut he forced words through the rage and the rippling darkness behind his eyelids.

Who am I? Peter Bishop.

Where am I? I don't know. Am I at the village by the river? No. There were books and tables. Ryan had been pointing a gun at him and calling him lieutenant. The library. The Vatican.

Why am I doing this? He touched me. The dragon touched me.

Breathe. In through your nose. Out through your mouth.

He flexed his fingers on the cool of the tiles and felt them dig through the marble like a child digging through beach sand.

It doesn't matter who you are.

The voice was recognizable now, and while Bishop still didn't fully understand what was happening he could at least put a face with the voice.

You will let me out.

No. Bishop rammed the word into the darkness in his mind. One unshakable standard in the military was you don't negotiate with terrorists, and from what he'd seen this thing was just that.

You will...

No. Again he used the word like a club and slammed it into the bundle of anger and rage pushing it back into a corner of his mind.

"Bishop?"

Blinking, he opened his eyes. He was still kneeling on the broken floor of the Vatican library. It shouldn't have surprised him, but with everything going on lately he hadn't been sure if he was going to open his eyes on a desert cave, a Bedouin camp, or a little village next to a river. It was nice to see a library. Libraries had always been places of calm.

Taking in a few deep breaths he leaned back and looked up at Ryan, "Is your last name Sidney?"

"I..." Ryan was still pointing his sidearm at him, and a look of confusion washed over his face.

It felt good, for that small moment, to have someone else be confused about the world they're living in. "It doesn't matter. Actually it's nice having two different names. Helps me keep things straight."

"Dude." Larry stepped into his line of vision.

"I didn't hurt you, did I?" They'd just met, but Bishop liked the guy. He'd jumped in to help without asking for anything in return, and while Bishop hadn't known this scenario would happen at the time, it still mattered to him that the new guy was okay.

"Hurt me?" Larry looked down at himself, patted a few spots and winced at one of them. "Nah," he looked back at Bishop, "I'll be fine. I get hit by flying tables all the time. It's the unfortunate life of a history doctoral candidate. You, on the other hand," he waved his hands at Bishop who was standing up, "you grew horns. It was the coolest thing to ever happen to me in this library. It might be the coolest thing to happen in any library."

"Excuse me." The priest stepped between Ryan and Larry. Looking over at Ryan he said, "You can put that away." Ryan looked momentarily guilty and tucked the pistol back into whatever secret compartment he had behind his back. "Also," the priest nodded his thanks, "in the future, if you could refrain from sneaking firearms onto the premises we would all be grateful."

Turning, the priest looked Bishop over. "I know we met earlier in the Cardinal's office but," he took a step forward and extended his hand, "I am Father Oni. Kashala Oni."

Bishop took his hand and gripped it. Looking into his dark brown eyes he felt like he was holding onto a lifeline. He could feel calluses, and the father's grip was strong. "Peter, Peter Bishop."

Father Oni nodded as they released their grip, "Peter, I assume the possessed person you were referring to earlier was yourself."

Larry snorted and tried his best to hold back a laugh.

The priest gave a small smile to the overly obvious statement. "We should vacate the area before Vatican security comes to deal with the situation. Normally, I would let them do their job, but after what I just saw I don't think they have the right tools to deal with it." He stepped past Bishop and looked over his shoulder, "Follow me please."

Peter rose and looked around as they headed for an exit and was thankful to note that the destruction he'd caused had been very localized. Most of the damage was contained to a six foot circle. In fact, it looked more like a small meteor had hit rather than a person had lost their mind and grown horns. The reading table was broken in half. Chairs were no longer chairs, but now some very expensive form of firewood. The worst part was the floor. Delicately inlaid marble work, that could have been a thousand years old, was shattered.

Heading down a hallway toward an exterior door Father Oni looked over his shoulder, "What was it that caused the manifestation?"

Before Peter could speak up Larry answered, "There was a manuscript going over religious finds by British and Spanish mapping expeditions in the late nineteenth and early twentieth centuries. Peter had described a fresco or mural he'd seen and the one on that page was the closest representation of it."

The Father held the door open for them then followed out onto the side of the Vatican opposite St. Peter's Basilica. Gardens stretched away to either side, and through the trees Peter could just make out the governmental building they'd visited earlier.

"So, when you saw this picture…" Father Oni looked at Peter to finish the statement.

There's nothing he can do to help you. The voice was quieter than it had been. The deep tones of it were still recognizable from his conversation with the dragon, but it wasn't yelling and trying to destroy things this time.

Taking a deep breath to still the jangling of his raw nerve endings, "He wants out."

They walked onto the grass and sat on a bench overshadowed by expertly groomed tree branches. Father Oni nodded, "And who is he?"

"That's what we were trying to figure out in there," Peter waved a hand back toward the library.

Nodding, the father replied, "And why you needed to see the Cardinal." It was a statement of fact, and seemed to settle something for the older priest. "I'll go and see what I can find from this manuscript you…" he glanced over at Larry.

Smiling, Larry held out his hand, "Larry Boggs."

"And you are?" The priest turned to Ryan who was standing slightly behind them and looking out over the paths leading from the main building they'd just come from.

"Ryan," he locked eyes for a moment with Peter, "Ryan Sidney."

"Ohhh…" the Raven's voice coming from directly behind his head caused Peter to twitch, "So they do have the same name."

Everyone leaned slightly away from Peter, and Ryan's hand trailed toward where he'd secreted his weapon away to. Peter sighed, "Sorry, just a little twitchy at unexpected noises."

They all seemed to let out a collectively held breath and Father Oni stood, "If you wouldn't mind waiting here. I'll come find you when things have calmed down."

As they watched him walk back to the door the Raven's voice poked Peter in the back of the head, "So we trust that guy now? And who's the guy grinning at you over there? Why hasn't Sid, I mean Ryan, shot him yet? He looks annoying. His smile is annoying. Who would smile at a time like this? It's creepy."

Peter looked at the two guys standing around him. Ryan was still, apparently, doing overwatch as if some bad guys were going to pop out of the bushes at the Vatican. Stopping himself Peter realized that might have a solid chance of happening. They'd popped out of vans at the airport. He wasn't really sure what to think about the entire situation with Ryan. He was here, but he had a doppelgänger on the other side, and they even had the same name. From the little interaction Peter had with either of the men, they seemed to have the same personality, and even the same job description. Nothing had led him to believe he couldn't trust Ryan, he just wasn't sure how far down the rabbit hole of this situation he would be willing to go. Was he the kind of guy to only do the job and nothing more, or would he stick with him as they wandered through a swamp full of crazy.

"So," and then there was Larry, "you grew horns." Larry slid onto the bench beside him.

"Wait," Peter could feel the raven's breath on his neck as he said, "you grew horns again? I missed that? That's my favorite part."

"So," Larry paused, "I should stop saying so, but my mind is having problems dealing with what just happened. I mean, I've done a lot of studying and reading and listening to old people lecture about medieval stuff, but I never once even started to consider that possession was true, and if it was true I just thought it was some kind of schizophrenia or bi-polar disorder. But, dude, you full on broke the building and grew horns."

"Yeah," Peter didn't really know what to say.

"Back at the airport," Peter looked over as Ryan spoke up, "I could see something was happening, but I was too far away to notice any physical changes." He stopped his constant checking of the area and looked at Peter, "When the captain sent us I thought... Well," he shook his head, reached back and touched his weapon to check it was still secure, "to be honest I didn't really care and didn't really know what to think about it."

Peter cocked his head and raised an eyebrow at Ryan. Of all the people to let it slip that they were connected to the military he figured it would be him, not Ryan.

Shrugging back at him Ryan said, "Look, I'm trying to process what just happened, or should I say, what has been happening."

"True," Peter nodded at him, "and as long as we don't use any specific names then it shouldn't be a problem to discuss some things openly."

"Yeah, but he grew horns." Larry looked back and forth between the two other men.

"What kind of horns?" The Raven stepped from the back of the bench and onto Peter's right shoulder.

"Why does that matter?"

"Well," Larry and the Raven answered at the same time, Larry beating the Raven slightly, "It kind of proves you aren't insane doesn't it. I mean, if I was in your position, especially with the military being involved, I would be doubting my own sanity, or at least trying to explain it all away so it didn't end up on some report."

"I assume you were talking to me and not whoever this guy is," the Raven said. "The horns are important because, well, because if they look like his then it kinda proves who is bothering you on this side, doesn't it."

Peter really didn't want to know, but the Raven was right and he needed to know. He needed to close all the loopholes and figure this all out. The only way to do that was to know. He closed his eyes and asked, "What did the horns look like?"

Peter kept his eyes closed, refusing to look at the others. He could hear the smile on Larry's face as he replied, "They were black and started just behind your hairline. They came up about an inch to an inch and a half before following the contour of your head then swooping up to a really sharp point."

"Were they ridged and kinda rippled?"

"Yeah, and they reflected the light kinda like…"

"Like an oil slick in the parking lot of a grocery store," Peter finished.

"Exactly."

The Raven's beak tapped him in the side of the head, "Those are his horns. Why are you growing his horns? This is crazy. Not as crazy as why what's his name over here won't stop smiling, but still crazy."

Peter lowered his head and covered his face with his hands.

Larry patted him on the back, "No worries man, we'll figure this out."

Ryan grunted, "What do you mean we?"

"Look, I can tell, mainly from the fact you kept calling him lieutenant, that you two are military of some kind, and this is not the kind of thing the military handles well. You need me. I know everything there is to know about this era of stuff. Well," Larry waved the hand he wasn't uncomfortably rubbing Peter's back with, "everything except for what specifically is happening to you, but I am an expert at finding information. I have spent way too much time in library's looking through books no one else cares about."

Turning his head, Peter made eye contact with Larry. There were certain standards of acceptable behavior between men. Rubbing his back for too long was breaking one of those, and Larry knew it. Peter liked the guy, but him coming along with them to wherever this went was out of the question. The point had been to keep this all quiet and get it taken care of. Smashing up the Vatican library was bad enough. Letting some overly talkative academic who didn't totally understand personal space come with them was beyond the pale.

Standing up Peter stretched and walked over to Ryan. "One main question keeps bothering me."

Ryan raised an eyebrow, "You mean other than…" he waved at the general location of the Vatican library.

"That's a bit more than I can deal with right now," Peter said. "It's outside my, how should I put it…"

"Professional experience," Ryan finished for him. Peter wasn't sure if he was referring to himself or just feeling what Peter was going to say.

"Exactly. They don't actually train you to deal with supernatural incursions in OCS. So I can't really evaluate and deal with that right now. It is bothering me but…" he shrugged, and Ryan nodded back. "What's bothering me, are the guys at the airport. Have you had any contact with the captain? Did anyone tell you about a possible threat like that?"

Ryan shook his head, "I thought about getting in touch with the ship and having them run some kind of search except…" he shrugged. "We were told to keep things under wraps."

"Something's obviously wrong with this situation, and I'm not talking about me growing horns."

The Raven chuckled next to his ear, "I really wish I could have seen that."

"I agree," Ryan said, "but there's nothing I can send them to look up. I didn't find any kind of identification in the short time I had to look them over. I did snap a picture of one face, but the others were a bit indisposed."

Peter nodded, remembering tossing them around the runway. "I doubt a group throwing around that kind of firepower out in the open is going to give up after one try."

"True." Ryan returned to scanning any approaches to their current position. "I would tell you to secure a firearm of some kind, but you just did that," he nodded at the Vatican library, "so I'm not too worried about you being able to defend yourself."

Peter shrugged and turned away. Larry stood up and Peter waved him off, walking into the stand of trees behind the bench. He needed a quiet moment to think and to have a conversation with the Raven who was currently poking holes in his shoulder. "You just left me there."

"Well," Peter felt the pressure as the Raven shifted his weight from one foot to the other, "what'd you expect me to do? I might be big and black but I'm not facing off with a dragon. Did you want me to scratch him in the eye or something?"

"I don't know, but it would have been nice to have someone there with me. I thought…" he sat down on the grass and leaned back on a tree trunk, resting his head on the bark.

"You thought what?" The Raven hopped off his shoulder and landed on his outstretched right leg. "I put myself in danger to warn you, didn't I? I could have just flown in the other direction and called it a day, but no, I hustled back and warned you at great personal peril to myself."

"Sure," Peter said. Closing his eyes, he took a deep breath and mentally searched the darkness behind his eyelids. There it was. Huddled at the back of his consciousness. It was as if you knew someone was behind you, and you didn't want to talk to them, but you knew they were just standing there staring at the back of your head.

He had the distinct feeling that if he acknowledged it things would be bad. The technical military term for things being bad beyond reason involved swear words, so he continued to ignore it and focused on breathing.

Chapter Fourteen

Bishop sat up and shaded his eyes from the sun. He had lain, and was now sitting, in the middle of the dirt road leading into town. A building lay collapsed in on itself in front of him and another to the side was on fire after its chimney had been caved in by a passing dragon's tail.

He usually thought of himself as a smart man, but when the world has stopped acting logically it sometimes takes a moment to pull things together. Bishop had never been in a situation where things, the world itself, didn't act according to well established rules of cause and effect. This wake up, however, finally started to make some sense to him.

This world, he thought, was something like another state of consciousness. When he fell asleep, or passed out, he came here. The passage of time in either world didn't seem to happen normally while he was in the other. The only thing that still bothered him about this theory was how the Raven, and now the dragon, could come across. If they were just part of his subconscious then how was he smashing holes in the floor of the vatican library?

Sid walked up to him and extended a hand, "You okay?"

Bishop took the offer and pulled himself to his feet. Mentally checking himself for any injuries, he found nothing. "I think so." He patted his chest where the dragon had tapped him with a claw the size of William Wallace's claymore. "Yeah, nothing's broken or bleeding."

Sid nodded and looked back to the townspeople hauling buckets of water to the burning house. "We should be moving on before they decide to blame us for that."

"Why would they? We didn't do anything." Bishop looked around for the Raven. Normally, they were close together when he skipped over to another world.

"Why would they?" Sid looked incredulous, "A dragon shows up, breaks peoples homes, and goes directly for you, almost as if you're the reason it's here. It touches you, then just flies off."

"He flew off?" Now it was Bishop's turn to be incredulous.

"Yep. I was over there," he waved at a stable, "and could hear him saying something to you. Then he reached out, gave you a love tap, and flew away."

"None of this makes sense." Bishop closed his eyes and found the presence still huddled like a goblin in the back corner of his mind. What would happen if it came out here?

"We agree on that, but for now," Sid started walking along the river, "we need to not take the main road into town to meet my friend."

Bishop followed him, then stopped to look over his shoulder, "Shouldn't we help them?"

"No," Sid kept walking, "it's not our business, and like I said, they'll be looking for someone to blame, and it's obviously you."

Leaving things alone was not one of Bishop's strengths. He'd never had a formal reprimand but he had been firmly talked to by his commanding officer multiple times about rushing in when it wasn't any of his business. He'd given up his food to refugees and had caused a stampede, his CO called it a flood. Separately, on deployment in northern Africa, there had been a collapsing building, and he thought he heard people in it. After rushing in he'd found himself surrounded by unhappy, and heavily armed, people who had no love for the US military.

Seeing a house on fire, and walking away knowing it was somewhat his fault, hurt his insides. Sid was right, however, and the last thing he needed was to end up in some form of jail, waiting to be hung for his crimes against this tiny village. Plus, what would happen if he died here? Did he just wake up in the real world, or did he have some brain aneurysm and die there too?

A flutter of wings and weight settling onto his left shoulder was followed by, "I can't figure out where he went. You said he took off back toward the forest?"

Sid nodded.

"I mean it's not like he's little and can just hide somewhere. He's a giant, horrifying, black lizard with wings." The Raven fluffed his feathers and knocked the side of his head against Bishop's, "Welcome back to the real world."

"So he just vanished," Sid said. "Or were you too frightened to actually follow him?"

"That's the stupidest thing I've ever heard." The Raven leaned out and looked at Sid walking on the other side of Bishop. "Of course I was scared. Do I have to point out again that it's a dragon? Because it's a dragon. Were you not scared? I didn't see you standing out there trying to fight it off."

Bishop stopped walking and hung his head. "I can't do this."

"Can't do what?" Bishop turned and started to jog back toward the wreckage. "Oh..." the Raven bobbed along on his shoulder.

"Seriously?" Sid's voice echoed off the buildings and Bishop glanced over his shoulder to see him standing, watching Bishop jog away.

"You're probably no good at putting out fires." Bishop directed the statement at the Raven hanging, slightly painfully, onto his shoulder, "but what you could do is go up and see if there's anyone injured and point me toward them."

"You know, Sid was right, people are going to be angry and they'll blame you. Also, people don't tend to trust talking ravens."

"Why would that be?"

The Raven either didn't catch the sarcasm in his voice or deliberately chose to ignore it, "I don't know. I really don't". With that he launched himself into the air and started circling his way above the rooftops.

Reaching the edge of the destruction, Bishop started looking for a place to help. He could grab a bucket and start passing it along. Thankfully the fire had started fairly close to the river and the townspeople seemed practiced at dealing with this situation, which made it obvious when they stopped passing buckets along and started pointing at him.

Having just walked across a desert at night with people he at least marginally trusted it hadn't really occurred to him that his clothing was a bit anachronistic and didn't help him blend in at all. It was something he'd vaguely thought about, and might have dealt with in town, but it hadn't been a problem until now. He couldn't blend in.

"Over here." The Raven's voice jolted him out of his head and he turned away from the stares and the finger pointing to see what the bird wanted.

The Raven was sitting on the corner of a house and as Bishop got closer he fluttered down and around it. On the other side Bishop saw a few people laid out on the ground with some women tending to them. One figure, at the end, had his hands crossed on his chest and his eyes closed. No one was tending to him.

A young boy was surrounded by an older woman and a girl that might have been in her lower teens, except Bishop really wasn't good at determining age. The boy was screaming and crying as he approached. None of them looked up at him and he was able to get a good view of the boy's condition. At first the odd angle of the boy's arm made Bishop think it had broken, but the placement of the angle at the elbow joint led him to believe it might just be dislocated. The pain would be almost unbearable and Bishop wasn't sure how the boy was still conscious.

"Excuse me," Bishop placed a hand on the older woman's shoulder. She twitched and turned toward him. "I know how to fix that."

She stared at him and wouldn't move.

"I understand." He gave his best reassuring smile, "it looks like his elbow is dislocated. If I could just get a look, I've been trained to fix that."

Part of being a lieutenant was training, not only in first aid, but in dealing with locals who might not want the US military around. The training was specifically in how to give aid when the local population really didn't want to be near you. Some groups hated you for religious reasons, some were just scared because you were an outsider, while others had political reasons.

Bishop put his palms up to show he carried nothing dangerous and continued to give a slight smile. You didn't want to smile too big because then you looked insane and even more dangerous. The smile needed to be what a parent would give to an injured child to let them know the hurt wasn't that bad, and the smile had to reach your eyes. That was a difficult part for some military members to learn.

"Please," he took a small step toward the boy, "I have been trained on how to deal with this exact injury."

The older woman bit her lip and took a small sideways step to clear the way. He could tell she didn't trust him, and he understood. He also understood that she might not care what had just happened with the dragon. Fixing her son was more important. Having a child cry out in real pain, and not be able to do something about it, had to be the worst possible situation for any parent.

Kneeling down he ran through a quick first aid check. Bishop didn't need to check on the boy's responsiveness, it was obvious by the screaming and crying that he wasn't unconscious. The next two, burns and bleeding, were quick thankfully. You could smell a burn long before you could see it, and there was none of the tell tale burnt human smell. Normally, he would touch the person to check for hidden bleeding areas, but with no blood on the ground where they'd laid him down, and none on the clothes or hands of the women, he could rule out any hidden cuts for the time being.

"All right," he turned back to the older woman, "I'm going to touch his arm and make sure nothing is broken." She nodded at him and he ran his hands, as gently as possible, over the boy's twisted arm. As he suspected there were no lumps or odd angles anywhere other than at the elbow. "Good, nothing is broken. Now I'm going to need you to hold him as still as possible and you," he nodded at the younger girl, "will need to hold right here." He pointed at the boy's bicep. "Hold tight." She nodded at him as her face drained of color.

Great, he thought to himself, she's going to pass out. I can only deal with one emergency at a time. Grasping the boy's forearm, and placing his other hand on the elbow joint itself, he nodded at the two women. Leaning over he smiled at the boy and said, "What's the smell of the color blue?" A look of confusion flickered over the boy's face and in that moment Bishop pulled with one hand and pushed with the other. A loud pop echoed in the small space and was not accompanied by a scream. Bishop looked over to see the boy's eyes rolled up in his head. He couldn't give him any anesthetic, but he'd tried to distract him for a moment. Thankfully, he'd passed out.

He looked over at the older woman, "You'll need to wrap his arm in a sling to support it while he's awake for about two to three weeks."

A peck on his leg was followed by the Raven's voice, "Incoming weirdness."

The women's eyes bulged and Bishop was sure if they'd been standing they would have ran away. When you're not used to a talking bird, it can be a bit disconcerting.

Glancing over his shoulder Bishop was only momentarily surprised to see Larry doing a quick walk over to them. He stopped a few feet away, glanced over his shoulder then back to Bishop, and said, "Take me with you."

"I…" Bishop looked down at the Raven then back up at Larry, "what?"

"Look," Larry looked around again, "I've been stuck in this town all my life and I don't want to be buried here. You just talked to the dragon. People are freaking out about it. Some are talking about sacrificing you to get it to go away, others said you must be some kind of god. I just want to go with you."

Standing, Bishop leaned, and held out his arm. The Raven hopped up, and with a little flap of his wings landed on his forearm. Lifting him up the Raven hopped from his arm to his shoulder. During this process he took a moment to look Larry over. He knew who he was in the other world, and he assumed with everything going on that not much would be different here. It seemed even the general personalities were the same, even if the clothing styles weren't.

Larry looked younger than Bishop felt he should. In the other world he was constantly talking about doing research for some masters or doctoral degree, but he didn't look old enough to be doing that. Part of Bishop's problem was the group of people he worked with on a daily basis. Some guys under his command were barely eighteen years old, while others had stalled out at that rank and were in their thirties. Larry, he was fairly sure, wasn't still in his teens, but someone getting a higher degree, like he claimed, should be in their mid to upper twenties, or even in their thirties. This was a guy who was going to have his age perpetually misdiagnosed.

"And what's your name?"

Larry nodded like this was a completely understandable thing to ask, "Laurence."

Bishop glanced at the Raven then back, "That makes sense."

138

"Really?" Confusion slid across Larry's face.

"Do you mind if I call you Larry?" Bishop looked back over at the two women, who had done exactly the right thing and decided to ignore whatever was going on with him and focus on the boy laying on the ground.

"Uhm," Larry shrugged, "sure."

The Raven chuckled and said, "Great, and how can you help, Laurence?"

The full body twitch convinced Bishop that Larry really wanted to both run away from the talking raven and at the same time really wanted to be a part of whatever all this was. Swallowing he said, "I know where they were sending guards to try and catch you. They assume you're going to need to head through town because you're not going to walk back out into the desert."

This version of Larry didn't sound as confident to Bishop, but if you've been raised in the same tiny village all your life, it's going to make a difference to your personality. The other Larry was full of bravado and knowledge. Maybe this one was too, but there had just been a dragon, so some leeway had to be given.

"Sure." Bishop looked over at the Raven, "Could you find Sid for me?"

The Raven pushed off and headed up. Bishop started walking and motioned for Larry to follow him. "This is going to sound strange, but so far everything for me has been strange. I have no problem with you coming along. I'm not a god, and that was the first time I've ever met a dragon."

They stopped and looked both ways when they emerged from the neighborhood. The fire seemed to have been contained with only some white smoke rising from the building. The river was in front of them, and the road he'd come in on was off to the left. Glancing up he saw the Raven circling over something to the right, so he headed that way. "A friend of mine said he was taking me to someone here in town who might have some answers to my questions."

"Oh," Larry nodded knowingly, "I know who he's talking about. You're not going to make it there."

Bishop looked over at him, "Why not?"

"Well, like I said, they want to grab you and have some words about houses being broken and fires starting."

"You know I didn't have anything to do with that?"

"Do I?" Larry looked around, deliberately not making eye contact. "The only dragon in existence comes to our little town and heads straight for you. It proceeds to have a nice chat with you, after smashing some homes and setting things on fire, then leaves. A person might think you had something to do with that."

"Honestly," Bishop saw the Raven land on the edge of a building up ahead and headed toward it, "that is one of the reasons I wanted to get some answers."

"Right, which is also one of the things they thought as well, so there will be guards waiting just in case you head over there."

The Raven hopped from the rooftop and drifted down to land on a smallish furry animal who shook enough to dislodge the bird. Bishop stopped and looked down at the dark brown four legged creature. "Well, that's handy for you, but Larry here says they've posted guards outside the home of this information broker you were taking me to."

The animal's shoulders rolled in a shrug, then he turned and started walking down an alleyway leading into town. The Raven hopped along on the ground next to him, "We could try the same trick we used back at the oasis."

Bishop nodded and looked at Larry out of the corner of his eye to see how he was reacting to the situation. It would be understandable to have a negative reaction to a talking raven and a random animal guiding him into town. Larry looked from the hopping raven to the trundling animal then over to Bishop, "This…"

Bishop smiled and kept his eyes pointed straight ahead, "You asked to come with us."

"I…" Larry nodded, took a deep breath and kept walking.

They stopped at the corner of the building and Bishop looked out onto a connecting street. Across the dirt road and down a few buildings to the right stood a log built home no different from many of the others he'd seen when looking down from the ridge before they'd crossed the river. It was one story and wasn't large. The entire structure was maybe thirty feet long by twenty feet deep. The roof was bundled grass and probably had bugs and a multitude of small rodents living in it. The front had two windows covered in wooden shutters and one door. On either side of the door stood men with old helmets and equally old spears in their hands.

"See," whispered Larry, "guards."

Bishop felt sure, or at least fairly sure, he could take both guards. These were farmers who happened to be holding a spear instead of a plow. They were not at all as intimidating as the Bedouin swordsmen he'd encountered back at the oasis, but he didn't want to hurt random people unless he really had to. "Okay," he glanced down at the Raven and Sid, "you two know what to do. Once the guards are out of the way, we'll see you inside."

The Raven looked up at him with one dark eye, "Close the door and open a window. It'll look less suspicious."

"And if anyone knows anything about looking suspicious, it's you." Sid said as he walked toward the left alleyway alongside the target house.

Larry looked from the little mammal to Bishop, "Did he just..."

Bishop smiled and nodded. It was nice to have someone along who was more freaked out by the situation than he was. It seemed he'd come to find talking animals a normal thing, and he couldn't wait to see Larry's face when little fuzzy Sid turned into big tough Sid.

The raven and Sid made short work of the guards. It was easy to convince them someone was trying to talk to them and lead them off long enough for Bishop and Larry to make it, unseen, to the front door. Bishop tried the latch that served as a door handle, and finding it unlocked let himself in.

With the shutters closed, the room was dark to his light adjusted eyes, but he could see that someone was sitting at a table just a few steps in from the door. "I'm sorry." Bishop glanced around at the rest of the room. This seemed to be a mix of a kitchen, living room, and dining room, with a door leading off to what must be the only bedroom in the small home. "We didn't mean to just barge in."

"Really," her voice reminded Bishop of some teachers he'd had while growing up, "and I suppose you just accidentally got rid of the two men standing outside my door, and fell through into my kitchen while walking by."

Great, thought Bishop, not only did she sound like a middle school English teacher, but she was sarcastic too. Hopefully they'd come to the right house or he was going to feel very silly in a moment.

Larry stepped around him, "We are sorry ma'am, but this gentleman needed some answers and I felt it was necessary to bring him."

"It is good to see you Laurence," She said.

Bishop's eyes had adjusted to the dim interior light, enough to see his estimation of her wasn't too far off track. She absolutely looked like an alternate world version of someone's seventh grade English teacher. Her black hair was streaked with gray and pulled back into a single loose braid. Her shoulders were covered with a blanket knitted in patterns of black and red stylized forest animals to keep off the cool of the morning. A tapping at one of the shutters reminded him of his job and he walked over to open the window just enough to let in the Raven and a struggling fuzzy Sid.

She let out an exasperated sigh, "First you barge into my home and say you didn't mean to, and now you let in a herd of wild animals."

"We're not a herd," the Raven replied as he landed on the kitchen table. Tapping one foot on it he looked over at Bishop, "This is quality wood." Hopping to the edge he looked over at the legs of the table, "Nice. You see where the legs are joined to the table top? That's some quality work."

"Thank you," she replied. "It was my late husband who made it. He always took pride in his handiwork."

Bishop expected a reaction from her like from so many other people when confronted with the existence of a talking raven, and yet she didn't even blink.

"Well," she gestured to the other chairs scattered around the table and the room, "take a seat. We might as well get started." Turning she called back through the door, "Alexandra dear?"

Bishop heard shuffling from the back room then a head poked out through the door, "Yes, grandma?"

"Could you make us some tea please?"

"Yes, grandma." A girl, that to Bishop's eyes could have been in her teens or her twenties, stepped out into the kitchen area. Getting out a kettle she filled it using a hand pump at the sink.

"It will take her a moment to get the fire lit," the grandmother said. "While she's working on that I should check to see if Laurence here took the time to tell you who I was."

"Well, actually," Bishop glanced down at the furry little form of Sid on the floor. He couldn't think of a reason to not tell her what was going on. It was, actually, the reason they had come. "It wasn't Larry who brought us. It was Sid."

"Larry?" She looked back and forth between Larry and Bishop. "Oh, I see." She let out a low chuckle. "So, where is Sid?"

Bishop pointed down at the fuzzy animal sitting on the floor.

She nodded, "I thought as much," she said to the animal, "but you wouldn't tell me the last time you were here."

Sid rolled his shoulders in his familiar shrug, "I was trying to keep it to myself as much as possible."

She gave him a nod, "I assume you found one of the scales then?"

Sid grunted.

"You always were a talker." Sid grunted again as she turned back to Bishop. "And what's your name dear?"

Bishop wasn't sure, culturally, what an appropriate greeting was here. She seemed like some kind of wise woman, and that usually brought with it a good amount of respect. Enough that they'd posted guards outside her home. Should he bow? Should he just extend his hand? He went for a middle ground, gave a slightly deferential nod, and said, "Peter. Peter Bishop."

"Well, Peter, I assume your friends here, including this marvelous specimen of raven," at that the Raven stopped hopping around the table watching Alexandra try to light the fire, and fluffed his feathers out to their fullest extent, "have brought you here because they said I have some kind of answers for whatever problem you've been having."

Her voice was slightly a question, but mostly a statement, and Peter nodded. "I'm not sure even where to start with my story, but, not to be rude, no one has told me your name."

"Of course they didn't," she shot a look at Larry and even leaned over and made eye contact with Sid. "I'm Cua."

Again, Peter nodded. The name matched her.

Cua smiled at him, "I'm assuming, with that style of clothing, that you're American."

Peter's eyes flared open and his heartbeat tripled, "You know about America?"

She leaned back in her chair, "My family immigrated to the United States back in the sixties. We made the choice to help the Americans in their war against the northern Vietnamese, and that meant we couldn't keep living there."

"That makes sense," Peter's voice cracked, "but…"

"But how did I know you were from America? How did I get here? How did you get here?"

"Yes," he wanted to shout and jump up from his chair, but all he could do was hold eye contact and hope.

"First, I need to check something." She leaned forward and gestured for him to do the same. "Your hand please." He extended his right hand and she took it in both of hers. It felt like she was going to read his palm and tell him he was destined to have a very short life, but she closed her eyes and started squeezing.

The words dropped from her mouth like frozen water and shattered around him, breaking his vision of the world. With each word, cracks ran though the sky and down, creating fissures through which all he could see was darkness. Then a soft white and pink light started pulsing through, overwhelming the dark. It reminded him of something, but he couldn't focus.

Yes…

The voice in the recesses of his mind whispered and Cua's eyes shot open. "Wait…" The light from the cracks flashed, blinding him and drowning out her voice.

Chapter Fifteen

Bishop's eyes shot open as his head knocked into the tree behind him. Sucking in a deep breath he tried to steady his heart rate and take in his surroundings. There were trees. Reaching up and rubbing the back of his head he could confirm that there were trees. He was sitting on the grass. Letting out the breath, he realized he was back at the Vatican. He must have fallen asleep while waiting.

"Raven?" He'd gotten used to having someone come back and forth with him. It helped.

"It's the weirdest thing." The Raven was invisible, and no one else could hear him, but it wasn't like he was communicating telepathically. Bishop heard the words and felt the weight of the bird as if he was there. "When something happens and we blip back and forth, it's like I just blinked. Blink, change of scenery. The first few times," Bishop felt his toenails as the Raven landed on his leg, "it seriously freaked me out. Now, it's like, hey you've magically ended up in a new reality, and I'm all like, who cares, happens to me all the time."

"I know how you feel." Bishop twitched his leg to let the Raven know he was going to be standing up, and when he felt the weight leave he levered himself up and stretched.

"So," the raven landed on his shoulder, "that lady had to have been a witch, am I right?"

Bishop frowned, "Did you understand anything she was saying before I came back over to the real world?"

"Nope. All gobbledygook."

"Did you see anything strange when she was saying it?"

"Everything felt really heavy for a second. Then poof, blink, and here I am, back in some messed up version of reality."

Walking back around the few well groomed trees Bishop saw Larry sitting on the bench chatting with a girl while Ryan leaned against a tree.

Stepping out of the trees and nodding at Ryan, Bishop walked over to the bench. "How're things looking?"

Larry smiled up at him and Bishop was reminded of the absolute absurdity of the existence of two Larrys, or a Laurence and a Larry. He had resigned himself to the oddness of Sid and Ryan being the same person, but then this happened and made things extra bizarre.

A flutter of invisible wings and a weight on his shoulder was followed with, "Seriously. Now it's just getting ridiculous."

"Peter," Larry guestured back and forth to the girl sitting next to him, "this is Alex. She was just telling me about coming here from the US to practice archery with some big name Italian coach."

The Raven squawked, "She looks just like the other one. This is getting stupid."

Indeed. Peter twitched. It seems reality is having trouble adjusting to the situation.

Those were the most words, and the most understandable words, the dragon living in his head had spoken since this all started. Normally it was like a bad monster movie in there. I angry, it would say. I smash things.

It's because we've actually met now and it's more than just my overwhelming emotional state you're experiencing.

"You okay?" Larry was looking at him with a concerned expression, and Bishop couldn't blame him.

"Yeah," he smiled at the two on the bench, "just thought I heard a wasp."

"Oh, that was good," the raven whispered unnecessarily.

The girl, her name was Alex if Bishop remembered correctly, chuckled, "You go all the way around the world with this idea that things will be magically different in another country and end up with wasps still being jerks."

Larry laughed, "They are jerks, aren't they?"

"Wait," the Raven continued to whisper, "wasn't the other girl's name Alexandra?"

"Bees at least give something amazing to humanity," Alex said. "Wasps just fly around looking to hurt people."

Wasps were actually some of my favorites. Fiercely defending their homes. Not putting up with others.

Bishop took in a deep breath and held it for a moment. He wasn't sure how he was going to be able to handle more voices in his head, even if the crazy one was now sounding a little bit more educated and a lot less murdery.

"Larry, can I talk to you for a moment?" Bishop turned and walked toward Ryan.

"Uhm, sure," he smiled at Alex and walked over to join Bishop and Ryan.

"First off..."

"Tell him he's funny looking," the Raven added a squawk. "Not for any reason. I just want to see the look on his face."

Your sense of humor hasn't changed, little brother.

"Look," the raven let out a rolling sound close to a growl, "disembodied stupid voice. You think you're big and special, but you're just a jerk like that imaginary wasp. You don't know me, so stop acting like you do."

"Yes?" Ryan had crossed his arms.

Bishop shook his head to clear it of other conversations, "Why did you let her sit down? I thought you were doing overwatch."

"Yeah," Ryan gave a nod, "for bad guys. I can tell from here she's not carrying a weapon."

"That's not the point. If something does happen and I get…" Bishop shrugged his shoulders, "overly stressed like back in the library…"

"I thought about that," Larry said.

"And?"

"And, I figured we needed to look as normal as possible. You know," Larry shrugged, "blend in."

"I still think it's weird we have so many duplicates," the Raven said. "I mean seriously is your world just a bad copy of mine?"

A metallic sound caused both himself and Ryan to look. A hammer blow of sound hit Bishop in the chest and was joined by a flash of light that fried his vision.

Larry screamed, staggered backward, and fell over. Bishop dropped to one knee so he would be less likely to lose his balance. The effect of the multiple flash-bangs wasn't as pronounced as it would have been if they were inside a room, but it still gave the dark clad bad guys some momentum.

Through his light dazed eyes, Bishop saw multiple shapes emerge from the trees to his right and left along with others coming around the corners of buildings in front of him. A grunt next to him led to a black clad soldier hitting the ground a few feet away. Looking through his watering eyes he could just make out Ryan kicking the downed goon in the head while pulling his pistol out from his back holster.

Goons to his right advanced past Alex huddled on the bench, and Bishop instinctively reached for his own service weapon only to be sadly reminded he wasn't carrying one. Alex flopped down off the bench and wrapped her arms around the ankles of the advancing goon pulling hard. With his feet gone and all his momentum pushing forward, the goon had nowhere to go but face down.

Bishop mentally applauded her, but knew as soon as the mercenary got his bearings she would be getting a bullet in an uncomfortable place. Being someone they'd just met he was especially surprised to find her joining in. This wasn't her fight. Standing up, and taking a step forward, Bishop lashed out with his right foot and caught the guard on the chin.

"Down!" A rough voice barked at them and Bishop looked up to count two more, each, on the right and left and three advancing from the front. "I said, get down!"

No.

The voice of the dragon rippled through his mind, and Bishop was uncomfortably reminded he had the honest to goodness spirit of a dragon hiding in his head.

Reaching down with one hand Bishop picked up the comatose goon and flung him one handed at the two advancing from his right. Simultaneously he heard shots to his left and assumed Ryan was dealing with that situation. Putting a foot on the edge of the bench, Bishop pushed hard and watched it fly across the grass audibly breaking the leg of an oncoming goon.

Extending a hand he said, "It's Alex, right?"

She nodded up at him and took his hand. Pulling her along, Bishop found a paved trail and followed it to a small outbuilding of what looked like a palace. He hoped Larry was smart enough to get out of harm's way. At this point Bishop assumed whoever these guys were, or whoever they were working for, were looking for him specifically. The only reason he dragged Alex along was to get her out of the line of fire. If he could find a good place to stash her around here, then he could get back to Ryan and hopefully help out.

"What's that sound?" Alex leaned out away from the column they were hiding behind and shielding her eyes, looked up.

Her pointing it out brought the buzzing sound to the front of his mind. "I sure wish I had something like an amazing raven that could fly around and tell me if there were any bad guys coming."

Alex looked over at him and cocked an eyebrow, "That's a specifically weird thing to wish."

"It really is." The Raven said from his right shoulder. "Ohhh, you mean…" He stopped talking as he took off.

That one has always been odd.

You're telling me, Bishop thought back.

I know him, but I don't remember. It's been a long time since clarity of thought was a thing to be sought after.

"I think it's a drone," Alex had leaned back out. "Yep, it's a drone."

The Raven's feet slid along his shoulder and disappeared for a moment then a flapping wing hit him in the side of the face and the feet grabbed on, "They're coming fast."

"From where?"

Alex looked at him and pointed up, "The drone's over there, dude."

"What?" The Raven knocked his head against Bishops, "You want me to point? I'm invisible. What good would it do?"

Three black clad soldiers appeared through a stand of trees. One took a knee and opened fire. Bishop, recognizing the kneeling position, shoved Alex behind the pillar. Chips of real marble cut into his cheek as the M4 rounds dug furloughs in the pristine white of the column.

Bishop's first thought was how angry the Vatican was going to be. His second thought wasn't actually his.

I will crush them.

There was the Mr. Grumpy Pants Bishop remembered, but he also remembered Mr. Grumpy was right. He could crush them.

Bending his knees Bishop dug his toes into the edge of the marble patio and launched himself. His shoulder connected with the first bad guy, and Bishop rolled over him, landing on his feet facing the kneeling goon. Striking the ground, Bishop watched a wave of earth ripple out and knock the mercenary off his feet. Flicking his left hand back, he grabbed the web harness of the one he'd bowled over. Reaching out with his right he watched black tendrils extend from his fingers and wrap around the one trying to stand up. Yanking him back and pulling the one in his left hand around, Bishop slammed them together. It was a satisfyingly deep thud as the two hit each other.

A scream was cut off behind him and before he turned a mental image bloomed in his mind.

This.

He could see the one remaining goon holding Alex. He was taller than her by almost a foot, exposing most of his head. He held a nine millimeter pistol to her right side temple. The chipped column was touching her left side.

Here, here, or there.

The goon's head was highlighted in a slight hazy glow, as was his right leg, and his gun arm and hand.

Bishop's first thought was to put one of those black tendrils through the goon's eye and be done with it, but the still totally human part of him didn't want to scar Alex for life by having dripping brain matter get in her hair. Moving onto the next best action, Bishop decided on the gun hand.

Turning around, Bishop saw the scene with his own eyes. The dark was his friend. The shadows were a connected part of the dragon that lived in the back of his mind. They rippled with the opalescence of dragon scales. The shadow of the column stretched and filled the pistol pointed at Alex. It wrapped around the mercenary's hand and pulled it back away from her. Bending his wrist, Bishop forced the goon to point the gun at himself. Alex squirmed out of his now loosened grip and ducked to the other side of the column.

He will die. They should all die.

Bishop flicked his hand and the goon flew toward the next pillar.

Alex, eyes wide, walked slowly toward him. Her hands patted the air in front of her, "Hey, man, uhm…"

Alex and the world were lit in shades of gray. The trees were a dark mass over his shoulder, and the only light was thin as though someone had thrown a blanket over the sun. His breathing was slow and deep. The wet smell of grass, the ever present throat coating smog of Rome, none of it reached him. Flexing his hands, he could feel the claws dig into his palms, and knew it would take one swipe to end this thing walking toward him.

"Uhm," she stopped half a dozen feet away, "It was Peter right?" She tried to smile at him, "I know I said I came to Europe hoping things would be different but this is taking it a little far. All the bad guys are gone. Do you think you could…" she shrugged, "I don't know, pull the claws back in?"

A sharp pain shot through the side of his head, "Hey, knucklehead." The Raven jabbed him again with his beak. "The crazy doppelganger girl has a point. Also," another sharp stab, this time on his ear, "I still do not understand why we keep seeing doubles of people. Is there a double of you somewhere running around in my world?"

"You…" Alex bit her lip and looked from his eyes to the top of his head. "You actually have horns. Could we, I don't know, get to know each other a bit better before I ask you why you have horns." She tried smiling at him again.

I will be free.

The pressure in his mind was building. A memory flickered like an old fashioned reel to reel movie running too slow. Watching from the top of a hill as fire fell from the sky and consumed a village built of mud brick.

I will burn it all.

"Hey," the Raven's beak grabbed his earlobe and pulled. "Snap out of it. Think about something else. Think about kittens. You people like kittens, right?"

Think about something else. Think about something else.

Keeping her smile as big as possible and extending her hands out Alex walked toward him. "I don't know you, but I know you're a person. I know you tried to get me to safety." Reaching out she put her hands on the sides of his face. "Take a deep breath, and when you let it out, you'll be better."

Closing his eyes Bishop blocked out the black and white world around him. The cool of her palms pressed in and he knew he was still himself.

I am me.

It felt a little silly to say that, but this was the first time he'd had another voice living inside his head.

Who am I?

A series of mental images rushed through. His mother and father around a campfire handing him a marshmallow to roast. Helping his Grandpa tear down an old shed in the backyard of their house in Nebraska. Mowing the lawn because he knew his Grandma would always give him money for that. His first kiss and how much wetter it was than he expected.

I am me.

I am still here.

Chapter Sixteen

Bishop's stomach lurched and his inner ear told him he was falling. The back of the chair tipped and his arms flailed trying in vain to maintain his balance. He hit the ground at the same time as a thump caused the front door to crack.

"What?" The Raven hopped onto Bishop's chest.

Larry jumped from his chair, two knives materializing in his hands, as a second thump and crack threatened to remove the locked door from its hinges.

Sid rolled sideways and hugged the wall next to the door. The air around his fuzzy form shimmered.

Bishop brushed at the raven, who squawked and hopped back onto the table top, then rolled off the chair and pushed himself back to his feet.

The old woman across the table turned her head and yelled into the open door, "Alexandra!"

"I'm over here Nana," the girl crouched next to the fire she'd just managed to start.

"Good girl." She twitched her head in the direction of the bedroom, "Now get your bow and check the back windows."

As she ran for the open back room, Bishop patted his pockets, again wishing he had his service pistol. He also wished he could manage to stay in one place for long enough to figure his life out. Jumping back and forth, while getting easier to recognize and deal with, was seriously messing up his ability to keep everything straight.

He could feel the presence of the dragon in the back of his mind again, so did that mean everything was fine back at the Vatican or was he still struggling with that? Things seemed to pause in place as he went from one world to the other. Except for him and the Raven. Why the Raven, he wondered as he looked around the room for a weapon to fight an enemy he didn't know. He assumed it was an enemy. Normal people don't knock so hard they break your door.

"Is it the police?" Bishop looked at their host.

She shook her head, "The local constables wouldn't break my door down. They know better than that."

A high pitched scream came through the wall at the back of the house, followed by the voice of Alex, "Nana, there's men with torches trying to set fire to the house."

"And?"

"And they're hiding now."

"You didn't kill him, did you?"

"No Nana," Alex's voice sounded impatient. "I only shot him in the shoulder so he couldn't throw the torch."

"Good girl." Cua turned back around as the door gave a final crack and fell into the room.

The first person through the door was greeted with an arm across his throat by Sid, now full sized, standing next to the opening. Two more men attempted to push through. One tripped on the prone, gagging, body of the first man, and after Sid delivered a swift punch to the back of the head he joined him on the floor.

The next man swung a sword at the exposed arm of Sid, and had it deflected by a quick move of the left hand knife by Larry. The right hand knife followed it with a flicking motion to the intruder's sword hand. The man's thumb hit the floor only a moment before his sword did.

"There," the raven squaked at Bishop. "Get the sword."

Bishop twitched forward to grab it but stopped himself. He didn't know how to use a sword, and in such close quarters was just as likely to injure one of his comrades as he was to hurt one of the assailants.

The window to the right of the door shattered and a rock bounced across the floor. A moment later a flicker of brown zipped past his head as an arrow buried itself in the far wall. Larry flattened himself against the wall between the door and the window while another rock destroyed the only other window in the room.

Bishop knew the next thing would be either an assault through all three points of entry, or more torches to set the building ablaze and force them out into the open. They could cover an assault easily. Sid could hold the narrow door against anybody, while Larry and himself covered the two windows. There didn't seem to be any chance of an attack coming from the back of the house with Alex putting arrows through people, which made him think back to the real world.

On his mental list of things to figure out he added a question asking why there were doubles of certain people, and it was quickly climbing the ranks. It wasn't number one, or even number two, but it was getting up there.

The personalities and capabilities of the doubles seemed to be at least somewhat in sync with each other. This meant the Larry he'd met back in the library might be carrying some knives, and knew how to use them. It also explained why Alex, held hostage by a gun toting mercenary, and witnessing a guy grow horns and throw things around with shadows, hadn't flinched.

"Rawk," the Raven's call cracked through everything crowding his mind. "Roof's on fire."

"Of course it is," Bishop said as he turned to Cua. "Will they hurt you?"

"They might take issue with my granddaughter at this point," she pushed her chair back and stood up, "but I don't think they would be crazy enough to take a shot at me." Scooping up her fallen shawl she yelled back into the room, "Alexandra, sweet heart, we need to leave."

"Coming Nana." The girl calmly emerged from the back, attaching a full quiver of arrows to a belt at her waist.

Bishop glanced around. Three points of entry and exit. The two windows weren't suitable for a good exit since you'd have to jump through them, and there was the possibility of getting caught up on the broken glass, leaving yourself at the mercy of anyone with a bow and arrow. The benefit of the single door was now going to be a hindrance with them all needing to exit at the same time, and quickly with the amount of smoke coming through the thatched roof.

"Covering fire." Bishop turned to Alex, "I need you to send some shots out and convince them to keep their heads down. I'll take point and head toward the closest threat. Sid, I need you to peel off in the opposite direction and take out the next. Larry, run like crazy and try to get behind them while we distract them from the front. Hopefully, she's right," he inclined his head toward Cua, "and we don't need to worry about them trying to put an arrow through her as she exits her now unfortunately burning home."

They all gave a quick nod and Bishop slid to the edge of the door. Sid made room for him and stacked behind him with his hand resting on Bishop's shoulder. Leaning close Sid said, "The closest one I saw was left and down the alley. There may be more than one of them in there…" He left the statement hanging implying he was worried about Bishop's ability to deal with more than one at a time.

Remembering what happened getting out of the helicopter, then at the tent with the dragon scale, and finally, just recently, at the Vatican, Bishop was growing ever more certain he could handle more than one bad guy at a time. He was a bit worried about the presence huddled in the back of his head, but worries could wait till better times. Right now he needed to clear some corners and alleys.

Glancing over at Alex he caught her eye and twitched his head to the nearest window. She nodded, stepped through the broken glass littering the floor, raised her bow and sent an arrow flying. Immediately she dropped her right hand to her belt quiver and pulled another shaft. That one was joined a moment later by a third. Two yelps followed her volley, and she shook her head. "Sorry about that last one," she rolled her right shoulder to loosen it up. "It caught the edge of the building and missed."

Bishop realized he was staring in awe when he should have been moving out, using the covering fire to advance, but he'd never seen someone do what she had just done. Shaking his head he reached up and tapped Sid's hand then ran out the door, looking for the alley to the left Sid had spoken of.

As he rushed across the dirt street, he noted the difference between this fight and the most recent one in the other world. This one felt better, he'd had a chance to gather his wits and make a plan. Everyone was acting as a team, even though he didn't know them that well. Back at the Vatican it had all been reaction with no chance to stop and think. They'd never had a chance to work together.

A face appeared around the corner of the alley ahead and Bishop drew back his fist and rammed all his running speed through the punch. The shock of the hit ran up his arm and jarred his shoulder, but the effect was perfect. The body, ragdoll limp, flew into the three men standing behind him disrupting any plans they'd had to stab him with the swords and spear they held.

Using his left foot as a pivot he planted it on the wall of the alley and pushed off at full speed. Lowering his shoulder he rammed into the sternum of the lead guy, who'd just pushed the unconscious man off him. The impact knocked him back into the other two, causing them all to stumble. Bishop stepped forward, planted his left foot, rotated on it, and lashed out with his right, taking the leader hard in the crotch.

As the man crumpled to the ground, Bishop mentally acknowledged the unfairness of it all. There were certain unspoken rules of fighting between men, and one of them was not to kick the other guy in the crotch. However, when someone is actively trying to kill you, and sets your friend's house on fire, all rules are suspended. Fighting to save your life, and the lives of those under your command, was more than just a sparring match. There were no rules.

Reaching down, he grabbed the falling man by the back collar of his shirt and did something he now knew he could do, but would never have considered at any other time in his life. Lifting the man with one hand, he threw him into the chest of the next. Tossing people around was quickly becoming one of his favorite tactics. No normal person knows how to react to another person, especially one who's on their side, being thrown at them. Do you dodge and just let them hit the ground, or do you try to catch them?

The men must have known each other because he tried to catch him. Bishop would have stopped and watched. It was almost comical, especially in that split second when he realized he still had a sword in his hand, and you could see the question cross his mind of how he was supposed to catch him with a sword in his hand. Taking

154

one long step, Bishop jabbed out, flattening his left hand to spear the man in the throat. Then followed up with a right hook, sending him crashing into the wall of the alley.

Lowering himself instinctively on the follow through from the punch, he felt the whiff of the spear point from the final man slice the air where his torso used to be. Spiraling his right arm up and around he wrapped it around the haft of the spear, pinning it between his arm and his side. Grabbing it with both hands he pulled. A quick thinking soldier would have simply let the spear go and let Bishop fall on his back, but these were not the quick thinking kind. Bishop was starting to wonder if they were even the soldier kind.

The man was yanked toward him, holding onto his spear with the look of a man holding onto the last plank of a sinking ship. Whipping his head forward, Bishop slammed his forehead into the nose of the wide eyed man on the other end of the spear. A crack was followed by an immediate release of pressure on the other end of the spear.

Leaning back, Bishop surveyed the alley. Flipping the spear around he planted it in the dust and leaned on it. With no more immediate threats, Bishop wasn't quite sure what to do. Normally, he would have radio contact with his platoon, and could check on their progress, or at least tell them not to shoot at him as he emerged from the alley. As it was, he had no idea what was going on elsewhere, and was honestly worried about leaving the alley and getting shot by Alex.

Deciding to give everyone else a minute to clear things up, and not having any reservations about their ability to do so, Bishop decided to play battlefield detective. Of the men in his little alley, only one of them was partly conscious. He decided to save that one for last, but didn't want him getting any ideas about leaving early, so he glared at the slumped figure and whispered, "Stay," in the grumpiest way he could.

Flipping over one of the others and looking him over, Bishop didn't see anything out of the ordinary. The guy had the basic pants, shirt, and shoes of someone living in a little village in a time period that seemed to be something like late medieval or early renaissance. He wasn't a history buff so sorting out time periods based on clothing styles wasn't going to be exact. Also, he seemed to be in an alternate dimension and their fashion choices might not coincide with the real world.

Patting him down, Bishop didn't even find some kind of a coin purse. Granted, he hadn't had to buy anything yet, but you never knew when supplies would be necessary. Moving to the next victim, he found the same set up. Basic clothing, a normal weapon, or at least what Bishop believed to be normal. Swords must be expensive, even in an alternate version of the world. After checking over, and finding nothing, on the third man, Bishop decided to turn to his only awake attacker.

"So," he squatted down in front of the man who had propped himself up on the wall of the alley, "I'm going to be quick about this. Why did you attack?"

The man squeezed his broken nose and glared at Bishop, "The dragon is free."

Pursing his lips, Bishop nodded, "That's a fact, true, but that's also not a reason to attack a woman's home. So," Bishop leaned forward and tried to be a little menacing, "again, why did you attack?"

"The dragon must be free to do his job, and you must die."

Bishop stood up. "You want me to die because the dragon talked to me, and that single conversation is somehow stopping a giant overwhelming dragon from doing its job. Whatever that may be."

"He has obviously chosen you, and…" the man trailed off then shook his head, wincing and putting more pressure on his broken nose. "You won't trick me into revealing the truths."

"Right," Bishop nodded. "You probably don't even know them yourself."

Leaning against the wall, Bishop tried his best to take stock of the situation. Fanatical dragon cultists, he knew it wasn't the best word but at the moment it was all that would come to him, were trying to kill him for reasons only cultists would know. Separately, fanatics with unknown motivations were trying to kill him back in his world.

"Hey," a rawk was accompanied by weight and raven feet digging into his shoulder. "Why are you hanging out back here by yourself?"

Glancing over at the Raven he was momentarily surprised to be able to see him. Pushing off the wall Bishop said, "I was a bit worried Alex would poke a hole in me if I stepped out."

He started walking toward the exit for the alley and the Raven grabbed and tugged on a lock of hair, "Nope, can't go that way."

"Oh," Bishop turned around and headed for the other end of the alley, "I kinda thought I was joking about her shooting me."

"It's not her. Although that would be funny. It's that." The Raven bobbed his head toward the sky.

Looking up through the thin gap allowed by the walls of the alley Bishop saw heavy smoke drifting through the sky. He knew Cua's house was on fire, "Look, I feel bad about the house and I understand if she's a little, or a lot, irritated about it right now."

"It's not just the house. Well, it is the house, but it's more who's shown up to try and put out the fire at the house."

"Oh, right. We don't exactly need a crowd, and all the questions that would come with it." Bishop walked out of the alley and onto the dirt thoroughfare leading along the river.

Everyone was waiting at the river's edge. Most didn't look any worse for the fight they'd just been in. Larry had a bruise across his left cheek that would, most likely, turn amazing shades of yellow and purple, and Alex was playing with her hair where it was curled and burnt slightly shorter from being too close to the fire in her house.

Catching him looking, she shrugged, "Nana needed some of her things brought out of the house."

"Oh, sweetie," Cua patted her granddaughter on the shoulder, "it'll grow out."

Alex made eye contact with Bishop and flared her eyes for a moment. He gave back a small smile and, "Thank you, Alexandra, for your help back there. You jumped in when it wasn't necessary. You most likely knew some of those men, and will have to live around them again."

"True," she nodded, then smiled, "and it actually felt good to put an arrow through some of them."

Cua nodded, "You won't need to worry about our relations with our neighbors. Those men are some of the worst in town and I, for one, have been looking for a good reason to get them kicked out for some time now. Setting fire to my house, while ridiculously annoying, is a great reason to shove them out and let the desert take care of them."

"No prison time?" Bishop asked.

"Prisons are too expensive," Cua answered. "There's one room we can use as a holding cell before a trial, but no one just gets put in prison here. You either get punished and released or shoved out to the desert."

Sid stepped into Bishop's line of sight, "Look, it's good chatting and all, but people are going to start coming around and asking awkward questions."

Cua nodded and locked eyes with Bishop, "Your friend is right, so here are some quick answers. When I was little, my family was on a trip. Part of the trip was a tour through an archeological dig. I thought it was boring. At one point the person taking us on the tour showed us a pile of things that had been taken from the dig. Among those was a crystal. It was about a hand's length and in the light seemed to glow a pinkish white. I wanted to touch it even though we had been asked to keep our hands to ourselves, and I knew my mom would be upset. When I reached out, it was sharp and one edge cut me. The ground changed, moved, and I fell. When I opened my eyes

I was here. Well, not here in town, but here, in this world. Eventually, I made my way to this town and made a life."

Bishop was nodding along with the story, "The crystal I came across was a lot bigger than the size of your hand, but it was similar."

She waved her hand, indicating the world around them, "I don't know much about this place or why those crystals would bring us here. I did find, up at the monastery, a monk who would answer some questions. He was stubborn and wouldn't answer everything. I was young and angry and might have hit him in his mouth when he told me the answers I was looking for weren't for me. Maybe you can get more answers out of him than I could, especially with the dragon roaming around and all."

"How did you do that thing," Bishop paused, "where you sent me back?"

"Is that what happened?" Her eyes widened. "To us it just looked like you fainted for a moment. You didn't go anywhere."

"I did." He looked around at his companions, new and old. He knew the raven would understand, but explaining all of this to Sid and now Larry and Alex, would be difficult.

"It's one of the things the monk did tell me. If someone ever showed up looking like they came from home then I could do that and it would give me proof or not, and it looks like it gave me proof."

"So," Bishop couldn't believe he was about to say what he was about to say, "to get the answers I need to go find a monastery and talk to a monk."

"I know," Cua nodded and smiled at him, "it's all a bit much, but the monasteries are really the only places in this world that kept track of the past. Libraries aren't a thing here."

"And where would this monastery be, exactly?"

"Laurence, have you ever been to the monastery?"

Bishop looked over at his new companion who shook his head, "No ma'am. My dad talked about it, but my mom couldn't see any sense in going that far for no good reason."

Cua sighed and Bishop was fairly sure she rolled her eyes, "That sounds like your mother. If there was no coin to be had, it wasn't worth the trip." She looked back at Larry, "No disrespect meant to your mother."

Larry smiled back, "It's no disrespect to speak the truth ma'am."

"Well, be that as it may, the monastery is off the main road." She turned and pointed through town, "Take the main road up into the mountains. When you come to a cliff on your left, look for a crack in it with a trail that goes in switches back and up. That trail will lead you to the monastery. I would tell you to say old Cua sent you, but he might still be sore about the punch in the mouth."

"Thank you." Bishop thought for a moment then added, "Do you mind if I borrow your granddaughter? She was amazing back there, and I could use the help."

Cua turned to look at Alex, "It's not my decision. She's a grown woman now and can make her own choices."

"Oh I can?" Alex raised an eyebrow at her grandma.

Cua frowned at her, "Don't give me sass right now girl."

Alex turned and looked at Bishop, "Sure, I'll go with you. I've never been more than a mile or so outside of this town. It would be nice to see other places."

Bishop smiled, "Thank you." Turning his head he looked over at Larry, "What about you? Still want to tag along after what's happened so far?"

Larry grinned at him, "It's because of what's happened that I want to come along. My Mom wants me to be the town scribe. It's a good steady paying job, she would say. So, between sitting and writing down what other people say all day, and traveling with someone who talks to dragons, I think I'll choose the dragons."

Bishop laughed and remembered a shirt one of his men on the ship had bought while in port. It said, "cool story bro... needs more dragons". Well, here he was, with more dragons.

Chapter Seventeen

"Dodge!"

"What do you think I'm doing?"

The target's body guard loomed large in the monitor as the drone pilot tried to flick the machine sideways and avoid his pistol fire. The screen tilted then showed a rotation of the sky and ground until the only thing showing was an extreme close up of grass.

"Number three has hands on a hostage."

"They were told not to take hostages."

"He seems to be improvising."

"Can you blame him? I mean did you see what the target did to the other two?"

"His camera's down, and his vitals are all over the place. He's unconscious."

"Do we have any drones left?" The commander in the ops room glanced over at the soldier in charge of the drone team.

"Yes sir. Just one."

The commander sighed. He was glad none of this was coming out of his pocket. Those drones were expensive, and he hadn't expected the body guard to be such a good shot. "Where is it?"

"We landed it on top of the library building and were using it for wide angle visuals."

"Do you still have a view of the target?"

The main screen, currently showing the health read outs of all the men engaged in the fight, switched to a color feed showing the area just outside the Vatican library. "Only the bodyguard, sir."

The commander nodded. The main target had fled into the trees and, if the vital signs and body cams could be trusted, had just finished taking out three of his men. "Send a message to the suit and let him know it was another failure."

A moment later Patrick walked into the room. He nodded at the commander.

"Sir," the commander nodded back. "Two dead from bullet wounds, and all others unconscious. We have one drone left but at present we can only see the bodyguard. The last drone footage we have of the primary target was…" he paused looking for the right word, "disturbing."

"Good, good," Patrick smiled.

"Sir?" The commander looked from the screen showing all his men as incapacitated or KIA, then back to Patrick.

"We need to drive them indoors, commander." Patrick pointed to the large digital map of the Vatican they had pulled up on a screen to the right. "We need to be able to control their points of movement. Out in the open they have too much freedom, but indoors they have to worry about collateral damage and innocent bystanders. Then when they try to escape we'll have the exits all controlled."

The commander nodded, "That would explain the second group."

Patrick briefed him on the follow up plan and the secondary follow up plan in case that plan went wrong. There was a good chance it would. He still wasn't sure about the extent of this lieutenant's powers and thought it preferable to have a few backups in place just in case.

"I need to make some calls." Patrick nodded his goodbyes to the soldiers and headed back to his cabin. He really would need to make some calls. He did have some contacts inside the Vatican, but not many, and unmarked soldiers shooting the place up would cause a response. They couldn't trace it back to him, but any kind of response right now would slow down his operation. He didn't need for it to go away, he just needed it to be slowed down a bit.

Sitting down at the desk in his cabin he took a moment to look out the large sliding glass doors at the turquoise of the Mediterranean and on to the green Italian countryside in the distance. Reaching up he took a framed picture down off the edge of his desk and stood up. The calls would wait for a moment. Sliding open the glass he stepped out onto his balcony.

"You would've loved this view." He glanced down at the picture of a brown haired girl. A sprinkling of freckles crossed her nose, lending a perfect frame to her wide toothy smile. "We're almost there, sweetheart. Almost there…"

Chapter Eighteen

The office was cramped with the five of them in it. "It seems you're in need of more help than was previously assumed." The priest had been the first Vatican official to show up after the gun fire with the mercenaries. Thankfully he'd been willing to pull them inside and temporarily shelter them, but only after some serious begging.

Separately, Bishop was having a hard time keeping his reality straight. The last thing he remembered was leaning against a tree when the alternate world version of his group had stopped to camp for the night. They'd stepped off the main road and into the cover of the trees to set up what little equipment they'd taken from the village after the fight, and he must have drifted off. Finding himself back here with Alex leaning over him and Ryan running through the trees followed by Larry was jarring. After the gunfire and fight outside the library, Father Oni had shown back up and hurried them all inside and eventually into this small work space.

Father Oni had sat down behind the only desk in the room, and Bishop had let Alex take the only other seat. "Is it that obvious?"

Giving him a small smile, the lines at the corners of Father Oni's eyes grew deeper for a moment, "I have few options in this situation, you understand. Technically," he stopped himself and sighed, "more than technically, I should have left you to the security forces. However," he raised a hand to forestall any comments, "after having seen what I did in the library…" He left the statement hanging.

Bishop had taken over the speaking part of this trip from Ryan when it became clear to Father Oni that Ryan was no longer the one who needed to be talked with. "Yes, we understand, and, again, thank you very much for bringing us here instead of taking the more obvious route."

The father nodded, "The modern Vatican doesn't view these kinds of events in a very positive light. They're trying to claw their way into a more modern stance and the presence of demonic possession here on the grounds of the Holy See itself would set that back, at least in the eyes of the media. Their response to you would have been…" he paused for what Bishop could only think was dramatic effect, "harsh."

The priest looked around at the group then leaned back in his chair, "So, what exactly were you hoping to achieve here?"

Bishop glanced over at Ryan, wondering just how far he could go with the information before getting into trouble, "We were told to look up the Cardinal and he would be able to help without raising too many red flags."

"And by we, you mean all of you?"

Bishop smiled at this but before he could answer Larry spoke up from next to the door, "I met them in the library and was helping them look things up when all of it got a little bit nutty."

The priest rolled his hand in the air.

"Right," Larry nodded, "by nutty I mean…" he paused and looked to Bishop who nodded for him to continue. "Well, he grew horns and smashed some things I didn't think a normal person could smash."

The father's deep black skin crinkled as he raised one eyebrow. "I saw what happened in the library. What I want to know is why you have joined them in all this, as you say, nuttyness."

"Well," Larry paused and looked around at the others in the room, "my life has been one long expectation. My mom always expected me to do this, to go to college, to get a fancy degree, to have a stable paycheck. I guess if I thought about it, I'm here because I want to do something amazing."

The priest was giving small nods in response to Larry's statements then asked, "But you don't know these people?"

Larry shook his head, "No."

"And yet…" The priest let the statement hang in the air.

Larry shrugged and didn't respond.

The priest looked from Larry to Alex, "And you miss?"

She also looked up at Bishop, and he was overwhelmingly reminded of the Alex from the other place. It was silly because he was almost sure they were exactly alike, but at the same time he wasn't sure of anything lately. The other Alex had jumped right in when they'd set off from her small home town. It had been evening when their group had said goodbye to Cua and slipped through town and down the road into the forest beyond.

Alex hadn't said much at first, but when they were out of sight of town she started asking questions and didn't stop until they made camp under the bows of a giant pine tree. Her favorite topic was the talking raven, but that was closely followed by Sid's ability to shape shift. The fact that Bishop was from the same place as her Nana was also greatly explored, especially since she had never been quite sure if Nana was telling the truth or if it was all some kind of morality lesson she was trying to teach her granddaughter.

Back in the real world, Bishop smiled at her, "So, you're good with a bow?"

She gave him a quizzical look and nodded, "Yeah."

"And do you have a Nana?"

"Doesn't everyone?"

"That was a dumb question," the Raven said in a stage whisper to his right ear.

It was a rather ridiculous way to suss out whether she has more than a physical connection with the other version of herself.

"Grumpy dragon voice is correct," the Raven noted.

Bishop shrugged and gestured for Alex to say whatever she wanted to the priest.

Nodding, she turned back, "Lots of black clothed guys with guns came and started shooting at us. Peter grabbed me and dragged me away so I didn't get shot. Three of them found us, and he took care of them."

"That's leaving out a lot," said the Raven. "The best bit was when you snapped that guy in the face with some crazy shadow tentacle, like you were the octopus demigod of darkness. No, wait, of ink. Because, you know, octopuses have ink."

The priest nodded, "Were there horns involved."

Again she looked up at Bishop. He wasn't sure if she was trying to cover for him, or if she was worried he would transform and kill everyone. Either way he smiled again and said, "Go ahead. It's not going to change anything now."

Looking back to the priest she nodded, "Horns, yes. Some of the side of his face had turned to what looked like black scales."

"Really?" Bishop wished he could see what was going on with him, but, for some reason, he never stopped to find a mirror when he went crazy.

Our connection is growing stronger.

I don't really want our connection to grow stronger, Bishop thought back at the rumbling voice in his head.

Alex shrugged at him, "It was a bit scary, but I could tell you were only trying to protect me."

"And what were these black clad mercenaries doing exactly?" The priest asked.

Bishop looked over at Ryan, "Any ideas?"

"Well," Ryan looked around at the strange group huddled in the tiny office below the Vatican library, "they're not normal terrorists, that's for sure."

"Normal?" Larry leaned forward from the back wall, "What definition of normal are we using here? It's fairly obvious they would only show up, whoever they are, for something, and that something must be Peter."

The Raven chuckled, "If anyone here would know the definition of normal, it would be that guy. I can see him wearing a sweater vest and slowly stacking books until everyone around him dies of extreme boredom."

Remember, little brother, he ran through the door of a burning house to fight enemies who had him greatly outnumbered.

"In a different world," the Raven clucked in the back of his throat. "I mean, do we even know if they're anything like each other?"

Bishop met Larry's gaze, "Larry's right. Most likely, whoever they are, they're after me. I am the only variable here."

"Well," the priest looked around at them all, "we can only handle one emergency at a time, so let's focus on the one in front of us. Hopefully the Vatican security can deal with the intruders for now and we can focus on your problem." He paused and waited for most of them to give a nod, "So, did you make any progress with your research before things went sideways?"

Both Larry and Bishop nodded and Bishop let Larry speak since he wasn't sure what book it had been that had set him off. Larry detailed the book and the section, adding emphasis to the image that was the main culprit. Knowing what the priest specialized in, Bishop hoped he would be able to point them in a better direction.

Father Oni sat and thought for a few moments then nodded to himself. "In the essence of time we'll need to split up. Larry, you've been through the stacks correct?" Larry nodded at him. "Miss," the priest looked over at Alex, "are you willing to help us in our time of need?"

Alex took a deep breath, "My name's Alex." She seemed to think about the situation for a moment then nodded, "I'd be happy to help."

"Good." The priest smiled at her, "If you could go with Larry and help him, I would appreciate it. I know the popular ideas of helping with a possession don't include looking through a library, but the best thing we can do now is narrow down exactly what is going on, and do it as quickly and quietly as possible."

Bishop pressed his thoughts toward the presence lurking in the back of his mind and mentally said, why can't you just tell me what's going on? We shouldn't have to do research to figure out what you are. Just tell me what you are. Silence met his request.

"I don't know if he can," the Raven said, for the first time seeming to read his thoughts. "I get the feeling he's just a bit of a disembodied ghost. Like, somehow, that great big dragon put a piece of himself into your brain, but it's not the whole thing."

The Raven is not wrong. I know that I exist, but I can't remember...

"Peter?"

Bishop snapped back to the here and now, "Sorry, I was in my own head. It's all a bit overwhelming."

The priest stood up and took in a deep breath. Letting it out he smiled at Bishop. Bright white teeth gleaming and projecting as much of a sense of calm as possible, "I am impressed with how well you have kept yourself together in the situation. I've known fully trained priests to fall apart at the first sign of true possession."

Heading out the door, they went down a short tan hallway and up a narrow set of stairs. A door at the top of the stairs led back out into rooms filled with books.

"Alex, Larry, what you're looking for is to the left." Bishop must have missed the details when he was having his own internal conversation with an invisible raven and the dragon who was currently possessing part of his brain. Father Oni turned to him, "We are going this way. I believe the picture you saw can lead us to a series of translated cuneiform texts." They began walking down the tiled hallway between shelves of books. "Have you ever heard of the statue of Ozymandias?"

Bishop nodded but it was Ryan who spoke up, "Wasn't he the one who basically said, my empire will last forever. Look upon how awesome I am."

"Yes, and no. That Ozymandius is a poem written by Shelley. It's a fantastic poem about the frailty of human ambition. The real Ozymandias is better known to us today as Pharaoh Ramses the second. I believe some of the translated hieroglyphics from one of the temples he built can lead us to the right cuneiform texts."

"Right." Ryan looked over at Bishop and shrugged.

The Raven shifted his position on Bishop's shoulder, "Cuneiform. I like that word. It's fun. Have you ever seen cuneiform? It looks like a raven was dancing in wet clay. It's my favorite language. That and Chinese. Why do I know what Chinese writing looks like?"

Bishop really wished he could have a conversation with the Raven. He was the only person, person being an emotional term in this case, who really understood both parts of what was happening. He did have a monster living in his head who was being a little more talkative, but he felt having a conversation with the problem might not get the best results.

Cuneiform was one of the first fully developed written languages. It developed after everything happened.

The voice always surprised him, and it didn't help that he was trying to split his attention between what was going on with the books and some dragon in his head. It was also super weird that the thing who just half a day ago wanted to see the whole world burn was now wanting to have a pleasant conversation about the history of an ancient language.

"Peter," Father Oni had stopped, "do you mind if I call you Peter rather than Bishop as your college does?"

"No," Bishop hesitated, "that's fine, but what should I call you?"

"Father Oni would be traditional, but in this situation I understand you may need something quicker and a bit less formal, so Oni would be fine."

"I like him." The Raven was still trying to whisper. Bishop wasn't sure why since no one else in this world could see or hear him. "He's the same color as me and that instantly makes him more reliable. I bet he has some raven in his family tree."

You know that's not how humanity works, right?

Bishop was glad the dragon had said something because he was a bit concerned. On the other hand, how much should he really expect a raven to know about human biology?

Father Oni pointed to a row of blue spined books at shoulder height, "These are a catalog of anything considered supernatural during the reign of Ramses the second."

"Not to sound uneducated," Ryan looked between the two others, "but isn't basically everything from ancient Egypt considered supernatural? I mean they worshiped crocodile statues."

And cats.

The Raven's feathers rippled across Bishop's cheek and ear, "And that's why I don't like them. Who could worship those no account, bird hunting, arrogant, fuzz balls?"

I like cats. They take time to think things through, and they're very clean.

"Ugh," the Raven tapped the side of Bishop's head, "did you hear this guy? Literally citing all the reasons why cats aren't good. They sit around and think forever rather than acting, and they lick themselves. Everywhere. I, on the other wing, am a raven of action."

Father Oni nodded with a slight smile at Ryan, "To that extent you are correct. This section is a bit more specific, however. This section only applies to things of the supernatural sort that we might classify as either directly and provably demonic or so out of sorts with the rest of Egyptian mythology that it needed its own classification. The book Larry showed you a picture from was an offshoot of studies done in this section, but because we can't go and grab that book right now we shall begin our search here."

Bishop looked over the blue clad books, "Why can't we get that one?"

Ryan stared at him hard for a moment, "Really?" Bishop looked back at him and shrugged. Ryan sighed and said, "You smashed the whole room. Very loudly smashed it, I might add. That place should be crawling with security and who knows what other people. If we go wandering over there and ask if we could just grab that one book off the floor in the middle of all the carnage, there might be some questions."

Father One nodded emphatically, "A lot of questions, and asked with bars between you and the person asking them."

His shoulders slumped a bit. Bishop's mind had been so split between other worlds, voices in his mind, and a raven going on about how he didn't like cats, that he was having problems tracking with a normal conversation. "Of course. I'm just a little off my game today."

"I don't know," Ryan gave him a friendly shrug, "you took out what looked to be a very highly paid mercenary team with your bare hands. I would say your game's doing all right."

Bishop gave back the standard man to man nod and said, "Thanks." Turning to Father Oni he said, "So, basically, we skim through these looking for something I recognize then use that as a reference leading to more specific books."

"Yes," Oni said. "From your description of the image in the other book I was able to narrow it down to this section, but from here we need to do some serious sifting."

"How did you mentally narrow it down to here?" Bishop looked around at the thousands upon thousands of books.

"If you're implying that I know my way around all the books in the Vatican's library, then dispel that notion," Oni waved a hand at the multitude of books. "There are entire sections here which I have never visited. My specific calling does mean, however, that I need to be versed in the literature of some topics very well. You just happen to have fallen directly into my bailiwick."

Ryan reached for the last book in the row, "It's been a while since I passed a world history class…" He looked around, "Is there a table with some chairs, because I'm not standing and reading through the entire supernatural history of Egypt."

Father Oni pointed out a few reading nooks tucked away between shelves along the hallway they were in, and they started skimming their way through one book at a time. Soon, Bishop had three books in front of him opened to specific passages. They needed him to verify anything they'd found before they moved onto the specific connected volumes in this section of the library.

Two out of the three sounded very promising. Both were from Ryan. It turned out being in his line of work, whatever that was, needed a certain amount of natural IQ. His ability to skim and synthesize complex information was impressive. Bishop knew it was more than just natural IQ. That was a good starting point, but training and hours of practice taking multiple sources of information then being able to sift them for the common threads, was a truly learned skill. Looking up at the back of the possible mercenary, or intelligence operative, Bishop reassessed the soldier. Physically he was a tank, solid and able to plow through a problem. Thankfully he wasn't mentally a tank. Hopefully Sid, on the other side would show the same mental acuity. He was going to need to convince both of them to stick around through all of this. There was no way he could make it through without support. Every good lieutenant knew that.

*   *   *

"Do we have visual or just audio?" Patrick wasn't normally in the opp center, but this time he wanted to know what happened immediately so they could react to it in real time.

The main screen on the wall split into four smaller views and video of book shelves came into focus. He'd known they were supposed to have video, but they'd been having problems with the signal getting out of the Vatican buildings. Those walls were thick.

"We could lose the view at any time, sir." The soldier sitting at the control board looked on the young side. All the men here had been vetted and had all served time in a regular military unit. Most were American, but some hailed from other parts of the world. More and more lately American soldiers were looking for a more profitable way to continue their career. The skills they'd learned were difficult to master, but didn't translate naturally to civilian life, and they didn't want to waste all the time and effort they'd put into all of it.

"I understand. As long as we can keep the audio link up, we should be fine." Patrick turned to the commander, "I'm not trying to step on any toes." There was a fine line between maintaining control and letting people get on with their job. He wanted to let them know he was the one sitting at the top of the mountain, but didn't want them to get grumpy with him for interfering.

"I understand sir. I'll try to keep you in the loop."

Patrick nodded. He didn't need an explanation for anything. This was too important to him to leave simple knowledge to someone else. He'd taken the time to learn what each system did, and what each display was reading out. The time it would take to have someone explain a graph to him just so he could react to it would cause him to be minutes too late and was unacceptable.

Glancing around at the monitors, he picked the one showing heart beat readouts from the team in the library. "Could you replace that visual with an overlay of the map showing the positions of everyone on sight." He wasn't asking if it was possible. He knew it was.

The soldier at the console glanced up at the commander who nodded back at him. The screen flickered to an operating system then after a few clicks a black and white schematic of the library popped up with a glowing blue dot marking the position of each operative on site.

A camera check a few minutes ago had shown positive visuals on each exterior door. They didn't want to draw attention to themselves so the drones had landed and were silently acting as stationary cameras. The map showed at least two dots close enough to each door to be able to react to any attempt to leave the building. They had been instructed to simply block the doors and not engage if the target attempted to leave.

Patrick was fairly sure, after watching the last few interactions with his men, that the lieutenant could simply tear the doors out of the walls if they were locked, but he was also betting he wouldn't. He wasn't used to his new abilities yet. They weren't what he thought of first. His mind was still programmed like a normal human. If a door was locked, you tried to find another way around.

"Contact."

Looking back over to the main monitor he saw one of the new companions of the lieutenant. They hadn't taken the time to look up background information on the male. All Patrick knew was how he'd tripped one of his men in the fight earlier, and now here he was helping with some kind of research.

Talking with Marcus, they decided their target, Lieutenant Bishop, was trying to find some information on whatever was happening to him. It was the right move to make, and a smart one to come here specifically. Patrick had done his fair share of research here when all of this had started. The section they were currently in contained any number of books Patrick had found invaluable in their search.

The unknown male looked up from reading and their operative simply extended a hand and tapped the small taser to the back of his neck. The target stiffened and started to fall out of his chair. Catching him and pushing him back so he leaned against the wall, the operative pressed a needle into his arm and injected a small amount of a chemical designed to help with sleep. The combination of the electrical shock and the drugs had a chance of causing a heart attack, but Patrick was willing to take that risk.

One of the other sections of the monitor showed the same action with the female that had joined the group after the most recent failed attack. He really would need to look up their names and information. It was impressive how Bishop had been able to recruit such a disparate group of people to his cause, especially when his cause was so obviously strange.

The girl had been standing at the shelves and had to be quietly carried to a reading nook after being rendered unconscious. If everything went well, they should wake up a while later with a lot of aches from the taser and a bad case of cotton mouth from the chemicals, but no other problems, aside from the possible heart attack.

These two weren't the main problem. They could sound the alarm and maybe trip up a few of his men, but the main problem was who they referred to as the bodyguard. As opposed to the ones they'd just knocked out, Patrick had tried all of his channels to figure out who this man was. So far he'd had no positive replies. The few responses he'd gotten had simply said someone with that name and description didn't exist. It bothered him. Having an unknown like the female they'd just knocked out was one thing, but this obviously highly trained bodyguard was going to cause problems.

They had two plans in place. If they could get close enough they would attempt to incapacitate the bodyguard, but Patrick believed the other plan was the better of the two. If they were separated enough, and if they had a good window of opportunity, Patrick believed they could just ignore the bodyguard and go straight for the lieutenant. Hopefully, they could knock him out and remove him from sight before the bodyguard even noticed anything had gone wrong.

The camera view from the third agent swung around a corner and showed the lieutenant sitting at a desk in a small alcove. The desk was covered with books. Some were closed and stacked off to the side while a couple were open, and he was currently flipping pages on the closest one. Patrick wished he could take a closer look. He was certain he would recognize the books. It did give him a certain feeling of comradery with the lieutenant. They both sat in the same spot. Booth looking for the same answers, even with a little bit of the same sense of urgency, just with different motivations.

Seeing he was alone in the hallway of bookshelves, Patrick leaned over and said into a microphone, "You have a go to retrieve."

The lieutenant, on the monitor, looked up and nodded as their operative approached, "Father, what can I help you with?"

Their agent, dressed in the simple garb of a lower level priest, replied, "Do you have your library card? I just need to check some things."

"Oh," the lieutenant started patting his pockets and didn't notice the taser until it touched his neck.

Chapter Nineteen

Bishop snapped awake. The first rays of sunlight hitting his face through the bows of the pine tree he was sleeping under. The others, aside from Sid who was already up and chewing on something, blinked awake to the sounds of Bishop yelling and kicking the tree they'd slept under.

Larry looked at him, eyes peeking out from under the blanket he'd pulled up over his head during the night, "Uhm, what's wrong?"

"Did something crawl into your blanket?" Alex sat up on the other side of the camp. "Something crawled into my blanket. I don't really want to think about what it was. I got up to go pee and it took off."

"No," Bishop thought about his response, "I think the interaction with the dragon's having some side effects."

"Oh," the word quietly came out from under Larry's blanket.

Alex nodded sagely, as if this was something she'd been expecting, "Nightmares I bet." She glanced from Bishop to Larry, "Something like a dragon gets into your head and who knows what's going to happen in there."

The Raven landed on a branch of the pine tree a few feet away, "What was that?"

Bishop looked up at him, "Why didn't you warn me? I thought you were hanging around and keeping an eye out or something?"

The Raven hopped down to another branch, "Why?"

"Why would you keep an eye out?" Bishop raised his hands in a grand mock gesture, "Maybe because of the bad guys that might be attacking at any moment."

"Look," the Raven cocked his head, "some guy, who by the way looked exactly like every other guy in that place, walked up to you all polite and stuff. Then he pulled out this thing, and I thought to myself, wow that thing looks interesting, then he touched you with it and pow, here we are." The Raven fluffed his feathers, "In all that, what exactly did you want me to do?"

"I'm sorry," Larry finally sat up, but kept the blanket firmly pulled up to his chin, "what are you two talking about?"

Bishop looked over at Larry, then at Alex, "My magic talking raven friend and I are just having a disagreement about something that happened before we met you."

"Yeah, I am a magic talking raven, and this stuff definitely didn't happen here." The Raven hopped down onto the ground and started walking toward Bishop's pack, "Now, do you have anything good to eat in this thing?"

On their way out of town the day before, Cua had acquired some packs and supplies from friends who owed her favors or were just friendly. Bishop shewed the Raven away, "Go find something's dead eyes to eat."

"I looked." The Raven hopped up and tried to get a look into the pack, "Do you know how much harder it is to find things to eat when all these trees are in the way? Well," the Raven walked over to Alex's pack and started pulling at the drawstrings to open it up, "it's hard."

Alex stood up, walked over, and untied the drawstrings.

The Raven gave a low croak, "I was about to get it."

"I know you were." She smiled at him and dug around in her pack. Pulling out a strip of dried meat, she tossed it to him.

Snatching it out of the air the Raven beat his wings and landed on the lowest branch of the pine tree. Bishop walked over to him, "You could at least say thank you."

"Oh," he'd been holding the meat steady by pinning it onto the branch with one foot, "sorry. I don't normally hang out with humans." He bobbed his head at Alex, "Thank you. You can be sure that if I find something suitable I will bring it right back for you."

Bishop wandered away from the group as the Raven ate his breakfast and the others started to do the same. Light conversation trickled out to him from under the bending large bows of the evergreen they were camped under.

He wasn't sure what to do. Granted, he hadn't really been sure what to do about anything for a while now. Even his sense of time had gotten warped. Stopping and thinking about it, he realized time was moving differently depending on where he was. Back in the real world, it hadn't even been a single day since he'd woken up in the medical wing of the ship and had a very disturbing conversation with his Captain. They'd landed in Italy, taken a bus to the Vatican, and gone through the library. It was still the same day. It was just barely after lunch on the same day.

Here, however, multiple days had passed. He'd fallen asleep in the desert under a sage bush and woken up in a Bedouin camp. Then he'd woken up the next day in a cave, and walked through the night in the desert. Now here he was, another brand new day. That was, he ticked them off on his fingers, three, now four, days here to just one day back home? He was almost certain that when he woke up back home it would only be moments later, or at least that's the way it seemed to work before.

This situation felt different though. Someone, most likely one of the group of mercenaries who'd come after him two times now, had taken the time to dress up like a priest and knock him out. Who knows where they were dragging him to right now, and why hadn't something amazing happened to protect him.

"Seriously," he mumbled to himself as he heard the sound of water and headed toward it. "Are you there?" He tried to press his thoughts toward the constantly hovering presence in his head. There was no response.

"Right. When I don't want you around you pop out and destroy a section of the Vatican library. When I do want you around you're not even a glimmer." Picking up a rock and throwing it into the small creek he'd found, he said to the water, "I don't have anything figured out. Nothing. And why is this happening to me? I am literally nobody special. I am a gear in the great machine of the US Navy. The only people who know I exist are a few guys in my platoon and my commander."

His mind started tripping through multiple fractured thoughts about family and religion and how he was feeling picked on by the universe. The mental pictures and statements flickered by so quickly he didn't even need to finish thinking each thought before his mind jumped to the next, like hopping across a frozen river while the ice was breaking up under his feet.

"Peter?"

Looking up from the burbling water he saw Alex moving through the bushes and trees. She was younger than him, he thought, though probably not by much. It made her the youngest of the group. Bishop was fairly certain Sid, or Ryan, or whatever his name in this reality, was the oldest, and he got the feeling Larry was right there with himself at the same age.

Alex had her long dark hair pulled back into a slightly off center ponytail, and as she stopped next to him he saw she wasn't that much shorter than he was. Back at Cua's house he'd assumed she was rather petite, but it turned out he was just a bad judge of such things. He figured it didn't really matter how tall she was if she could constantly put an arrow on target.

"So," she bent over and picked up a rock from the edge of the creek, "life's a little bit crazy."

He chuckled and watched a swirl of whitewater create a perfect whirlpool on the back side of a rock in the creek. "To say the least."

"You seem to be handling it well."

"I don't really have a choice do I?"

174

"Sure you do." She tossed the rock and it landed with a satisfying plop in the middle of the creek. "I've wanted to get out of that little town for as long as I can remember. I would throw fits and scream and cry, to try and get my parents or my Nana to take me somewhere, anywhere, other than that small boring town. Looking back on it, now that I've made it out, I think I would've had more success with a different approach."

Bishop picked up a stick, tossed it in, and watched it float away. It brought back memories of his family racing sticks dropped into any river they could find from one side of a bridge to the other. "And after your one day of freedom?"

"I think me throwing little, or maybe big, tantrums actually proved to them I wasn't ready for anything outside of town. If I had made a different choice it would have shown them I had a little bit more maturity and could handle a trip." She tossed a stick into the water and it immediately was caught in an eddy of water and trapped against a rock. Looking over at him she said, "I think we all have a choice about how we handle a situation. You could be throwing a tantrum, but instead you're trying to find answers."

Bishop let that statement quietly sit with him for a moment, then said, "Thank you, Alex."

She smiled, looking over the creek, "No one's ever called me that. I like it. A new name for a new adventure." Glancing over at him she hesitantly said, "Speaking of adventure and such things, that was a fairly lame excuse about the argument you were having with your raven."

Bishop sucked in a deep breath and let it out through his nose, "It was. There are more things going on here than just a dragon stopping by for a chat."

"I thought so. We've never had a dragon around here before, but I didn't think it would show up and talk with someone, and then nothing else would happen."

"You're a wise woman Alex."

She snorted out a single laugh, "That's new. My friends, my family, and random strangers now that I think about it, all say I tend to talk too much, and none of it would be considered wise."

"So maybe you express your wisdom differently than others."

She grinned, "Or louder."

They both laughed, and Bishop realized, in that moment, all his muddled thoughts about this situation had calmed. It wasn't that he had anything new figured out. There were no epiphanies during his conversation with Alex, but he realized having companions, maybe even friends, made all the difference. He didn't need to have it all figured out as long as he had people with him who were willing to help.

"Thanks." His voice was quiet and almost drowned out by the murmuring of the creek.

She shrugged, "We all noticed you'd walked away."

"And you drew the short straw?"

She looked over at him, confusion on her face, "Uhm, no? What does that even mean?"

"It's a way of choosing when no one actually wants to do the thing, or have the conversation."

"Oh… no, that's not it. Sid just looked the other way, Larry said something about not knowing what to say or how to talk to people or something like that, and the Raven had his mouth stuffed full of dried meat, so here I am."

"Well, thanks anyway." He looked around and tried to make a mental note of the scenery. It was beautiful here. The bright dew covered green of the grass and bushes contrasting with the darker shades of pine. The flashing, rippling, creek. It was a painting waiting to happen. "We should get back, and start down the road."

It didn't take much time to bundle up the few possessions they'd brought with them. For Bishop it consisted of only a rolled up blanket some friend of Cua's had given him. No pillow meant he'd needed to use his arm, and with no sleeping mat he'd had to make the decision to either lay on the one blanket he had and stay off the ground or sleep on the ground and try to conserve some warmth with the blanket on him. Needless to say, it hadn't been a comfortable night. Except, he didn't remember any of it. Had he tossed and turned? Had he woke up in the middle of the night because he'd rolled onto a rock? No memories at all. After falling asleep he was right back in the other world. It might be a blessing in disguise. Who knows what was happening to his unconscious self back in the real world. All he knew was they were walking down a dirt road in this world.

"Sid…"

Sid looked over at Bishop as they walked.

"You seem to have made your way around these parts before. Have you ever been to this monastery?"

He shook his head, "I knew it was there. Most people around these parts do, but if you aren't specifically looking to improve your soul, or whatever a monastery does, there's no need to head up there."

"I was told," Larry turned and walked backward to face them for a few paces, "it has nothing to do with true religion."

"Let me guess," Alex chimed in, "the priest at church told you that."

"Well, yes," Larry slowed down until he was walking side by side with her, "but why wouldn't he know?"

"Oh, he knows everything. At least according to him." Before Larry could get a word out of his mouth she went on, "It's a tiny town, with a tiny church. If he really was as wise and knowledgeable as he constantly lets on, then why is he there and not in some big cathedral in some big city?"

Before Larry could respond Bishop put his hand on his shoulder to steer the conversation back, "Why would he say it's not part of the normal religion?"

"Well," he gave a sideways glance at Alex to see if she was going to interrupt him, "none of the clergy ever goes up here. They come through town, see that everything's working the way it's supposed to, and head right on out."

"Okay, but how do you know they don't stop here on their way out?" Bishop asked.

"Because I listen."

"He means," Alex pointedly didn't look over at them, "he hangs out around the church a lot and eavesdrops on what they're talking about."

Larry blushed, "Not intentionally. It's just that the church is the only place in town with more than one book. The priest lets me read them and sometimes, maybe, I hear what the visiting clergy is talking about. None of them ever talk about coming up here. One of them, in fact, talked about how the," he put one hand on his hip and pointed a finger of the other hand into the air to mimic the old priest, "old religion," he let his hands drop, "shouldn't even have a monastery anymore."

"Raven," normally Bishop would just need to turn his head and ask, but ever since Alex had given him a strip of meat he'd insisted on riding on her shoulder. "Do you know anything about the monastery?"

The Raven looked over at him, "I think I know what a monastery is, but beyond that, unless it's dead and lying in the sun back in my treeless wonderland, I have no idea."

Bishop again searched his mind for the voice. The weight of a presence was still huddled in the back rooms of his mind, but no one was talking. The way the Raven had put it the other day, or the other moment in a different world, made some sense if you didn't think about it too much. The presence in his head was simply a small copy of the real thing and couldn't interact very much on its own. Or maybe it was just brooding for some unknown, multiple reality, I have a dragon living in my head, reason.

They found the fork in the path easy enough. It wasn't a well traveled trail they turned onto, but it seemed to be maintained, or at least not choked with weeds. It was a sharp uphill turn and within a few minutes even Alex was out of breath. The last words out of her mouth were to ask the Raven to ride somewhere else, or to, and she put this more delicately than Bishop could have, use his own wings instead of just hitching a ride.

Eventually the path turned into stairs and as they came around a copse of trees a large building came into view. Its resemblance to a Tibetan monastery was uncanny. Bishop, however, wasn't one to scoff at these kinds of things since he'd met multiple people who were exactly the same between two separate realities. Apparently you could get used to anything, no matter how ridiculous it was.

It was tucked away between a cliff face climbing up the mountain on the left and a sheer drop back down to where the creek had become a river on the right. The white walls and red tile roof contrasted sharply with the slate gray of the cliff face and the dark green of the few pine trees scattered around the grounds of the building. Multiple windows looked out from the separate layers of the monastery, with the roof of the first layer eventually becoming the floor of the next. In the far back, perched at the edge like a peninsula surrounded by air rather than water, was a square, white tower, capped with a bright red pyramid shaped roof.

Bishop immediately wondered what was in the tower. In all the stories boys make up in their minds, the tower has either the treasure or the solution to the mystery hidden in it. Some would say that's where a main character would be imprisoned, but that's a ridiculous statement to anyone with an imagination. Towers like that were way too cool to use as a prison.

The stairs stopped almost fifty yards from the main gate, and the top of the stairs were framed with pillars. Actually, as Bishop approached them, out of breath from the climb, he noted they would more rightly be called obelisks. Laying a hand on one he traced the carved images crawling up to the pointed top.

"They're the same."

Larry stepped up and looked, "The same as what?"

Bishop hadn't really meant to say it out loud and was slightly surprised someone had heard him, however, "You might know better than I would. Actually," he turned to face his traveling companions who had all stopped for a breather at the top of the stairs, "do any of you know about a collapsed temple at the oasis a couple days walk from town?"

Standing next to him, Larry reached out and touched the carvings, "Any temples from the old religion would have been struck from the records of the church. I don't remember reading anything about them."

Alex stood from where she'd been resting on the stairs and walked over, "The church really doesn't like people thinking about what came before them. They probably have records of where all the old temples were located just so they can keep an eye on things, but our little town wouldn't have had anything like that."

Bishop turned to his shapeshifting companion, "Sid?"

Sid lowered the water skin he'd been drinking from, "Sure, everyone who trades or travels across the area knows about that place." He shrugged, "There's nothing special to know."

"Any idea what it was, or why it was pulled down?"

"Remember when I told you my grandma would always tell us stories about the beginning times, and how the dragon would roam around doing stuff?" Bishop nodded and Sid continued, "That's the old religion. It was centered around the dragon. That's why so many people are freaking out about a dragon roaming around, and why, once word gets out, the church will be coming for you. They don't really like competition."

Alex looked over at Bishop, "Why?"

"I happened to take a look through the ruins before pulling Sid out of a cage."

"What?" Alex and Larry both looked over their shoulders at Sid.

"Story for another time," Bishop looked over as the Raven landed on the top of the last step. "Anyway, inside were all these carvings and pictures. A lot of them looked just like this."

"I knew it." Larry stepped back and looked up and the obelisk, "I knew this place had to do with the old religion."

"If the church doesn't like competition," Bishop looked back at Sid, "then why is this still here?"

Sid shrugged. He didn't seem like the kind to care about something unless it directly had to do with him or whatever his current job was. If this was anything like back in the real world, his job would be something of a mercenary. Having the ability to change shape would seriously help with that.

"Who knows," said Alex. "Maybe they don't care as long as it keeps to itself. I haven't exactly heard of anyone coming from here and trying to convince people that the church is wrong, and like Larry said, no one ever comes here."

"Or," the Raven hopped a few steps farther and stopped at a silver line crossing the wide pathway to the front gate, "they couldn't get in."

Bishop wanted to keep looking at the obelisks but realized it wouldn't make any difference since he, and apparently everyone else, couldn't read the inscriptions. Instead, he walked over to where the

Raven was still staring down at the silvery line in the stone walkway. It glittered and reflected the sun like water in a creek as he walked toward it. Squatting down he realized it was a ribbon of metal, maybe even silver, and it stretched farther than just the walkway. Standing up he tried to follow it with his eyes. It arced away in either direction, and he assumed, formed a circle. He wasn't sure how, or if it even connected anywhere, since the monastery was built directly onto the sheer rising wall of the mountainside.

A shadow blocked out the sun for a moment and Bishop heard Alex swear. Glancing back, he saw them all looking up. Following their line of sight he watched as the dragon settled itself onto the rock face of the mountain just to their left. It perched there, grasping onto small rock outcroppings Bishop never would have thought could hold the weight of something that large. It's wings were extended, twisting, keeping its balance. Eventually it settled in. It was too far away to be a threat, and there was no way Bishop was going to climb up those rocks to ask what in the world was going on.

Stepping involuntarily away from it, he crossed over the line. The air shimmered and he felt the muscles in his shoulders and neck relax. Taking in a deep breath and letting it out slowly he realized something was different. Looking up at the dragon he searched his mind. The lump of separate consciousness that had been living in the basement of his mind was gone.

The Raven let out a rwack and landed hard on Bishop's shoulder, "Who is…"

Glancing over to where the Raven was looking, Bishop twitched, almost knocking the Raven loose. Standing to his right was a man. He was dressed immaculately in a black pinstripe suit with a gray button up shirt, a silver vest decorated in a scale pattern, and a matching black tie. Dark black hair was slicked back and parted perfectly around two very prominent glossy black horns. His feet were bare exposing black scaled toes ending in reflective claws. His hands hung straight beside him, and were surprisingly human after seeing what his feet were like.

Leaning over the Raven whispered, "Those are the same horns as you get when you go all crazy."

"Right." On the one hand, Bishop was glad to see how it all looked when things had been, as the Raven put it, going crazy. On the other hand, "You." Bishop walked up to the man, "You were in my head."

The man nodded, then gave a slight bow, "I would say, at your service, but I'm not."

Bishop stepped forward and punched the man in the nose. The swing dislodged the Raven who fluttered around Bishop's head then landed on his other shoulder. The horned man's head snapped back, but that was all the reaction he gave to the assault.

A groaning and creaking noise drew his attention momentarily away from the horned man. The barn door sized gates of the monastery slowly opened. He guessed it was only a matter of time before any monks living inside noticed a giant dragon and a group of people on their doorstep. From the small opening in the doors Bishop could see a man dressed in a flowing black robe exit. It took only a few moments for the man to get close enough.

"Of course it's you." Bishop threw up his hands and began walking toward the gates into the monastery.

The Raven leaned forward peering at the approaching monk then broke out laughing.

The monk slowed as Bishop approached and extended a hand, "Welcome honored guest…"

Not slowing down, Bishop walked past the monk and through the gates into the monastery. Inside was an open entryway with some seating scattered around the edges next to fountains that bubbled pleasingly. The walls were whitewashed and gleamed where the sunlight made it through the open windows. At the back of the room a stairway led to the next level of the monastery and Bishop, without pausing, headed up.

"Any idea where we're going?" The Raven looked back over their shoulders to see the others hurrying to catch up.

"Nope, but my guess is, if this is some place dedicated to worshiping a dragon, they would have some books or scrolls or something like that."

"Why not just ask father what's his name back there?"

Glancing back down the stairs Bishop saw the monk, or priest, or whatever he was, closing the main doors. His dark skin and short cropped hair matched exactly with the priest back in the Vatican library. "I guess I shouldn't be surprised. Everyone else has a double. We wouldn't want him to be left out."

"And," the Raven hopped on Bishop's shoulder, "he was working in a library so this one should also have something like that."

Bishop nodded, "That's what I said."

"No," the Raven looked around as they exited the stairwell, "you said the monastery should have something like that. I'm saying everyone else who's doubled has matched in some way, so it only stands to reason that the guy with some answers back there should also be the guy with some answers over here."

"It's all just a bit too convenient." Bishop slowed and looked around at the new room, trying to decide where to go.

"Really?" The Raven nudged him toward the next set of stairs, "Because I don't think anything that's happened so far has been convenient."

"You think it'll all be in that tower at the back?"

"No," the raven said. "I mean, something will be in there, but a library needs more room than that."

"True."

"Peter!" Alex's voice echoed up the stairwell. "Slow down."

Bishop stopped at the next landing and waited. Panting, one hand on the wall for support, Alex stopped at the top of the stairs. "Seriously." She held her free hand up and waved at him to sit down on one of the many pillows or couches around the room. "You need to wait for the rest of us." Looking down the stairs then back to Bishop she shook her head, "I'm fairly sure Larry's going to die. I might die." Stepping farther into the room she collapsed onto a large pillow resting against the wall. "Sid looked like he was just taking a pleasant walk, and you," she pointed a finger at him like it was one of her arrows, "who runs up two flights of stairs after climbing a mountain? And," she leaned toward the stairs and looked down, "who's the weird looking guy you punched in the face?"

Voices carried up from the level below. Bishop recognized the voice of the priest from the Vatican. Maybe the Raven was right. Maybe he should just ask. There was no way he was going to wander around this place and find answers to anything. He'd just been so angry. The monster in his head could have left at any time? Another duplicate from his world showing up here. Taking a deep breath, he remembered what Alex had said back at the creek. He did have a choice about how he reacted to situations, and choosing to punch the horned monster in the face had been the right one.

Glancing from Alex to the stairs Bishop said, "There was a giant crystal that blew up and got a bunch of pieces in me. I was infected with part of the dragon's mind, I think. The guy back there is that part of the dragon's mind. He's been a real jerk."

Alex tilted her head, "I get the feeling that is the short version."

The Raven hopped to a table in the corner of the room, "Oh, totally the short version. It leaves out all the duplicates, and the other world..." he paused in front of a golden statue of a cross legged man with a bowl in his outstretched hands. Sticking his beak in he pulled out a gold ring. Setting it down on the table he pushed it forward with his beak. "Put this in your pocket."

Bishop stepped up to the table, "Why? Is it magical, or going to be important later?"

"No," the Raven looked up at him, "I like it, and I don't have any pockets."

The others slowly straggled up the stairs. Alex had been right about Larry and Sid. The former looked like he might puke with every new stair and the latter didn't seem to care at all. Sid had taken the precaution of coming up the stairs behind the horned man, and Bishop mentally thanked him for that. Sid didn't know who this new figure was, all he knew was Bishop didn't seem to like him.

The priest came up last, stopped at the top of the stairs, and smiled at Bishop, "Welcome…"

"Sure," Bishop frowned a little. "Look, I'm assuming your name is Oni, or something like it. It's nice to meet you except it's not really because I'm getting a bit tired of whatever these games are." The monk started to say something and Bishop held up a hand to stop him, "I would like the answers to be straightforward and lack any type of riddle or mystery."

"And," the raven hopped to the edge of the table, "we would like something to eat."

"Well," the monk, who had folded his hands in front of him and waited patiently for Bishop to finish, nodded, "I would love to give you answers. This is a unique time, especially with our other guest." He tilted his head to indicate the horned man. "The problem is, I don't know your questions."

"Really?" Bishop walked over to a window looking out over the entrance, "With that sitting out there staring at us, you're saying you have no idea what we're going to ask about."

The monk took in a deep breath and walked over to look out the same window, "The dragon has returned. It's been thousands of years. What I know tells me this is not a good situation." He turned and looked at Bishop, "There is nothing in my information about you. I have knowledge of the past, of what the dragon is, and why it was gone for so long, but I don't know you or this one." Again he nodded at the horned man.

"That one," Bishop turned to look at the strange horned guest, "is some type of representation, or fragment of, the mind of Mr. Dragon out there. He's been living in my head for a while. Isn't that right old grumpy pants?"

The man nodded, "As the monk said, I don't have all the answers either, but you are correct in saying who I am. I am the dragon, or at least a part of him. I was fractured and unstable when we first met, but when you interacted with my whole self, things were, how can I say it, put right."

The monk looked between the two of them, "So," his gaze stopped on the nicely dressed avatar of the dragon, "can I safely say that you are acting as a direct representative of the dragon?"

The man inclined his head, "More than that. I am the dragon. Here, in this place, with the magics holding it all together, I am able to present myself in this way. I thought it would be helpful for all involved to have a real conversation."

Bishop looked at them both, "Okay," he paused and rubbed at his temples. "First question. Why are you in my head at all? Why me?"

The dragon nodded at the question, "A valid question, and let me be clear, I am not trying to be confusing. The answer to that question has a few separate moving parts. Let me start with, why you. I don't know. I am no longer privy to the counsel of the Ageless One. I don't know why He designed for you to be the one standing there at that moment in time. I would ask my little brother here," he pointed a thumb over his shoulder, indicating the Raven who'd gone back to digging through the bowl of shiny objects, "but, if nothing's changed, he's had about as much interaction with that realm as I have lately. I could make some statement about how you've obviously been chosen, but I truly have no idea.

"How I ended up inside your mind, however, I can answer. First, some visual help would be useful." The dragon turned and headed up the next flight of stairs. This time the top of the landing split off into multiple directions with doors and a long hallway ending in another flight of stairs. "If I remember correctly, granted it has been a very long time..." he walked to a large door carved with the same symbols from the obelisk and temple and the tunnel leading into the cave with the crystal and pushed it open. "Yes, here we are."

The room was large, and for all intents and purposes seemed to be a library. The walls were partially lined with shelves. Books didn't fill them, but instead they held massive amounts of rolled up scrolls. Some were simply rolled and tucked in with others while in other places they were held in wooden tubes or tucked into cubby holes. Between the shelves were pictures. On the far wall the pictures were multiple stained glass windows stretching from floor to ceiling. The sun was currently on the other side of the building, but even with the defused light coming through, the windows cast multi-hued rippling light across the room. The pictures between the shelves were anything from painted directly onto the wall, carved from stone or wood and leaned against the wall or done as a mural, tiled with chips of colored rock. They seemed to have been collected from multiple locations and brought here.

"Ahh," the dragon looked around, "I was just going to use the windows, but I see other pieces have been added since I've been gone."

The monk moved into the room and looked around, "Welcome to the library. The additions you noticed are from the temples. We tried our best to recover whatever we could before they were torn down or burned."

Larry was already at the nearest shelf, hands folded behind his back so as not to touch anything accidentally, and trying to read one of the labels that had been conveniently placed on each shelf. "Pre dynastic archipelagian politics." He glanced over his shoulder at the monk then at Bishop.

The dragon shook his head, horns shimmering in the light cast by the giant windows. "I'm sorry, we don't have time for that." He turned to one large stone leaning against the wall. It was painted with small red figures holding what looked like ropes in their hands. The ropes led to a larger figure, wrapping around it and holding it in place. "Each of these tells a version of the same story. Some have more detail, some are very, how should I say, primitive, but in all, it's the same story. The story of how I got here, which in turn leads to the story of how you got here."

He turned and looked at Bishop, "I don't mean to turn an answer into a tale, but the only way to understand it, is to tell it all. If I simply said there was a magic rock, then you would ask why it was there, and what it has to do with you, or me. So rather, I will start at the beginning. Well," he looked over at the raven for a moment, "not quite the beginning, that's a bit too far back."

Looking around he waved for them to find seats if they wanted. Sid had already settled in, and Larry looked torn between listening to a dragon tell a story and looking at all the scrolls in the room, but eventually decided on a chair. Alex, met eyes with Bishop. They both seemed to shrug and mutually decided nothing else could be done at the moment so why not. Bishop picked a seat halfway into the room and Alex deliberately walked behind the dragon and sat down there. Smiling at her, Bishop was starting to think she might be the smartest one in the group.

"My job for millennia was to, how should I put it, help with the…"

He hesitated, and in that hesitation the monk said, "He was death. Not all the time, mind you, but still he was the one that, when things needed to be done, he did it."

"Not the way I would have phrased it, but succinct."

"If a town needed punishing," the monk went on, "for whatever reason, he was the one sent in to drop a meteorite on it."

"That..." The dragon shook his head, "That did happen." He turned and looked at the first of the stained glass windows. It showed a man, robbed all in white. His right hand was outstretched and droplets of fire fell from his fingertips.

After a few moments of silence the monk continued, "After thousands of years going about his job faithfully he decided enough was enough. We believe there was one event in particular that led to the decision. He was called on by the Ineffable one to, how should I put this, remove all the children of an entire nation."

The dragon let his head droop. After a few moments of silence he turned, "I went through with it. It was my job after all. It was what I was created for, and there's no getting around that. Well," he looked over at where the Raven was poking his head into a scroll, "that's not entirely true, but it wasn't the choice I was prone to make. However, somewhere in the middle of it all..."

The monk stepped in again, "We aren't sure, even here in the middle of all the research and study on the topic, exactly what happened. The being who once was that," the monk gestured to the white clad figure in the first window, "became that," and he pointed to the next window. This time the central figure was the dragon they all recognized. Fire bellowed from its open mouth and his wings visibly stopped the rays of light coming from the sun so only darkness was below it.

The dragon stepped over and placed a hand on the dark panes of glass, looking up at the dragon etched in shades of gray and outlined in ribbons of lead. "I went mad. It's a hard thing to say, especially for one of my kind. We have seen madness in our ranks before, but not like this. Their madness was one of calculated choices and arrogance, this..." he shook his head, "this was something different." He looked over at the monk. "To be honest, I haven't felt this lucid and talkative since it happened. I don't know why that is." Looking over at Bishop he tilted his head, "Maybe it's you acting as a sort of filter, and maybe, Peter, we both need some answers."

The monk looked between the two then turned to the final window, "The civilized nations of the world were in chaos. There had never been a dragon in the world before. They didn't know what to do about him. They couldn't kill him."

"Believe me," the dragon said, "they tried."

"The weapons of the day just weren't up to the task of removing one of the immortals," the monk said. "However, while they couldn't kill him, they could bind him. That had been proven."

"I don't remember a lot..."

"I remember the shiny thing." Everyone looked over at the Raven, now standing on the head of a cross legged statue. He looked

186

at the last window, the light streaming through glimmered in multiple shades of red. Pink, rose, orange and burgundy rippled across the shelves and carpet. "I remember they asked me to find the best one. Why do I remember that?" He looked at Bishop then over at the dragon.

The dragon shrugged, his shoulders rising and falling slowly, "I don't know, little brother. I didn't even know you were involved until right now."

"There was a man," the Raven looked around the room, "he said something to me and I..." his feathers ruffled and he quickly tucked his head under his wing.

The dragon stared at the Raven for a moment, "The shiny thing was the crystal."

Bishop had been staring at the last window. He hadn't realized what it was when he came into the room. Too much focus had been on the dragon himself. What was he going to do? What was he going to say? Now, however, the crystal glinted at him from the stained glass of the window and from the pictures of his memory. It was standing in the middle of a cave surrounded by terrorists. A man raised a trigger for a claymore. Shivering he looked back over to the dragon and made eye contact.

"They bound me inside the crystal." The dragon pointed up at the window and all the people ringed around the crystal. "Working together they found a way to catch me and bind my spirit."

"So," Bishop stood up and walked over to the dragon, "we're inside the crystal? We can't be." He looked back up at the window, "It blew up."

The dragon nodded, "And this is where things get murky. My memory of that time is, shall we appropriately say, fractured. I know I was in a cage for a long time, then something happened and I was able to fly again. I could feel you out there. I was angry and wanted to burn everything."

Bishop nodded, "I remember."

"I found you once, at night, but you disappeared. I tried to follow you, but only part of me succeeded. Then, I found you again in a little village by a river, I was able to..." He sighed and shrugged.

"No," Bishop shook his head, "you don't get to just end the sentence there. Why are all these people the same as the ones back home? Why am I being tossed from one world to the other? Is this all in your mind? Is it all in my mind?"

The monk reached up and put a hand on Bishop's shoulder, "It's not all in your mind, and it's not in his. I'm not even sure I know what you mean by the people being the same, but I do know this is a real place."

"So," Bishop looked again from stained glass window to stained glass window, "you're basically the angel of death."

The dragon shook his head, "There's no such thing as the angel of death. There's no being responsible for the deaths of all people, or similarly responsible for ushering the souls of the dead off to their proper places in the afterlife. No one being, excepting Him of course, can even be in more than one place at a time."

Bishops shook his head, "Semantics," he looked over at Sid who shrugged then nodded. "Whatever, you dealt with killing people when they needed killing."

"If you want to put it that harshly and ignore all of the reasoning behind what I did..."

"And eventually you did something even you couldn't handle, so you snapped." Bishop walked over and put a hand on the second window. Looking up at the image of the dragon he knew exactly what was going on. "It's what we call post traumatic stress disorder. Most people with it have a hard time dealing with normal life. Certain sounds have a chance of setting them off, or it might be the bumping and jostling of a crowd that does it.

"I had a buddy who was driving a humvee when they were hit with a roadside improvised explosive. He still can't get behind the wheel of a car. He's tried, but every time his heart rate shoots through the roof, and his breathing goes crazy. A few times he sat there and tried so hard that he caused himself to pass out from lack of oxygen."

"I am one of the immortals." Bishop looked over and the dragon had his arms tightly crossed, "I am one of the strongest beings in this universe. I didn't have a mental breakdown."

The floor jolted under Bishop's feet and several scrolls tumbled off the shelves. A moment later a second concussion ripped through the room, causing the wooden panel to tip away from the wall and crash to the floor.

"Look," Bishop pointed to the dragon, "just because you don't like what I said..."

"It's not..." The dragon flickered. He was there then not and back again. "The boundary is..." He flickered again and was gone.

Everyone was on their feet and Sid grabbed the monk by his shoulder, "What is happening?"

"This way." The monk led them out of the library and back into the hall. Looking out the windows they could see a mass of people milling around in the space between the stairs and the gate. "We believe, as you heard in the story, that this place was partly designed to be his prison. He'd lost control and the people of your world locked him up here. It only stands to reason that any prison would have..."

The floor shook again causing the monk to lose his balance and grab for the wall.

"Guards," Sid finished for him.

The monk nodded as he straightened up, "Or something like that. Some kind of mechanism to try and contain him if he were to ever slip his bonds."

"Well where'd he go," Sid pointedly looked out one of the windows as they hurried past.

Bishop noticed the lack of a giant black dragon, "He's right."

"Yeah," Larry said, "why couldn't he just burn them to little bits of ash?"

"This has never happened before." The monk pulled a key from a pocket in his robe, steadied himself with one hand against the wall and unlocked a simple looking wooden door. Behind it another set of stairs led up to another floor of the monastery. "We always assumed there were defenses built into the system, but we didn't know what." He led them up the stairs and into a hallway that Bishop realized, when he looked out the windows, was actually an enclosed bridge leading to the tower they'd seen earlier. "Before the church decided to tear down all the temples there might have been information located in those about all of this, but they're long gone into the fires of religious zealotry."

They stopped at another locked door at the end of the bridge. "Wait," Bishop put a hand on the monk's arm, "I'm here to figure out how to fix this, and while the story back there was nice and all, I still haven't heard anything about getting him out of my head for good and getting back home."

The monk turned the key in the lock and opened the door, "This," he paused and locked eyes with Bishop, "wasn't supposed to happen. There's nothing in all of our literature about your situation. I'm sorry. The best I can do is point you in a good direction." They stepped through into a circular room dominated by a curving staircase descending from floor level down into darkness. "You need to figure out the mechanism used to trap him here. It might be that is also holding him in your head. Maybe," the monk nodded to himself, "maybe you took the place of the crystal when it was destroyed. Either way you need to find his original cage and study it."

"Great," Bishop looked over his shoulder at his companions, "and where is that?"

"I have no idea," the monk shrugged.

"What?" Larry stepped up to within a few inches of the monk's face, "There are things, or people, or whatever, out there trying to kill us, and the one thing this monastery was literally built for is knowledge of the dragon, and you don't know where he was locked up?"

Inside, Bishop grinned at the man's reaction. It was good to see someone else was as frustrated as he was about the situation, and it was always nice to have someone else lose their cool for once.

"You have to know something," Alex stood with an arrow knocked and pointed back the way they'd come, and again Bishop was grateful she was with them.

"True," the monk nodded at her. "The order here at the monastery was always about gathering knowledge, especially after the destruction of the temples. Others of our order were worried we academics would become too curious in our search for answers."

"They thought you'd set him free," Sid said.

"Not intentionally, and not to just set him free on the world again, but," the monk nodded, "yes, they were worried about us wanting to get too close to him."

Alex loosed the arrow and a scream echoed down the hallway and bounced around the stone room they stood in, "You should have closed the doors behind you," she said as she readied another arrow. "What's the point of having locks on all of them if you're just going to…" she let another arrow fly and it was followed with an accompanying cry of pain.

"Down and out," the monk pointed. "Follow the river to its source and there will be a single building. Inside you'll find a map. It should lead you to his cage."

Half a dozen steps down and Bishop heard the door into the room close and lock. He had no problem with the monk, or the priest in the other world, and hoped everything would be okay. If they, whoever they were, were really after him, to stop him from letting the dragon out, then they should leave him alone, hopefully.

The stairs weren't lit, and after a few turns the light from above faded then disappeared entirely. "So," Larry's voice floated down from above, "I have some questions."

Chapter Twenty

Crusty gunk stuck his eyelids together, and when he tried to reach up and wipe it away his arm wouldn't move. Trying again only caused a twinge of panic as he realized both his arms were strapped down. After a few deep breaths he tried to assess his situation.

Starting with how he'd gotten here which made him realize now he had two different reasons for being anywhere. He remembered the library at the Vatican, and how someone, obviously dressed as a priest and not really being a priest, had knocked him out with something. On the other side of things, he'd slipped. They'd made it to the bottom of the stairs and out the door. A lot of questions had flown down those stairs, and he'd tried his best to be honest, but the whole situation was insane, so he wasn't sure if honesty really was the best thing at that moment.

Beyond the door was a river, just like the monk had said. Crossing the river had been the problem. He remembered stepping on what looked like a solid rock, and the feel of it shifting under his foot. Now, here he was. What happened if he died over there? Did he die here, or could he not die over there because all that would happen is him waking up over here? He didn't really want to test out the theory.

In his immediate situation Bishop could feel the thin pad and flat rack of a medical gurney. They'd drugged him and strapped him down to a gurney. There were straps across his legs in multiple places. One stretched across his chest, and others kept his arms down at the wrists. Taking a deep breath he scrunched his face up and finally got his eyes to pop open.

They hadn't strapped his head down so he had a modicum of movement to look around and assess his situation. The room he was in obviously wasn't a room. Someone had converted the back of an ambulance into something resembling a mobile command center. The cabinets that usually housed the medical supplies had been converted into computer racks and video monitors.

Over his head, where he couldn't see, would be the driver's seat, and with all the bumps Bishop assumed they were actively driving somewhere. He had to assume there were two men up front, one driving and another in the passenger seat.

The crackle of a communications set led to a voice, "How's traffic?"

"Oh, it's about as good as can be expected for an afternoon in Rome. Do you see any accidents or problems on your end?"

"No, everything's clear."

"Good, then the ETA should hold true."

"The boss wants a word with Marcus."

"Sure."

A new voice came over the line, "Marcus, can you pull up a video feed, please."

A third voice, one who Bishop assumed was Marcus, replied, "Sure, just give me a moment." Movement above his head told Bishop the passenger was attempting to extract himself from the front seat and move back into the main cabin. Closing his eyes and trying his best to settle his breathing, Bishop hoped that Marcus wouldn't notice he was already awake.

Clicking on a keyboard had Bishop picturing someone entering their username and password. It was followed by a few distinct clicks of a mouse then, "Hello, Patrick."

"Marcus. I just wanted to have a look at our esteemed guest."

"Of course. Will you be waiting for us at the site, or should I let you know when we get there?"

"There's no reason for me to wait. I'll head out to the helicopter when we're done here. Less chance of anything going wrong if we do this as quickly as possible."

Bishop slowly raised an eyelid and tried to get a look at the monitor, but Marcus was sitting in front of it and he couldn't get a good look. Presumably this was the man responsible for the mercenary attacks on him. He couldn't imagine why someone would go to these lengths to get him. Then the events of the past day seemed to crash down on his mind, and everything simplified. Well, he said to himself, everything about these attacks simplified. There were still some very outstanding pieces of information that were not simplified at all, but for the immediate situation it was clear. Power. He had it. Some guy named Patrick wanted it. Simple.

"Hang on Patrick," Bishop snapped his eye closed as Marcus turned. "What are you doing awake so soon?"

Both of Bishop's eyes opened and he looked directly at Marcus. Now would be a great time for a dragon, a real dragon, living in his head to pop out and trample this place. He saw fear creep onto Marcus' face as Bishop started straining against the straps holding him down.

A little rage and smashing anger would be helpful right about now, Bishop thought. Reaching back into his mind he searched for that knot of presence that had haunted him since waking up on his ship, and while it was there, it was only a tiny echo of what it had been.

Fear and joy flashed through him at the same moment. Maybe, when the fancy suit dressed version had popped out of his head to have that conversation at the monastery, he hadn't been able to get back in. Maybe he was gone. Separately, if he was gone, then how was he going to get out of this, and how would he convince crazy pants on the monitor over there that he didn't have the magic juju living in his head anymore?

A shrill beep snapped him back to the immediate situation. Warmth flooded up his left arm and overwhelmed his senses. Reaching for that small echo of the dragon his last thought was, where'd you go?

*   *   *

The cotton mouth was the worst. Larry rethought that. The cottonmouth was bad, but after three large glasses of water he was feeling better. The worst was the spot they'd tasered him. The muscles were still trying to cramp up in his neck. If he tilted his head a little too much to the left every muscle on that side from his shoulder blade all the way to whatever was on top of his head tried to clench up and run away screaming.

Come to think of it, the headache had been pretty bad too, but the four Ibuprofen he'd taken with the second large glass of water was finally starting to kick in. "Any luck?"

Ryan shook his head and continued typing furiously on his phone. Standing up Larry walked over to where Alex was stretched out on the floor, her arm across her eyes and a jacket acting as a pillow. "How you feeling?"

A groan was followed by, "Remind me why I agreed to help?"

Larry squatted down next to her, "The adventure of a lifetime?"

"Why did I forget about the other part of adventures of a lifetime."

"And what would that be?"

Her arm dropped a little and she looked up at him, "The part where things happen and people get hurt." She tried to sit up and Larry pushed her back down. The color in her face had gone from a deep tan to a white that would match the priest's collar. She laid back and put her arm over her eyes again.

Ryan and the priest had found them unconscious, and ever since waking up there had been an ongoing argument between the black frocked father and the soldier about what to do. The priest insisted on contacting the authorities, and said this was no longer a matter of helping someone possessed with a spirit. Ryan, on the other hand, said he was under orders to keep this away from the very same authorities for as long as possible. Neither one of them knew where Peter had gone. Everyone assumed he'd been kidnapped since he was the only one missing.

Larry's mind was trying to sort through all the possibilities and situations, "So," he stopped squatting and just sat down next to Alex, "they were obviously dressed to look like priests."

"How can you even talk right now?" The words groaned out of Alex like someone pressing down on a bellows.

"Well, I've got a bit more meat on my bones," he patted his tummy, "so the drugs get diluted a bit. Anyway," he stretched a leg out, "they would have needed a way to get Peter away from here in a hurry without anyone suspecting anything. My first thought was your generic white kidnapper van, but that wouldn't have worked because they would have been noticed speeding."

"And what if they just went the speed limit? It's not like we're going to give chase or anything."

"Sure, we aren't, but what about Ryan over there? For all you and I know he could be all kinds of James Bond."

Her shoulders moved in an exhausted shrug, "So, no standard van."

"Right."

"It would need to be something that could run red lights if necessary."

"And be big enough to carry him all tied up."

"And have equipment to knock him out again if he woke up." She uncovered her eyes and looked at Larry, "Are you thinking what I'm thinking?"

He nodded, "An ambulance."

Ryan finally looked up from his phone as Larry explained their theory, "That is…" he tucked his phone into his front pocket, "That's really smart actually. The problem is figuring out where it's headed. I've been trying to call in some favors and see if anyone can look at the traffic cameras around here, but everyone wants to know why."

"Can't you just tell them someone's been kidnapped?" Larry said.

"Then they would ask why the authorities haven't been informed. I was in the process of thinking up a good lie for that question when you walked over."

"Father?" Larry leaned around a bookshelf corner to see the priest sitting at one of the reading nooks. Books were open and scattered across the small table. Larry recognized them as the ones Peter had been pouring over during the course of their search in the library. Father Oni looked up and Larry walked over to him, "Does the Vatican have its own personal internet?"

The priest nodded, "We do have our own internal network, yes."

Larry nodded then turned back to Ryan, "If we went back a decade all of my skill at finding historical information would simply be on how to use a library, and not to brag at all but I am pretty good at using a library. Today, in the modern day world, however, I also need to be really good at interfacing with different digital mediums and internet search programs."

Ryan cocked an eyebrow skeptically, "Are you saying you can hack into Rome's traffic system through the Vatican network?"

Larry smiled and shook his head, "No, I'm not a computer analyst or programmer, and contrary to popular media hacking actually takes a long time and some handy USB drives with already written programs on them. What I'm saying is the Roman network makes reports, and I've run across these on accident before. Those reports are digitally filed so reporters have freedom of information access to where fires have happened or where police are going…"

"Or," they looked over to see Alex finally standing up and leaning against a bookshelf with her eyes covered by her hands like a weeping angel, "where ambulances ran a red light."

"You'll need to get to him in a hurry." They all looked over at Father Oni. He held up one of the books and Larry recognized the image as being similar to the one he'd shown Peter earlier that day.

"Aren't those Myan?" Larry leaned over and looked at the image closer, "Those are Myan hieroglyphs, but…"

The priest set the book down and held up another one. This image had no writings around it, but the inscription beneath it, "This one was found in Wales. Apparently one of the old English castles built there to conquer the area caved in and the crew sent to check it out found these in the caves underneath."

"Okay," Larry leaned back, "so this thing we think is inhabiting our new friend is a world traveler. Why does that need any more of a rush than just him being kidnapped by obviously bad people?"

"In each one of these," the priest tapped multiple books across the table, "a tale is told. Sometimes just in pictures, and sometimes in words, but always the same tale. The creature, if let out, will destroy."

"Will destroy what?" Larry asked.

"Anything," Father Oni looked them over, "everything."

"Well," Ryan dug in his pocket, pulled out a bottle of Ibuprofen, and offered it to Alex, "all the crazy possession stuff aside," she waved it away mumbling something about ulcers, he shrugged and put it back in his pocket, "this is, in effect, the same as some terrorists getting ahold of a bomb, and I know how to deal with that."

Chapter Twenty One

"How long was I out?" Bishop rubbed the side of his head where the river rock had cut him.

Alex walked on one side of him and Larry on the other just in case he had any leftover vertigo from being knocked unconscious and almost drowned in the river. Looking over at him Alex said, "It was only a few minutes."

Rolling his shoulders to release some of the tension, something odd occurred to him. Looking around he asked, "Has anyone seen the Raven?" Thinking back, the last time he saw the black feather ball was in the library of the monastery when he'd tucked his head under his wing.

Alex pointed up, "He flew over a little bit ago. I assume he decided not to take the long dark stairs with us and just jumped out a window since, you know, he can fly."

Larry chuckled then looked over, "I hope he's okay. I like having a magical talking raven along. Makes everything seem less real, and somehow easier to deal with."

A flutter and nails biting into his shoulder were followed by the Raven saying, "I'm also handsome and have great eyesight, which brings me to the people hiding in the trees around the next bend in the river."

There was a distinctive twang from behind him and the world seemed to freeze for a moment. Turning his head Bishop could see the arrow emerging from a dense stand of trees off to what would have been the right side of the trail as they were walking down it. The tip was metal and reflected the sun like a fractured piece of light. The shaft had bent slightly under the pressure of being released, but was starting to straighten as it flew its way toward the center of his back.

He thought about trying to catch it, mainly because of the cool factor, but settled for brushing it aside. It was the more practical maneuver once he saw two more tare through the foliage and speed toward him and his companions. His mind reeled in surprise, not at the attack, they had been expecting something like that since they'd escaped the monastery, but at his ability to react to it. The pressure to figure out how he was doing this was drowned by the need to remove the immediate threat first, so he moved.

Branches scraped past his shoulders as he bull rushed his way through. Multiple shapes loomed out of the darkness where the trees blocked the light. A faint glint to his right warned him and he ducked under a sword swing then lunged toward it, punching the first attacker in the ribs under his outstretched sword arm. The inhuman force of his fist lifted the man free of the ground and slammed him into a nearby tree. The crack of his impact didn't sound wooden.

Reaching back he snatched the fallen sword up, twisted and threw it. Halfway through one revolution the side of the sword was met by the twisting block of another. Bishop followed the throw and tackled the man. His shoulder slammed into the spot directly beneath the rib cage forcing all the breath from his attackers lungs and driving him to the ground.

A scream caused him to look up in time to see Larry pull two knives from the back of a third man then disappear back into the woods. Looking back down Bishop saw blood seeping around where the man's head had met a rock on the ground, and he rolled off the body picking up the man's now unused sword.

Shoving through the brush, Bishop burst back onto the trail in time to see a bear backhand a man so hard he flew off the road. Kneeling in the middle of the trail Alex drew an arrow and sent it into the trees. Not seeing anyone, Bishop wasn't sure what she was doing, but the accompanying yell reminded him not to doubt her.

Rushing past Alex, he focused on the two men still advancing toward the bear, who Bishop assumed was Sid. It was nice to see he could transform into something a little more useful than the little marmot he'd been earlier. Of the two men advancing, Bishop decided to focus on the one in front. He was the first soldier he'd seen that was carrying a shield. The man behind him and just off to his right was wielding a long spear, and it looked, as a duo, that they could be very effective. The shield and sword in the front providing cover for the spearman in the back to stab you while you were trying to deal with the shield.

Bishop still wasn't sure how anything he was doing was working. He had a vague idea that in the real world his newfound powers, the flickers of shadow and claws, were because of the dragon living in his head. Here, however, it was different. He could hit a man so hard it made them break. He'd heard, and watched, an arrow fly as if in slow motion. Each time he'd come out of an encounter, not just surprised that he'd won, but sure that something on him would be hurt, and pleasantly surprised that it didn't.

Knowing all this, or at least hoping for all this, Bishop took a running leap. Planting both his feet on the face of the shield, he kicked. His flying momentum and the inhuman force of the kick sent the shield bearer crashing back into the spear holder. Having landed on his side, Bishop rolled to his feet, lunged, and drove the point of his sword through the staggering spear man.

Letting go of the sword, he watched it fall, still embedded in the other man. The shield bearer wasn't moving so Bishop let him be.

Turning, he checked on Alex who was still scanning the tree line along the sides of the trail for anyone attempting to sneak by Sid and himself.

"Don't shoot," Larry stepped from the woods waving his hands in the air. "I think that was all of them." Stepping up and looking down at the shield bearer he said, "They don't have any markings, or official emblems."

The Raven landed on the shield and looked at himself in the poor reflection of its surface, "They have the markings of dead guys."

"Well," Alex stepped between them and looked over at the spearman with the sword sticking out of his chest, "if what the monk and the guy with horns was saying was true then they could just be…" She trailed off and the only sound was a bear pushing its way deeper into the woods.

The Raven hopped to the top of the sword sticking from the dead spearman and looked over at where Sid was disappearing into the trees, "Should I wait and ask him if he wants any of this, or should I just assume he's leaving it all for me?"

"Really?" Alex poked the top of her bow at the Raven, "they're dead. Leave them be."

"Apparently he likes his privacy," Larry said watching the lumbering bear form of Sid finally vanish behind a screen of leaves and branches.

"Maybe it hurts," Alex said.

Larry nodded, "I hope not."

"But they are dead," the Raven looked from Alex back to the spearman, "they don't really need all their bits and pieces anymore."

"So," Bishop pointedly ignored the Raven, reached down and picked up the fallen spear, "first, let's get some distance between us and these guys."

"What about Sid?" Alex looked off into the woods.

"I'm pretty sure he can find us," Larry said.

They walked single file in silence for a few minutes until Larry stepped up beside Bishop, "You really think those guys back there were just this world's way of stopping you from doing something with the dragon?"

"And what," Alex squeezed next to them, barely fitting on the narrow trail, "are you going to do with the dragon?"

"I already told you," Bishop sighed, "I have no plans to let this dragon go anywhere. I just want to figure out how to get it back into its cage."

"Then why don't they just let you do that?" Larry asked.

"Yeah," Alex leaned forward and looked past Bishop to Larry, "if they don't want it getting loose then why don't they, whoever they are, just let you get on with putting it back."

"I think it's broken," Bishop said.

"What is?" Alex asked, "The world?"

"Kinda," Bishop shrugged. "One of the things they said back there is true. The crystal, whatever it was, is gone. It shattered into a million pieces."

"What does that mean?" Alex asked.

Bishop threw his hands up, "I don't know. Look," his hands dropped back to his sides, "I'm good at making plans. I'm good at being part of a team and leaning on other people's strengths when I don't know what to do, but here, with all of this…" he waved his hands at the world around them. "I have guesses, but that's all they are. I don't know anything about dragons or ancient beings who got ticked off because they had to kill some people then went crazy."

Alex stepped forward, turned and walked backward down the trail for a few steps until Bishop stopped. "Then make a guess. We decided to help you, to come with you, and none of us know what's going on."

"That story," Larry pointed back toward the monastery, "is all well and good, but it doesn't help us with the here and now. I've grown up with my nose in a book. My mom wants me to be an accountant, everybody needs an accountant, she said. I came out here, with you, because…" he trailed off. "I don't know, it just felt right, and it still does."

Bishop took in a deep breath. The smell of the pine trees surrounding them was beautiful. For a moment he let it clear his head and focused on that fact. Then, letting his breath out, he said, "There are just so many moving pieces. Is this place just a prison built to hold an angry dragon? What happened when that prison broke? Are those guys back there real or were they just some magical construct cooked up by the prison to stop me?"

"Are we real?" Alex asked quietly.

Bishop nodded at her, "All that matters is that you're real to yourself. If you think you're real then you are."

Larry nodded, "I agree with that."

"Why?" Alex looked over at him, "Because some church book said so?"

"No," Larry looked up as a cloud drifted across the face of the sun blocking the light for a moment, "because the other alternative is frightening, and" he looked back down at them, "there's enough frightening things happening right now."

"So," Bishop put a hand on each of their shoulders, "we focus on what we can do and what we do know. It doesn't matter where the bad guys come from, only that we don't let them kill us. It doesn't matter if this world is a made up projection, only that we need to move through as if it were any other place."

Alex nodded once, "We find the tower and get the map."

"Then we find the cage and figure out a way to put the dragon back in it," Larry said.

Sid stepped out of the woods, "You also need to figure out how to be quieter."

Bishop tilted his head toward the shape shifter, "Good to see you're okay."

Sid shrugged, "Got a few scratches, but nothing to worry about."

The day went smoothly after that. The Raven rejoined them and Bishop decided it would be best for everyone if they didn't ask him what he'd been doing. As the sun dropped toward the horizon, Bishop started to worry about the other world. He knew if they had to bed down for the night he would be transported back, and he didn't really know what was going on over there. The dragon had been absent, but just as they were knocking him back out again with whatever IV drug they'd given him, he swore the lump in the back of his mind had stirred.

"I don't think we should break for the night until we find the tower." Sid hadn't said anything since stepping out of the tree line and rejoining the group.

"I was thinking about that too," said Alex, "and I agree with Sid. If people are going to be popping out of the trees to kill us I think we need to keep moving."

"And how are we supposed to see the guys hiding in the trees if we keep walking along in the dark?" Larry asked. "At least if we make a camp we can set some traps or prepare for the inevitable attack."

"Set traps?" Alex looked over at him, "What kind of traps do you have? Or do you plan to make some from twigs and leaves?"

"Maybe I was," Larry crossed his arms and kept walking.

"Well, I think," Alex motioned for them to stop, "the greatest of all ravens should fly ahead and see if we're even close to the tower."

They all looked at the Raven perched on Bishop's shoulder. He looked from Alex to the sky then back, "Fine, I'll take a look."

After he jumped into the sky and disappeared beyond the trees they began walking again. Larry settled in next to Bishop and asked, "Do you think there will be people at this tower?"

Bishop shrugged, "The monk didn't say anything about needing to convince people to give us the map."

Larry nodded, "So a deserted tower then. It'll probably be locked."

"I'm sure we can figure out a way to break in if we need to," Bishop said.

Larry smiled, "I always wanted a reason to break into a tower."

The Raven circled back over them a few times then dropped down to land on a branch a few yards down the trail, "There's a little bridge across the river up ahead, then more stairs, then the tower."

"You think we can make it before it's too dark?" Bishop asked.

The Raven thought about it for a while then said, "Not before the sun goes down, but not too long after that."

The creek burbled and rippled appropriately as they crossed it, all the while watching for more silent assassins waiting in the trees around them. The narrow path started to rise then turned from a dirt track to creek stones used for steps.

"Really?" Larry stopped and put his hands on his knees, "Why can't they just build their fancy tower down here where it's nice."

Sid patted him on the shoulder and kept walking.

A few minutes later the sun had dipped below the horizon, earlier than expected, but being on the wrong side of the mountain did cast a shadow over them. They reached the landing at the top with a smattering of twilight still giving definition to the landscape.

The tower was immediately apparent, and would have been no matter what the quality of light. It was a single square structure rising at least fifty feet into the air. Windows marked the side of it, but with no light coming from them they were only deeper black marks leading up to the flat topped roof.

No gate blocked the way, and with only a simple door which Bishop could just make out, he saw no reason to hesitate and stepped out from the top of the stairs. The ground shifted beneath his feet and he caught himself with the spear he'd picked up earlier. A groaning sound from in front of them drew his eyes to a rise in the ground about fifty yards away that hadn't been there before.

"Are you kidding me?" Bishop turned and looked from Larry, who'd spoken up, to the growing hill in front of them. "Of course there's a thing."

"What do you mean, a thing?" Bishop tried to focus on what was happening but the dimming light only served to highlight the area in various shades of gray.

"A thing." Larry shrugged and pulled his two knives out from where they hid in the small of his back. "You know, a guardian kinda thing that we all should've assumed would be here."

"And why," Bishop saw Alex put an arrow to her bowstring as she looked at the now cracking ground, "would we have known something would be here?"

"It's a special tower isn't it?" Larry rolled his shoulders and started to sidestep to the left. "It's got some super secret map, right?" Looking over his shoulder to make sure he wasn't in Sid's way, Larry continued to the left until he blended in with the shadows, "Of course there would be something guarding it."

Alex huffed, "And why didn't you think to bring this up to the rest of us?"

Larry's voice was a whisper in the darkness, "I assumed if I had thought of it you would have too."

Bishop turned to the Raven on his shoulder, "You have better eyesight then we do. What is it?" Is the darkness that was leftover at the end of twilight all Bishop could see was a mass of something darker than the surrounding area. It seemed to shake and he could hear the crumbling of dirt and rocks dropping to the ground.

"Well," the Raven leaned forward, "it's big."

"Really?" Sid's deep voice rolled over them. "Anything better than that?"

"Look," the Raven tried to glare at Sid, but since Bishop's head was in the way it didn't work, "I saved you from a cage so show a little bit of gratitude."

Sid grunted in reply then shook himself. The air around him rippled like heat waves rising from pavement as his outline changed. A few moments later a massive bear stood on its hind legs occupying the space where Sid had stood.

"Right," the Raven shuddered, "enough of that."

"But seriously," Bishop raised the spear he'd acquired, "can you see anything in a bit more detail?"

The mass in front of them reared up and lunged forward. The Raven leaped from Bishop's shoulder, "I'll look from up here and let you know."

Alex's bow string twanged and Bishop could hear the arrow ping as it connected with something solid and ricocheted off. Sid roared, dropped onto all fours, and ran toward the thing. Turning to Alex Bishop yelled, "Wait," as she was drawing back another arrow. "Is there any way you can set something on fire?"

Pausing and lowering her arrow she glanced around then back up when the roar of a bear was followed by a meaty thud, "I can light an arrow on fire, but there's nothing around here that would catch if I shot it."

She was right. Looking around, Bishop didn't even see a useful dead tree. What there was around looked way too alive for a single flaming arrow to do anything to.

"Hey," Bishop jumped and spun his spear narrowly missing Larry's face. "Whoa," next to them Alex let another arrow go with the

202

same ricochet result and Larry raised his hands to ward off any other unintended spear thrusts from Bishop, "it looks like a manticore."

"A what?" Bishop turned back toward the shadows and hoped Sid was doing all right.

"A big thing that looks like a lion and has the tail of a scorpion."

"Then why aren't my arrows doing anything?" Alex raised another and fired.

Bishop heard a grunt of pain, "Sid needs help." Raising his spear he charged the monster in the darkness. Taking deep breaths with each step he pushed forward as fast as he could. Nothing had been normal since that mission in the cave system, but in this moment with the wood grain of the spear shaft digging into his palm, normal didn't matter. Do the job in front of you, had been his mantra for years. He knew he wasn't anything special. He knew he was just part of a larger machine, both in the Navy and in life, but sometimes being special didn't matter. Sometimes the bullets were flying and you simply had to do the job in front of you then move on to the next. If you kept doing and doing then eventually something would change, hopefully for the better. In the meantime you protected your squadmates.

Things were different here, in this strange world. He was faster and stronger. Gathering the shredded remains of his thoughts he balled up all of his pent up frustration from the past few days, gathered it all in his chest, and pushed it out through his arms. Lunging the last few feet he jabbed the spear forward at the side of the beast.

Larry had been right. It was four legged and from this close did resemble a thick maned lion. It moved faster than something the size of a pickup truck should have been able to and his spear thrust caught only air. From the corner of his eye Bishop saw something twitch toward him, and dodging to his right he swiped with the spear, deflecting the black barbed tail away from his face.

"Push it toward the trees," the raven's voice floated out of the darkness above him, but Bishop couldn't spend a moment trying to see where he was.

"What trees," he swiped again with the spear and stepped forward as the tail lashed out again.

"Over your right shoulder."

"Great," dropping to a knee, Bishop felt the air move as the tail whipped over him. Thrusting out with the spear he felt the point of it connect with the beast's side but saw it slide along the fur not penetrating.

From the other side he heard the roar of the bear again and saw the tail flip up preparing to strike down onto his friend. Jumping from his crouched position Bishop wrapped the spear around the tail and grabbed the other side of it. Using it as leverage he pulled the tail down with him as he fell. Letting go he rolled and yelled, "Sid! Head toward the trees behind me!"

Standing up he jabbed with his spear and at the same time saw an arrow glance off the side of the beast. Turning and ducking he saw Sid the bear rumble his way past, on the way to the stand of trees the Raven had said were over his shoulder. He assumed Larry had some plan in mind, but didn't know what difference the little knives he carried could do against something that seemed impervious to damage.

Turning, the manticore slammed its shoulder into Bishop, sending him tumbling across the grass. Pressing his free hand against the ground he pushed off and lunged to the side just missing being stomped on by the leaping monster. Pivoting, he sprinted toward where he could just make out the dark shape of trees against the now starlight sky.

A rumble Bishop associated with a helicopter turning on was directly behind him and at the last moment Bishop grabbed the branch of one of the oncoming trees to help him turn while at full speed.

A yell snapped Bishop's head around and he saw the last moments of Larry's fall from a nearby tree as he landed squarely on the monster's back. His arms rose and fell as he jabbed his knives repeatedly at the neck and shoulders of the lion. Behind him Bishop could see the massive black scorpion tail rise. Preparing to jump, Bishop knew he would be too late to stop the fall of the poisoned stinger.

An arrow ricocheted off the shoulder of the beast directly next to Larry's head and he rolled off, falling to the ground. The striking scorpion tail, descending to kill Larry only a heartbeat before, stopped mere inches from the manticore's back.

Rolling to his feet and dodging behind a tree Larry yelled, "Did it work?"

"No," Alex fired off two more shots, aimed directly at the monster's face, "he stopped."

Bishop could hear Larry repeat what must have been the only two swear words he must have known as he dodged between trees and disappeared back into the darkness. A familiar roar was followed by Sid slamming into the manticore's side, turning its attention away from where Larry had been only a moment before. Bending almost in half the Lion opened its mouth wide and clamped its jaws down on Sid, lifting him from the ground like a chew toy. The crack of a bone was followed by Sid flying through the air and slamming into a tree.

Alex screamed and ran toward Sid's still form, firing arrows as she ran. Larry reappeared from the shadows beneath a pine tree and attacked the manticore's back leg, hoping to somehow draw its attention away from the defenseless man. Twitching its tail, it swept Larry off his feet and sent him tumbling, while at the same time it gathered itself and jumped. Alex screamed, standing over Sid's still form, and fired two more shots as the leaping beast dropped toward her.

Screaming, Bishop shot forward. Rage, red hot, and pulsing like a heartbeat flooded through him. His scream turned to a roar and ripped through his throat like a rockslide. Slamming into the side of the beast he wrapped his spear holding left arm around the top of it and his free right hand around the bottom, grasping the fur on its underside. A tree snapped at the sideways impact of man and beast and Bishop heaved up with his bottom hand flipping the monster over and away.

Tossing his spear into his right hand he pushed his rage, burning and alive, into it, setting it alight. Stepping forward and planting his foot he threw the burning spear directly at the side of the rising manticore. It screamed as the spear pierced its once invulnerable hide.

Turning, Bishop locked eyes with Alex. She nodded and raised her bow. Gathering the heat of his magical anger Bishop flung a hand out and arrow after arrow flickered to bright orange life as they leaped across the open darkness to bury themselves in the now stumbling monster. Turning its head toward them it let out a roar only to find two flaming arrows sprouting from its now open mouth. Staggering, it slipped and fell onto its side. Stalking forward, and ignoring the flaming footprints he was leaving behind, Bishop reached out and pulled the spear from the beast. Stepping around to its head, he raised it high then rammed it down through a watering eye. A final twitch and the manticore lay still.

"Peter!" Alex's voice cut through the anger induced fog in Bishop's mind. Turning he saw her and Larry leaning over what Bishop could only imagine was Sid's body. In the darkness all he could make out was a lump on the ground.

Running to them he looked down to see a man where only a moment ago a bear had lain unconscious. "Is he..."

Larry's head was resting on Sid's chest and he glanced up, "I can hear his heartbeat."

"Good," Bishop looked around. The only light was the slight flickering orange left over as the fires of Alex's arrows and his spear slowly died out. "The tower. Let's get him inside." Looking down at the slightly twisted form of Sid he knew this was going to hurt the man, but he wasn't about to take the chance of trying first aid out here. "Larry, you take his feet. Alex, keep guard and shoot anything that's not us."

"I'm almost out." She twitched her head toward her quiver to indicate the three arrows left.

Bishop nodded, "I trust you." Anything other than an impenetrable manticore he knew she could take down in one shot.

"Don't shoot," the raven dropped out of the darkness above them, "I checked the windows and no one seems to be home."

Bishop waved for Larry to grab Sid's legs then he scooped him up under his armpits. The two walked the distance to the door of the tower while Alex scanned the darkness.

Once there, she tried the door and shook her head, "It's locked."

Without putting Sid down Bishop leaned back and with the last remnants of the anger left bubbling inside of him from the fight with the manticore, kicked the door. It cracked down the middle, and Alex pushed the half hanging front he hinges inward while leaving the other half to hang from its twisted lock. Squeezing through the half open door they were greeted with an entryway that mimicked the one from the monastery. Pillows lined the walls with short tables arranged to serve visitors.

"Alex…" Bishop nodded toward some pillows.

She arranged them as best she could to make a kind of bed and they laid Sid down. Running through his medical training, Bishop found no bad puncture wounds or gashes. Sid was bleeding from a few minor cuts and abrasions on his torso, but surprisingly where the monster had bit him, nothing was life threatening. The worst were the broken ribs. Just looking, Bishop could see, even in the dark of the unlit room, where a part of Sid's rib cage was curving at the wrong angle.

"I," Bishop glanced at the others, "I don't know what to do about that."

Alex pursed her lips, obviously trying to think, and Larry stepped up, "He's a shapeshifter, right?" Bishop and Alex just looked at him. "Well, if he can change the shape of his body, including his bones, into an entirely different animal, then maybe…"

He left it hanging, but Bishop understood what he was getting at. "So I guess we wait for him to wake up and ask him." He looked over at the broken door, "I'll keep watch over him. You two start to search this place for a map."

Alex looked around, walked over, and picked up an oil lamp from a table. Shaking it she said, "Sounds nearly full. Does anyone have a way to light it?"

Chapter Twenty Two

Bishop woke to the smell of aluminum and diesel fumes. Blinking he tried to make the darkness go away, but he quickly realized it had nothing to do with him. His hands and feet were untied, but he was in a metal box of some kind. Feeling along the walls of it he found dents and gashes that almost penetrated the metal.

Focusing, Bishop searched for the feeling he'd had back in the other world. He remembered the strength and the speed and how he'd been able to bottle his energy up and push it out through his arms. He didn't want the emotions and the anger. That seemed to be the way toward fire, and while that was helpful when fighting a manticore, he didn't think it would be as much help trapped inside an aluminum box. Mentally, he created a picture of energy running through his body. He channeled it toward his right hand then pressed the tip of his index finger to the deepest gouge he could feel. With a pop he felt his fingernail break through the metal skin.

Pulling his hand back a thin ray of light illuminated the darkness of his prison. His right hand was black and covered with reflective scales. The claw at the end of his index finger curved and the underside of it looked sharp enough to frighten a tyrannosaurus rex.

"It's dark in here." The Raven's voice made him twitch. "Where are we this time? Obviously not back in the tower, which, by the way, it had been my idea to try and get the crazy monster to sting itself. It would've worked too if Larry hadn't chickened out so fast." Bishop felt the Raven walk over his leg then heard a sharp metallic ping, "Ouch. Yep, that's metal."

"Hey," a voice drifted in through the small hole Bishop had made, "did you hear something?"

"I hope not," a second voice replied.

"Seriously, dude killed the driver and everyone in both escort cars before Malcom was able to put him back down."

"He's been quiet in there for a while…"

"Look, let's just get this thing off loaded."

"I'm seriously glad we didn't take it down the river like they'd wanted to."

"I know, right? With him trying to break out every five minutes, I think a boat would have been a bad idea."

"Not that I'd mind this guy being at the bottom of the Tiber, but we wouldn't get paid if he was."

"Or, even worse, we'd only get paid if we got it back up from the bottom."

I hate water.

Bishop twitched again and almost said a few swear words.

"And why is that?" The Raven's feet landed back on Bishop's leg. "I thought you were huge, dark, and scary. What problem could you have with water?"

Bishops felt the presence in the back of his mind again. Larger than he'd remembered.

There was an event.

Bishop's mind flooded with flickering images of homes, some simple mud others made of stone or wood, being washed away by a tidal wave. People trying to stay afloat but eventually being sucked under by the swirling mass of dark water.

"Oh, an event," the Raven said, sarcasm dripping from his beak, "and where were you when we had an event? Off pouting somewhere because you remembered you were a horrible plague on humanity?"

The disconnect caused by the monastery, and the subsequent attack by the prison's guard system, made my reaction slower than I'd wished, but I did show up.

Rattling and scraping noises echoed down from the top of Bishop's prison. Clicks were followed by a voice from outside the box, "It's hooked up."

"So," voice number two was fading, "once we get there do they have a crane…"

The Raven's feet hopped off his leg again, "I can almost see through this hole…" Bishop rolled slightly as the vehicle they were in started a tight turn to the right, then after a few moments began backing up. The light from the hole went away, "And we're backing into something."

So insightful.

"Look," the raven's sharp toes audibly scrapped on the metal floor, "if you're so big and amazing why don't you tell us where we are."

Because I'm stuck in here, and can only see what Peter can see.

A few moments later they came to a jerking stop. Multiple footsteps and voices converged on the aluminum box that was his prison. Bishop had been part of hooking things up to helicopters and flatbed trucks so many times in his military career that he could easily picture what they were doing. The rumble of a motor was followed by a jerking ascent coupled with sway as they left the back of whatever truck they'd been on. Swinging to the side they came to a bobbing halt maybe a dozen feet from where they started. The slap of hands slowed the swing of the box until it was steady enough to descend.

Bishop could hear voices calling out commands, but they were muffled by distance and the aluminum skin of his prison. A solid thud brought them to the ground and he waited for something to happen.

"Ow," the Raven hopped back onto his leg, "that's hot."

A sizzling sound was followed by waves of heat and light breaking in from the edges and corners of the box, and once those were low enough there was a metallic clang as the top was pulled off by its still connected chain. The sides fell away revealing a warehouse full of people and equipment. To the side was the flatbed truck and next to it a small crane, the metal lid still dangling from the end of the cable. Around him Bishop saw four metal posts connected with white and blue strips of cloth. Tracing it quickly he saw it was connected to a heavy electrical cable and knew the strips were a kind of electric fence designed to keep him in.

"Uhm," the Raven transitioned to his shoulder as he stood up, "they know you can jump right?"

Beyond the electric fencing rose four metal towers, each easily twenty feet tall. A white rounded device with a hole in it, looking something like a large camera, sat atop each one.

A blinking red light on each tower one by one turned solid green. "Well," the Raven said, "that could go either way. Green is a nicer color than red."

"It is good to finally meet you." The voice was familiar and Bishop turned to see a man in an impeccable gray suit step up onto a platform to his right. The man removed his jacket, draped it over a handrail to his right, then began rolling up his sleeves, "You definitely put a dent in our timeline, but we both know that was not your intention, and not really your fault either."

Holding out his arms another man started to hook medical looking wiring up to his wrists, "The men we hired to get into that cave weren't exactly the best, but sometimes you have to work with what's available. They weren't told to blow the place up, and frankly, the claymore they used was not helpful in any way."

Bishop's eyes traveled back over the setup in the warehouse, "What is all this?" He didn't ask why he was here. It would be ridiculous. He knew why he was here. There was a dragon living inside his head.

The raven nudged the side of his head, "Just dragon out a little bit, jump over the fence, and throw them all into a wall."

"All of this," the suit nodded to the man who'd finished hooking the wires up to a console a few feet away, "is the best modern representation we could make of the ritual that trapped the dragon in the first place."

The dragon inside Bishop's head moved making him feel slightly nauseous.

I don't remember. Why don't I remember?

"Those ancient people used the best materials they had available to them, and unwittingly hit on something only modern science is just now beginning to understand. The crystalline structure you found in that cave, and which was blown up by over eager hired terrorists, was the perfect medium to trap his consciousness. Today, computer companies are working on ways of using the same type of structure to store massive amounts of data for thousands of years without losing any of it."

"So," Bishop was torn on how much he should stick around to listen to or if he should just do what the Raven suggested and get this over with, "they sucked his mind into the crystal."

"Yes," the suit leaned over and said something quietly to the assistant at the console, "then that consciousness was transferred to you when all those shards jabbed into your skin."

Bishop mentally tapped the dragon and shot a mind picture of what they were going to do at him. He didn't want to wait for an obvious moment, and the Raven was right, he just needed to get out.

"You will be free of this." Bishop paused and looked back up at the suit. He stood there with white, blue, and red wires snaking away from his outstretched arms, "I know this has been a trial for you. I know life has turned upside down. Stand still and let me do this. It will remove the dragon from your mind and place it in mine. You see, you accidentally proved a theory we'd been operating with. The human mind is far more complex than any crystal could be, and therefore is far better at containing a separate consciousness."

Bishop let out a laugh, "And what would you do with a super powered dragon living in your head? Help the poor? End genocide? I think your goons proved the lie to any philanthropic motives you might put forward." Bishop felt the dragon growing in his mind, pushed that feeling into his legs, and jumped.

The shock of the electricity caused his muscles to spasm then clinch. The fall wasn't bad since he'd only made it a few inches off the metal floor of the deconstructed box he'd been standing on. The Raven was gone, having taken off at the assumption the jump would work.

"You didn't really expect it would be that easy did you?" The suit said. "One thing we did find, again thanks to your unusual intervention, is that super powered or not, electricity still restricts muscle movement. Now maybe, if you were an actual scale covered dragon things might be different, but there's no reasonable way to test that theory."

That was unexpected. I believe I can work through this, but you would have to trust me to take over, and I know, with what has happened in the past, that might not seem like the best alternative.

Bishop unfolded his cramping arms with an effort and pushed himself up to a kneeling position. One hand still rested on the metal floor, "Then why are you doing this? Just for power? Are you some movie villain that's going to rub his hands together and cackle at any moment?"

"No," the suit acknowledged a thumbs up from the assistant at the console. "I understand how you might think that because of the methods used against you. However, this is for a better purpose. You see, death is misplaced, misused. It runs rampant with no sense of purpose."

I am not death.

"Sometimes death makes mistakes." The suit nodded firmly to the assistant, "But I don't need to explain any of that to you."

There was a humming and the four towers and the pods on top of them, which Bishop thought might be cameras, began glowing. Heat flooded his body and he flinched away from it. The white pods at the tops of the towers moved and tracked his location.

The dragon rose up in his mind. The rage Bishop had become used to, and now knew wasn't his own, built up and then was pressed back down by the pounding of the heat coming from the towers.

"We never found a full explanation of how they did it." The suit's voice drifted through the pain in Bishop's mind, "But what we did find were fragments in multiple places. Once we put them together we had an almost complete picture. It seems they used light to compress him. We hoped the lasers would do the same. I suppose we are about to find out."

An explosion rocked Bishop off his knees and with his muscles still cramped from the massive jolt of electricity he'd received earlier, all he could do was lay on his side and watch. One tower toppled as flames licked at the base of it. A moment later, another explosion, this one on the far side, dropped a second tower. Rolling as much as he could, Bishop watched as the falling structure smashed through half of the electrical fencing keeping him trapped.

A yell from a black clad mercenary drew his attention and he watched as an arrow suddenly sprouted a few inches above his collar bone. Another mercenary tried to point to where the arrow had come from and fell grasping at the calf muscle on his left leg. Without seeing him, Bishop knew Larry had gotten hold of a set of knives.

Two more explosions drew the mercenaries' attention toward the back of the room where they watched flames engulf the diesel generator that must have been the backup for the electrical system.

212

Hands roughly grabbed Bishop under the armpits and lifted him to his feet.

"You need to be able to run," Ryan's voice was quiet but emphatic.

Pressing into the dragon essence in his mind he pulled it into himself, using it to supplement his electrically cramped muscles. "Which way?"

Ryan pointed to a door to the left of the main roll up doors of the warehouse and they started to run. The thump of a large caliber gun rang out twice and stopped. Bishop looked over his shoulder and saw Alex running along the catwalk just behind and above them, firing arrows over her shoulder like some modern day Valkyrie. Turning back he watched Larry slide to a stop and hold the door open just long enough for them to get through, then slam it shut and ram a bar into the crack at the bottom, jamming it shut.

Ryan continued to run past and looked up as Alex leaped from an open widow twenty feet above them. Bishop watched her trajectory as Ryan grabbed one corner of a tarp stretched out and tied to multiple crates and pallets in front of the warehouse. Yanking on the corner of the tarp then relaxing it, Ryan caught the falling girl and then eased her to the ground. Rolling off she gave a thumbs up and flashed a giant smile at Bishop.

"Now that," Larry ran past them on his way to a waiting van with it's doors open, "is what I call a rescue."

Bishop buckled in as the van took the first few turns fast enough to worry him about it staying upright. "So," Alex leaned around from the front passenger seat and looked back at him, "you okay? Did they torture you or something?"

Bishop smiled at her and shook his head, "No, they drugged me and locked me in a box for a while, but no torture."

"Awesome," Larry grinned from the seat next to him. Alex glared until the grin faded and he said, "I mean it's not awesome that you were drugged and locked in a box," the grin returned, "but it is awesome they didn't torture you."

Bishop leaned back in the seat and closed his eyes. Breathing deeply he tried to get his mind to calm down. He knew things were moving quickly here, but if he could just make the jump back to the other world he might be able to fix everything. If what he'd seen about the jumps remained true then not much time, if any, would pass here while he was figuring things out on the other side. The problem was, he needed to be unconscious. The transition had only happened when he'd either fallen asleep or been knocked out. How was he supposed to do it on purpose?

Chapter Twenty Three

"This is crazy." The Raven landed on his chest and Bishop's eyes twitched open. "I mean one moment I'm flying around some room, invisible and not quite sure what I'm supposed to do, then things start blowing up and madam arrow over there is sticking people..."

Bishop looked around the room and saw Alex stretched out on gathered together pillows, asleep. Larry and Sid were absent, which gave him some hope about Sid's well being. "Where's..."

"And then pow," the Raven jumped on his chest for emphasis, "I'm back here. I mean, seriously, how does this work? I know it, obviously, has something to do with you, but if you could just leave me out of it for a while I would really appreciate it."

"Hey," Bishop sat up, displacing the Raven who hopped to the ground, "do you know if they found the map?"

"How would I know that? I've been having my soul ripped out and tossed from world to world like some kind of child's ball that gets tossed from one place to another." Walking over to the sleeping form of Alex, the Raven hopped up onto the pillow next to her ear, leaned close, and whispered as loudly as he could, "Hey..."

Twitching, Alex swiped a hand around her head and landed a solid backhand blow to the side of the Raven, knocking him off the pillow. Sitting up she fumbled around next to her, picking up her bow and looking around the room with one eye still closed.

"Ouch..." the Raven fluffed his feathers out and glared at the girl. "What's that for?"

"Oh please," Bishop stood up and stretched, "you deserved that."

Alex looked from Bishop back to the Raven and lowered her bow. Rubbing her eyes she asked, "What time is it?"

Bishop shrugged, "I have no idea. I was going to let you sleep, but Mr. Raven here decided he needed to ask you some questions."

"Whatever," the Raven hopped in a little circle, "don't you blame me for this. You're the one who had questions. I was just smart enough to wake up the person who might have the answers."

"Right now," she flopped back onto the pillows, "you two are too much. I'm going to try and get some more sleep, and if you," without looking she pointed at the raven, "wake me up again, I'm going to put an arrow through you."

"Well," Bishop hesitated for a moment then asked, "since you are awake right now, is Sid okay?"

Turning her head to look at him, Alex gave a little nod, "Yeah, when he woke up he must have done something, but I wasn't here to see it. By the time I got back from looking for the map he was up and being his normal sternly quiet self."

"Good," Bishop nodded to himself as she rolled back over.

Walking away as quietly as possible, Bishop went through the door at the far end of the entryway. Stepping through into what he assumed would be a hallway or a room, he was met with a slight feeling of vertigo. The interior of the tower was hollow with a set of spiral stairs corkscrewing up the center of the massive empty space. At regular ten foot intervals the stairs met a landing and a short bridge led off to a platform attached to the outer wall. Walking around the space and looking up, Bishop could see no support for the stairs or the platforms other than the stone they were resting on. The stairs had no railing or stopgap measure to make sure you didn't fall to your death, other than leaning toward the middle of the spiral and hoping you didn't step wrong.

The whole area was lit by a few torches on the ground level and one or two of them at each corresponding bridge as it rose to the top. He could see at the first landing that a fireplace was built into the wall of the tower, and he imagined that once all of them were lit the open space would be bright with flickering orange light after the sun had gone down. Windows all along the space would give it natural light during the day, but they would also let in wind and rain and even birds, but he didn't see any hint of the mess that would cause.

Obviously, no one was living there and the only movement Bishop could even make out was near the top. He assumed it would be Larry still going through as many books as he could find. Sighing, he placed his foot on the bottom stair and started up.

"This place is amazing," the Raven let out a rolling sound that could only be compared to dropping rocks on a hollow log. Bishop looked over in time to see him flying tight spirals around the central staircase. "A raven must have built this," he said as he swung past Bishop.

Placing his hand on the central column that held the stairs up he started to climb. The silence brought his mind back to the transition from his world to this one. He wished he knew how he'd done it. There was no way he could have fallen asleep. The adrenaline had been pumping through him along with the leftover rage he'd borrowed from the dragon. At least this time, the word borrowed made sense. Other times he had it thrust on him, but at least now he knew it wasn't his, and he knew it was one of the ways of accessing whatever it was the dragon could give him. Lighting a spear on fire for example.

"Hello," the voice echoed down from above him and Bishop fought the urge to lean out and look up to see if Larry's face peeking down like a disembodied ghost. "This place is amazing. Come up here, I think I've found the map."

"Of course it would be at the top," Bishop muttered to himself. He wasn't scared of heights. No one working on an aircraft carrier could afford to be scared of heights, but he did have a healthy respect for safety measures, and this place had none. As he passed the first little bridge he noted the lack of handrails leading over the bridge to a small sitting area with a bookshelf. He'd been right about the fireplace.

Each level was basically the same, and he assumed each bookshelf would hold a different selection of material. Some levels were larger than others and contained a bed and a wardrobe, and after he passed the fifth one he realized something must be wrong with his perception. From the outside the tower didn't look tall enough to house all these levels. He remembered seeing the windows as they'd come to the top of the stairs, and there hadn't been this many.

Reaching the top, Larry waved at him from a platform that circled the entirety of the top level of the tower, "Weird isn't it. It's like it's bigger on the inside." Leaning over the edge Larry pointed to the torches, "I thought it would help if I lit those on the way up."

The ceiling above them was made up of large wooden beams that formed a cone shape. The beams were covered over on the top with wooden planks, except for one spot where a ladder extended up through it. Larry pointed over to the ladder, "Sid went up through there to keep an eye out for any, how did he put it, approaching issues."

"So he's feeling better?" Bishop tried not to look down as he crossed the small stone bridge out to the platform. He wouldn't lie to himself. When Larry had leaned over the edge earlier, it had definitely caused his stomach to clench.

"Yeah. None of us saw it, since you'd fallen asleep, but when he came walking up here nothing was wrong. I even insisted on seeing that spot on his ribs…" Larry shrugged, "Must have been right that he could fix himself. I asked him and he didn't really want to talk about it, so Alex and I just let him go."

"She's trying to get some sleep down in the entryway."

"I tried to talk her into using one of the actual beds set up, but she said she didn't want to roll off to her death."

Bishop nodded, and completely agreed with her sentiment. "So, did you find what we're looking for?"

"Yeah, at least I think so," Larry waved him over to a small table with three chairs around it. "At first I thought it would be easy. There's not too many things to look through here, but then we ran into a problem."

Bishop gestured for him to continue and Larry tapped the table top. It was covered with maps. From what Bishop could tell there were at least seven maps spread out over the small table top.

Larry started leafing through them, "It turns out the monks here really liked their maps. Thankfully most of them were labeled and we could just put those back. They had maps of monastery locations, city streets, countries I've never heard of before, even whole continents I've never heard of before. There was one labeled in big black letters with the title the Myan city of Tikal."

"Really?" Bishop leaned over and looked for that map.

"Yeah, why, do you know that place?"

"Not really, but it is from the other world."

Larry thumbed through the maps on the table and brought out one. Laying it down on top of the others he shrugged, "Do you think it means something?"

"It's from my world and they have a map of it, so yes, I think it means something." Bishop looked over the map and noted the buildings with their labels. A main roadway entered the map from the bottom right corner and intersected a triangle of roads also at their bottom right corner. Along the bottom of the triangle were a series of temples, each with their own name. One stood out among the others. In the center, with walls surrounding it, was a pyramid labeled the temple of the lost world.

Looking back up at Larry, Bishop asked, "Is there anyway to take this with us?"

Larry grinned, "Absolutely."

"Good," he couldn't help but smile back at him, "also, I have to say, dropping down on top of that manticore was amazing. If I could give you a medal and pin it on you in front of thousands of people with music playing, I would."

Larry sat up straighter, his shoulders pushed back, "Thank you. It was a long shot, but I did remember reading that the only thing that could pierce a manticore's hide was its own tail."

"And you came up with the idea of dropping out of a tree onto it?"

"No, that was Alex…"

Bishop reached over and slapped him on the shoulder, "Who cares whose idea it was. You were the one to jump on the back of a giant monster."

Larry beamed and nodded, "Well," a small blush creeped up his neck and he fumbled through the maps again, "here is the one we think leads to the cage." Laying it down on top of the Mayan map, Larry pointed to a spot close to the top right. "We are here, I think."

The map was of a large island. Toward the center of it was a desert with an oasis marked at the edge of it. To the right of that, a river defined the meeting point of the base of some mountains and the edge of the desert. Following up from a small dot marking what must have been the village, Bishop found the monastery then the tower Larry had pointed to.

"There's a trail marked out leaving the tower and heading this direction," Larry traced a light brown line with his finger to the coast line. "Here we would have to find a boat of some kind because the only other mark is out here." He tapped his finger to a small dot out in the water.

"It would make sense to have the cage out away from populations," Bishop said. "How long of a walk do you think that is?"

"Well," Larry waved at the edges of the map, "they didn't include a key, which would have been nice, but we can estimate from our own trip. I think we camped about here on our first night out from town," he pointed to a curve in the trail leading from the village to the monastery, "then it took us one whole day from the monastery to this tower. That should mean we could make the coastline…"

"If we start when the sun comes up," Bishop loved maps, and a good part of his job, being a lieutenant, was to use maps, "we could make it there by sundown."

"Assuming nothing else attacks us on the way."

"Right," Bishop reached out and started rolling the map up, "assuming that."

The assumption mostly proved right. Bishop and Larry had hung out on the roof with Sid until the first light of day was showing in the sky. He assumed it was rising in the east, but with a different world inhabited by dragons and manticores he really couldn't be sure. They woke Alex and started off.

Pushing them hard to make it to the coastline before sunset, Bishop had worried they would start to tire and complain. Frankly, he'd expected Larry to be the first one, but Alex would push on while Sid just didn't seem affected by anything. He'd been pleasantly surprised when no one had asked for any kind of rest except at mid day when they'd stopped to eat and drink the little they had scrounged from the tower.

With the pace being as hard as it was no one was really in the mood for conversation, except for the one time Larry had asked Sid if he could turn into a manticore now that he'd seen one. Sid had simply told him he didn't feel like experimenting with his life. Larry nodded as if he truly understood, then looked at Alex, and shrugged.

Bishop felt he did understand. With everything happening to him lately, especially with his own body, he knew what it felt like to risk, and if you didn't need to then why push it. He really had no idea what would happen if the dragon really came out back in his home world. It didn't seem to be a problem here. Maybe because the dragon was actually out and flying around here. The point was, did he really want to risk changing his own body when he didn't feel he needed to.

The sea, or ocean, or whatever body of water they were coming to, eventually became a smell on the wind. It reminded Bishop of his job. It wasn't a bad thing, but the faint smell of salt water was definitely, permanently, attached to his job. At this point he probably could have led them to the coastline just by his nose alone, but they followed the trail they'd found as it wound its way around. Most likely, it was avoiding sudden drops off a cliff, and that was a good thing, even though it felt like it was wasting precious time.

His assumption was that no time had passed back in his world. At least it seemed that was how this all worked. The hope was he would be able to find whatever was used as a cage for this dragon and that would lead to him being able to get it back into the cage, thus getting him out of his head. Back in his world, with no psychotic dragon trying to break free, he could head back to the ship and give the captain a clean bill of health.

Whatever the crazy man, who he thought was named Patrick, had wanted would be gone. Back on the ship he would have an entire crew of military personnel to watch his back and hopefully catch the madman whenever he showed back up.

The trail ended at a small community on the coastline. Looking down on it from the final ridgeline it looked like it couldn't have more than five hundred people living in it. Multiple docks stuck out into the water with small to medium sized fishing boats moored to wooden posts. It obviously wasn't a tourist or transportation hub, but whoever had built the tower must have wanted it that way.

"Makes sense," Bishop assumed the Raven had fallen asleep, "you don't want to put your great big secret dragon right near a big city." Ruffling his feathers and rubbing his beak with a wing the Raven looked around. He'd been hopping from one person to the other throughout the day. Mainly he'd stayed with either Alex or Bishop, but from time to time he'd tried to chat up Larry or Sid. Sid normally swatted at him after a few seconds while Larry would start asking him questions about where he'd come from and did he know if his parents had been able to talk, then the Raven would just flutter back over to Bishop or Alex.

"Well," Larry looked down onto the fishing village, "it seems fairly obvious what we need to do."

"Find an inn and get some dinner and sleep," Alex said.

Larry sighed, "No, we need a boat."

Alex looked from Larry to Bishop then finally to Sid who just shrugged at her, "It'll be dark by the time…"

"And something will show up and try to eat us," Larry finished the sentence for her.

"We were lucky," Bishop said. "The only ones so far was that small group on the trail."

"And they looked like they'd been running the whole way," Larry added. "We've got a little bit of a lead on whatever's trying to kill us. I think it was surprised when we survived the manticore. If we give it all night then something big is sure to show up."

"We don't want to endanger the village," Sid added quietly.

Alex looked at him for a moment then slowly nodded, "Fine."

"Anyway," Larry started back down the trail, "if the map is accurate at all, then the island shouldn't be that far off the coastline."

Finding someone with a boat wasn't hard. Finding someone that would let them use their only source of family income and food was another thing altogether. Eventually, they came to one older man who was willing to let them use his boat in exchange for something.

"There's nothing out there except death," the man's wrinkles around his eyes were so deep Bishop assumed they were used as shade while he was out on the water.

"So no one ever goes to the islands?" Larry asked.

"Some have," the man shaded his eyes with a hand and pointed out where they could just make out a difference in the horizon. "When I was young there was a man, had himself a family too, who got it into his head that there must be treasure of some kind out there. Never came back."

"Great," Alex pushed Larry with one hand, "there's defenses out there. You still want to go now?" She gestured at the setting sun.

"With the dragon gone, and those defenses running after…" Larry paused and looked at the old man, "anyway, they're most likely not there anymore."

"Anyway," Bishop gave his best shut up stare to Alex and Larry, "what is it you would like us to do for you in exchange for the use of your boat?"

"Well, I'm not getting any younger, and the sea is always going to be hard. I've got no real family to support me when I can't fish anymore…" he left the implication hanging there.

"We don't have any money on us, but whatever we find out there," Bishop looked back to the slight change along the watery horizon, "we will give you the most expensive thing we can bring back."

The old man extended a hand and Bishop shook it, "When it gets dark in a few minutes there will be four stars in a row crossed over

220

with two other stars. The bottom of that crossing will point to the island. Well, at least it will for the first few hours. After that it kinda drifts up and to the left, so it'll be up to you to get there before then, or you'll miss it and be out in the open ocean."

"Great," Alex threw her hands up in the air.

"Don't worry," Bishop patted her on the shoulder. "It was literally my job to work on boats before this." He said it to calm her fears, but in reality he was exaggerating a bit. Maybe a lot. Not that he hadn't worked on boats, but the boats he'd served on had nothing to do with navigating by the stars. They had this wonderful thing called GPS, and if that failed, you used a compass and all the modern navigation equipment built into a U.S. Navy ship.

The small sail on the boat wasn't going to be much use since the only wind was blowing toward them. There were four oars and everybody pitched in, mainly because they wanted to get to land as quickly as possible. They had no real problem keeping in sync with each other as they rowed, again being pushed by the desire to not be lost in the ocean at night.

The horizon quickly darkened and the stellar cross the old man had told them about became readily apparent. Aiming for it and pulling hard on the oars quickly brought them within sight of the island. It loomed over their rowing shoulders, rising higher and higher, a mass of deeper darkness against the star lightened night sky.

"Can anyone see a spot to land without being smashed by rocks?" Bishop asked as they called a halt to rowing for the moment. Poking at the Raven sitting at the prow of the boat, he'd been alternating between that and the top of the mast while they rowed, Bishop said, "Maybe someone who can fly would like to take a look and guide us in safely."

"Oh," the Raven looked back at him, "sure, why not." Leaping off the boat he quickly disappeared into the raven colored sky. A few moments later a flutter of wings in the darkness announced his return. "Okay, so you're gonna wanna go to the side of the big sharp rock that's coming up and slip around the back of it. There's a spot against the cliff there where it looks like people have attached boats before."

"Which side?" Bishop asked.

"I don't know." The Raven shrugged and looked back toward the island, "The side with less sharp rocks."

Larry leaned over the edge of the boat and tried to see what the Raven was talking about, "Not very helpful."

"What'd you expect?" The Raven hopped over to the oar Larry had been holding, "I'm a raven not a compass."

"Okay," Bishop slumped down in his seat. "Let me think. Do you know the difference between left and right?"

"I know what right is," the Raven hopped back to the bottom of the boat and walked along to the front. "What's left?"

"Right," shaking his head, Bishop looked over at Alex, then at Sid, "Who has the best eyesight?"

Sid shrugged, "I can't do an animal with great eyesight, if that's what you're wondering."

Bishop nodded, "Alex it is then." He pointed toward the prow of the boat where the Raven was again acting as a figurehead, "We need you to watch for us. Tell us which way to go."

She nodded and made her way forward. Squatting down she grabbed the edge of the boat and leaned forward. Looking over at the Raven she said, "Did you happen to see if one side or the other had more of the smash us kind of rocks?"

The Raven rolled his feathered shoulders, "Maybe that way," he waved his left wing, "had less stuff, but it was hard to tell looking down at it. The water was moving and, if you hadn't noticed, it's kinda dark."

"We're drifting," she called back over her shoulder. "Head slightly to my left then straighten out."

For the next hour they did minor course corrections and found themselves navigating water worn rocks sticking up out of the dark sea. Bishop could understand why people trying to explore here could end up dead before even setting foot on the place. Eventually they found their way around what the raven called the big rock, which to his credit was about the size of a small house, and saw a small pier with an iron rod jutting from the stone face of a cliff rising up into the darkness.

Tying up the boat they stepped out onto the small dock, "Well," Larry walked up to the cliff face, "I've got good news and bad news." As Bishop approached it he saw what Larry was talking about. "The good news is," he gestured to metal ladder rungs that had been hammered into the stone of the cliff face, "there's a way up. The bad news…" Larry trailed off as they all looked up at the rusted iron rungs rising above them. "I'm sure they're fine."

"Sure," said Alex, "they look regularly maintained."

"They were put here to help guard against the escape of a magical beast." Larry reached up and tugged on the first rung, "They're probably just camouflaged to look like this so people won't explore around here."

Bishop took a deep breath and stepped up. The best way to move things along, at a time like this, was just to do it yourself. The others would either follow or not, so gripping the rung he pulled himself up. The ladder was steady and strongly attached. The only thing that bothered him after the first dozen or so was the rust digging into his palms.

Eventually he reached the top and pulled himself up onto an expanse of green turf. The landscape tilted down from the cliff top into a kind of bowl. Larry climbed up next to him, "Well that's not natural." The island was ringed in gray stone cliff, but the interior was the soft turf they were standing on. "I wonder if the way we came up is the only way?"

Turning around Bishop extended a hand to Alex and helped her up onto the soft grass. She looked around, "It's a bit dark, but I assume what we're looking for is down there."

Sid waved Bishop off and hauled himself up onto the top of the cliff. They all looked around for a moment then Bishop headed down the gentle slope to the lowest point of the island. There were no trees or bushes to get in the way, or to even make the walk interesting. It was like the island had been carpeted, and Bishop was tempted to take his boots off and feel the grass squish between his toes.

By the time they reached the bottom most part of the bowl that made up the island the moon had risen enough to grant some light to their discovery. Two stone pads rose above the perfect grass, each about ten feet square. On top of each rested a metal cage. The bars reflected back the silver moonlight and were obviously not made of iron. Back in his world Bishop would have assumed they were some steel alloy, but here, with magical dragons and manticores rising up from the earth, they could be anything.

The nearest cage had two sides obviously broken and destroyed. Walking up and touching it Bishop had to come to the conclusion that explosives had been used. In some crazy way it made perfect sense. It had been a claymore explosion that destroyed the crystal, and if those two things were connected then it would stand to reason the cage had been blown open.

Larry leaned over and picked something up. Holding it up to the moonlight he turned and showed it to Sid, "Dragon scale?"

Sid walked over and looked closer, "It's not exactly like mine, but yes, it is."

"They're everywhere," Alex picked up three of them and held them up.

"I guess they would be," Larry waved the one he was holding at the hole in the cage.

"Right," Bishop walked around the first cage, "and if that one had been holding an ancient and terrible dragon then," he pointed at the other cage, "what's this one for."

They all walked around to the second cage. The door stood open. Larry lifted the lock, dangling from the wide open door, "Cut clean through."

It was easy to see what was inside since the cages had no walls to block the view, only reflective silver bars. Alex leaned through the door anyway, "A writing desk?" She leaned back out and looked at them, confusion on her face.

The Raven hopped into the cage and up onto the desk that was settled against the back corner of the open cage. Looking around he leaned over and held up a writing quill in his beak. Dropping it, he hopped back down to the wooden chair then onto the floor, "Nothing under here, except..." he came out from under the desk and walked in his ungainly raven way back to the door. In his mouth he held a long shimmering feather. Setting it down he backed away from it, shivers causing his dark feathers to ripple, "I don't like it."

The feather was almost two feet long and could be called white, except its white wasn't a color, but more the definition of the slightly shimmering light emanating from it. "So that's it?" Bishop asked. "Look around for writings or a building. Something to explain how they maintained this, or how to get him out of my head and back into here."

Alex turned in a slow circle, "They had to have contingency plans for getting him back into his cage, and why are there two of them?"

"It had to be someone's job to come out here and check on things, right," Larry started walking past the second cage. "That means there should be a building for them to stay in, or some kind of place to keep a snack at least."

For the next few minutes they all looked. Bishop turned to ask the Raven to fly over the island, but found him staring at the glowing feather and decided to give him a minute.

"Nothing." Bishop waved his hands at the island, "Why is there nothing."

"Maybe," Larry squatted down and poked at the soil under the grass, "maybe it's underground. Maybe there's a section of this that pulls up and reveals a set of stairs going down to some cave."

"Or maybe," Sid's deep voice carried over the waving unnaturally perfect grass of the island, "there's nothing here. If the prison was built by those on the outside, maybe the directions aren't here."

"Right," Larry stood back up, "why would you keep the plans for the prison inside the prison."

"Separately," Alex held up the feather and waved it slowly, "I think this is important. I mean look at the effect it's having on him."

She nodded toward the raven who still hadn't stopped staring at the feather.

"Yes but he likes anything that's shiny," Bishop said, "and that's the shiniest thing we've ever seen."

Alex shrugged, "I still think it's important." She pointed it at the broken cage, "One cage holds something dark and hard, while the other holds something bright and soft. That seriously has to be a metaphor for something."

"Well," Bishop nodded his agreement to Alex and walked a few paces away from the cages, "I, for one, don't want to row back to the village right now." He also knew if Larry was right, and it made sense about the plans being outside the prison, he would need to head back to the minivan currently driving like crazy around the suburbs of Rome. Lowering himself down onto the soft grass he folded his arm under his head and used it like a pillow.

"This," Larry laid down a pace away, "is the softest bed I think I've ever had."

Alex sighed, "Now I know why they didn't have a house around here to sleep in. My bed at home was straw with a blanket thrown over it. This is amazing."

Bishop found himself smiling, more glad than they could realize that they'd all stuck with him this far.

Chapter Twenty Four

"What do we do next?" Bishop heard Larry's voice at the same time as the van rocked to the side, almost losing its grip on the road.

"Well," Sid's voice was calm as he turned the wheel sharply, squealing the tires around a corner, "they have a helicopter so what we do next is…" He slammed on the breaks at the same time as something punched the side of the van, shattering the window next to Bishop. Instinctively he turned his back to the window and threw himself over Alex.

"Everybody out," even under pressure Sid's voice had a measure of calm to it.

Bishop watched Alex slide open the van door and realized she hadn't undone her seatbelt. Grabbing the back of her shirt to stop her from trying to jump out, he reached down and pushed the bright red button first on hers then on his. He wasn't sure what to expect when they jumped out, but it seemed this Patrick had decided to stop being subtle.

A helicopter hovered overhead with three armed men hanging out the open door, while around them were parked multiple black SUV's, with one of them having been modified to have a fifty caliber machine gun mounted on the top. Dozens of black clad mercenaries were pouring out of car doors and raising their weapons, and walking between them, calm as a rich man at the horse races, was Patrick.

"Bravo," the man in the perfect suit gave a small clap, "I did not expect your friends to be so effective, or, honestly, to even show up." Stopping just behind the front line of AR-15 wielding soldiers for hire he locked eyes with Bishop, "Now, lieutenant, this game is over. I have much more important things to be getting on with. You will give up and come with me. As I said before, all I want is the dragon. You, and your friends, can go about your life after that."

Bishop shook his head, "I don't trust you. I don't trust what you would do with this, or with my friends, Patrick." He emphasized the name, trying to throw it out there like evidence before a jury. Bishop knew that after all of this there was no way Patrick was going to let them just walk away.

Patrick nodded, understanding the statement for what it was, "I've read everything about you, lieutenant Peter Bishop. You've never really lost anything, or anyone important to you." Quietly he said something to the mercenary beside him then looked back to Bishop, "When you do, maybe then you can judge me." Turning he walked back into the crowd.

The mercenary he'd spoken to raised a hand, "You will surrender, lay down on the ground with your hands and feet out, or we will open fire."

Without looking, Bishop knew Ryan had a gun in his hand, Larry would have a pair of knives, and Alex already had an arrow nocked and ready to pull. What he didn't know was what to do. Part of him wanted to fight it out. To punch the bad guy in the nose. It was one of the reasons he'd signed up with the Navy in the first place. Another part of him worried about his new friends. The manticore hadn't been willing to accept surrender. This monster might, maybe.

A scuffle and a yell to his right snapped his head around. Two mercs had grabbed Alex and Larry, guns to their heads, and were dragging them back toward their lines. Patrick stepped up and raised his hands. "I will not let you be the one to take everything from me again. I have worked too long, and sacrificed too much on the altar of these ends to see you snatch it away because of some misplaced moral certainty. Now give me the dragon, or I will kill them."

Out of the corner of his eye Bishop saw Ryan, pistol raised, and knew he could take out one or maybe two of them before everything tore apart. "You know," the Raven's voice was calm and sure beside his ear, "looking at that feather I remembered some things. One of them is where it came from. The other is just how big the real dragon actually is."

Bishop gritted his teeth as his emotions mingled with the deep rumbling of the dragon as it rose from the back of his mind. The color leached from the world as he took in a deep breath, "You want him?" His voice was a whisper in the silence of the standoff, "Fine."

The roar shattered the windows in the SUV's. His perspective changed, rising above street level, as he flicked one hand and sent the helicopter spinning into an apartment building. Dropping a wing, he shielded Ryan from the storm of bullets coming from behind him, while at the same time two dark tendrils shot from nearby shadows and punched perfectly round holes in the mercenaries holding Larry and Alex.

A small part of his mind watched in wonder as Larry spun and grabbed two pistols from the vest of the nearest fallen soldier, then disappeared around the back of a nearby truck. He lost track of Alex and hoped she wasn't in the line of fire as he sucked in a deep breath. If these pretend soldiers were going to be nice enough to bunch themselves together then who was he to ignore the invitation. Breathing out, the blast of flame covered an area as large as two middle class suburban houses. Soldiers screamed and ran while vehicles and the pavement they rested on bubbled and liquified.

Flicking his tail he cleared the road behind them, then reared up looking for Patrick. A few mercenaries were still in cover trying to get in a shot at him or Ryan. He watched as one then the other sprouted an arrow, but nowhere did he see the man in the suit.

Dropping back down he let out one more bone shaking roar, then turned his attention inward. The rage covered his mind like a thick blanket, but he knew it wasn't his. It was hard to think, and there was a thrumming desire to keep going. Destroy it all. End it. None of them deserved this place, this world.

Turning his head he watched Larry slip from an alley and look up at him, grin spreading across his face like a child on Christmas morning. The rage wasn't his. The anger at the world wasn't his. He put it away.

"You have magic clothes." Larry tucked the two pistols into shoulder holsters he'd acquired from somewhere.

A hand touched his shoulder and Bishop looked over. Alex, bow in one hand, asked, "Are you okay?"

"Is he okay?" Larry let out a laugh, "He just, literally, and I'm using the word literally correctly here, turned into a dragon and back again."

Bishop nodded at her, "I think so."

"We need to get off the street," Ryan still had his pistol up, scanning the surrounding area.

"He's right." Bishop turned and looked at the carnage around them.

"Well," Larry slapped his shoulder, "where to now?"

www.ingramcontent.com/pod-product-compliance
Lightning Source LLC
Chambersburg PA
CBHW030821210726
48290CB00002B/702